Give Her the Stars

by Marilyn W. Lathrop

Published by
Felix River Publishing
at CreateSpace
e-book available on Kindle, Nook,
Kobe, Apple and Smashwords

Cover image and design created by
John H. Turkle
johnturkle@gmail.com

Felix River Publishing
P.O. Box 351
Dexter, NM 88230
felixriverpublishing@gmail.com

MarilynWLathrop.com
overtheedgescifi.blogspot.com

The characters in this novel are fictional. Resemblance to any actual human being, living or dead, is purely unintentional.

This book is intended for teens and older.

Some of the places described in this book are real, others have been adjusted to fit the needs of the story and others are totally fictional. If you live in New Mexico or happen to visit the state you might be able to find some of the locations.

If you enjoy this book, please post a review somewhere and/or recommend it to a friend. Thank you!

1

Elise Ramos stood on the sidewalk outside Buffalo Exchange longing for an outfit she couldn't afford to buy. The coveted garment was a white, gauzy halter dress with broad, friendly floral hints. Sunlight picked at the beadwork in the bodice with come-hither allure. A matching, flirty wrap hung around the headless mannequin's neck. On the floor, a pair of strappy, heeled sandals promised days strolling in air-conditioned shopping malls and nights dancing. Elise twisted in place, back and forth, imagining the swish of the skirt around her legs, her eyes moist.

You're full of nonsense, she thought and wiped her nose.

Max, her two year-old son, fidgeted in his stroller, kicking his sandaled feet one after the other. He jabbered in his private language, pointing east, down Central Avenue. He grinned and yammered some more.

Elise sighed. A stressful visit from her ex-husband, the latest in a series that would probably stretch through the years into the distant future, had sent her out of doors seeking relief. Dogged by feelings of failure and shame, she'd hurried out of her apartment to stand here and dream. Except, at the moment her dreams seemed a futile hope. Always out of reach, on the horizon, taunting her. A better future, a beautiful dress, leisurely strolls and nights dancing--sheer foolishness.

Student loans, visits to the Roadrunner Food Bank, struggling to find and pay capable, kind baby sitters and being forced to leave Max with strangers. Working retail. Gabriel and his abusive, controlling ways. That's reality. Not that stupid dress.

The struggle to live by faith, keeping her eyes on the

Lord and not her problems, characterized her life. Not that dress.

"Self-pity, what a waste of time," she muttered under her breath. "God help me. I am so tired."

Max squirmed to look up at her. "Dink." He said.

Elise tousled his hair. "Ok honey, we'll go home and get a drink." But she didn't move.

For several minutes the strange sensation someone watched her had nudged her consciousness. Intruding into her reverie, like a persistent poking finger. That sensation had, oddly enough, kept her from bursting into tears right there on the sidewalk. While she'd stood rooted to this spot, the feeling had increased until now she couldn't ignore it. She turned to meet the rude person's stare.

About fifteen feet away, in front of the Zinc Wine & Bistro, stood an amazingly attractive man wearing a brilliant white shirt with brand new, well-fitting jeans. Not the saggy kind she despised; the kind often topped by a band of colorful underwear that made men's legs and buttocks look flat and misshapen, this man's jeans showed off his muscles the way jeans were supposed to.

Wow. Nice, Elise thought, touching a finger to her lower lip.

The man's dark-chocolate cowboy boots matched his hair. The belt sported a tasteful buckle, not too large, not too small, shiny silver in the sun. The shirt fit perfectly too, emphasizing his chest.

Her heart shuddered at the sight of him. She bit her lip. What a beautiful man. Where did he come from?

So many other, more attractive women strolled down the sidewalk or breezed through the store's entrance, surely he looked somewhere else. Elise scanned her surroundings. No, his gaze remained fixed on her.

Maybe he's looking at someone standing right behind me. Elise spun to check.

Nobody. He can't be looking at anyone but me. She

gnawed her bottom lip.

A ray of afternoon sunshine struck him for an instant, illuminating him separate from the rest of the world. As if Heaven announced, "Here is your destiny." This was the unmistakable and persistent sensation her friend Lolly would label a "God moment."

Girl, you've gone mad, Elise thought, even as her heart fluttered with hope.

She tapped her chin. This man possessed a fabulous head, what her grandmother would have called, "well shaped;" a firm mouth, expressive eyes and intelligent brow. His tousled hair took the edge off the "Holy Ground" sensation. It seemed so incongruent with his dashing costume and the ray of sunshine that she decided perhaps he was real.

The man smiled and lifted his foot to approach her. One step, two...

Suddenly conscious of her shabby broomstick skirt and store brand, three-to-a-pack, t-shirt, Elise pointed the stroller west, away from him and walked briskly toward Girard Avenue.

The man followed. "Miss," he called. "Miss..."

Elise stopped. Her heart pounded with violent energy and her face burned.

He stopped in front of her, the picture of smart, masculine elegance and bowed. "My name is Lendar Marl. Please forgive me, you look remarkably like someone I've met before." His baritone was laced with a lovely accent that loosed a thrill through her being.

Her pulse thumping like a tympanum, Elise frowned. "Really. Well, I'm sure I've never met you before. I remember faces." After a moment she added, "I'm Elise Ramos and this is my son, Max."

Lendar studied her with a genuinely, puzzled expression. "Perhaps you are correct. Though your name is vaguely familiar, I do not remember where I've heard it. It is possible I am mistaken, but if I may, will you permit me to buy your son a lemonade?" With his opened hand he pointed down the street. "The Taco Bell serves acceptable drinks."

Elise choked on the snigger that now demanded release. This fellow, who moments earlier had basked in a ray of sunlight on what she had perceived as "Holy Ground," had just uttered the name "Taco Bell" with complete sincerity and lack of guile. Taco Bell when Brasserie La Provence, an upscale French restaurant, stood right behind him. Hilarious.

Clearly this man was out of synch, dressing like a romance novel cover model and going cheap for Taco Bell. Where is he from, I wonder? His accent intrigued her--a wonderful, western European kind of sound with a hint of Spanish. And when he smiled, the smile reached all the way into his eyes.

Could God be answering my prayers at last?

Rule #1: never consider a man whose smile did not brighten his eyes…which, taking the converse, meant she absolutely *should* consider any man whose smile reached his eyes. Lendar's smile not only reached his eyes, it seemed to fill them up and bounce right back from his retina.

Elise sighed. Trapped by the very rules I invented to protect myself. In the next instant she thought, No, don't be so negative. God does answer prayer! He does! If only you believe!

Lendar had the appearance of a thrill without the bad-boy edginess that normally attracted her. Something sure and steady in his manner; something overwhelmingly masculine in that sureness and steadiness suddenly generated a new kind of attraction she'd never experienced before.

Oh God, he's wonderful, she thought, in a sudden moment of unbridled exuberance.

Yes or no? Lemonade at Taco Bell or not?

Rule #10, "Trust God. Which means, be willing to take reasonable risks." Besides, Max is thirsty, he's paying and Taco Bell is a busy, public place. She offered a faint smile. Hope he's not judging me by the same criteria. That was one cold smile.

Her hands suddenly sweaty on the stroller's handles, she said, "Thank you. Some refreshment would be nice."

He bowed and gestured, a kind of 'well, then, let's go,' sort of sign.

Interesting. Never saw a speaking person sign like that before.

They crossed Monte Vista Boulevard, Lendar obviously wanting to take command of the stroller, possibly fulfilling the criterion behind rule #8: "If he's not polite, run away," or maybe rule #3: "If he creeps you out, he's most likely a creep."

Does he creep me out? No, not really. How could a creep be simultaneously nice, elegant, masculine and goofy?

At the restaurant, he opened the door and stood aside. Ok, definitely, possibly, fulfilling the criterion behind rule #8. He bowed as she passed. Elise threw him a quizzical look.

When he joined her in line to order, she said, "Your accent sounds Spanish, but it's different from what I usually hear around New Mexico."

Lendar's hand went to his chest and his torso tilted, as if he were about to bow once again. "Oh, yes, Castilian Spanish," he lisped.

Elise's brow wrinkled. "Is bowing a common practice where you come from? I thought it was just Japanese who bowed."

Lendar replied, "I suppose bowing is a deeply engrained habit. I've been in service my whole life."

Elise squinted at him. "Service? Not military, right? Are you a butler or something?"

"I am a gentleman's gentleman. An anachronism in a modern world, no doubt, but I provide necessary ministrations for my lor...boss." Lendar's neck and face flamed red.

Elise giggled. A man who blushes so easily can hardly be dangerous.

Lendar's grin spread across his entire face and his eyes

fairly beamed. "And, what is your profession, if I may ask? Or, perhaps you have made motherhood your profession?" A fresh wash of red flowed over his face. "Forgive me, I meant no implication that motherhood..."

Elise waved her hand. "No worries. Feminism has mostly run its course, thank God, and a woman can choose motherhood with no shame. I'm an art student at UNM." She paused, bit her lip, then added, "Divorced."

She thought, Oh gak, why did you have to go and do that? Now he'll ask you out.

Maybe he'll ask you out.

Don't you want him to ask you out?

What if he doesn't ask you out?

Arrgghh.

The teenager at the counter glared. "May I help you?"

Lendar replied. "I apologize. We've been chatting and neglected our menus. Could we please have a few more minutes to decide?"

The teenager snapped. "If you're not ready, move to the back and let someone else order."

Lendar leaned his direction. "Actually, three large lemonades please."

The teenager counted the cups, handed them to Lendar and stated the cost. Lendar paid him and led the way to the beverage dispenser where he filled all three. "I have erred. Max needed a smaller size, did he not?" Chagrin played on Lendar's face.

Elise waved. "Don't worry about it."

Lendar carried all three cups and followed Elise to a table. She noted his hands, large enough to manage the three drinks, but soft, as if he had never done any serious labor in his entire life. She wrinkled her nose.

No, Elise, she told herself, don't be a snob. He already told you what he does for a living and such a person would not have work-worn hands. Soft hands don't mean he's lazy.

He hurried to the wall where the highchairs were kept

and returned. He peeled napkins from the dispenser and wiped the highchair's seat.

Hhmn, thoughtful, but I guess if he's a butler he's supposed to act like that. "Is your boss here in town?" Elise asked, hoisting Max from his stroller.

"No, I am here alone." He paused, then added, "I am on vacation. New Mexico is a delightful place. I have traveled to Sandia Crest. Once I rode the tram, the second time I journeyed there by motorized conveyance, ah, car. I plan to visit the aquarium tomorrow. Perhaps you might join me?" Lendar wore a look of hopeful expectation.

Well, how about that? He asked you out. Wow. Don't break rule #10. "Ah..."

To buy time, she helped Max with his straw. He blew air into the cup and laughed, delighted at the burbling sound. Elise admonished, "Max, don't do that. Just drink it, please, honey."

"Is Max short for Maximilian?" Lendar asked with evident interest. She couldn't help but be charmed by his accent and his elegant manner of speech. He was so polite! And he seemed genuinely interested in Max!

"Maxfield for Maxfield Parrish, one of my favorite artists." Elise replaced Max's cup to the tabletop, fished a toy from her diaper bag and offered it to him.

Lendar said, "Unfortunately, I'm not familiar with his work."

"He was an illustrator, born in 1870 and died in 1966. Very romantic work."

Lendar nodded. "Do you plan to become an illustrator?"

Elise shrugged. "Probably just a debtor to the student loan system working at Wal-Mart." Her shoulders slumped. She couldn't seem to help herself. She thought, I could use a good cry, then pushed the idea away. What a blubbering baby you are, she decided. A sudden blast of air-conditioned coldness emphasized her slouch, easily punching through the thin, cotton fabric to her skin. She shivered.

Lendar's sympathetic expression proved too much for her to bear. Elise studied the condensation collecting in the wax over the Taco Bell logo on her cup. She blurted, "It's time Max and I went home."

"Eat," Max said. "Wanna eat. Prease eat, Mama."

Lendar hopped up from the table and rejoined the line at the counter.

Elise's face burned. Everyone is watching. Ugh. She glanced down at the hands folded in her lap, winced, then cast a challenging glare about the room. Actually few had taken note of her, but she was painfully aware that the refrigerator at home contained only a handful of eggs and a mostly empty gallon milk container.

Lendar returned with a "Grande Meal." "Plenty of food and choices. Forgive me, but I'm unfamiliar with the menu options. This item was the simplest selection. I hope something in this collection will prove suitable."

Max reached for a taco. "'Ungry, now."

Lendar winked at Max. "I'm hungry too, Max."

Elise tore a soft taco into bite sized pieces and placed the bits on a napkin for Max.

He stuffed a piece into his mouth and reached for his lemonade, his fingers wriggling just out of reach. "Dink, prease."

Absently, Elise held the cup for him.

Lendar chomped into a hard taco. Lettuce, meat and cheese scattered over the table.

With the splattered lettuce and meat decorating the Formica, the situation suddenly felt normal. Lendar wiping up the mess with his napkin, happily chewing; Max blissfully sucking his straw and herself surrounded by happy males. If only it weren't just a momentary thing.

Elise tackled a bean and cheese burrito. The food at Taco Bell was ok, but if Lendar thought this represented real Mexican or New Mexican food, she needed to educate him.

Little Anita's? Maybe Sadie's on 4th Street... Better yet, Hippolita's…yeah.

Already planning a second date? What are you thinking girl? Get a grip on yourself!

With his mouth full, Lendar asked. "Will you accompany me tomorrow?"

Max popped another piece of soft taco into his mouth and copied Lendar. "Gro 'morrow," he said and offered a wide-mouth grin showing the half-chewed food.

Lendar rewarded Max with a similar broad smile.

Elise shook her head. She should scold him, but Lendar had spoken with his mouth full and rewarded his rudeness with a grin. Good heavens, I thought he was polite. Just look at that masticated mess. Both of you! Ugh.

Max he's not your father, Elise willed her son to comprehend, somehow, silently through osmosis maybe. But, she had to admit she couldn't remember the last time Max had beamed with such happy abandon. "Yeah, we'll go. What time?"

Lendar slapped his hands together. "Max is a young master, does he take an afternoon nap?"

Surprised Lendar would know such a fact or even consider it an issue, Elise nodded. "One o'clock thereabouts."

Lendar's frown was slight. He wiped his fingers on a napkin and slugged down some lemonade. "How about 3 of the clock?"

Unconsciously, Elise mimicked him, wiping her fingers and drinking some lemonade. "Sure. 506 Prin...how about I meet you there?"

Lendar fell back into the chair. "Very well. 3 of the clock post meridiem." He leaned forward and grasped his second taco. "Would I be correct to guess this food is a knock-off of original cuisine?" He said the words "knock-off" as if they were foreign, as if he'd just learned them. His mouth curved up more in one corner than in the other, in a self-deprecating sort of way. He looked positively charming, boyish even.

Elise giggled.

As if reading her thoughts he asked, "Would you know where persons might dine on true Mexican food?" He studied her through his brows. His expression was somehow simultaneously suggestive and naïve.

"Sure." Oh, that look is so sexy, Elise thought. Her body warmed at the fantasy of his embrace. I bet he smells real nice.

Lendar grinned, both corners rising equally--a smile of delight. "Then, that is where we shall dine once our adventure at the aquarium is complete."

Elise felt a dreamy, intoxicating sensation she hadn't experienced since she'd had a crush on Jay Ogelvie in Jr. High. Lendar has the most fabulous eyes, not quite green, not quite blue; eyes that seem to generate their own illumination, as if light comes from inside. Long, dark, sexy lashes.

Elise winced and settled back in her seat squelching the weightless, foolish folly of adoration for no good reason. She looked down at her cup again, at the logo where water droplets had gained enough weight to create a trail down the side. Tears. Hurts in the past, fear to trust. Oh, God, I'm scared. She cleared her throat and stared at her hands.

Lendar turned his attention to Max, holding the straw so he could drink.

"Some genuine New Mexican food would be nice," Elise managed at last.

Lendar's smile seemed to express understanding and compassion for her plight.

She shifted uncomfortably. Don't make assumptions about me, buddy, she thought irritably. Aloud she said, "Max and I need to go."

Lendar immediately jumped to his feet, stuffing the uneaten tacos and burritos into a sack. Without a word he slipped the food into her diaper bag. He bowed, then blushed. "I know bowing is not customary, but apparently I am a creature of habit. Such a failure...such rudeness is inexcusable in a gentleman's gentleman." He cut a second bow so short it turned into silly bobbing. "I will see you tomorrow at the aquarium."

Elise might have laughed if she weren't so mortified. "Thank you for the meal and the nice chat," she said, lifting Max from the highchair. She buckled him into the stroller, stuck his lemonade into his hands, snatched up her own and walked out.

2

Bruce Keaghan, Elise 's neighbor, sat in a rusted lawn chair outside his efficiency apartment. "Hey, Elise. You have a nice walk?" He clutched a dog-eared copy of Stanton Friedman's book, *Flying Saucers and Science*....

Elise offered a faint smile. "Yes, I did." She fished keys from her diaper bag and unlocked her door. "You doing ok, Bruce?"

Bruce grinned. "Doing fine. Turned down for the three jobs I applied for this week."

"Don't take it personal, Bruce."

His grin faded. He shrugged. "Hard not to. But hey, I'm not starving…yet."

Elise nodded and pushed the stroller into the apartment.

She bathed Max in the kitchen sink, brushed his teeth and dressed him for bed. His crib stood at the front window. He played with the curtains creating flashes of light in the otherwise darkened room. He peered through the glass, then pointed. "Lolly," he said.

Elise flipped through her sketchbook resting on the kitchen table. "Yes, Lolly is coming." She turned her attention to the sketches.

Her instructor had assigned a minimum of ten sketches per day, sketchbooks and sketchbooks of drawings for the summer semester. One week left and she was behind twenty drawings. He'd frowned the last time he'd checked her work. He'd scribbled: "more elaboration; more invention." She sighed. That's so explicit, so clear. She couldn't seem to discern what he wanted or put her heart into the sketches.

A knock on the door. She jumped. "Oh, Lolly's here." With her Murphy bed tucked into its closet on the east wall, her apartment offered a nice open living area. She crossed the linoleum-tiled expanse and opened the door.

"Hey, Elise. Talk to you later Butch." Butch was Lolly's nickname for Bruce. She breezed in, sweeping Max out of his crib and nuzzling him in the neck. "How you doing, Max?"

Max giggled and tried to stick a toy's arm up Lolly's nose.

"Max, that's not good. Don't do that, not even to yourself," Lolly scolded before kissing him, then blowing a raspberry on his cheek. "Things up the nose are not good. No, no, no."

Max smeared his face against hers. He tried pressing his lips onto her flesh to duplicate the pressure of lips and air she'd just applied to his skin and failed, only making a slobbery kiss.

"Ah, Maxie, we'll be sweethearts forever, won't we," Lolly mumbled. She set him down on the floor. "Elise, I'm in the mood to model for you this evening, if you like."

"Ok."

"What's up with you, girl?" Lolly perched on Elise's rickety office chair. "You look down."

"Oh, I met a guy." Elise tacked a wan smile to the end of her remark.

Lolly whistled. "Hallelujah! It's about time. What's he like?"

Elise shrugged. "He's rich, well, if his clothes are any indication. High-class, white shirt, leather cowboy boots and a nice belt buckle."

"And?"

"And what?"

Lolly frowned. "And, what does he look like? Who cares if he's rich if he's not good looking!"

Elise threw her hand in Lolly's general direction. "Pshaw, Lolly. You know being a good man is way more important than appearance or money."

Lolly propped a fist on her hip. "So tell me, is he a good man?"

Elise sighed and plopped onto the couch. "There's a distinct possibility."

"And?"

"And what?"

Lolly shook her head. "How come that don't make you happy?"

Elise shrugged. "Except for talking with his mouth full, he's exceedingly polite. Ugh!" She propped her chin on her hand then drew an arc from her mouth toward the floor. "His mouth was full like a slob."

Lolly shook her head. "Talking with his mouth full. So he's not perfect. He can join the club. Tell me more."

Elise grimaced. "He has chocolate brown hair, it's all curly and messy, like he doesn't know what to do with it." She paused and gulped. "He looked like romance novel cover model."

Lolly waved her hand back and forth. "You're kidding, right? Did he have a ray of sunlight beaming right down on him like he was the Son of God come forth or what?"

Elise screwed up her mouth like she'd just eaten a lemon. "Yeah, actually he did."

Lolly laughed. "Girl, that's hilarious. Are you sure they weren't filming a movie over there? They do that all over town. I've seen them more than once."

Elise shrugged and leaned over her knees. "It's insane, Lolly, completely insane. Normal people don't meet like we did. It's not…normal. I mean, I was 'picked up.' Me, picked up!" She pointed at herself and offered a lopsided grin.

Lolly sniggered, then her face turned serious. "You think there's something automatically wrong with him because he noticed you on the street?"

Elise shrugged. "He was wearing creased jeans…"

Lolly's rich, brown skin wrinkled in a frown. "Is there something wrong with that? Are creased jeans, like, some kind of sign he's a jerk? Besides, what do you mean, "creased jeans"?"

Elise winced. "Cowboys iron their jeans to make a nice crease front and back. Normal people only do that with dress slacks, but for cowboys, their best pair of jeans *are* their dress pants. So they crease them."

Lolly ticked her index finger back and forth. "Oh, ok. Keep going. But I have to tell you, girl, I don't see cause for glum here."

"They were brand new, not saggy or distressed or any of that..."

Lolly nodded. "I know how much you hate those worn out pants people spend good money for. Sheesh, Elise, this guy sounds terrible. No wonder you're so depressed!" She spluttered her lips emphasizing her sarcasm.

From the floor, Max copied her, attempting the spluttering sound, and added, "Momma depressed."

Elise threw Max a look, then nodded. "Yeah. Well, no such shabby chic for him."

"And?"

"And what?"

Lolly poked the air. "Look, you'd better tell me all about this guy 'cause I'm getting tired of interrogating you."

"There's not a lot more to tell. We went over to the Taco Bell, he bought us lemonades, he bought a Grande Meal and he invited us to go with him to the aquarium tomorrow."

Lolly's large, umber eyes widened. "You said, "yes," right?"

Elise grimaced. "I said, yes, I'd meet him there."

Lolly stretched her shoulders and rested an elbow on Elise's desk. "I'm sneaking over there to get a look at this guy. What time's your date?"

Elise frowned. "No you're not. Wait until we find out if he's more than just a passing fantasy."

Lolly eyed her friend. "Urumph, what's the matter with you?"

Elise's hand dropped from her chin to hang from her knee. "I'm just scared as hell, that's all." She attempted a smile.

Lolly's right eyebrow crawled up her forehead. "Girl, you afraid of getting hurt. Well aren't we all."

Elise sighed. "I know it's silly. But I didn't turn him down. Don't you think that's an improvement?"

Lolly snickered. "You mean an improvement over how you treated Doug Wells? Yeah, that's an improvement. But Doug Wells weren't no catch. And if you don't give this guy a proper chance I'm going to twist your arm until you give me his phone number and I'm calling him myself."

Elise relaxed into the couch. "Didn't get his phone number."

Lolly shook her head. "Guess that settles that. For now. We'd better get busy if you're going to meet your ten sketches per day assignment."

"Alright."

3

Later, instead of finishing the essay for the final in her Art History class, Elise scoured her closet, completely emptying it onto the bed, looking for something, anything that wasn't worn out. All she could find was a sundress a woman at church had given her.

She hung the dress from the molding around the wide doorway into the kitchen and sat down at her desk to work. Elise read the assignment aloud: "'Compare and contrast two works from one movement or period.' Which?"

Elise made desultory efforts at research in the handful of books she'd brought home the day before Mr. Lendar Marl had walked into her life and scribbled a few notes. Periodically she glanced at the dress, groaned and scribbled more nonsense. "Ok, I know what I'll write!" She hacked at her old-fashioned electric typewriter and wasted two pieces of paper before giving up. She ripped the paper out of the platen and muttered, "Don't panic! You still have time, it's not due until Wednesday."

She read a passage from her Bible, then ducked into the bathroom and stared at her reflection. She stuck out her tongue at the young woman looking back at her. Thirty minutes spent brushing her teeth, applying body lotion and slipping into an oversized t-shirt ended with another agonized rumble through the closet.

Elise pulled her bed down from its slot in the wall, then spent the night tossing and turning, her mind churning with hope, fear and anxiety. By morning, she was exhausted.

After breakfast, Elise hauled laundry to the Laundromat across the street. Bruce kept an eye on Max, watching him play in the gravel that constituted the apartment building's yard. Laundry finished, it was time for Max's nap. While he slept, she tried drawing again, managed a few pathetic sketches and gave up. In the end, she realized she'd spent half of Max's nap sitting at the kitchen window staring into the back yard where a concrete block fence and some neglected grass provided the view.

I'm wasting my time! Might as well get ready. When Elise slipped on the sundress she groaned. So, absolutely and utterly not my style.

One more search through her closet, attempting to see her garments from a different perspective--maybe she'd failed to see a combination of skirt and top or jeans and top--netted nothing new. Tears pressed at her lids. No time for a cry fit! Think positive! At least you're not going naked. And the color does look good on you.

She sighed, applied her make-up, then allowed herself one spritz of the perfume she reserved for special occasions.

She fed Max a warmed-over burrito while she nibbled at a taco, her appetite quashed in a knot of anxiety. A finch twittered on the concrete wall, then flitted upward. Max laughed with his mouth full.

Elise admonished. "Oh no honey, don't do that. It's rude."

"Rube," Max said and stuffed another bite into his mouth.

After lunch, she dressed Max in a garage sale outfit she'd been saving for church. Slipped his sandals on, doused him and herself with sunscreen and left.

Bruce's apartment window leaked forlorn Dr. Dog into the air as they passed. The summer heat herded them down Princeton to Central Avenue. They boarded the bus.

Max stood on the seat and tapped the window with his fingertips. "Dah, dah, dah," he chanted as if counting.

Elise watched the passing scenery with little interest. Wish I'd gotten my work finished.

At last the bus arrived at their stop. Lendar waited nearby, at the edge of the parking lot, pacing like a caged cat. Her spirits lifted. He seemed so boyish, like a kid at

Christmas. Oh my, does he really like me that much? She placed Max on her hip, slung the diaper bag over her shoulder, hooked the stroller with that arm and stepped off the bus.

Lendar strode to meet them, his face beaming. "Hello!"

Immediately, Max leaned his direction, arms outstretched.

Elise wanted to turn around and board the bus, but it was already gone. Men don't want little babies crowding them, she thought, wishing she could make Max understand. To Lendar she said, "Hello. Oh, my, I don't know why he's doing that. He's never done anything like that before. Max, honey, maybe Mr. Marl doesn't want to hold you."

Lendar's grin verged on ridiculous, but it faded to a question. "I'm pleased he likes me. I like him also." He seemed to imply all men should love other men's children as well as they loved their own. Lendar opened his palms and received Max into his arms.

Max smoothed Lendar's hair. "Messy," he said, tucking the tendrils behind his ear. His pink tongue touched his lip.

Lendar didn't seem to mind Max's ministrations; in fact, he seemed to bask in the attention, as if he craved it. The smile that played about his lips was soft and brimming with joy. He daubed Max's nose. "You may try to tame it, Max, but it won't stay." He turned to Elise, the friendly kindness now extended to her. "How was your trip?" he asked.

"Trip?" She grinned and flicked her wrist. "Oh, we just get on the bus down by the university and sit tight. No big deal." Her heart clenched.

"Ah." Lendar took the stroller. He made some kind of a sign that reminded Elise of purposeful walking. "Shall we? It will be more pleasant inside the aquarium."

Suddenly shy, Elise dropped her eyes to the ground, then gazed back at him. "Yes, it is warm out here." Sunlight made a silver flash at his wrist, catching her attention. She admired his well-shaped hands and wrists.

His wristwatch proved a fascinating piece of jewelry, the time and date hovered over what looked like a slide show one might see on an idle computer monitor. A view outside some snazzy, Mediterranean style house with ugly landscaping; a glimpse of the Sandia Mountains…looks like the Northeast Heights. Views here at the aquarium. She glanced toward the parking lot. The images seemed to come from that point of view. Her eyes dropped back to the watch, then wandered up his arm.

He'd rolled up his sleeves to just below his elbows, the white cotton accentuating his olive skin where dark hairs made silky lines she suddenly longed to stroke. Her voice went husky. "Nice watch; interesting slide show. I've never seen a watch like that before." And your eyes are amazing.

Lendar nodded. "Let's me know what's going on." He cocked his head and waited, as if expecting more queries. When she kept silent, he turned his attention to Max who squirmed with excitement.

Elise stared at him, bemused. How many men have that kind of technology, I mean even the well-to-do?

"Rook," Max said, pointing.

"That's a roadrunner, Max." Elise pivoted to catch sight of the bird and watched the cuckoo consider his options, the little tuft on his head alternately fluffed and flattened. Her heart delighted in the sight of him.

As a child on her grandparents' ranch, Elise had managed to tame one by feeding it little balls of hamburger meat and exerting a kind of patience she hadn't known she'd possessed. Eventually, that adult roadrunner had returned with his mate and family. Six roadrunners gadding about the dusty yard behind the ranch house tame enough to allow her within two or three feet. Grammy had been impressed.

Elise's eyes teared. She hadn't seen her grandparents in a long time. Maybe the roadrunner was a sign things were changing for the better.

Lendar turned to give Max a clearer view. "There he

is."

Max giggled and bobbed.

"Now you want down, is that it? It's no use, Max, a fence separates us." Lendar strode away. "Let us find the entrance before he leaves."

By the time she'd caught up with them, they'd crossed the parking lot and Lendar had let Max down to toddle where he chose. He headed straight into the plaza toward a bronze park bench where a statue sat. He grasped the metal slats. Glancing back at Lendar and Elise, he yelled, "Hot! Herp prease."

Lendar lifted Max onto the bench.

She smiled. Lendar's patience seemed to have no end. Hopefully, that characteristic wasn't just a façade.

Max poked the statue in the eye. "Bink!"

Elise chuckled. In that moment, for her, the bronze figure stood in for all those men who hid behind deceitful façades. Men like Gabriel, her ex-husband, and Frank, her step-father. "Honey, it's a statue. It's made of metal. He can't blink."

Max poked the eye again. "Bink," he commanded.

Lendar laughed. He offered his hand. "Come Max, we will purchase our tickets."

Max raised his hands and wriggled his fingers. "'Endar," he said.

Elise thought, What is with that child? Why does he give this stranger his trust? To Lendar she said, "I've never seen him do that before."

Lendar winked. "It is a sign."

Elise's hand went to her throat. "A sign?" Oh God, a sign, a sign from You? Her breath caught.

"A sign that I'm, what is it called, oh yes, a sucker for small children." Lendar grinned.

Elise relaxed as they strolled across the plaza to the ticket box. She smiled. "I doubt you're a sucker for anybody."

Lendar ducked his head so he could meet the clerk's

eyes and slipped cash under the payment window. He glanced at Elise, then spoke to her, though he now looked at the clerk. "Not for everyone, just small boys and beautiful women." He turned those fabulous, aquamarine peepers on her, slicing through her defenses like lasers.

Elise's heart leapt into her throat. Her knees threatened to buckle. To feel this man's lips...Oh my goodness, am I falling for Lendar Marl already? She dropped the diaper bag from her shoulder to her hands and bounced it against her knees. Hope and anxiety alternated just as frequently as the bag lapped against her legs.

Max chased in a circle, "Whirr, whirr."

Feeling shy, she looked back at Lendar. His clear, delicious water-blue eyes flared like the flame from an acetylene torch. Her chest felt hot and moisture popped to her skin.

He asked, "Which shall we visit first, the gardens or the aquarium?"

Elise shrugged, struggling to catch her breath. "What do you want to do?"

"Aquarium. Max will probably enjoy it the most. By the time we finish in there, he might be tired." Lendar's baritone sounded friendly and thoughtful, as if his only concern was Max, but his face testified to a different story: he wanted Max to sleep, so they might be alone and focus on each other.

Focus on each other...ah, her imagination could go crazy with that phrase! Elise stared. Could you be the man I asked God to give me and Max?

Lendar wriggled his fingers at Max who immediately grasped the digits. "Let's go in." He pushed open the gate and held it. Max scampered straight for the fountain where he splashed until he was soaked.

Elise stopped beside Lendar.

"He's a very intelligent child," Lendar said matter of factly.

Elise knew her pride in Max glowed on her face. "Yes,

he is. You seem to understand children remarkably well. Do you have any?"

Lendar shook his head. "No. I am not a father. I have never been married. I have been in service my whole life. As a consequence, I have tended numerous children."

"Exactly what do you mean, "in service?" I haven't met anybody in that line of work before."

"I manage my boss's correspondence; care for his garments; purchase things he needs; occasionally I cook for him, but usually he prepares his own meals. He enjoys cooking. I track his business and financial affairs, other, similar tasks." Lendar led Max into the air-conditioned aquarium building.

Happy as a puppy, Max scurried to the Rio Grande cutthroat trout exhibit. "Frish," he hollered, jumping up and down, begging to be picked up.

Elise whistled, then teased, "Sounds like a wife."

Lendar lifted Max for a better view and grinned. "My boss's new wife doesn't have time for these tasks. She has her own duties."

"Oh." Elise's imagination ran with this new information: a wife with her own duties and Lendar to take care of the house. Wild.

Max tugged at Lendar's collar. "Rook, frish," he said.

"Yes, Max, Rio Grande cutthroat trout," Lendar said and read the placard beside the exhibit. "New Mexico's state fish…"

Wistfully, Elise thought, Wonder what it would be like to not worry about money? "He must be rich, your boss, I mean."

Lendar frowned, then his face softened. "Yes, I suppose he is."

Max bucked, as if he were attempting to get a horse moving. "Gro."

Lendar said, "Very well then, young master, we will move on." He turned to Elise. "You have work?"

Elise shook her head. "No, well, sort of. I have work-study, about twenty hours a week. I do word processing and things like that. Mostly I'm a student."

"Yes, you mentioned that yesterday. An art student. Illustration? Painting?"

"Painting." Like I'll ever make a living doing that! A small frown tugged at her lips.

"Your studies do not please you?"

"Not sure how I'm going to earn any money as an artist." She smirked. "As I said yesterday, debtor to the student loan system working at Wal-Mart."

Lendar seemed puzzled. "Why did you choose that field?" Before he could hear her answer, he hurried to follow Max to the next exhibit. He glanced over his shoulder, offering Elise an apologetic look.

Watching him sprint away, Elise muttered. "Good question. Why did I select that field?"

Lendar called. "The stingray are over here…"

Elise sped up and joined them. Max already perched on a vantage point with Lendar's arm looped loosely around him. The two males grinned at her. They even looked like father and son. She suppressed a gasp.

"Amazing creatures," Lendar muttered, watching the animals flapping through the water.

Their movements reminded Elise of flying birds. With chagrin she realized she found Lendar's delight in them annoying. "Yes, they are amazing." Suddenly tired, she thought, if I had my sketchbook, I could draw stingrays and be closer to my required number of sketches. Lendar could watch Max, he's so obviously good at it. In the next instant, she felt a pang of guilt for her selfish wish to take advantage of his skills. Then, she felt irritated that so much of Lendar's attention had been devoted to Max. What a ninny you are, run around by emotions like a slave.

"So, why did you select that field?" Lendar's brow cocked. His eyebrow ridges rose strong over thin cheekbones split by a generous mouth.

That mouth, Elise thought, the earlier desire for a kiss returning. To taste those lips... Duty, exhaustion and desire churned within her, a gooey mess in the mixing bowl that was her tired brain. "Following my dreams I guess. They say if you follow your dreams, do the thing you love, you'll be fine." Elise shrugged.

"You do not sound convinced."

Elise shook her head. "I have responsibilities now..."

Lendar's expression turned pensive. "Let's go over there." He pointed to the darkened hallway leading to the eel caves. He collected Max and the stroller.

Elise followed slowly, suddenly jealous of Mr. Lendar Marl. Look at him, he comes out of nowhere from his cushy life and sweeps Max off his feet. Max has ignored me this whole time. What about me? Tears threatened.

Stop it. The trouble with a pity party is you're the only one in attendance. She raised her gaze from the floor to discover Lendar eyeing her quizzically. She attempted a smile.

The dark eel cave and the huge ocean tank were her favorite parts. She could sit for hours watching the eels peering from their holes and then watch the sharks and colorful fish make their circuits. Her mind returned to her sketchbook. If only I'd brought it.

Maybe I'm not really cut out to be an artist.

She tagged along behind Max who rushed through the sea horse exhibits and past the tube containing alien looking jellyfish into the large room facing the ocean tank. Lendar kept pace.

Elise parked on the thick, concrete steps designed for an audience and watched the animals swim while Lendar worked his charms on Max. It was a lovely scene. Just what she'd been praying for. So why are you so jealous, annoyed and distracted? Elise sighed.

You're just never satisfied.

Lendar left Max standing at the aquarium wall. He

strolled toward her, his masculine form silhouetted against the light-filled, blue water. He came as if stalking her, as a cat on the prowl. When he settled next to her, his cologne floated into her nostrils in a waft of moving air. It was a scent like no other.

Apparently he could read her moods as if they were flashing neon signs in the dark. "Elise, what is the matter?"

She shrugged. "Tired, just tired."

Lendar looked away, then back. "We finish in here, dine, then I'll take you home so you may rest."

Elise knew her eyes watered. Guilt dripping from a bad leak. "I hate for you to do that. You're on vacation."

Lendar offered a lopsided grin. "What? Being on vacation gives me the right to be selfish?"

She knew her smile was small, but maybe it finally reached her eyes. "You're far from selfish."

Lendar studied her, but she tore away to watch Max. A sea turtle drifted past. Lazy. Nothing much to do but swim in circles all day.

After a moment, he said, "This is one of the best aquariums I've ever seen."

"Uhmn. Yes, it is a nice one." Her whole body thrummed, longing for his arms. His nearness overwhelmed her earlier sensation of fragmented worry and exhaustion. Now she felt only warmth and ease.

Oh God, I am falling for him! If this man isn't in Your will, please send him away.

Max ran along the thick, transparent wall chasing a shark.

"You have work you need to do today?" Lendar asked. He bent a knee and rested his wrist there, the hand hanging loose. The other leg went straight, the cowboy booted toe pointing at the ceiling. A casual, manly pose. Just look at those boots, nice ones.

Cowboy boots reminded her of her grandparents' ranch. Sweet desire welled within her. Somehow, in that moment, she knew she'd see that ranch again and Lendar would help her.

She answered, "Yeah. I am supposed to draw ten sketches a day and I have a canvas at school I need to finish. And an essay for Art History…" One kiss and I would forget all about it…throw my whole three and a half years at UNM Fine Arts College away. "It's the final week of school coming up. Kinda nerve wracking."

His body angling for a bow that never materialized, Lendar said, "In that case, we have lunch, discover your sketchbook and your canvas and complete those tasks. I offer my assistance in whatever capacity most benefits your efforts." He flicked a hand, accentuating his statements. He seemed so certain that with his help she could accomplish anything.

Elise shook her head. "You don't have to do that." She almost laughed at his ridiculous formality.

Lendar flashed that completely disarming grin. "What else am I to do? A man on vacation; nothing planned for this whole day except to spend it with you. You have work to finish. We'll get it done. I achieve my objective and you achieve your objectives. Besides I'd like to see your paintings." That wonderful, crooked smile again.

Elise sighed.

Max approached, his hand tugging the seat of his pants.

She chuckled. "Diaper duty. Excuse me, we'll be right back."

When they rejoined him, Lendar insisted on a turn through the aquarium gift shop where he bought Max a T-shirt and Elise a necklace. He chose some gift items, one for himself and one each for his boss and boss's wife. For the sake of her unfinished work, they ate in the aquarium café rather than somewhere less convenient.

"The hamburger is a uniquely American sandwich, is it not?" Lendar asked, his mouth full. He looked so charming, his hands dripping with mayonnaise, his face decorated with obvious enjoyment. She could almost see him salivate with delight. And I don't even seem to mind that he's being so rude at the moment. How can a guy who is so over-the-top polite chew with his mouth open like that?

Max mimicked him, jabbering something unintelligible with French fries on full display.

"Max," Elise scolded, tapping his hand as he reached for more. "Don't talk with your mouth full."

Lendar blushed. "Ah, forgive me. I did not realize talking with one's mouth full is impolite in this country. Where I come from talking with one's mouth full indicates he enjoys the food or, at the least, enjoys the company." He winked.

Elise giggled. "That explains it. For awhile there I couldn't figure out how you could be alternately so polite and so rude."

Lendar shook his head and wiped his mouth. "In the future I will endeavor to observer proper conventions."

"Rube co'ven'ns," Max laughed. Together he and Lendar slurped their milkshakes.

4

Outside, in the aquarium parking lot, Lendar walked toward a brand new, shiny red, Cadillac Escalade. The color immediately activated the pleasure center in Elise's artistic brain that loved mixing paint and found the sight of certain colors as satisfying as a piece of creamy chocolate. It wasn't until he'd loaded the stroller in the back that Elise remembered Max needed a car seat.

"Oh, Lendar. Max can't ride in this car without a car seat." She loosed a dejected sigh.

"No worries," Lendar said. He opened the rear passenger side door and waved his hand. "A car seat."

Elise's fingers went to her lips. "You're amazing. Are all men in service like this?"

Lendar scooped Max from her arms and placed him in the seat. He spent a few minutes fiddling with the straps. "No, not all." He glanced her way, his serious expression faded to a wan smile.

Elise thought he might say more, but he didn't. He opened the front passenger door for her, then skirted the grille to climb into the driver's seat. The smell of new leather delighted her; it seemed to promise a better future.

"Did you know they make a deodorizer that's supposed to make an old car smell like new?" Elise asked.

Grinning, Lendar turned the key in the ignition. "I didn't know that. That's amusing. I wonder if that product functions as advertised."

Elise relaxed into the seat. "I have no idea." She thought, Oh boy, I could get used to this!

Lendar drove toward the parking lot exit. "I await your instructions."

"Oh, turn left onto Central," Elise answered, her heart in a quandary. What are you going to do now, let him see your shabby apartment? Might as well! If he wants to end it because you're poor, better now than later.

Oh please, don't end it.

Elise closed her eyes. The air-conditioned coolness pelted her with refreshing moisture. Oh please don't end it, not yet, she repeated.

Music filled the vehicle, something with a classical hint, totally new to her. "That music's delightful," she said, eyes still closed.

""Spaceman's Fugues" by Reeser Peland," Lendar said from some far away place.

""Spaceman's Fugues"?" Elise muttered dreamily.

"He's not known in the United States, not at all." Lendar drove on.

The fugue, an interweaving of repeated melodies, lulled Elise into deeper and deeper relaxation. The next words she heard were, "We're at Central Avenue and University. Where do I turn now?"

"Oh, I fell asleep!" Elise sat bolt upright and shook her head. She glanced to the back seat where Max snored. She smiled at Lendar and touched a tendril of his hair before she could stop herself. She almost topped the gesture by saying, "You're a sweetie," but cut her words short, just in time. Oh gak, getting so familiar after only a few hours!?

"Madame," Lendar said gruffly. "Your affection is welcome, but I must focus on traffic." He winked.

Elise giggled. "Oh, you just went through the light for Yale. You need to turn right on Princeton. It's coming up soon."

"Ah, here is it." Lendar made the turn.

"Keep going on this street. The number is 506."

Lendar cocked his brow at Elise. "You'll help me sight the location?"

Elise smiled. "Of course." In a few moments she said, "Here. Park along the curb here." She leaned forward, staring. "Wait. Those women are from my church." She scooted below the dashboard.

Lendar threw her a quizzical look, then focused on some buttons on the dashboard.

Elise watched. "This vehicle has more knobs and buttons than any I've ever seen before."

Lendar winked again. "Luxury model." He turned one dial and a small screen popped up. On the screen the two women walked toward a white, Ford Crown Victoria parked behind the Escalade. The two women climbed in and sped away.

Elise's eyes widened. "Nice."

Lendar chuckled. He stepped into the street and came around to Elise's side. After he'd opened her door he said, "Max is still asleep. I hate to disturb him."

Elise turned and glanced over her shoulder to observe her son. "I'll fetch my sketchbook and be right back."

Lendar nodded and waited for her to climb out. He shut the door and returned to the driver's side where he leaned against the shiny red metal. The window rolled down.

Bruce sat outside his apartment. He raised a hand in greeting to Elise. "A couple of women were here. They left you this casserole." He offered it half-heartedly.

"Bruce, would you keep it? I don't have any room in my refrigerator for that right now." Elise fished her keys from her diaper bag.

"Thanks Elise. I told them you were at school working on a project." He glanced in Lendar's direction. "Didn't realize you had more productive pursuits!" He smiled, the expression turning suggestive.

"Oh, Bruce. Be nice. He's a great guy. We just got back from the aquarium." Elise opened the door. "He's a complete gentleman," she said, pausing at the threshold.

Bruce straightened. "I hope for your sake he is, Elise."

Elise frowned and stepped into the darkened efficiency. She snatched up her sketchbook. Next, she stuffed pencils into her paint box, closed it and clutched its handle in the other hand. Outside, she slipped the sketchbook under her arm, the paint box into that hand, pulled the door shut and locked it.

Bruce's door stood open. He'd already taken the casserole into his kitchen and placed it in the oven. Elise hurried away, just as he looked up from the table where he placed a napkin and silverware.

Lendar opened the door for her and went back to the driver's side. "Where now?"

Elise bit her lip. "How about we look for parking in the visitor's lot at UNM."

Lendar started the motor. "Sounds fine. Do I retrace my route up Princeton?"

Elise nodded. "Yes." She'd forgotten to pick up anything for Max. She had plenty of diapers, but he might need a snack. Somehow, that problem just didn't seem important. She felt secure, provided for and protected. O, Lord, let him be the one You sent and not a phony, Elise prayed silently.

Lendar found a driveway several doors south and turned around. Javier Maldonado stood on the sidewalk leaning on an old Pontiac. The Pontiac's spots of rust colored primer contrasted with the sea-foam green that had been a popular color in the late fifties.

Too late to slink down and hide. His angry scowl let her know he'd definitely seen her.

"Damn." Elise said before she could think.

"Pardon me?" Lendar asked.

Elise started to say, "Nothing," then thought better of it. Let him have every opportunity to end this sooner instead of later, she thought. "Javier Maldonado. My ex-husband's best friend!"

Lendar cocked his brow again. Elise found the expression very sexy. He asked, "Is that individual a problem?"

Elise shrugged. "I don't know. He'll probably tell Gabriel, er, sorry, no probably about it, he definitely will tell

Gabriel. And Gabriel is a double-barreled jerk."

Lendar laughed. "Double barreled jerk? Is that an expression referencing double barreled shotguns?"

Elise nodded. "You shouldn't underestimate Gabriel. He's mean." Her eyes felt wet. Exhaustion, emotional turmoil, whatever the excuse, tears rolled down her cheeks. "After Javier talks to him, he'll come and bully us. Even though we're divorced, he's very possessive. I don't know why, but every time I try to find him to collect any child support he's disappeared, but if I meet someone nice or try to move to a new apartment, he's suddenly there, breathing down my neck." The tears flowed one by one down her cheeks.

Lendar scowled. "Any man who bullies a woman and child is a coward."

Elise whispered, "You don't know what he's capable of. And you can't protect me 24/7."

Lendar gave her that cocked brow look again. "Elise, I can and will." He shrugged, flicking a hand away from the steering wheel making some kind of sign with his fingers. His lip curled with disdain. "Bah, let him try."

Elise fished a napkin from her diaper bag, but Lendar's silk handkerchief interfered. She took it, wiped her eyes and blew her nose. "Lendar, you just really have no idea!"

Dear God in Heaven, I guess if Lendar isn't the one for me, Javier and Gabriel will run him off. But Lord, I don't want them to run him off! Oh Lord, help! They'll kill him or at the least beat him up!

Holding the handkerchief a few inches from her face, Elise cried, "Lendar, he's hateful. You don't know what he can do!"

Lendar pulled over and parked. "Elise." He paused, staring out the windshield for a moment before resuming. His brows furrowed, he studied her expression, his face earnest. "A man does not bully women and children, such a person is not a man, but a brute. And brutes, I can handle." He winked. "I'm a trained professional."

Elise's eyes widened. "Butler, valet types have to do that sort of thing…I mean, the body guard thing?"

Lendar laughed. "Elise, butler and valet only begin to describe my duties." He checked the street for traffic and pulled away from the curb.

5

Elise clutched Max in her arms. She breathed deeply and smiled. The painting studio smelled wonderful. Only an artist could find the odor of turpenoid and oil paint one of the most intoxicating perfumes in the universe. With mingled hope and trepidation, she tugged her canvas from its slot.

Lendar took hold of the opposite stretcher bar and gazed at the painting with evident interest. Suddenly nervous, Elise bit her lip. I hope he likes it! The painting was a landscape based on the Sandia Mountain foothills. She'd taken the hints of human forms she'd seen in the rock formations and emphasized those qualities until the setting morphed into figures. Lendar met her eyes, his eyebrow cocked in that amazingly attractive manner of his.

Elise pointed toward an empty easel not far away. "Please put it there."

He placed the picture and took Max. "Shall Max and I watch, or shall we go outside and play for awhile?"

Elise frowned. Suddenly she feared letting Max out of her sight. Lendar was a stranger. Though he'd made extravagant promises, he hadn't had opportunity to deliver on any of them. He might turn out to be some kind of mass murderer. She'd always heard mass murderers usually gave the impression of being really great guys. She gulped and answered, "Stay in here for now, if you don't mind."

Having said that, she was confronted with the reality that Max and Lendar hanging about in the studio would be infinitely distracting. "On second thought, let's go outside and I'll just work on my sketchbook. I can do this later."

Lendar had already allowed a squirming Max down onto the floor. He took his small hand. "As you wish."

"Ourside," Max said, pointing at the doorway and the pair walked into the hall.

Elise winced. It would have been nice to have that canvas finished today when she had someone to watch Max.

Stop it! Stop it! Tormenting yourself no matter what you choose. It's stupid.

She hesitated. Finish the painting or not? Is he really a mass murderer? A guy who blushes and bows? I mean seriously.

Well, what do you know about him anyway?

Nothing.

Nothing except he's really cute and I want to kiss him. Arrggghh.

Lendar and Max waited.

A couple of students passed by, seeing Lendar, they flicked knowing glances into the studio, then walked on. Except, they couldn't really know what was going on, could they? They probably thought it was some kind of a lover's quarrel; maybe husband and wife quarrel.

Don't you wish!

Patience continued to be characteristic of Lendar...so far. He seemed not the least perturbed at her stalling. Elise's heart softened. Just look at the two of them, they're like a matched set. Except Max isn't patient.

Max struggled to tow Lendar away. "Gro," he repeated.

"Well, what did you think of the picture?" Elise asked, her voice pinched.

Lendar swung Max onto his hip and strolled back into the studio. He paused before the canvas. "I have a feeling you've painted some place that may actually exist. But you've endowed the pink granite with a sense that it is living, a kind of blending of rock and flesh. I think you achieve that effect quite well."

Not only did his observation leave her breathless, but so did his intense expression. Lendar's not a man to fool around--get to the point and say it! If only her professor could see what she tried to achieve. He'd only made a crack about creating pornography and passing it off as landscape.

Elise's hand went to her throat where her pulse pounded under her fingertips. Lendar understands my work! I'd begun to wonder if anyone ever would.

Oh, God, is he real? Did You send him to me? He's so gorgeous.

Lendar suggested, "Why don't you pack up your canvas and bring it along? You can work at your apartment. I'll watch Max there."

Elise frowned. There wasn't space in her apartment to do that. When the bed was pulled down from its closet, there was barely room to get between it and the couch. The desk occupied the area on the north side of the bed and Max's crib the south, right in front of the clothing closet. Nowhere to put anything more, adding something that really only fit when the bed was put away just made a cramped space worse. "No. I'll work on it later. I'm behind on my sketches, we can do those."

Dejectedly she slid the canvas back into its slot. She felt inspired, like she could really accomplish a lot. But it would be foolish to put her trust in a man she'd barely met, only known for a few hours; a man her son trusted from the moment he laid eyes on him; a man who paid attention to the slightest details and tended so thoroughly to not only Max's needs, but her own; a man who understood her art…

Elise sighed. Yes, you're a complete ninny.

Outside, she sketched while Max and Lendar posed. Somehow Lendar made such sport of the task that Max happily co-operated. Soon, several five-minute sketches enlivened the pages of her sketchbook. Elise grinned. I can turn a couple of these into great portraits of Max! Way cool. This is probably the best sketching session ever.

"Time for supper," Lendar announced, apparently noting Max nearing exhaustion.

While they'd worked, the sun had wandered low on the horizon and twilight filled the plaza outside the art building.

"Good idea," Elise said. With the sketches finished, she felt more confident she could at least complete the essay after dinner.

"Where would you like to eat?" Lendar asked.

Max reached for his mother. "Dink."

"Yes honey, I want a drink too, but first we need to change your diaper." Elise looked for a grassy spot.

Lendar intervened. "Why don't we go back to the Escalade and you can change his diaper there?"

Elise nodded. "Ok. If you don't mind the odor."

Lendar shrugged. "Only temporary, I'm sure."

Elise nuzzled Max in the neck and kissed his cheek.

Max giggled. In the next breath he said, "Dink."

Elise pecked his cheek again. "Yes, honey, I know." To Lendar she said, "How about Hippolita's on Juan Tabo?"

An eager smile spread over Lendar's face. "Real New Mexican cuisine?"

Elise chuckled. "Yes." A gentle breeze carried cool moisture from a strip of freshly watered grass. Max molded himself to fit against her. "You're tired, aren't you honey?"

Max shook his head. He scanned his surroundings, stared at Lendar for a moment, then rested his head on Elise's shoulder and popped his thumb into his mouth.

Lendar seemed distracted. His eyes took on a far away kind of look, as if he were watching something in the distance.

Elise looked around, but couldn't see anything out of the norm. Wonder what's going on with him? Startled, she realized she'd already come to expect Lendar's undivided attention. Wow. Pensive, she watched her feet as they walked toward visitor parking. She grinned. Maybe he's a poetic, dreamer type.

They left the cool places and strolled onto hot asphalt where the sun's collected warmth radiated into the air. But, in the shadow of the architecture building the pavement had already turned cool. They shared companionable silence. For the first time it occurred to Elise that she didn't feel compelled to fill the gaps in conversation with talk.

Lendar unlocked the Escalade with his key fob and opened the driver's side passenger door for Elise. She laid Max down in the seat and unsnapped his pants while Lendar went around and opened the doors on the passenger side.

A breeze drifted over the middle seats, the new car smell mingling with the scent of something blooming nearby and hot, wet diaper. Lendar climbed into the driver's seat, leaving his door open. She glanced up and caught him punching buttons on his cell phone. She heard something whiz past her. She spun to see what it might have been but could see nothing. What's he doing? Judging by his expression, the text message, or whatever he'd discovered on his cell phone, didn't please him.

There's definitely more to this guy than what's on the surface, she thought. Next, she realized that thought didn't disturb her. Interesting. When I'm not looking for some excuse to be worried, I don't worry, I feel completely safe. Hmmn. Wonder if serial killers' victims feel like that?

Face it girl. When you were with Gabriel you never felt this safe!

Looking back she had to admit she'd ignored the warning signs he'd unwittingly given her. Back then, instead of working herself into a fit of worry, she'd made excuses for his behaviors and rationalized away the evidence that should have made it painfully clear that he was no fit husband or father. She smirked.

It's kind of dumb to make yourself feel insecure!

Elise kissed Max on his forehead, then whispered in his ear. "That marriage was all a stupid mistake, except for you."

Max smiled and pawed at her cheek before smearing her face with slobber.

Hugging him tightly, she went to the other side and strapped Max into the car seat. Over Lendar's shoulder she could see the scene he viewed on his cell phone. That's the house where we saw Javier. Elise squinted. Look at that, there's Javier on the sidewalk next to that Pontiac holding a can of beer and jabbering at Gabriel. Lendar must have felt her gaze, because, somehow, the image disappeared from the screen.

She dropped her eyes quickly, as if she'd had her attention fixed on Max the whole time. "'Bout ready," she said brightly, then looked up at him.

Lendar's smile seemed thin, as if he wondered what she might have seen. At last he said, "Excellent. I'm famished."

Once she was seated and buckled, he found the restaurant on his GPS unit and they left the parking lot. "Spaceman's Fugues" by Reeser Peland still played. It was like no music she'd ever heard before.

Soon as I can I'm going to do some research at Zimmerman or in the SUB on the public use computer and find out about that composer, Elise decided.

She studied the man named Lendar Marl. Had his choice of that particular driveway, Javier's driveway, been as random as it had first seemed? He used some kind of mini cam to watch the church ladies walking to their car. She'd assumed the camera was like one of those advertised for backing large vehicles, but what if this Escalade was more than a "luxury model," what if it was more like one of those armored SUV's wealthy Mexicans drove to protect themselves from drug gangs and kidnappers? Those were equipped with all sorts of high-tech stuff.

Who was his boss anyway? What kind of world did Lendar Marl normally work in? Was it the kind of world filled with people who partied on yachts in the Mediterranean off the coast of Greece where the waters were so deliciously blue? The kind of world where his boss might attend a fashion designer's cocktail party at the Louvre after hours? Or fly into New York just to attend the Metropolitan Opera? The kind of world where he regularly contended with paparazzi or stalkers and fended them off?

Elise peeled her eyes away and stared out the window at passing traffic, wondering.

Lendar seemed content in the silence.

Actually, come to think of it, comfort in silence was a good sign. Maybe, instead of finding things to worry about, she might try finding things to be glad about.

Elise looked at him again. His profile portrayed a solid, reliable sort of guy. Without realizing she said it aloud, she blurted, "Who are you?"

The night was young, not quite full dark, but Lendar's face was hidden in shadow. He asked, his voice gruff, filled with an intensity that took her breath away, "Are you ready to find out who I am?"

Elise gasped. "Oh!"

He turned his attention back to traffic. A thin line of light edged his forehead, nose and chin like a contour in a drawing, white on blue-black. When he glanced at her, the white line shifted to his cheek and jaw, the remainder of his face hidden in shadow, but his eyes seemed to bore through her with a laser-like power. "For now, Elise, know this: you are the most beautiful woman I've ever met in my entire lifetime and I intend to win your heart." He returned his attention to the road, the remnant of his laser-like gaze burning through her skin and into her bones.

Oh, man! That's...that's...intense. Breathe, girl breathe.

His chiseled face, his unruly hair, his strong shoulders and well-muscled legs, the thigh twitching as he stepped on the brake at the light, the large, capable hands on the steering wheel. A deluge of masculine mystic, intelligence, confidence, charisma and beauty threatened to drown her in a way she'd never experienced before.

And he hadn't even kissed her yet!

Swoon. That was the word. Swoon. Yes, she could swoon, just like those Victorian women in their too-tight corsets! Oh my God, she prayed, is he Your will?

As if sensing her thoughts, Lendar's eyes flickered over

her, his lips at once, firm with resolve and soft with longing. His attention returned to the road again.

Max burbled, bringing her back to reality, but this was a new reality that included a man named "Lendar Marl."

This is reality, everything before now was just the lead-up.

I'm really riding in this fabulous car with the most wonderful man in the world! Elise's hand went to her throat. She hardly saw the cars or buildings, only the colors, the bright shapes that were the taillights, headlights and illuminated signs of Albuquerque. A place that had suddenly become the most enchanted city on earth.

At the restaurant, Lendar held Max on one arm and her elbow with the other. His firm touch bringing a glorious sense of unity with him, as if they were one being, walking through the parking lot and into the restaurant. What an amazingly wonderful sensation, Elise thought. They stopped just inside the door, next to the "please wait to be seated" sign.

The hostess held menus. "Three? Highchair?"

"Yes," Lendar answered. Now his fingers moved to the small of her back where tingling delight wrought a scrumptious connection. As long as he touched her, they were one, moving in perfect unison. Nothing was ordinary. Not the tiny flower arrangements on the table, not the chatting diners, absolutely nothing. She belonged to another world.

Girl, you're falling hard, Elise thought, realizing she wanted to fall completely, with utter abandon.

Lendar pulled out a chair for her. Placed Max in the highchair and made sure he had a gadget to play with, something from his pocket, a small, articulated toy animal.

Who was Lendar Marl? Where did this perfect man come from? She stared at him, her neck stretched like some ridiculous crane.

"My name is Ann, I'll be your server tonight. What would you like to drink?"

Elise blinked and studied her menu. "Ah, I'll have the

raspberry tea."

Lendar smiled. "I'll have the same. Lemonade for the young master, please."

Nonplussed, Ann paused. "Oh, you mean your son." She smiled. "Ok, I'll be back with your drinks and take your order." She walked away.

Lendar grinned. "I'm at your mercy, Elise."

Elise gasped. Her heart already thumped with reverberations from Ann's words, "your son." She meant "your" as in plural possessive; she meant our son! She thinks Max is our son. And Lendar hadn't corrected her. Could it be that he liked the idea? Aloud she blurted, "What? You're at my mercy?"

To his grin Lendar added a cocked eyebrow; a look that apparently could bring warmth to her inner being every time.

Elise stared while her heart thrummed like a tightly wound spring ready to pop loose. How could he be at my mercy? What on earth does he mean? Oh God…surely not! Could he? Will he?

Lendar spoke, that delightful Spanish/European sound thonking her head like a stray tennis ball. "Though I've been here several months, I don't believe I've ever enjoyed an authentic New Mexican meal. Please, what do you recommend?"

Elise coughed to cover her bewilderment. Oh gak. He just wants to know what to order. Aloud she breathed, "Ah, let me see." Her eyes bounced off the menu, as if they were ping-pong balls, right back to Lendar's face, attracted like plastic wrap to static electricity. He was electricity. He was magnetism. Her heart might float right out of her body if she were to open her mouth more than the tiniest amount. She cleared her throat. "How about the blue corn, cheese enchiladas with red chile sauce." She said the words then felt her face twist into a ridiculous smile, like some fool. You are a fool!

Lendar folded his menu. "Very well, I'll try it. And for

Max?"

Ok, it's just the menu. You can handle this. She took a breath. "I think the lite omelet would be good for him, maybe with some green chile sauce on the side." She could hardly believe it. She'd managed to sound intelligible while her lungs fluttered like caged birds. She stared downward at the menu, senseless.

"And for you, my lady?"

Elise's head snapped up. My lady? Every system in her body froze, including her brain.

Lendar's eyes seemed to smolder with promises of love. A curl hovered over his brow like a question mark, like a finger beckoning her to draw nearer. His lips opened slightly, as if preparing for a kiss.

Unconsciously, she leaned just a little closer and licked her lips.

What are you doing? Get a grip!

Covering her mouth, she coughed again. Breathe, girl, breathe. "Ah, I'll have the guacamole burger…no, I'll have the same as you except with green chile instead of red."

Lendar smiled and folded his hands on the tabletop. "Ah, you will let me try the green chile then?" Those fabulous hands with their fine black hairs and clean, pink fingernails. Not one ring on any of his fingers.

Elise nodded, stupidly, wondering if spittle collected on her lips and a dull cow look had taken charge of her face. I don't think I've ever felt this way, no, I have *never* felt this way before in my life. I'm in love. Oh, God, what if he turns out to be a rat? Oh, Lord God, take him away from me tonight if he's a rat, please. I can't bear it if he's a rat. Oh, God!

The waitress returned. Lendar gave her their order, then reached across the table and took her hands.

Swooning. Yes, swooning. I'm turning into a complete, tongue-tied idiot. Swooning, right here, in front of everybody and their dog, and I don't care. His hands were so warm and dry. Crackling. That sensation of unity of flesh returned. She could lose herself in that. Give it all up, right now, this minute. Oh God, stop me from being an idiot, please!

"When will you graduate from University?" Lendar asked.

"What?" Elise gasped. Experimentally she touched her bottom lip with her tongue. She was convinced her mouth hung open, wet with slobber.

"How long before you graduate from UNM?"

"Ah…" Elise struggled to collect her wits. Now what was it he had asked her? Oh yes, when do you graduate, that's it. "This is the summer semester, if I pass all my classes, I can graduate in May, next spring."

"Not so very long."

"No, not really, though at the moment it seems very far away." Suddenly, Elise had to know, "When does your vacation end?"

"Seven months left." His not blue, not green eyes fixed on her like iron filings to a magnet. "I have the option to extend." His expression seemed to ask, "Do you want me to extend?"

Elise gushed. "Oh, wow. That is so amazing! Your boss can give you a year's paid vacation and extend it?"

Lendar rubbed her knuckle with his thumb. "He is a most generous employer. When the time is right, you shall meet him."

"What?" Elise blinked.

Lendar cocked his head, then leaned a little closer. She could feel his body heat. His cologne mixed with warm male musk and refried beans from nearby tables to fill her nostrils with excitement. His lips moved, she stared, struggling to hear him while they lured her closer. "When the time is right, you shall meet him. Both my boss and his wife."

"Meet who?"

"My boss and his wife."

Elise blurted, "Really? Why would they want to meet me?" His breath tingled across her skin, little prickles creating eddies of succulent sensation. I'm going to sigh like some silly bug-eyed girl from some absurd romance movie. Cue the violins. Sigh.

Lendar released her hands and relaxed into his seat back. He smirked. "Don't you want to know who I am, Elise?"

Max waved his arms. "Dink, mama, dink prease."

Oh, baby, I forgot. I'm sorry." She helped Max drink. Without thinking, Elise picked up the toy he'd dropped to the floor, took a baby wipe from her diaper bag and cleaned it before handing it back to him.

Lendar watched in quiet amusement. "My boss is also my oldest friend. We have been together since infancy."

"Infancy?" Elise's mouth twitched.

Girl, you are turning into a complete nincompoop. Infancy?

What sort of people know one another since infancy, especially a boss and his butler? How does that happen? Weird.

Lendar nodded, that wonderful European/Castilian Spanish accent flowing over her like perfume. "Yes, our families have been associated for centuries. My father serves his father. And my brother served his brother until the day he died saving him from a fire." His face darkened, likely with the memory of that day.

"Oh my, your brother is dead?"

Lendar nodded again. His face etched with an old familiar sorrow. "Yes, my brother, only in his teenage years; a dreadful day. We have always suspected arsonists, but never found proof."

"Oh, that's terrible," Elise said, feeling the horror of the incident only remotely. It seemed to her that the three of them sat in a sort of protected haven, a bubble shielding them from the ravages of time and awful things like fires and jealous ex-husbands. Maybe the whole restaurant existed within that bubble. The lights, the colors, the scents everywhere were heightened beyond anything she'd ever experienced.

"Please, tell me more about your home." Wide-eyed, she blinked, surprised that comprehensible words came out of her mouth.

Lendar looked wistful. "I haven't been home for many years. It is a beautiful place, very ancient. The house is in a valley. A stream runs not far away. Graceful trees centuries old shade the house. We have vineyards and livestock. I suppose by American standards it is a hobby farm, but we produce fine cheese and some excellent wine." He offered a wan smile.

Elise's eyes watered. This was all too much. Some kind of European villa somewhere. Oh God, when you answer prayers you answer them in spades! She managed to croak, "It sounds lovely."

"Oh, yes, it is very lovely. The house is quite old, you see, all the rooms stand in a row facing the hallway along the front." His fingers hovered over the table, as if he drew the floor plan there on the tablecloth. "The kitchen is a separate building which my father has joined with a glassed in breezeway where my mother grows herbs. The bedrooms are on the second floor, all facing the hallway, similarly to the ground floor. A spectacular view of hills rising to the mountains fills each window." Lendar stopped. "Bah, listen to me going on like this. It must be tedious for you."

Elise shook her head. "No, it's not boring at all." I could live there. Romantic, bucolic, serene. Spend my days painting landscapes and my nights in bed with... She blushed and dropped her eyes.

Ann arrived with their food. "Red, blue corn, cheese enchiladas for you sir, omelet with a side of green chile for your son and green, blue corn, cheese enchiladas for you ma'am. Will there be anything else?"

Lendar glanced at Elise, then replied. "Please, refresh our drinks and more than that, nothing for now. Thank you."

Ann offered a polite smile. "Enjoy."

Lendar cut into his food with obvious anticipation, then

slipped it into his mouth. "Delicious," he said, his mouth full. He covered his lips with a napkin. "Forgive me. It seems I am a creature of habit."

Elise giggled. "I'm glad you like it." She cut Max's food for him and daubed the bites with green chile sauce. She handed him the fork and helped him feed himself.

Max stubby fingers struggled to manage the utensil.

"Well done," Lendar said, when Max succeeded.

Max grinned and tried again. This time the bite slid to the floor. "Oops." He pointed and dropped another bit just to watch it fall.

Elise laughed. "Honey! Watch out, you're dropping food."

Max picked up another piece of omelet and deliberately dropped it. He clapped his hands. He reached to try it again, but Elise snatched the plate away. She glared at him, but Max only laughed. She offered him a drink. He swallowed, then stretched his fingers toward his food. Elise fed him a few bites, before turning her attention to Lendar whose smoldering expression remained, now veneered with amusement.

"He's a delightful child," Lendar said.

"He can be," Elise answered. "Except when he drops food on the floor."

Lendar waved his hand "The food will be disposed of and the floor cleaned. He will learn. You are an excellent teacher." His face turned serious. "How may I contact you?"

Elise stared at her plate, then attacked her food. Gak, he wants my number.

Well, don't you want him to have your number? How else is he going to ask you out again if he doesn't have your number?

Girl! He knows where you live.

So why don't you give him your number?

After several bites, she spoke. "I'll give you my cell phone number." She set the fork down and fished in her diaper bag for a piece of paper.

"Elise, I can enter it into my unit." Lendar already had his impressive cell phone out of his pocket.

"Is that an I-phone?" Elise asked. "I've always wanted to see one of those."

"You may take a look, but first your number?"

"505…of course you have to put a one in front of that. At least, I think you do."

Lendar entered the number and handed Elise the phone.

She played with it for a minute. How do I get to that section where he was watching Gabriel and Javier? Man, I don't know how to operate this thing.

Lendar had left his photo collection on display. All she could do was flip through the images. Most were New Mexico landscapes, but there were a couple of her and Max. Duh. Nothing more.

Any special features, like the series of images she'd surreptitiously caught over his shoulder, were carefully locked away from her prying, not that she was capable of unlocking them anyway. She had no experience operating fancy phones. Besides who could make sense of his strange icons. Weird, like cuneiforms or something. They don't look like anything I've seen before.

She kept flipping through pictures until she reached the beginning of the set, an image of herself with Max in his stroller standing in front of Buffalo Exchange. The woman in the picture appeared vulnerable and worn. She stared at the camera, wide-eyed, as if about to bolt. It must have been taken that moment when Lendar called, "Miss," and she'd prepared to run. She handed Lendar the phone leaving that picture on the screen.

Funny, I don't remember him snapping any pictures.

Elise swallowed the niggling question about how that picture was taken. "It's a real nice phone," she said. "That picture of me and Max at the aquarium is pretty good. Could I have a copy?"

Lendar grinned. "Yes, you may. I'll print it for you tonight." He looked at the phone, astonishment washed over his face. He stuffed it into his pocket, glanced at Elise and then back at his food, his face an unreadable mix of emotion.

Hmn, for once he looks like the one who's overwhelmed.

Elise picked at her enchilada.

I'm overwhelmed, totally out of my comfort zone. She lifted a morsel into her mouth with her fork. Maybe I kinda like it. She winced. He probably wonders what the heck he's doing with a loser like me, she thought.

Unwilling to clean up any more omelet from the floor or be forced to discipline Max in the restaurant, she spoon-fed him the rest of his omelet. While she held his cup for him, she surreptitiously watched Lendar.

Lendar stared at his food, looking dazed, as if he'd just seen an alien from outer space or some dead person walking. Gradually he seemed to sort through whatever had assaulted his brain. His face transformed, as if he'd just awoken from a coma. A smile played about his lips and he resumed eating.

This time Elise felt compelled to fill the silence. "Lendar, what are your plans?"

He made a pucker-shrug of his lips. "Eh, many things. See New Mexico. Perhaps Colorado. The Royal Gorge Bridge. Pikes Peak. I have yet to visit Chaco Canyon or Jemez Springs. Carlsbad Caverns. The Gila Wilderness." He paused. "Perhaps you might be willing to accompany me…when you are available, of course."

Elise replaced Max's drink to the table and folded her hands in her lap and hunched her shoulders. Oh, how I'd love to do that, see all those places. Aloud she said, "Well, I do have to be in class and finish my assignments."

Lendar cut through his enchilada with the side of his fork. When he looked up, he smiled. "Naturally. Now, please. You see, if I can help you in any way, it is to my benefit because it will free you to accompany me." He gestured her direction, then toward himself as he spoke.

Elise blushed. I've never met a man so willing to help, even in his own "selfish" interests.

Ok, girl, face it. Guys aren't this sweet to losers, which confirms the fact that you're not a loser. Serial killers might be a different matter.

Like you know anything about serial killers!

Besides, you already know you're not a loser. You're a queen in God's Kingdom, even if you don't have any physical evidence of that yet. So stop telling yourself you're a loser!

This man is The One. Now where did that notion come from? A fresh flush of red rushed her face. This is only the first date! Get a grip!

Elise bit her lip. "Ah, here, try this enchilada with green chile." She used her clean spoon and scooped up a sample for him.

Lendar leaned her direction, his mouth ready.

She'd intended to place the food on his plate or hand him the spoon, not feed him. Heat crept up her neck. She stuck the spoon into his mouth before the trembling at her shoulder could transfer to her hand. Whew! Man, who woulda thought feeding a man could be so stressful, gak, and erotic!

Forgetting his earlier promise, Lendar spoke with his mouth full. "Delightful. I like both flavors. Is the red chile a different species from the green chile?"

Elise shook her head. "Ah..." she sucked a breath. "Not necessarily..." Ok, breathe. "Ah. Usually the green is picked earlier from the same plants where red is harvested later in the season."

Lendar spooned some refried beans into his mouth. "I must have these recipes."

Elise laughed. Tension released, she said, "Green chile is addicting. There are people all over the world who order frozen green chile to be shipped to them from New Mexico."

Lendar cocked his head. "Really."

Elise nodded. "Oh yes."

Lendar bunched runny cheese together and pushed it onto his fork with his knife. "Hmn, well, I could come to crave it, yes, I think I might."

They ate in companionable silence for several minutes. Elise asked, "So, your parents are still living?"

Lendar's expression clouded. "They were alive when I left home."

Elise frowned. "They've died since you've been on vacation?"

The clouding thickened. "Probably."

Elise stared. "Why don't you know? Aren't you in contact with them?"

Lendar wiped his mouth. "No, our home is very remote and communications are not easy." He shrugged and drank.

That dark look...was it grief? Yes, I think it is. Puzzled, Elise stared at her plate, collected a smidgen of refried beans to go with her enchilada and popped it into her mouth. Absently, she chewed while her mind churned. She could picture no location in Europe where a fancy villa such as Lendar had described could be out of range of modern communications. And he had access to all sorts of high tech stuff. How could he be out of touch with his folks? What is with this guy?

Lendar stopped eating. He stared at his plate, then looked straight at her, his face the picture of boyish, innocent pleading. "Elise, will you give me a chance? Will you be patient with me until I can reveal all to you?"

Elise set her fork down and held Max's drink for him. Max seemed droopy. Well, duh, he's tired. Yes, but you're distracting yourself; you're focusing on Max instead of Lendar's questions.

He's hiding something.

Why can't men just be simple?

Arrgghh.

Her heart thudded and the restaurant seemed to fill

with haze. She set the cup down and folded her hands in her lap. Well, what else are you going to do? If you say, "No, I'm not going to give you a chance," it's all over! You don't want that do you?

Besides, you want the same opportunity, to be given a chance, to not be written off. You haven't exactly told him everything either.

Maybe there's a perfectly logical, not terrifying explanation.

It's not like he's telling you it's none of your business, he's just asking you to wait. He must have a good reason for asking you to wait.

Before she could dither any more, she blurted, "Yes, I will."

Relief flooded Lendar's face, a fresh rush of masculine lusciousness. "You could not possibly understand how delighted I am to hear you say that, Elise." He seemed about to say more, as if he were prepared to add "beloved," or "darling," or "my love!"

Gak! Oh God, oh my God. God please....please, make this real forever. Elise clutched her hands together in her lap, the physical expression of her pleading prayer.

Serious peacefulness, almost monkish...no...more like a warrior at home in his skin, spread over his features. Oh, God, he's so sexy! She lifted a hand. It hovered over her plate tentative, hesitant. She wanted to take her index finger and draw the line of his brow, draw his cheek ridge and his lips...press her thumb into his mouth and...

Lendar took her hand and pressed it between his palms. Her small fist disappeared within his grasp. It didn't feel confined or threatened, but content and protected. My whole body, Elise thought, take my whole body. He pressed her fist against his cheek, then stared at her, those eyes searching, as if he could pierce her flesh. And suddenly she wanted him to do just that. Instantly, her face burned brilliant red.

"Elise," he said slowly, then stopped. His mouth opened again, but nothing came out. It closed, though it remained ready to kiss or speak or something…but nothing happened. He seemed bewildered, frustrated, excited and grief stricken all at once.

What is the matter with this guy? She felt certain her eyes glazed over. The warm oneness she'd enjoyed only moments earlier fizzed into scattered memory.

He let go of her hand. "Forgive me." His face suddenly lost radiance, as if the sun had set and left him in twilight. His eyes were mournful, his mouth flat.

"Why?"

"I long to reveal all, but at the proper moment, in the proper place. Now," he made one of his strange sign-language movements, "in this restaurant, neither criterion is met."

Elise rubbed her forehead and then sipped her tea. "Ok."

Ann reappeared.

"Would you care for any dessert?"

Lendar glanced at Elise, then replied. "No thank you, the check please."

Ann nodded. "More tea?"

Elise replied. "Yes please. And I need a take-out box."

"I'll be right back with tea, a box and your ticket."

Lendar's eyes gradually lost their mournful appearance, but his hands remained distant. Finally, he spoke. "This has been a delightful day."

Elise nodded. "Yes, it has. Thank you." She smiled.

You were rushing too fast anyway. No. Correction. I was rushing too fast. All in my head.

Lendar was talking, his voice filled with resignation, as if backing away from some wonderful prospect. "…but Max needs his rest. I'll take you home." After a swallow of tea, he asked, "May I call you tomorrow?"

Elise felt her heart flutter. It didn't seem to care if she rushed. In fact, her heart recommended it. "Yes."

He grinned, then looked at his cell phone. "Please, excuse me a moment." Lendar left the table in search of the restroom, or so Elise presumed.

Ann returned with the check, handed Elise a foam box, poured tea and left.

Elise scooted her food into the box, then studied the restaurant. Patrons lifting their forks and sipping their beverages; families chattering happily under a blanket of music. I could really get used to this, she thought.

She cleaned Max's hands with a wipe while he jabbered in his private language.

Lendar returned. He read the ticket, then slipped sufficient cash to pay for the meal and tip into the wallet. "Are you ready?"

Elise nodded.

Lendar gathered Max into his arms. When they left the restaurant, he took her elbow again, same as before. And that sense of oneness returned.

6

Lendar helped Elise into the Escalade and strapped Max into his car seat.

Max clung to his neck. "No wanna," he said.

Elise turned and tugged on his sandaled feet. "Max honey, we have to do it this way, if we don't we'll get into trouble."

Lendar unclasped Max's hands. His face marked with determination and a hint of sadness.

Max wailed. "No wanna." His fingers flailed helplessly.

Lendar glanced her way, his expression verging on anguish.

Elise unbuckled and slipped into the middle seat. "Honey, I'll sit beside you. How's that?" She leaned her head his direction and placed her arm over him. The position was awkward, but he calmed down.

Lendar hurried to the driver's seat and started the motor. He checked for pedestrians or cars in his way, then backed out.

Max was tired. He'd become quiet during the latter part of the meal, idly toying with a bit of green chile on his high chair tray and absently drinking his lemonade. He was a good boy to sit so patiently, waiting instead of crying in his exhaustion. By the time Lendar joined traffic on Juan Tabo, Max already slept.

Elise didn't speak. She knew Lendar checked on her occasionally in the rear view mirror, but she stared straight ahead. I'm so tired. I'm not going to get that essay done tonight. I'll have to work on the painting tomorrow, somehow. Thinking about her unfinished work only made her feel worse. Oh God, why does all this goodness have to be mixed with a bunch of dreary work?

Traffic was light; they arrived at her street within

minutes. He slowed. The nearer they came to her apartment the more he seemed in a quandary, as if analyzing something and grappling with a decision. Finally, he glanced back at her and stated flatly, "Elise, when we arrive at your apartment, stay in the vehicle."

Elise's eyes widened. "What?"

Lendar stopped at a stop sign. "When we arrive at your apartment, stay in the vehicle." His voice carried an unmistakable tone of warning.

Elise bit her lip. "Ok. I'll stay in the car."

Lendar went through the intersection and then let the Escalade edge forward on momentum. "I'll adjust the windows so you can see out, but none can see in. Understand? I know you're tired, but we have an unpleasant surprise waiting for us."

Elise nodded. "Oh, you mean Gabriel and Javier. You've been watching them on your cell phone. Do you have some kind of camera planted in my yard somewhere?"

Lendar grinned. "Elise, you are a wonder."

Elise gazed at headlights approaching the intersection. They flashed through the passenger window arcing through the Escalade as the unknown driver made the corner. "I thought so. I happened to get a look when I was changing Max's diaper at the university."

"I suspected you might have." Lendar chuckled and stopped by the curb. His wrist resting on the steering wheel, he turned to look at her. "No matter what happens, stay in the vehicle." He made a chopping sign, his hand a blade slicing the air.

Elise bit her lip and nodded.

Lendar put the Escalade in park.

Bruce sat outside his apartment, insects swirling around his porch light. He held a motorcycle magazine up in the bulb's yellow rays, then turned a page. Two figures and the Pontiac stood silhouetted against the porch light at Javier's house. Sure enough, it's Gabriel and Javier. Oh, Father, please send angels to protect us. Bless You Lord, thank You.

Lendar stepped out of the Escalade, shut the door and leaned against it. The lock clicked. He folded his arms over his chest.

The moment stretched. Max snored peacefully. Bruce perused his magazine. The two shadowy figures, Gabriel and Javier, grew statue-like in stillness. Finally, one of them separated from the tableau. It was Gabriel striding with belligerent confidence toward Lendar, the awkward slap of his athletic shoes the only indication he was drunk. Javier trailed behind, stumbling, meandering as if he couldn't keep to a straight path.

They're both drunk as skunks, Elise thought, chewing a fingernail. Lendar said he could handle a brute, but can he handle two of them? Oh God, help!

Bruce lowered his magazine and looked up with interest. When he realized it was Gabriel stomping across the street, he stood and dropped the magazine into his lawn chair.

Gabriel pointed at Lendar. "My friend says he saw you with my wife. I don't like guys hanging around my wife."

Lendar made no reply.

Gabriel shouted. "Are you the guy dating my wife?"

Lendar answered. "I am courting Elise Ramos."

If a man's voice could freeze a person, Lendar's could. Wow, he's so totally in control. This polished, professional, rich man is doing battle for me! Yes, I could swoon, but then I'd miss something.

She gnawed another fingernail. What if this all goes very badly?

Oh, no, not that. Please not that.

Gabriel spat. "Elise Ramos is my ex-wife. Ramos, that's *my* name! And you're an asshole." He glanced back at Javier. "Did you hear that, Javier? He said he's "courting" Elise. Nobody uses words like that. The man is some kind of pansy-fluff asshole." To Lendar he snarled, "You sound like a wussy, British-prick-loser from some douche-y chick flick." Hands clenched, he glared at Lendar. "Asshole."

Lendar said nothing. His body seemed wound tight, yet completely under control. Every muscle tensed and defined even through his shirt.

He's so sexy! What if he whups Gabriel? Oh, man, that would be so nice! No more of Gabriel's awful bullying! Elise shivered, remembering her previous date. Gabriel had showed up the following morning, catching her as she was about to leave. He'd shoved her into the wall and called her names, but Bruce had knocked on the door asking questions until Gabriel left. She'd turned the guy down when he asked for another date.

Gabriel's eyes bulged and a vein popped into prominence on his forehead. He growled. "I'm here to tell you: hands off my woman, gringo." He moved a little closer. "She's my wife."

Lendar replied calmly. "You have no claim to Elise. She will do as she pleases."

Gabriel pecked at Lendar with his index finger. "Like hell she will. We have a kid together. No way she's going to corrupt my son, sleeping around like a slut."

Elise swallowed, her eyes tearing without warning. Javier disappeared behind a car parked a few doors south of the Escalade. Elise squinted, trying to see where he went, but failed. Uh oh, he's sneaking around behind! Should I tell Lendar…

"A gentleman never makes a public display accusing a lady and slandering her reputation," Lendar said, his voice an icy blast.

Gabriel laughed and lunged, a switchblade snapping into view, a sudden flash of silver in the faint light.

Elise screamed. Max woke up with a wail. She unbuckled him and hugged him tight, suppressing her own terror for his sake.

Lendar threw his forearm upward deflecting Gabriel's thrust, grabbing the arm with his other hand and twisting the wrist behind his head. In the next moment, he flipped Gabriel onto his back, his body making a resounding whack against the pavement accompanied by an "ooof," his breath knocked out of him. With his elbow pointing toward the sky and his wrist firmly in Lendar's grip, it was easy for Lendar to slide the knife from Gabriel's hand. He flung the blade under the Escalade.

Impulsively, Elise kissed Max on the forehead. Wow! That was a thing of beauty!

Lendar's baritone cut through the night. "You've had a bit too much to drink. Perhaps you should apologize and take your leave."

Gabriel hissed. "Like hell."

Near the front of the Escalade Javier roared, charging Lendar like a ridiculous, lumbering elephant. Lendar glanced up at him. In the next moment, Javier's knees jerked and he landed face down on the pavement, his bottom lip mashed in a stupid, drunken "o."

Gabriel craned his neck and whined in rage. "If you hurt him…"

Lendar's tone remained coldly formal. "Your friend also seems to have consumed too much alcohol. Perhaps both of you should go home and sleep it off."

Gabriel stiffened. "Let me go, you asshole."

Lendar gripped his hair and lifted his face upward. "You won't call me that again, Mr. Ramos." He tossed Gabriel's head in the direction of the asphalt and pushed him over with his boot. "Go home."

Gabriel rolled. He stopped in the middle of the street, got to his feet and broke into a stumbling run. Now reviving, Javier lay in a bloody mess, moaning. His girlfriend hurried to his side and helped him up. Together they shuffled after Gabriel.

Once the three had crossed the street and onto Javier's property, Lendar unlocked the Escalade and opened the door for Elise.

She set Max down in the seat, flung herself into his arms and kissed him on the cheek. "You were magnificent."

Lendar shrugged. "They were drunk. Didn't require much skill or effort."

Elise shook her head. "Nonsense." She let him go and turned to collect Max.

Max rested his head on her shoulder, his thumb searching for his mouth.

Elise picked up the carry-out box from the restaurant and her diaper bag. She studied Lendar's face. Should I ask him in?

He's just whupped your jerky ex-husband.

You'd better ask him in.

At last she murmured, "Will you come in?"

Lendar touched her arm, ready to pull her into an embrace, but he stopped. "I'll be there in a moment." His face and body were firm like a rock, her rock.

Feeling more desirable and beautiful than she'd felt in ages, Elise nodded, checked the street and walked toward her apartment.

Bruce waited on the curb. "You all right?"

"I'm fine. Max and I were perfectly safe in the car."

Bruce fell in beside her as she walked up the sidewalk. "I know, but that guy, what's his name?"

"Lendar Marl."

"Lendar must be a black belt or something. Maybe Jujitsu or Aikido. He just flipped Gabriel on his back easy as you please."

"Yes," Elise breathed. "It was amazing." She shot Bruce a wet smile and clutched his hand. "I need to put Max to bed."

"Ok, Elise, just glad you both weren't hurt." Bruce seemed to want to say or do more, but in the next instant his chin dropped and he went into his apartment.

Elise unlocked her door and hurried inside. Light and a few insects from Bruce's porch fixture scattered into her room. She decided it best not turn on any lamps. She set Max in his crib while she put the leftover food in the refrigerator.

Max whimpered from the crib. "Mama hug."

Elise fetched Max and covered his face and neck with kisses. "Time to brush your teeth, honey." She was standing at the kitchen sink with Max perched on the edge when Lendar appeared in the doorway. He placed her paint box on the end table beside the couch.

"Hi." Elise parked Max on her hip and he popped his thumb into his mouth. "I just finished brushing Max's teeth." She crossed the floor to stand beside Lendar.

He ruffled her son's hair.

Max's mouth made a popping sound when he tugged his thumb free. "Wanna seep," he said. He wriggled, holding his arms out.

Elise let him go to Lendar.

"Yes, Max?" Lendar asked.

Max hugged his neck. "Endar gro seep now." He kissed Lendar on the cheek with a damp, minty smack.

Lendar chuckled, delighted. "That's an excellent suggestion, Max, but first, may I speak to your mother?"

Max nodded and reached for Elise. "Gro bed."

Hands in his pockets, Lendar leaned against the doorframe.

Elise lay Max in the crib, changed his diaper and finished dressing him in a light t-shirt and short pants. She murmured into his ear, "I love you, honey." She kissed him and settled him on his stomach. His legs curled under his hips. She pulled the shade down to block the bulk of the light from the streetlamp and threw a thin blanket over him.

Lendar used his handkerchief to unscrew the porch light.

Elise shot him a quizzical glance.

"Too many insects," he said by way of explanation.

Bluish-white light outlined the sink, a chair and the edge of the kitchen doorway. On the opposite side of the apartment, illumination from streetlamps on the south shone through the lace curtains making a pattern on the sheets and Max's sleeping form. He relaxed, his legs stretching flat, his fists now lose and open, his breathing, soft and deep.

Elise waited. Now what?

Lendar murmured. "Come outside, I want to see what Gabriel will do."

She pulled her keys from her bag and joined him. He closed the door. A tree standing between Elise's apartment and Javier's house spread its blanket of darkness over them. The leaves' two-dimensional shadows swayed back and forth on the wall above their heads.

Suddenly the Escalade's motor started and it drove itself up the hill and around the corner. A flash and a puff of smoke marked the spot where the switchblade had once lain.

Elise stared, first at the moving vehicle, then at Lendar. How did he do that?

Lendar offered a faint smile. "Remote control," he said, and winked.

She nodded. "Ha, I'll bet. And you didn't touch a single button. You have a lot of high tech stuff, Mr. Lendar Marl. Better than anything I've ever seen."

Lendar shrugged.

Elise squinted at him. "What sort of person is your boss anyway? Some super rich oil prince with more money in his personal account than most countries?"

At first Lendar didn't answer, then he said, "Not exactly." He pursed his lips, then said, "I dislike keeping things from you, Elise, but I can't explain more at present." He looked down at her, his expression intense, as if willing her to be patient with him, to trust him.

She sighed. "You've been spying on Gabriel and Javier all afternoon and night. Do you spy on me too? Were you just pretending when you asked me for directions to my house?"

A crease appeared between his brows. He stroked the line of her jaw from her ear to her chin. He licked his lips, his eyes fixed on her mouth, as if he wanted to taste her. His whole body seemed to shout, "I want to take you into your hot apartment and ravish you."

Temperature in the immediate vicinity seemed to rise a few degrees. She suppressed a gasp and the usual internal argument, for once allowing herself to react without analysis. Oh, my!

Her body burned and she knew if he pressed, she'd be unable to resist. Her lips opened slightly and her breathing quickened. Oh, just forget that stupid question about spying and kiss me!

Lendar studied her face, from hairline to chin. "No, I haven't spied on you, Elise. But if Gabriel won't desist, I may be forced to keep watch over you every time you leave your apartment."

She stared. She wanted to feel his body hard against her. By force of will she pulled her mind from those thoughts and the precipice where she might lose self-control. "I believe you," she said. "I also believe I've lost my mind."

Lendar chuckled and opened his arm.

For a split second she hesitated, then she entered his embrace. The heat that had roiled off his body moments earlier now seemed carefully smoored. She felt safe, secure and comfortable.

He pointed at Javier's house. Softly, he said, "Gabriel's about to come out. Hold perfectly still." Together they watched a yellow rectangle appear in the darkened wall. Gabriel tripped across the doorjamb and onto the sidewalk.

She copied Lendar's quiet way of talking, her voice not a whisper, but yet barely audible. "He's angry; you made him look like a fool."

Though the neighborhood was quiet compared to daytime noise, it was by no means silent. A dog barked, a car rolled down a nearby street and a jet lumbered overhead while crickets sang.

Lendar's smile reached only one corner of his mouth. "He made himself look foolish, that's what infuriates him the most."

Gabriel paused beside his pick-up, an old Ford F-100 from the 70's. He looked up and down the street, presumably checking for Lendar's Escalade.

Wistfully, Elise muttered, "He used to have a 50's model pick-up he fixed up real nice. He had to sell it when he started doing drugs and lost his business."

"Oh really? He had a business?"

"He fixed up old cars, did hydraulics for low riders, after market upgrades that sort of thing. He was really pretty good at it. Javier was his detail painter, he used to do beautiful murals on hoods and doors."

Lendar grunted. "That explains why you married him." He paused then said, "Tonight he has lost face at my hand, but he's done far worse to himself."

Gabriel glanced their direction.

Elise's failed to suppress a sharp intake of breath. "Can't he see us?"

Lendar answered. "We're in the shadow of the tree. When he left the darkness under the eaves and went to his vehicle, he entered scattered light rays from the streetlamp. He's a bit light-blind, especially to motionless objects in the dark."

Gabriel climbed into his truck, backed out and drove north toward Central Avenue.

"Now he's gone..." Lendar pressed her body close.

She did not resist. She melted to fit his frame, her breasts touching his chest, her thigh pressed to his. She breathed his unique scent.

One hand meshed with her hair, cupped around the back of her head, the other at her hip. He buried his face in the hair just above her ear. "Elise..." he breathed.

Elise murmured. "Did you mean what you said in the car, about intending to win my heart, I mean, *really* mean it?"

His voice was laden with banked desire. "With every fiber of my being." His lips hovered over hers.

She closed her eyes, waiting for his kiss. She could feel his energy, the force of his desire; smell his musky scent. Nothing happened.

Elise's eyes popped open. His remained closed, his mouth still ready, his nostrils flaring. She waited, memorizing his face, the way it looked in this light with its plains and cliffs. His eyes came open. She stared at him, puzzled.

His expression anguished, he said, "Elise…I…I will call you tomorrow." He crushed her to himself then released her.

She stepped back. "Ok, that will be nice." A hesitant smile plied her lips. Why didn't he kiss me?

Lendar bowed. "Good night." The Escalade met him at the curb.

7

Elise watched Lendar walk away, his stride confident and powerful.

Why didn't he kiss me? He's so darn formal. She glanced toward Javier's house where all the lights had been turned off, then slipped into her apartment and locked the door.

Max slept soundly.

She opened the kitchen window and placed the fan on the windowsill where it could suck in the cool night air. Next, she opened the front window near Max's crib just a crack to give the air somewhere to flow and adjusted the blanket over him, just in case the moving air chilled him.

In the bathroom, Elise closed the toilet and sat on its lid. Lendar's words burned in her brain. She repeated them, already having committed them to memory. She stood and dug through the towels to uncover her journal. Sitting back on the toilet lid, she copied the words: "For now, Elise, know this: you are the most beautiful woman I've ever met in my entire lifetime and I intend to win your heart."

Her hands trembled and her heart shuddered. He's a man of incongruencies. He is so very polite, yet he chews with his mouth open. He has all this high tech stuff, yet he doesn't know if his parents are dead or alive because they're too remote. He wanted to kiss me, I'm certain of it, so why didn't he? Her body flamed at the remembrance of his arm around her, his hand tangled in her hair, his breath exhaled over her flesh, the breathing shallow and full of desire.

Why didn't he kiss me?

Her first thought was to find some flaw in herself to blame. Her heart thumped. If he hadn't kissed her because of some flaw within her, why would he fight Gabriel? How many men would knowingly enter a knife fight with a jealous ex-husband? No, there was no flaw within her, at least with respect to Lendar. If there had been, Lendar would never have made this declaration; he wouldn't have asked if he might call her tomorrow. Not kissing her must be a separate issue. So why didn't he kiss me?

The physical desire was there, she'd felt it in the electricity of his touch, in the trembling of his hand; she'd seen it in his lips, in his eyes that burned and searched hers…the love grew, but he waited for the right moment…maybe he was the rare man who wanted more than body heat…

Elise read the words again. Maybe Lendar didn't kiss me because he doesn't think he's won me yet. Maybe he hasn't. Maybe I'm not really ready to be kissed. Maybe when we twentieth-first century people put the kissing before the commitment it's a mistake. What a strange mix of old-fashioned chivalry and high-tech James Bond he is! A euphoric sigh escaped her lips. She clutched the open journal to her chest, as if she might press the words into her skin.

Wait! What if Lendar didn't believe in God? What if he rejected Jesus as Lord? Oh, God, please, not that. Elise gasped and pushed the worry away. Trust. Trust God. He's the One who brought us together. Just trust. The weight lifted.

Emotions running the gamut from worry, anxiety, fear, adoration and joy that had filled the day lumbered to a standstill in a thunk of physical weariness that demanded she sleep. The journal closed and hidden again under the towels, Elise washed her face and brushed her teeth. She went to the kitchen for a drink.

The backyard was as dreary as any other night, bathed in blue from the streetlight; the Payne's gray gravel, coarse and unfriendly; the concrete block wall brutal in its edges. But somehow the scene didn't depress her. Her reality now included something wonderful. She changed into her nightgown and pulled down the bed. As soon as her head touched the pillow, she fell asleep.

8

Someone knocked on the door. Daylight. Elise groaned and looked for the clock on the wall in the kitchen. 10:00 a.m. Oh great, I'll miss church, again.

Max clutched the crib rail, jumping up and down. "Lolly, Lolly," he cried.

Elise rolled toward the closet, took her robe from the hook and went to the door. "Hello, Lolly."

"Girl, you never sleep in like this, never. Must have been some kind of hot date!" Lolly breezed in, set the sack she carried on the bed and hoisted Max from the crib. "Max, my sweetheart." She blew her raspberry greeting on his cheek and tugged up his shirt to blow another one on his belly.

Max giggled and pulled her hair.

Lolly held him at arm's length. "Max, you are in need of attention. Pew-wee! You are odiferous!"

Elise took Max and spread a changing pad on the bed. "Oh Max, I'm so sorry. How long have you been putting up with this diaper?"

Lolly picked up the sack. In the kitchen she set it on the table. "Elise, if he'd been suffering for very long he'd have woken you up."

"I suppose you're right." Changing her mind, Elise took Max into the bathroom. "I'll be just a minute, Lolly."

"I'll start some tea."

After an initial wipe-off, Elise took Max into the shower and washed him thoroughly. When she emerged, both she and Max were dressed for the day.

Lolly had placed a cheese Danish, one for each of them, on saucers. She cut Max's into bite size pieces. She groused, "You haven't got any ice."

Elise helped Max into his highchair. "No, sorry."

"You can make ice in anything Elise. Empty sour cream

containers will work."

Elise shrugged. "If you drink a hot beverage, you don't notice the heat."

Lolly rolled her eyes. "Sure, whatever, but I like iced tea on a hot day. Sweet iced tea with lemon; like they serve in the south, where they understand these things…"

Elise acted as if she hadn't heard a word Lolly said. She plopped into one of her two kitchen chairs, a dreamy expression plying her face.

Lolly looked askance at her. "So. You going to tell me?"

Elise got up to take the kettle off the stove and poured hot water into the tea pot where Lolly had already prepared a couple of tea bags. "Hmn, well. We went to the aquarium, only that seems like it happened years ago. I just love the ocean tank, I could sit there watching those fish for hours…"

"Hrumph. Doubt you were watching the fish!" Lolly grumped.

Elise grinned. "We ate a late lunch in the café, you know, the one right next to the ocean tank, around the corner from the main observation area. It was a really late lunch, like four or something. We had hamburgers."

Lolly took a bite of her Danish. "Yeah, I've eaten there before. Their hamburgers are ok." She eyed Elise through her brows.

"Afterward, Lendar took me home so I could get my paint box and pencils." Elise touched her friend's forearm. "Lolly, he drives this fabulous Escalade. It's that delicious, cherry red Cadillacs come in these days. The seats were creamy leather, scrumptious. He played some lovely music on his CD player, or MP3 player or whatever it was, and I just went right to sleep."

"You fell asleep?" Lolly snorted.

"Yeah, well, I was tired. And the music was so relaxing. And the seats were just that wonderful." Elise sighed. "We came here. I got my paint box and we had to turn around so we could go back north and you wouldn't believe it: Javier lives only a couple doors south of here. He was standing in the driveway glaring at us."

"Really." Lolly looked disgusted. "A pimple on an otherwise delightful day."

"I wonder why I haven't seen him around before."

"Maybe he just moved in." Lolly frowned. "Actually, I'm not surprised you haven't seen him around, he probably sleeps all day."

"Oh, yeah, you have a point. Anyway, Lendar took us to the university. He likes my painting." Elise's face soured a bit. "Wish my professor liked it!" She paused. "Lendar and Max posed for me. I managed to make some great sketches. Then we went to dinner--really late dinner--probably walked in right before closing time. After that, when he brought us home, Gabriel was here."

Lolly whistled. "Wish that man would drop off the face of the earth."

"Lolly! That's not very Christian of you."

"Ha, look who's talking about what's Christian! You weren't in church this morning." Lolly pointed first at Elise, then at herself. "I was. I attended the 8 o'clock. The church police will be paying you a visit..."

"Yeah, well, they already have. They were here yesterday, Mrs. Halson and Mrs. Tafoya brought a casserole." Elise stretched her clasped hands across the table in a gesture of supplication. "Oh, Lolly, now I feel guilty I slept in. I have a lot of work to get done today. It hit me yesterday on the way to the aquarium...we only have one week of school left!"

"Tell me about it!" Lolly leaned the chair back on its two hind legs and opened the refrigerator. "Where's that casserole? I'm hungry."

Elise took a bite of her cheese Danish. "I gave it to Bruce."

"Ah, well, he probably does need it worse than you, though you're not exactly overflowing with goodies there, girl." Lolly kicked the refrigerator door shut. She shook her head. "A lot of work to get done? Don't wanna hear any more of your excuses." She put on a preachy, whiny tone. "You should be in church!" She pointed and wagged her finger at Elise.

Elise winced. "I know. I'll have to find some way to make it up. It's just that getting to church is not exactly easy. The worst part is it takes 45 minutes to get there, 45 minutes to come back and I don't have that kind of time today. Oh Lolly, I don't think Jesus would appreciate it if I flunked!"

"Yeah especially after you slept in!" Lolly shook her head. "Relax. You're taking me way too seriously! You haven't made a habit of skipping church. And I know your guilt will do my nagging for me." She smirked, then nibbled her Danish. "FYI: Friday evening I'm heading down to Cruces. My Aunt wants me to work for her for a while. Maybe only a month. Could be for the whole fall semester. She needs someone to fill in at her salon." Lolly's brown eyes met Elise's. "I think it's a sign from God things are changing for the better." She paused then said, "Speaking of things changing for the better, finish telling me what happened. When you got back, Gabriel was over at Javier's, right?"

"Yeah, he was. Ugh. And they were drunk." Elise paused, her face turning pensive. "I hope Gabriel's getting his tail whupped will put an end to his bullying. I hope things are changing for the better for both of us."

Lolly's lips and eyes wrinkled with pleasure. "Hhmn, so Mr. Lendar Marl beat Gabriel, eh?"

"Yes. We got back from supper. Max and I waited in the Escalade while Lendar got out. Gabriel cussed at him, then he flipped out his switchblade and tried to stab Lendar, only Lendar just plopped him on his back and took the knife away from him." Elise covered her smile with her fingers.

Lolly leaned back and lifted her upturned palms. "Wow. A knight in shining armor and on the first date! No sunbeams this time?"

Elise laughed. "No, not this time, silly. Don't have

sunbeams at night."

"Oh, moonbeams then." Lolly rolled her eyes again. "So, is he going to call you?"

"Yeah, he's supposed to call sometime today." Elise took a plastic cup from the cabinet and poured some milk for Max. "Here honey," she said and held the cup while he drank.

"Danks," he said, taking the cup and trying to drink by himself. Some milk ran down the sides of his face.

Elise snatched a towel, wiped his face and daubed his shirt. "Oh, honey, slow down!"

Max set the cup on the tray and accidentally sloshed milk. He sniggered with his mouth open, masticated Danish on display.

Elise sighed. "Ever since he saw Lendar talking with his mouth open, he's been terrible."

Lolly's eyebrows popped up. "Lendar chewing with his mouth open? I thought he was, like, perfection incarnate."

Elise rinsed the towel. "I doubt he's perfection incarnate, though at the moment I can't think of anything imperfect about him. I've only known he's existed for, what, 48 hours or thereabouts. Anyway, he said that where he comes from chewing with your mouth open shows you like the food or at least the company."

Lolly smiled, then looked at her watch. "So where's he from anyway?"

"I don't know where he's from."

Lolly's mouth fell open. "Don't you think you might oughta find out where this Adonis is from?"

Elise shrugged. "Yeah, it's on the list. He described his house for me. It sounds like some villa in Italy or something."

Lolly whistled. "Whoo-eee, girl. Just look at you glow. You're in deep aren't you?"

Elise nodded and grimaced. "Yeah, I am. I asked God to run him off if he wasn't the one for me and he's had every opportunity and a real good excuse. I mean," she sat up and waved her hands for emphasis, "how many guys will not only fight a jealous ex-husband armed with a knife, but want to call a girl the next day?"

Lolly smirked. "You have a point. Only one question left: did he kiss you?"

Elise shook her head. "Nope. Didn't."

Lolly nodded, thoughtful for a second while she toyed with her teacup, then chugged its contents. "Listen, Elise." She sighed. "I have an English paper to write today, but if you hurry down to the university I can give you a couple hours babysitting time. Maybe I can work on it while I watch Max."

"Oh Lolly!" Elise rushed around the edge of the table and hugged her friend. "Thank you. I desperately need to finish that painting."

Lolly blushed. "Eh, a few years ago, I was the friend in need. Now you are. Let's just hope we can keep taking turns at this friend-in-need business and we're not both friends in need at the same time. Take these other cheese Danish over to Butch on your way out and get your bottom over to the university. The day is burning."

Elise smiled. "Yes, ma'am, but I'd like to finish my tea first if you don't mind."

"Hot tea in 90 degree heat. You're insane, girl."

Elise agreed. "Yes, I believe I am."

9

Lendar will be here any minute, Elise realized after a glance at the wall clock. He'd called not long after she'd begun working and asked if he might join her. The thought of his imminent arrival released a burst of joy throughout her being.

While she painted, she wore a poncho made from an old piece of canvas. It was dotted with colorful splotches, not very attractive with its bulky shape and dirty edges, but she completely forgot to worry about that. The painting flowed easily and generously onto the canvas from the happiness in her heart. Softly, she sang praise songs to God.

She had no idea how long Lendar had been standing in the doorway before she felt his gaze and she looked up. His masculine form dominated the doorframe, his shoulder against the molding, his hands in his jeans' pockets. The blue cotton, striped shirt emphasized his healthy, tanned skin. He wore the same leather belt and cowboy boots she'd seen him wear the first time they'd met.

"Hi," she breathed. He looks so fresh and crisp; so gorgeous. She blushed.

"Ho," he said and strolled in. "How goes it?"

Elise smiled. "It goes well. I could finish in about a half-an-hour." She returned her attention to the painting, allowing her instincts to apply the colors while her brain freaked out. He's so handsome.

Lendar pulled a stool closer and settled there, one knee bent, the boot heel hooked on the stool's metal frame. "I thought this painting was good before, but it's even better now."

Smiling, Elise glanced at him, then daubed dioxide purple in the shadow of a rock. "Thanks."

After several moments, he wandered about the studio poking through other people's cubbies examining their work, studying canvases left on easels.

Elise ran out of cadmium yellow on her palette. She'd already squeezed the last bit of paint from the tube by bending it flat against the funnel that fed the paint through the nozzle then mashing the flattened tube's side against the opening to force out the last little dab. With her brush handle she managed to eek out another 1/8th teaspoon, but most of that stuck on the wood. She wiped it off on the palette then cleaned the brush handle with a rag.

That's not enough. She rummaged through her paint box. No more cadmium yellow. She went to the trash and sifted, checking for someone's throw-away palette to see if a bit of still moist paint might be available.

Lendar's voice interrupted her trashcan dive. "What are you doing?"

Elise's head popped up. "Ah." She reddened. "I'm out of yellow. I don't need much…"

"Let's go get some," he said.

Elise frowned. "Well. I don't have any money."

"I do."

"I hate for you to do that." More digging in the trashcan by the door proved useless.

When she pulled her head out, Lendar stood beside her, arms folded across his chest. "It's my pleasure." His face wore a mixture of dark intensity, er, maybe irritation, and light amusement.

"Oh." She went to the painting and stared at it. The yellow would finish it. If I had some yellow! Do I let him take me to the store? I need the paint, but if I let him get the paint for me…it's too humiliating. Besides I hardly know the man. Really? You hardly know him? Last night you wanted to make love to him and you didn't care about anything else! Arrrghh. What a bonehead.

Aloud, Elise said. "Well, it doesn't matter. I'm finished for today." She shrugged, an embarrassed smile on her lips. "Lolly only offered to keep Max for a couple of hours and I'm out of time."

"You are a proud woman, aren't you Elise." Lendar's gimlet eyes seemed to show hints of disappointment, sympathy and...disapproval?

Elise bit her lip. Oh Gak! Listen to that! He doesn't like prideful women. I never thought of myself as prideful. Maybe I am prideful. Now you've gone and done it, showed your true colors and he doesn't like what he sees. Just be glad nothing happened last night or you'd be even sorrier than you are now. Oh, God, help!

Carrie, a fellow student breezed in, rattling chains hanging from her black denim, cut-offs. "Well, Elise Ramos! How are you?"

"Hi, Carrie." Elise set her palette with its remaining paint in a flat, rectangular plastic container and reattached the lid. She slid it into the bottom of her paint box and replaced the fold out trays.

"Who's your friend?" Carrie hooked a thumb in Lendar's general direction. The hand was decorated with multiple rings and brilliant red nail polish.

Elise fanned the air. "Sorry, kinda distracted. Carrie Acosta, meet Lendar Marl. Lendar Marl, meet Carrie Acosta."

Lendar inclined his head with an aristocratic air.

Carrie whistled and looked him up and down. "Good work." She winked. In the next instant her eyes flickered over Elise's painting.

Elise sighed. Of course, Carrie referred to Lendar and not the art, but she kept up the pretense. "Thanks, Carrie. How's your picture coming?"

Carrie smirked and tugged her work free from its cubby. "It goes. You got any Alizarin Crimson?"

Elise went to her paint box and handed Carrie the half tube resting there. "Here, you can have it."

"Thanks." Carrie settled her canvas into an easel and tightened the brackets. "I hope I get an 'A.' My GPA could sure use it!"

"You will. You're good." Elise smiled, examining the bold, saturated hues that blasted forth from Carrie's easel.

"Thanks." She smiled briefly in Elise's direction, her white teeth framed by brilliant red. "Too bad you're not the professor." She winked.

As soon as she focused her attention on her painting, she forgot Elise and Lendar were even in the room. She plugged a pair of ear buds into her ears, already humming and swaying in time to her music while she loaded her palette.

Lendar watched Elise finish cleaning up. "Ok, I'm ready to go," she said. She clutched the paint box handle. He looks kind of disgusted and maybe a little bored, Elise decided.

Their footfalls resounded on the polished concrete floor. Sunlight beckoned through the safety glass in the heavy, exterior door a few yards away. Neither spoke. Maybe he's lost interest in me. Maybe he's only here to finish up an obligation.

You are such an idiot, she told herself. You really did it this time, he's probably deciding how to break it to you. Elise, I thought you were the one for me, but you're just too proud and I don't think I can take that long term. Sigh. She hung her head, watching her feet as she walked.

Lendar held the door for her and waited until she'd stepped on the landing. He followed her down the stairs.

She led the way toward Central Avenue, then stopped on the sidewalk beside Yale Park on Redondo. Now what? Ask him where he parked? Somehow, at the moment, asking Lendar that question seemed totally inappropriate.

Elise clutched the paint box with both hands and waited, her stomach suddenly sour. Central Avenue traffic crawled past on the opposite side of the grassy strip, heat from the asphalt alternated with cool moisture from the lawn in the playful breeze.

She squinted at him. "So. I have this terrible feeling you're mad at me."

Lendar answered. "No, not at all."

She felt as if she 'twisted in the wind,' as they say in the western movies. Now what, you going to ask him for a ride? Well, you wouldn't let him buy you paint! Elise hunched her shoulders and groaned inwardly.

Lendar observed her, a contemplative expression on his face. After a moment he asked, "Will you join me for a coffee at the Satellite Coffee shop?"

"I barely have time, but I think it'll be ok, especially if I take Lolly something." She winced. Oh, gak! You just said you didn't have any money! Now you're expecting him to buy Lolly something? Can't stop stupid, can you? Arrgghh! Elise cleared her throat and blurted, "Did you have a nice morning?"

"Yes. I had a fine chat with my boss. At my leisure all morning. Very nice. How was your morning?"

"Good, right up until I ran out of paint..." Oh gak, why did you bring that up again!? "You were there. Yeah. Well. Having you with me kinda makes the running out of paint not so bad. Especially now we're going for coffee and, yeah." She shrugged. "We wouldn't have had time to drive out to Langell's anyway. It's at least twenty minutes to get there, that's not counting being in the store. I'm pushing it to get coffee. I hate to impose on Lolly..." Elise stopped talking, remembering that proverb, 'even an idiot looks smart if he keeps his mouth shut.' Shoulda remembered it sooner! She stared at her feet for a moment. Finally, she cast a hopeful look at Lendar.

An amused smile played at Lendar's lips. He held out his hand. "Allow me to carry your paint box."

Elise blushed. "It's actually a tackle box for fishing. Paint boxes are expensive and flimsy, tackle boxes are cheap and sturdy."

Lendar grinned. "Elise you are a wonder."

"You keep saying that, but I don't see it. I think I'm completely silly. Ridiculous even. And a jerk for kinda forcing you to buy coffee for my friends and me." She squinched up her lip and looked up at him.

Lendar laughed. He took her elbow and pointed her toward Central. "One of the characteristics I enjoy most about you is your total lack of guile." He seemed quite pleased.

"What?" Now Elise burned from head to toe with embarrassment.

Lendar stole a glance at her, his eyebrow cocked. "Elise, you want to entertain your friends with food and drink, we will entertain them. Simple."

Elise thought, Ha, may be simple for you, but not for me! I can complicate anything. Just watch me!

They stopped on the sidewalk at the edge of the park now on the Central Avenue side. He studied her face intently. "Elise, the women I most commonly interact with, women who come into contact with my boss, they're very careful to shield their emotions. At cour…a whole class of people exists who learn from a young age how to mask their thoughts. Some of them have practiced hiding their true feelings for so long, I wonder if they even know themselves anymore. I find you quite refreshing." He cocked his head again and put on that melt-Elise smile, as if to say, "refreshing in more ways than one." He took her hand and kissed it.

Elise's free hand went to her throat. Oh, ok, I'm melting. "So what you're saying is every thought that passes through my mind is right here on my face." Awkwardly she touched her cheeks and winced. "And you *like* that?"

Lendar's smile was kind and delighted. "Exactly."

"Oh. Oh my goodness."

His fingers moved to her elbow, his attention directed toward gauging the traffic. His nearness and the delicious scent of his cologne joined with that renewed sense of oneness to become an envelope surrounding her, seeming to ward off exhaust fumes and insulate her from harm. Can it be he likes me just the way I am? That thought set her heart to thumping with renewed vigor. Joy flowed through her veins, dispensing happiness throughout her being.

He led her across the street to the median where they waited for another clutch of cars to sluice past. Feet on the sidewalk, they walked east to Satellite Coffee. He held the door for her and followed her in.

"Elise, pick whatever you think the folks back at the apartment would most enjoy." Lendar squinted at her. "That's Max, Lolly and Bruce, I'm talking about. The whole group." He made another one of his peculiar sign language movements with his hand. It was a graceful swirl, as if he gathered in something and hugged it.

Elise hunched her shoulders and giggled. "Ok. Do you know sign language or something?"

"We'll have the food and drinks prepared, how do you say, ah, yes, 'to go.' That will save time." He stared, then laughed. "Quite correct. I know a kind of sign language. But I've never studied American Sign Language."

"Ok." Elise giggled again. He's so adorable, that Spanish/European accent, his crazy hand movements, that suave, naïve way about him. Ah, delicious. She felt like a bubble loosely anchored to the earth. He wasn't angry with her or perturbed by her silliness--he liked her silliness. Amazing!

"So, in service includes sign language. I'm beginning to think you "in service" guys are the Renaissance men of the modern world." She clasped her hands together and beamed.

Lendar rubbed the bridge of his nose. "Well, we do have to acquire many various skills." His hand left his face in a flutter possibly creating another of his signs.

She placed the order for the group, he added his, then he gestured toward a nearby table. They sat down, listening to the music and people watching.

A moment later, Lendar rapped the table with his knuckles. "Elise, I'm having dinner this evening with a woman named Doreen Macintosh."

Elise's bubble popped. Suddenly she felt like a lump of

lead.

Lendar's expression verged between chagrined amusement and embarrassment. "I was courting, er, dating her when I met you. I feel it's only polite to speak with her and let her know our courtship is at an end." His fabulous gem-like eyes fixed on hers. "I liked Doreen, but no lasting affection blossomed between us."

"Oh." Ugh. There had to be something didn't there? Silly to think he wasn't dating anyone before me. "So you won't be able to hang out tonight." Half a lip curled downward in sorrow.

Lendar's smile was heavy with dusky desire, as if he longed to kiss her right here and now. "No. Ah, I won't be able to 'hang out' tonight." The smile changed to a bemused expression. "Hanging out rather sounds like we might behave like gorillas or chimpanzees." He shook his head and stood. "That's our number, I'll collect the food."

Elise watched his bottom and shoulders alternately while he walked to the counter where the server waited. Ah, she sighed, gorgeous. Doreen Macintosh. Ugh.

They left the coffee shop's ambiance and entered the noise and fumes of Central Avenue. Lendar carried the sack of food and the paint box; Elise carried the drinks.

"So, what's she like? This Doreen Macintosh?" Elise asked as they headed east on Central. The world now seemed dull and Albuquerque's busy noise annoyingly grating. The sun peered down, burning the top of her head and baking the concrete.

Lendar answered. "She's a professional woman who works for the state of New Mexico in the Public Education Department. She has a, what did she call it, yes, a 'Black Card membership' at Planet Fitness where she, ah, how is it said, yes, 'works out' three times a week and she attends a meditation club twice a week."

"Oh."

"Elise." Lendar stopped.

Elise spun around. Traffic rumbled past and pedestrians threaded by. The public setting made her feel on display. She wanted to say, 'Can't we talk about this in the car?' Instead, she stood like a leaden statue, her heart bleeding. She pictured her blood collecting at her feet and sizzling like the proverbial egg on the sidewalk. Her eyes stung and burned.

Lendar came closer. It felt as if he brought a soundproof booth with him, a weird type of aura that blocked out everything but her. He leaned her direction, his face so near that she could see the pores in his skin, the dark hairs preparing to make their appearance as five o'clock shadow. His voice was quiet, as it had been the night before, but somehow still audible, for her ears only. "Elise, Doreen Macintosh is a fine woman and I wish her a pleasant and prosperous future, but without me."

Elise's ears burned and she dropped her face to stare at the ground. A Golden Pride sandwich wrapper fluttered, half under her foot.

Lendar lifted her chin. His eyes seemed windows into the depths of his being where sincerity, admiration and something mysterious invited her to gaze more and more deeply. Basking in his aura, peering into his eyes, serenity coupled with hopeful excitement filled her and her spirit reinflated.

His baritone added music. "Elise, I meant what I said, I intend to win your heart as you have won mine."

Elise licked her lips, unconsciously stretching toward his partially opened mouth. "What did you say?"

Lendar's smile was gentle like a new leaf in spring. "I intend to win your heart. You've already won mine."

"Oh. How on earth did I do that?"

Lendar chuckled. "From the first moment I saw you standing in the afternoon light, I knew you were the woman I've been searching for. You are fresh, like a newly opened flower, honest and completely lacking in pretension. I cannot predict what you will say next, which delights me. Every emotion passing through your heart appears on your face." Gently he traced her cheekbone ridge and chuckled softly. "I believe you incapable of lying, which I find irresistible." Searching, he glanced from one eye to the other. "I long to learn more about you."

"Oh. Good heavens." Elise patted her chest. A new kind of burning flashed through her body.

Lendar cleared his throat. "Shall we move on? We don't want to impose on Lolly any more than we already have."

Elise squinted up at him. "Yes. Let's move on." Walking brought her back to reality, but the sky was no longer dull and the traffic noise had turned oddly soothing.

Together they crossed the street and passed in front of the UNM Bookstore. The bookstore reminded Elise that she probably could have gotten the yellow paint there instead of having to drive all the way out to Langell's. A quick look toward the store revealed a "closed" sign. Ha, they're not open on Sunday. Whew, saves you from being a total jerk.

She wanted to pump him for more gushy details about why he found her attractive, but instead she asked, "So, what's your boss doing today?"

"Ah, I'm not sure. We mostly talked about me." Lendar blushed.

"You did? Your boss wanted to talk about you?"

"Yes."

"Ok, what do you think he's doing today?"

"All I know is he told me he needed to sign off because his wife was waiting for him."

"What's her name?"

"Alma."

"Alma. Hmn. What's his name?"

"Anwic Berylin."

Elise gave him a side-long glance. "I bet his name would show up on Google."

"Probably not," Lendar said. "He's a very private

man."

Elise shrugged. "I'm not on Google either, but then I don't expect to be. I'm not private, I'm nobody."

"Really. You're nobody. I think you are Somebody to a few people in the world and the reality is if you are Somebody to a few people, you're actually Somebody."

"I suppose. Not that I want to be famous or anything."

Lendar teased, "So, you want to be famous?"

Elise laughed. "Lendar, I just said I didn't want to be famous."

"Oh," he winked and unlocked the Escalade with his key fob. "Not a famous artist?"

"No, just successful."

"Aren't they one and the same?"

"No, not necessarily. Though now you mention it, a successful artist is famous to his fans."

"In that case, you're famous. You have a fan." Lendar made a silly smirk and pointed at himself.

"Oh, get out." Elise blushed.

"In order to "get out" I must first get in." Lendar opened the door for her and waved his hand like a courtier.

The practiced aplomb with which he made the motions startled her. A nervous laugh escaped her lips. Weird. He did that so smooth like he's done it a jillion times. Where does a guy end up doing stuff like that?

Inside the vehicle, Elise chuckled softly while underneath her stomach twisted with faint unease. She stared out the window at the passing neighborhood. Bowing, courtly moves, sign language… What kind of a world does Lendar live in anyway? Is Anwic Berylin some kind of king or prince or something? They still have kings and princes in Europe, don't they? I know England does. People bow to the Queen of England don't they? Oh, God, what have You gotten me into?

10

It didn't take long to arrive outside her efficiency apartment building. Thankfully, Javier's house looked shut tight and Gabriel was nowhere to be seen. Lendar opened the door for her and helped her out. She gathered up her share of the goodies and led the way.

When she unlocked her door, Lolly looked up from the kitchen table where her looping handwriting decorated some college ruled paper. "Well, hello Sunshine!"

Lendar followed Elise into the tiny efficiency leaving the door open.

Max lifted his arms. "Endar."

Lendar hoisted him up and grinned while Max attempted to arrange his hair.

The way he looks, if Max were a cat, he'd be purring, Elise thought.

Noting Lolly's slightly irritated expression, she clasped her hands together, then released them to wave in Lendar's direction. "Lolly Lang, meet Lendar Marl, Lendar Marl meet Lolly Lang."

"Pleased to meet you." Lendar managed to avoid bowing, though Elise could tell he felt uncomfortable.

Lolly offered her hand. "Hello, Lendar Marl. Heard a lot about you, all of it good."

"I'm delighted." Upon finishing this remark, Lendar bowed to Lolly anyway and kissed her hand.

Elise giggled.

Lolly flushed red under her brown skin. "Er…wow. You do that on a regular basis?"

Lendar's face wore a look of formality contradicted by humble amusement. "In my world, it is the polite thing to do."

Lolly cocked her head and winked. "Let me into your world then! You got a brother, maybe a cousin?"

Lendar laughed. "I may know someone…"

Lolly leaned Lendar's direction. "Hmn, maybe we could double date or something."

Lendar smiled, but didn't answer immediately. Finally he said, "It might be arranged."

Seeing Lendar looking a little uneasy, Elise attempted a save, "Lolly, would you mind fetching Bruce?"

"Not at all." She threaded through the suddenly full floor space and went outside.

Elise brought the two kitchen chairs into the main room and parked them in front of the couch, then returned for Max's highchair.

"Elise, you should let me do that," Lendar protested.

Elise shrugged. "It's not heavy."

Lendar asked, "Shall we bring the kitchen table in here?"

Elise shook her head. "No." She went to the kitchen and fetched five melamine plates. "This will do."

Lolly returned with Bruce.

"'Uce," Max said holding out his opened palm and wiggling the fingers. He beamed at Bruce.

Bruce wiggled his fingers back at Max and made a goofy face. He wore a cotton camp shirt printed with 50's automobiles. A slight hunch touched his shoulders. After weeks low on cash, his blonde hair was beginning to look shaggy.

Lolly pointed at him. "Lendar Marl, meet Bruce Keaghan."

"Hello." Lendar stopped a bow in mid bend.

Bruce copied Lendar, performing the half-made bow precisely. Neither man offered his hand for a handshake.

Lendar chuckled. "Pleased to meet you."

Bruce's smile appeared and disappeared quickly. "Likewise."

"We brought refreshments." Lendar gestured toward the paper bags resting on the single end table beside the couch.

Max bobbed in Lendar's arms. "Eat!"

Elise handed Lolly a drink. "This one is for you. This one's for you, Bruce."

Lendar placed Max in his highchair, then watched, obviously pleased, while Elise handed out the selections. Soon the group was settled with drink and food. Everyone spoke at once. Uncomfortable silence followed.

Max laughed, jabbering something in his own language. He pointed at each of them, laughed again and stuffed a potato cube into his mouth. In the next moment, he dropped a bit of food onto the floor.

"Max!" Elise swatted his hand. "Stop that."

Max packed his mouth so full some food-rich drool edged down his chin.

"Max! Don't do that either," Elise exclaimed.

Lolly coughed back a laugh and spoke. "Max, you are a pistol."

Max pointed at himself and giggled. With his mouth full the word 'pistol' came out more mangled than usual. "'Iso."

Elise rubbed her forehead.

Lolly shook her head. "Max, that's just not polite at all. It's ugly. Stop it."

"'Iso," he pointed at himself, his smile fading in the heat of Lolly's frown.

Lolly deliberately removed her attention. Turning to Lendar she said, "I was born and raised here in Albuquerque. Where are you from, Lendar?"

"Andorra." He lifted his cup and drank.

Lolly pressed for more detail. "Andorra? Where's that?"

"It's a small nation between Spain and France." Suddenly Lendar looked totally ill at ease. He blinked and rubbed his nose.

Lolly frowned. "I've never heard of it, but then, I'm

pathetic at geography."

Bruce bit his toasted cheese sandwich and slurped his coffee. "What's the population of Andorra?"

"About 85,000. Mostly Catalan."

Bruce appeared thoughtful. "Fewer people than live in Albuquerque."

Elise asked, "Do you have any pictures of Andorra on your cell phone?"

Lendar shook his head, "No, but I do have a copy of the photo you requested." He peeled the picture of Elise and Max at the aquarium from his shirt pocket.

Lolly took it and gave it a look, then passed it to Bruce.

"Ah, the aquarium," he said. "Nice picture. Where's that dress, Elise, I've never seen it before."

Elise blushed and snatched the picture from him. "It's in the closet where it belongs," she replied.

Bruce grinned. "I thought it didn't really look like your style."

Elise shot him a look. At the moment, she wore jeans and a white t-shirt.

Lendar commented. "The color is perfect for her, don't you think."

Bruce shrugged. "Yeah, I guess so." He swigged his beverage. "What do you do for a living, Lendar?"

"I'm in service."

"Butler, valet?"

"Butler probably comes closest to describing my duties."

"Well, that could be everything and anything," Bruce said. "What about your boss? What's he do?"

Lendar rubbed his nose. "He has many interests. Management, import/export, employment services…real estate…"

Bruce frowned. "Import/export'd be a challenge from Andorra. Landlocked, not much of a railroad. And no airport."

"No railroad whatsoever." Lendar cleared his throat. "Andorra provides certain tax advantages. We have offices all around the world."

"Really. What's the name of the company?"

"Various companies all collected into one corporation. Would you like a brochure? Or perhaps a prospectus?"

Lolly glanced at Bruce and cleared her throat. "Bruce is looking for work."

Given what was turning into an increasingly hostile exchange between Bruce and Lendar, Elise elbowed Lolly. Don't need to blurt out Bruce's problems, she willed Lolly to understand.

Lolly frowned at her. "Well, he's been out of a job for a month. Maybe Lendar knows someone."

"Yeah." Sipping her beverage, Elise hid behind her insulated cup.

Lendar drank his coffee. "Oh? Bruce, what do you normally do for a living?"

"I'm a chef." Bruce winced. He waved his free hand. "Yeah, I know, it's rather a fad to become a chef these days with all the TV shows promoting that field, but yeah, that's what I am. Graduated top of my class from the Art Institute in Phoenix."

Lendar nodded. He stared at the floor, a contemplative expression on his face.

Bruce frowned and drank his beverage.

Max said, "'Endar, 'Uce friends." He nodded.

Elise and Lolly smiled.

Lendar's head snapped up. "Prophet Max," he said. Turning to Bruce, he said, "Bruce write me a one page autobiography or resume and I'll see what I can do about a job for you."

Bruce straightened, pressed his lips together, winced then finally managed a weak smile. "Thanks. That'd be great."

Lendar held up his hand and made a sign. "I cannot make any promises, please understand."

Bruce waved away his worries. "Gotcha. Just glad for another line on an opportunity." This smile seemed more genuine.

"Elise told us you were on vacation, Lendar," Lolly said. She took a bite of her salad wrap. "Where have you been so far?"

"Yes, I'm on vacation." His expression lost a little of its joy. "I've been in Albuquerque since February."

"Since February? This is July! How long a vacation are we talking?" Lolly asked. "And you haven't gone anywhere else?"

"A year-long vacation." Lendar rubbed his nose. "My first vacation in over 20 years of service."

Bruce nodded and grimaced. "Saved it all up for one big whopper. Doesn't work like that for ordinary people."

Elise glared at Bruce, but he ignored her.

"This is July, seven months left." Lolly grinned. "That's usually time enough to hatch something." She winked at Elise who turned beet red.

Lendar seemed not to have caught the joke. He contemplated his turkey sandwich, then bit into it. "Yes, seven months left." He'd started to talk with his mouth full, then covered it with a napkin. "Excuse me."

Lolly giggled. "Elise told us you people talk with your mouths open when you like the food or the company. Which is it now, the food or the company?"

Lendar hung his head, then raised it. "Both." He offered a boyish grin.

The ladies laughed, but Bruce maintained his frown.

"So…" Elise tried to change the subject. She glanced from Lolly to Bruce and back. "Lendar knows sign language."

Lolly lowered her cup. "Sign language? I'm learning sign language."

Lendar's face crinkled in a smile. "My boss has dealings with many signing persons."

"Deaf people?" Lolly sipped her drink.

Lendar sipped his drink. "My boss also…what is the phrase, ah, yes, he also 'wears many hats'."

Lolly's right eyebrow climbed her forehead. "And he works with deaf people?"

Again Lendar shrugged. "He works with all sorts of people."

"Import/ export, lots of different interests. Sounds like that rich, Greek guy Jacky Kennedy married. What was his name?" Lolly snapped her fingers as if the action would help her remember the man's name.

Elise shook her head. "Don't know. How come you know about that anyway? That was ages ago."

Lolly waved her burrito. "Oh, my mom was all into the Kennedys. I think she read everything there was to read about them. She has a huge coffee table book about Jacqueline Kennedy." She peeled back the paper from the tortilla, chewed off a bite and added, "I think it's called *A Thousand Days of Magic* and it's by one of the fashion designers. It's worth a fortune."

"Oh, ok." Elise rolled her eyes. "How is your Mom?"

"She's doing all right. She's living with her sister in Louisiana."

"Louisiana, I'd forgotten that," Elise murmured.

"And your Dad?" Lendar asked.

Lolly's face went bland. "He's doing fine. He's in New York driving a delivery truck. I haven't seen him in forever, but we talk on the phone every Sunday night." She focused on her burrito.

"Your parents are far away," Lendar commented.

Lolly's eyes dropped to some place on the other side of the room. "I was a senior in high school, going to the same church with Elise, when my parents divorced. Elise took me in and got me on my feet. I didn't want to go trapezing off to New York or Louisiana." She eyed Lendar and pointed at herself. "I didn't feel like running away even if my parents did."

Lendar asked, "You lived with Elise?"

"Elise and Gabriel, back when their marriage was good, except he never went to church. Then it all went to hell."

Lendar smiled at Elise. "So you're a benefactor too."

Elise studied her cup and mumbled. "No big deal, just what a friend ought to do, that's all." She straightened. "Hey, I thought we were interrogating Lendar!"

Lolly snorted. "Ha, we'll finish with him later. Meanwhile, I think it's a big deal. You were the only friend I had! None of my other friends wanted to deal with my emotional trauma never mind feed me on a regular basis." She rubbed her belly. "And I can eat!"

Elise smiled and patted her hand. "You were there when it fell apart for me."

Lolly smirked. "Yeah, after you helped me first. It wasn't as if I were some kind of noble person. I wasn't there for you when your Pop died."

"Pshaw," Elise said. "You hardly knew I existed when Pop died."

Lendar took a bite and chewed. "Where is your mother, Elise?"

Elise's eyes blurred. "Ah, don't know."

Lendar's sympathetic look was unmistakable.

Lolly rushed to fill in. "Ida disowned her when she married Frank. And he's kinda, like, afraid of crowds or something. You know, three's a crowd." She wiggled the fingers of her free hand. "Sick, if you ask me! But nobody asked me. So, yeah, I done said too much."

Elise looked at Lolly. Her expression verged between irritated glare and gratefulness, then her eyes went mournful and she dropped her gaze to her cup. After a moment, she drank.

Bruce placed his coffee cup on the table. "So, Lendar, tell us more about yourself."

"Ah, my father is also a butler. My mother occasionally helps him, but mostly she runs our family farm."

Bruce chuckled. "Wow, you have a farm. Cool."

"Yes, we have a small vineyard and produce enough wine to sell a small production, specialty wine."

Bruce seemed genuinely impressed. He eyed Lendar speculatively.

Lendar turned to Lolly, "So, Lolly, when do you graduate?"

"Ah, two years, unless I take summer school again, which I doubt I will, but who knows." She shrugged, a half-made smile on her lips implied more was involved than she was prepared to explain.

"And when you finish, what occupation will you seek?"

Lolly laughed. "Teach English in High School. Though at the moment, New Mexico can hardly pay for the teachers they haven't fired. Education in New Mexico is really bad right now. Really bad."

Lendar nodded. "Forgive me. When you say, "teach English," what do you mean?"

"Well, literature and grammar is usually what it entails. And writing. Spelling. Yeah." She gnawed away a section of burrito. A strip of tortilla hung from her lips. She stuffed it into her mouth. "Sorry," she said with her mouth full.

Elise and Lendar laughed.

Bruce interrupted. "Yes, Lendar, I'd like to see a brochure from your boss's company, if you don't mind."

Lendar reached for a napkin. "My pleasure. I'll bring one with me the next time I come."

Bruce nodded, his attention returning to his coffee.

The food disappeared and the drinks gone, the ladies got to their feet and began cleaning up. Max lifted his arms to be released from his high chair. Elise wiped his hands and face then let him out onto the floor. He went to Bruce and leaned on his knee for a while, then wandered over to Lendar. Absently, Lendar picked him up and parked him on his thigh.

"Hello Master Max, have you had a pleasant

morning?" Lendar asked.

Max pulled at Lendar's arm, plucking at his watch. "Rook. TV."

Lendar turned his wrist and allowed Max to lift it for a closer look.

Staring at Bruce, Max pointed at the watch. He laughed and said, "Rook."

Bruce squinted at the image and scowled.

Lendar checked the scene. "Elise, friends, let's step outside." He carried Max to the door, opened it and waited while the ladies filed past. Bruce refused to precede him. Lendar stepped out. Bruce made sure the door was not set to lock, then closed it.

Just as they reached the end of the sidewalk, where the small parking area serving the apartment building spread to the street, an ambulance and police car arrived. Gabriel's pick-up idled at the curb behind Lendar's Escalade, but Gabriel lay sprawled in the street, unconscious.

Elise covered her mouth with her fingertips, hiding a grimace somewhere between amusement and concern. "What happened?"

Lendar spoke with the same, barely audible tones he'd used the night before. "He tried to scratch my vehicle with his keys."

"Really."

Lolly frowned. She tugged on Elise's arm and whispered, "What happened?"

Elise held her fingers to her mouth to deflect her voice away from the street. "Gabriel tried to scratch Lendar's SUV with his keys, but apparently it's equipped with defenses."

Lolly nodded while her mouth formed an "o." At last she said, "Like an electrical shock?"

Elise nodded then shrugged.

Bruce, who stood behind the two women, scowled. He folded his arms across his chest.

The police officer triaged the situation then scanned the

handful of observers. "Anybody know who owns this Escalade or this pick-up?"

Lendar stepped forward. "That's my Escalade."

The policeman nodded. "Anybody know who this guy is?"

Elise joined Lendar. "He's my ex-husband and that's his pick-up."

The policeman bobbed his head and stepped aside for the paramedic. "We'll have this man transported to the hospital…"

Gabriel roused himself and struggled to a sitting position. "What the…"

The policeman crouched beside him. "Sir, can you tell me what happened."

Gabriel rubbed the back of his head. "Hell if I know."

The paramedic attempted to attach a blood pressure cuff.

Gabriel pushed him away. "Get away from me."

The paramedic eyed the policeman, then looked at Gabriel. "Sir, do you refuse medical attention?"

"Damn right I do." Gabriel curled his legs, made a spider-like posture and stood. He wobbled a bit, but maintained his upright stance. "I'm fine." His face blazed with fury; his eyes, pig-like beads. He scanned the watching group, the frown deepening when he discovered Lendar.

The policeman backed away a couple of steps, the paramedic copying him. "Very well, sir. You people clear out." He waved his hand at the crowd including neighbors across the street. He retreated to his car where he ducked into the window and removed a pouch.

The paramedics loaded up their equipment and waited at the bumper, just to make certain Gabriel was actually well enough to navigate.

Gabriel stumbled toward his pick-up.

The policeman approached him. "Sir, before you climb behind the wheel of that vehicle, you're taking a breathalyzer test."

Gabriel snarled. "Like hell I will. I haven't been drinking."

"In that case, you won't mind taking the test."

"Fine! I'll take the stupid test." Gabriel snatched the gadget from the officer's hand, huffed into it with practiced know-how and handed it back to the policeman.

The policeman studied the results. "Very well, sir, you may go."

Gabriel grunted and opened the pickup cab door. The policeman climbed behind the wheel of his vehicle and turned off his light bar. He wrote on a paper attached on a metal clipboard.

"He's taking down both license plates," Elise breathed.

Gabriel chugged water from a plastic water bottle, then poured some over his head. He wiped his face with a napkin and put the pick-up in gear. A jerk, a narrow miss, and he edged past the Escalade rolling south up the hill, around the corner and out of sight; the policeman following.

The paramedics mounted their running boards and hauled themselves into the ambulance cab, turned around in a nearby driveway and headed north.

Bruce quipped. "Apparently Gabriel finally met his match."

The ladies turned to look at him. His face was etched with pained amusement. They looked at Lendar.

Lendar rubbed the bridge of his nose. "Perhaps." He checked his watch. "It's time I go," he said. He offered his hand to Bruce. "Bruce, if I don't see you within the next couple of days, give Elise that document. Ladies, good day to you." He placed Max in his mother's arms. He took the boy's hand and shook it. "Until later, Master Max."

Max offered a limp wave. "Bye."

Lolly led the way back to the efficiency and went inside, but Bruce grasped Elise by the arm and stopped her. They watched Lendar walk across the street and climb into the

Escalade.

Bruce waited for Lendar to start his motor, then murmured earnestly, "Elise, Lendar seems like a nice enough fellow, but he's a liar."

"What?" Elise wrinkled her nose, then snorted in disbelief.

"Yesterday, at the library, I watched a video on Bing about how to tell if someone's lying. Excessive rubbing the face, avoiding eye contact; he did those things."

"Bruce, you're not exactly a trained professional in the lie detection business." Elise frowned. Lendar had looked really uncomfortable when he'd been talking about Andorra.

Max shook his head. "'uce not like 'Endar."

Bruce shoved his hands into his jeans pockets. "Whether I like him or not has nothing to do with it Max. Sorry, Bud, but you're just a little kid."

Max snuggled close to his mother looking over her shoulder away from Bruce.

Bruce sighed. "Elise, Lendar's got all sorts of high tech stuff normal people don't have. I watched that whole fight Saturday night. Something flashed right before Javier went down--like some force field knocked him down. Then Lendar drove that Escalade up the hill without touching it. I watched from my window. And that switchblade of Gabriel's, melted into a puddle. I have it in my apartment. And just today, Max saw what was going on out here on Lendar's wristwatch--that's super high tech."

"I saw surveillance footage on his wristwatch too, Bruce." Elise knew she used a hurt, defensive tone and regretted it. I am not an unobservant ninny. Well, not usually. Well, not all the time anyway. She bit her lip.

"Look, Elise, he's obviously in love with you and all that. He just glows when you're near him. But he's a liar." Bruce cleared his throat. "And deploying all this high tech stuff even before you've finished your first date, marginally creepy, if you ask me, like stalking and controlling."

Elise replied, "Bruce, think about it, the man is in service, he does bodyguard stuff for his boss. It's just routine for him." She waved an index finger. "Any guy who can give an employee a year's paid vacation has boo-coo bucks and probably a bevy of paparazzi tailing him 24/7!" She paused. "Heck, by our standards, Lendar has boo-coo bucks." She paused.

"Anyway, his boss is the kind of a person who's probably already bought his ticket for the first Virgin Galactic flight. He's probably had dinner in the undersea dining room at Burj al Arab where they put gold on your dessert. Lendar has to think about that kind of bodyguard and surveillance stuff all the time, it's part of his job. He's only trying to protect me." Elise spread her upturned palms. "Besides, guys with that kind of money…who knows what technology they might own, might even be better than the military who have to put up with whatever the lowest bidder gives them."

Bruce opened his hands and leaned her direction. "Elise, he lied about Andorra. That's when the face rubbing really got started. Andorra is not one of the big business centers of the world. Until just recently, their whole economy was based on sheep! It wasn't until they discovered the tourist industry and created a duty free zone that they started making any cash."

Elise shook her head. "How come you know so much about Andorra? I never heard of it before."

Bruce shrugged. "I spend a lot of time wandering through the internet when I'm at the library. I can tell you a lot about Luxemburg and Liechtenstein too, if you care to know. I got nothing better to do."

Elise touched his arm. "Bruce, he told me yesterday to be patient with him until he can tell me everything."

Bruce snorted, his face reddening. He stuffed his hands into his pockets. "What kind of crap is that?" He shook his head. "Hell, Elise. Who am I kidding. I'm an out-of-work, broke down, damn coward." He stomped off to his apartment.

11

Lendar called about bedtime, just as she finished the rough draft for her art history essay. "Hello, Elise. I hope this communication doesn't come too late."

"No, it's fine. Just trying to finish this essay." Man, he sounds tired and kinda depressed; his dinner date must have gone real bad. Bad for her, good for me. I hope.

"Oh, I don't want to distract."

"Too late. You already have, but it's ok. I was wanting interrupted." Chocolate, that's what his voice reminds me of, creamy chocolate with a touch of spice. Maybe some cayenne or something like that.

"I just wanted to say 'hello.'"

"Hello, Lendar." She giggled. "How was your dinner date?"

"When I told Doreen I would no longer court her, she was not pleased." He paused, strains of music, not the Spaceman's Fugues, but something else, something mournful and lonely, filled the gap. "Elise…"

The longing in his voice was unmistakable. Elise's heart rate accelerated and a bead of sweat popped on her forehead. How can one word communicate so much? Longing, tiredness, desire… She bit her lip. No sense putting of ugly.

Aloud she blurted, "Lendar, where are you really from anyway? Bruce thinks you lied about being from Andorra."

"It's a long story, Elise. Are you ready to hear it?" His tone communicated hope and dread.

What's he afraid of? And it's a good question, come to think of it. Am I ready to hear it? Do I really want my dream decimated right when I've barely begun enjoying it? Elise gulped. "Yeah. Might as well get the unpleasant parts over with."

Lendar chuckled. His voice went from tired and worn

to delighted. "Well, in that case, I'd like to take you and Max on a little trip and show you where I live."

"Oh, ok." What if this lying about being from Andorra is only the tip of the iceberg, what if… Oh God! "What if" is a bad place! Lord, if he has evil intentions, stop this trip! Please! But unless You tell me otherwise: rule #10, trust You. I can't let silly fears stop me!

Lendar was speaking. "…when is the earliest you may be available to depart?"

"When am I available? Oh. Wow. This is finals week. I can't miss." She mentally reviewed her schedule. "I won't be free until Friday."

"Friday it is then. I'll come and collect you and Max about 7, post meridiem. We'll be gone until Sunday afternoon, so plan accordingly."

"You're picking us up that late?"

"Yes, it's the best time for me. Is it not acceptable for you?"

Bravely she murmured, "Seven is fine." She gulped. "A weekend trip sounds cool."

"Cool? I've heard that expression several times before, I suspect it means 'delightful' or 'pleasing.' Am I correct?" Lendar's voice seemed infused with light, the sounds sparked in her brain like fireflies.

Elise tried the polite formality Lendar often employed. "Yes, you are correct." She cleared her throat. "Separate rooms, Lendar. Otherwise, forget it."

"Of course. You and Max will have your own suite."

"Delightful." She suspected her voice sounded clunky like wooden blocks. Ugh.

"Meanwhile, may I join you for lunch tomorrow?"

"Oh, that would be very nice. Will you be able to meet me in the SUB?"

Lendar asked, "The sub?"

Elise rubbed her nose. Gak. I'm rubbing my nose. Does that make me a liar? "Oh, sorry. Student Union Building. It's the big building to your left if you just keep going straight past the bookstore and Popejoy Hall heading north."

"I can do that. What time?"

"Eleven-thirty."

"I'll see you then. Good night."

"Night." Elise sighed and shivered with happiness. At least I have a week before my dream comes crashing down around my ears.

Monday Elise shared burritos with Lendar on the patio outside the SUB. They huddled in the patch of shade the metal umbrella provided.

"Where is Max?" Lendar asked, forgetting not to speak with his mouth full.

Elise pointed. "You did it again."

"What did I do?"

"You talked with your mouth full."

Lendar blushed. "Pardon me."

Elise threw a hand. "It's hard to break old habits and maybe I should learn to ignore it. The problem is, if we ever have a meal with anybody they'll notice."

"I do not want to prove rude." Lendar covered his mouth.

Elise laughed. "Yep. You did it again." Her countenance fell. There, in the crowd heading toward Central Avenue walked her mother.

"Elise, what is wrong?" Lendar turned to search the faces passing by. He glanced back to Elise.

"That woman, there, with the scarf on her head. That's my mother."

"I will go and fetch her."

Elise put her hand on Lendar's arm. "No. Sit. She doesn't want to see me."

Puzzled, Lendar stared at her for a moment, then tore his eyes away to watch Ida. "She looks much like you except her hair is darker." Lendar's brows were furrowed. "Why does she not want to see you?"

Elise studied Ida's face. She held her mouth in a straight line, a new pair of wrinkles was etched between her brows. The headscarf covered her neck and hid all but one clump of hair that peeked from under its white border. She wore harem pants and a long tunic in turquoise. Ida passed by their table. She was visible only a few more moments before disappearing in a clutch of students who poured from the student union into the plaza.

"Oh Lendar, I'm sorry. What did you say?"

"Why does she not want to see you?"

Elise shrugged. "I'm a Christian and Frank is a Muslim."

Lendar shook his head. "I do not understand."

"Muslims aren't supposed to even be friends with Christians."

"Why?"

Elise shrugged. "The Prophet Mohammed commanded it. Hmn, let's see, Surah 5:51."

Lendar pursed his lips. "Bitter?"

Elise's eyes dropped to her soda where she tugged the straw up and pushed it back down. "Yes, I suppose I am." She raised her eyes and bit her lip. "I need to forgive Frank."

"But you are concerned for your mother."

"Yes, yes, I am. He's insisted she give up all her best friends including me." Elise stood up, straining for one more glimpse of her mother. "Dad died when Max was 6 months old. She married Frank 9 months later. Max doesn't know her from Adam." She plopped back down onto the bench.

"I am certain I do not know her from Adam either, but it is a grief, to be sure."

"Yes, a grief." Elise sipped her soda, blinking her eyes to clear the sudden blurring. "What were you asking me? Something about Max?"

Tuesday they met Lolly at Frontier Restaurant.

Carrying a tray with his green chile burger, Lendar

quipped and pointed by jerking his head in the general direction of the far wall. "I'm fascinated with the art work in this restaurant."

Lolly chuckled. "It's the 'frontier' theme, but I heard that the owner loves John Wayne!"

Lendar asked, "Which portrait is his?"

Lolly looked at Elise, her eyes wide in shock, balanced her tray in one hand, then touched Lendar on his shoulder. "You mean to tell me you don't know who John Wayne is?"

Lendar paused in a doorway. "Please, ladies, find our table."

Lolly spluttered her lips. "Oh, no, you're not getting off that easy. Tell me how you can live in the 21st century and not know who John Wayne is!"

Lendar watched Elise and Lolly pass him, then fell in behind them. "Would you believe it if I were to say it's because I am out of touch with reality?"

Elise and Lolly laughed. Lolly said, "If you don't know who John Wayne is, you've hit that one on the head."

They found a booth and scooted into the seats, Lendar joining Elise on the same bench.

Elise pointed, "John Wayne's portrait is over there." She took a bite from her hamburger.

"Oh, I see. The large cowboy?"

"Yes, the cowboy." Elise's eyes crinkled in humor. "I suppose the longer he's dead the more and more people will not know who John Wayne is. I barely know who Groucho Marx is."

"Who is Groucho Marx?" Lendar asked, his eyes twinkling.

Lolly and Elise laughed. "We don't know!"

Elise swallowed more soda. "Actually," she cleared her throat, "he was a comedian. I know that much. And hilarious, from what I gather."

Lolly nodded. "Yeah, that's what I heard."

"If he's hilarious, then I would like to hear him,"

Lendar said, tugging the paper wrapped around his burger a little lower to free up a new section.

"Yes, so would I, but I think he's been dead longer than John Wayne has," Elise said with her mouth full. She covered her lips and looked at Lolly. Together they laughed.

Lolly chewed, swallowed and said, "He made movies. Let's watch one. Something like *Phantom of the Opera* or something like that."

Elise waved her hand. "No, silly, *Phantom of the Opera* is a musical, the movie you're thinking of is *Night at the Opera*."

"*Phantom of the Opera*, *Night at the Opera*, who cares!" Lolly sniggered.

Lendar gazed at Elise, then at Lolly, humor plying his features. "Yes, excellent idea, let's watch one of those."

"Say, Lendar, do you have any single friends?" Lolly asked, her eyes fixed on her paper cup. Shyly she raised them to meet Lendar's gaze, then she hunched her shoulders and giggled at Elise.

"I do." Thoughtfully he chose a French fry, then said, "Yes, I know the man who might be perfect for you."

Lolly giggled again, then her smile faded. "Well, if you know someone you'll have to bring him down to Cruces 'cause as soon as I finish up Friday morning I'm driving down there to work for my aunt for the rest of the summer."

"I'm sure something can be arranged if the gentleman is amenable," Lendar said in his polite, old-fashioned way.

Elise patted Lolly's hand and beamed.

On Wednesday, Elise planned to meet Lendar at the Which Wich restaurant. Arriving late and entering from the rear, she was surprised to see him at a table with a professional-looking woman wearing a power suit, her dark hair in a neat chignon. The turquoise and silver adorning her middle finger spoke old New Mexico class and wealth. Southwest Nicole Kidman with dark hair. Gak

Elise paused in the hallway next to the bathrooms,

hesitant. Oh Lord, help! He's found someone else!

The woman turned her head and Elise caught a glimpse of her features. Her heart fell within her rib cage. It felt listless and heavy, like dead weight resting on her diaphragm. How can he choose me instead of her? She's so beautiful. Her make-up looks professionally done, her complexion is flawless! Look at those hands…they're like porcelain. Look at those salon-perfect French nails! I probably have paint under my fingernails. Gak, I'm toast.

Elise realized she'd stopped breathing and stood on the verge of fainting. Carefully she drew breath and leaned against the wall next to the men's room to keep from sinking to the floor in an undignified head-between-the-knees posture. Only one problem: she actually leaned into a young man exiting the bathroom. "Oh, excuse me."

"Hello!" It was Kendall Grant from Drawing III. He'd spent three months stalking her, showing up at her apartment at odd hours and sending her flowers before Gabriel threatened to beat the snot out of him and she insisted he stop. His entire face announced he still found her attractive and that he mistook her near-faint for a change of heart. "Well look who's come around to see me," he said.

"Nobody has come 'round to see you," Elise groused. "Sorry, I bumped into you."

He crowded closer. "Oh, no problem, hun."

Elise pushed him away and careened into another man on his way to the restroom.

The second man frowned. "You giving this young lady a hard time?"

"Naw, she came onto me, man." Kendall wrapped a possessive arm around Elise's waist. "We've known one another a long time, haven't we hun?"

"Actually…" Elise began and unwrapped Kendall's arm. She considered kneeing him in the balls.

The other fellow snorted and pushed open the bathroom door. "Young people these days and in public for crying out loud!"

Kendall licked his lips. "I knew you'd come around someday."

"Leave me alone!" She closed her eyes and shoved...into thin air. When she opened them, Lendar had Kendall by the back of the neck as if he'd grabbed a kitten.

"The lady asked you to leave her alone," Lendar growled.

Elise gasped. Such masculine power in that fist and arm. Aahh...

"She came onto me!" Kendall twisted, jerking his shirt from Lendar's grip. "Who the hell are you anyway?"

Lendar opened his arm beckoning her to safety. "The lady is my intended. I suggest you apologize and abandon your suit and the premises."

Kendall's eyes widened at Lendar's formality and European accent. "What? You James Bond or something?" He squinted. "You a Spanish actor dude?"

Lendar's face softened with amusement. "Incorrect on both counts."

The young man shrugged. "Hey, no harm done. Just letting her know I still hold a flame for her." He raised both hands. "I apologize." He spun on his heel and scurried out the back door.

Elise rested her face on Lendar's shoulder. "Oh Lendar..."

Lendar kissed the top of her head. "Come sit down. Doreen's waiting." He led Elise back to the table where he pulled out a chair for her. "Elise, meet Doreen Macintosh, Doreen this is Elise Ramos. Elise is a fine arts major here at UNM. Doreen works for the New Mexico Public Education Department."

"Hello." Elise offered her hand.

"Hello." Doreen's handshake was disgusting. Her fingers felt cold and limp meanwhile her rich, brown eyes measured Elise with calculating, impolite directness, taking in her threadbare Oxford shirt, faded jeans and cheap canvas shoes. Disdain filled her face. "So you're Elise Ramos, famed art student and mother of young Max."

Reminding herself that the Lord Jesus commanded believers to love one's enemies, Elise kept her expression friendly. "No fame, but the rest is correct." On impulse, she grabbed Lendar's hand, glancing at his tanned digits intertwined with her pale ones. So steeled, she raised her eyes to meet Doreen's baleful glare.

Smirking, Doreen turned her attention to Lendar, her face instantly softening. With a nose that sharp and flesh that starved Elise would have doubted "soft" possible a moment earlier. Doreen drawled, "Lendar, as I was saying, I have tickets for the show this weekend. They're orchestra seats and I hate to waste them." She stretched her hand in Lendar's direction. "You know, I purchased them a couple of weeks ago…"

Ha, Elise thought, her eyes narrowing, throwing in a little guilt are we? A couple of weeks ago, like when we were still dating, you thoughtless weasel, you. Well, bring it on!

Doreen continued yammering at Lendar. "April's bringing her husband, Joseph. We can have dinner at the Artichoke Café and then head on over to Popejoy." She rested her elbows on the table, wrapped her fingers together under her chin and put on a flirty smile. "It'll be a lot of fun."

"As I told you a moment ago, Elise and I have plans for the weekend." Lendar stated flatly. A frown hovered on the edge of his countenance like a storm cloud on the horizon. Unconsciously he edged a little closer to Elise.

Elise stifled a giggle. A similar look had simmered on his face right before he'd flipped Gabriel on his back.

Doreen's expression soured before she caught herself and pasted on mask of friendliness. "Oh, you and Elise have plans." She said the name "Elise" as if the letters tasted like spoiled food. "Well, I'm sure that whatever you have in mind you can postpone until after the show." She glared at Elise.

"I appreciate the generous offer," he said, "but Elise and I will be gone for the entire weekend," Lendar replied patiently.

Doreen sniffed and pursed her lips. It looked as though she might explode, but after a moment her face turned friendly again. "Well perhaps some other time." She stood, clutching her Fendi handbag. "I'd better get going."

Lendar stood.

How does she afford a Fendi bag? Elise thought. I didn't realize state employees made that kind of money. Maybe she's like those *Sex and the City* girls who skimp on everything else so they can afford expensive clothes. Or maybe she has massive credit card debt.

Funny, Lendar doesn't seem to have any trouble not bowing to Doreen.

Doreen went around the table, placed her palm on Lendar's cheek, then breezed out, leaving a chilly draft of expensive perfume in her wake.

Lendar's hand edged up slightly, as if he considered wiping his face. He eased himself into his chair. "Let us sit a moment before we order lunch." The tension in his voice fairly crackled.

"So that's Doreen." Elise paused, then said, "The term 'battle ax' comes to mind."

"Yes, that's Doreen." Lendar pinched the spot between his brows, then cocked his eyebrow at her. "'Battle ax?'"

"Slang for domineering, bossy woman." Ooo, that cocked eyebrow is so sexy. Elise thought, her body warming and her skin beginning to tingle.

Lendar nodded, a smile struggling to make an appearance. "Yes, I believe you've, what is the term, yes, you've hit the nail right on the head." He exhaled and relaxed his fists. He studied Elise, his face marked by concern. "Elise, I believed myself shut of her, but it appears I was mistaken. I apologize for this intrusion...this rude intrusion."

"Yeah, that's a good point. How did she intrude?" Elise

rotated to stare at him straight on.

"She saw me as I entered this restaurant and followed me in." Lendar studied her expression. "Once again, I apologize. I am mortified."

"Pshaw. You can't control what she does." Elise waved a hand. "What I want to know is: how do you feel about her?" Her eyes widened and she leaned into his space.

Lendar frowned. "I feel that she should have a wonderful life somewhere far from me."

Elise chuckled. "Glad to hear it."

Lendar cleared his throat. "How was your morning?"

Elise smiled brightly. "Today has gone very well. I might actually get a "B" in painting. Er, I hope I will anyway. At least my professor didn't make any ugly cracks about my work like he usually does. He was pleased with my sketchbook, thanks to you!"

Lendar smiled. "I'm gratified."

"What's the deal with Doreen?"

"Ah, the deal? You mean what's her motivation?"

Elise folded her hands in her lap. "Yes," she replied.

"She imagines herself in love with me." Lendar wiped his forehead with his handkerchief, then continued. "The day I first saw you, the day we met, I'd planned to serve her dinner at my house. I'd already prepared lasagna ready to bake and purchased some bread. After I left you, I went home, put it in the oven and began making the salad while I awaited her arrival. She brought her friend, April." He ran his hand through his hair. The mass of healthy hair rose in shining waves between his fingers. Elise stared. She could lose herself in its thick strands. She sighed.

Lendar was speaking. "…April had driven to Albuquerque from Espanola to attend a rally with Doreen in Santa Fe on Saturday. Some kind of effort to fight poverty and end forced child bearing, I believe." He frowned.

Elise focused on his lips, hearing each word as a separate entity. He chose me instead of Doreen! Look at those wonderful lips! Her heart had gone from dead weight to weightless. His words are chocolate drops. Bursts of color and delicious chocolate scent exploded in her brain. Aahh, if he would just kiss me. That would be so fabulous. I could just melt.

Wait, are you nuts? Lendar's upset! He's talking about something serious! Pay attention! Her brows furrowed while her mind formed his words into sentences. At last she shook her head to clear it. "Fight poverty…ok…but what do they mean by 'forced child bearing,' I wonder."

Lendar's face darkened. "There is a philosophy that all child bearing is forced. Another philosophy states that if a woman becomes pregnant and she didn't want to become pregnant that a law forbidding her to receive an abortion would result in forced childbearing. Both are forced childbearing."

"Oh, I see." Elise pursed her lips.

Lendar's expression hardened. "Even if I hadn't met you, I could not have continued my courtship with Doreen."

"Oh?"

Lendar scowled. "Not after I learned she favors abortion."

Elise blurted. "Really? Why not?"

Lendar looked taken aback. "Tell me, do you agree with such a barbarous practice?"

Elise straightened and shook her head. "Hell no!"

"I presume the use of 'hell' indicates your vehemence?"

"Yep. You got that right. I was just wondering what you thought about it. Most guys are indifferent until they fool around and get someone pregnant."

"It is an abomination," he said softly, his voice barely audible. His eyes had gone from flinty, like storm clouds, to steely and hard, like ball bearings.

"What about cases of rape?" Elise asked, clutching her hands together in her lap. She suppressed a smile. He's not indifferent!

Lendar frowned. "Then the child bearing, if it came to that, would indeed have been forced, would it not?"

"Ok." Elise bit her lip. "I agree with that." She gulped. All right, so now you're going to tell him what you think, and it looks like he'll agree with you, but what if he doesn't?

Well, what if he doesn't? You're not going to change how you feel or what you believe, so just put it out there and if he dumps you, he dumps you.

Elise swallowed and pressed on. "As a Christian, love and respect for human life would demand I carry a child to term, even if I didn't want to have the child and regardless of how it was conceived. Though I have to admit, I would need a lot of grace, supplied by God, to carry a child conceived by rape."

She paused, then said, "When you think it through, it's not fair to kill a baby who is actually also a victim of rape. The girl should give the baby up for adoption if she can't bear to keep it, that's what I think."

At first Lendar didn't reply. He simply stared. "I've read that the argument is made that a person does not intend to have a car wreck when he drives a vehicle. Persons engaging in sexual intercourse don't intend to produce a child, therefore..."

Elise interrupted him. "Pshaw. Few people get into a car wanting to have a wreck, but if a person ends up having one, he is required to take responsibility for his actions. And 'responsibility' doesn't involve murdering the other people who might have survived the crash."

He grinned at her. But then his thoughts obviously turned in a new direction. Pensiveness stole over his features and it seemed he looked into some far away place. After a moment, he rapped the table with his knuckles.

"That knuckle rapping. Is that one of your signs?" Elise asked, pointing at his hand. She blushed. Suddenly feeling as if she'd intruded on a private moment.

Lendar looked at her, his eyebrow cocked. "Yes, it is."

"What does it mean?"

"Truth come out."

"Really." She tapped her lip. "Interesting. Around here when people do that it's 'knock on wood' kind of like sealing something away from bad luck."

Lendar's gaze lost none of its intensity. "You are a wonder Elise."

Her heart thwacked like a living balloon. "Oh am I?" What does that mean when he says I'm a 'wonder?' Elise's pulse thumped in her temples. He looks like he could eat me up he loves me so. A mischievous smile played at her lips.

Lendar's face edged closer to hers by slow millimeters. Time seemed to stop. Without realizing it, her lips parted. Will he kiss me? Oh Lendar, kiss me, just kiss me…she closed her eyes.

His mouth inches from her lips, Lendar murmured, "Ready to order?"

12

After lunch, Lendar stopped outside on the sidewalk. He seems moody and cloudy even.

Elise suggested, "Say, Lendar, how about going to church with me and Max tomorrow evening?"

"Very well. What time?"

"Church starts at 6:30 pm."

Lendar bowed. "I will come to collect you and Max at 6:15. Until then, farewell." He made one of his lovely signs and went south down the sidewalk.

Grinning, Elise watched him go. Feeling eyes on her, she turned and spotted a couple of fellow students staring. "What's with the dude? Like, why the bowing?"

Elise shrugged and replied, "He's old school." She spun on her heel and headed north, back to class.

On Thursday, Lendar arrived at precisely 6:15 p.m..

"How goes it?" He asked when she opened her door.

"It goes well. I might actually finish the semester with passing grades." Elise winked. "Let me fetch my diaper bag."

Lendar went to the crib where Max had been confined in order to keep his nice outfit clean. Max held up his arms appealing for Lendar's help to make his escape.

"Ah, Max, how are you today?" Lendar asked, lifting him from the crib.

Max tried to smooth Lendar's hair behind his ear, then slobbered on his cheek, a failed attempt at a raspberry.

"Max," Lendar murmured affectionately.

Elise looked up from stuffing her bag with clean diapers. I'm always startled that Lendar is so sweet to Max, she thought. Not since the final time when her Dad had held tiny, baby Max shortly before his death had any male, except Bruce, been so tender and loving to him. Yes, don't forget Bruce! We've been blessed to have Bruce's friendship.

Max's head was nestled against Lendar's shoulder and he toyed with the buttons on his shirt. Sensing she watched, Lendar looked up and grinned, his face boyish and laced with hints of feelings of awe. He seemed about to say something. Elise waited, but he closed his eyes and nuzzled Max.

Elise's heart surged, struggling to reach out to the two males, glad for their affection. She smiled, her eyes teary. "He really likes you." Thank you Lord.

Lendar used his index finger to try and lift Max's head, but the boy pressed all the more firmly into his shoulder. Lendar glanced at Elise and replied. "I like him very much."

Elise picked up a toy from the floor and set it on the end table. "But he's still his own man, isn't he?"

Lendar chuckled. "Wouldn't have it any other way." He opened the door and went out.

Elise set the door to lock and followed him into the early evening light.

Bruce sat outside his efficiency wearing an Isotopes cap and reading his Stanton Friedman book. He raised a limp hand. "Hi."

Elise smiled. "Hi Bruce. How are you this evening?"

"Fine."

"You want to go with us? We're going to church."

Bruce scowled. "No thanks, Elise." He stood, slammed his book shut and opened his apartment door. "I'll see you later." He went in and shut the door.

"Wow, he's crabby." Elise mumbled.

"Pardon me?" Lendar asked.

"Ah, he seems crabby." She shook her head. She ignored Lendar's questioning brow and reached up to clutch Max's hand. What's the matter with Bruce, I wonder? He's never been so grouchy and standoffish before. She peered at his curtained window, released Max's hand, then paused to gaze toward the road and Lendar's vehicle. "Did Bruce give you his autobiography yet?"

"Not yet."

Elise shielded her eyes from the sun and squinted at Lendar. "I'm surprised he hasn't."

Lendar shrugged. "Perhaps it's not ready yet."

Lendar opened the Escalade's passenger side door for her, then the door next to Max's car seat and went to work buckling Max in. "Do you normally attend church on weekdays?"

"No, I usually go on Sundays, but I kinda, well, actually, no kinda, I totally missed. I slept in. Yeah." She winced. "And Lolly gave me a hard time about it. You remember the two church ladies. Well, they were trying to be nice and let me know they care, but well, they were actually, sort of nagging me."

Lendar chuckled. "I am curious. I haven't delved into any of the religious experiences available here."

Elise stared. What is he talking about? Does he think faith is like going to a buffet where you sample different foods?

She watched Lendar skirt the front of the vehicle and climb in. She said, "We need to get on the one-way going east. I always forget the name, is it Lead Avenue Or Coal Avenue?"

"I know which road you mean." Lendar started the motor and turned around, once again in Javier's driveway. A golden glow highlighted the bottom of the curtains--lights were already on--but nobody peeked out. The place had the feel of nobody at home. Lendar seemed to take note, eyeing the house's façade before putting the Escalade in reverse. Looking over his shoulder to back out, he asked, "Have you had supper?"

"Yeah, we had a snack." Elise grinned at him and silently prayed. Oh God, please touch Lendar's heart and let him know You are real.

"Would you join me for supper after the service?"

"That would be great!" Elise beamed.

The one-way street was only a few blocks away. Lendar waited at the stop sign, then joined traffic. She loved the Nob

Hill neighborhood and the glide down the slope with the Sandia Mountains in view. "Turn left here."

Lendar parked and helped retrieve Max from his car seat. Elise dug through her diaper bag for the small case of earplugs she kept in a zippered pocket. Picking six of the foam plugs and clutching them in her hand, she slipped her diaper bag over her shoulder. "Here, take two of these. The music's loud."

"Very well." Lendar seemed a little surprised, but took two. "How are these employed?"

"Roll one between your fingers to mash it, then stick it into your ear. It will expand and fill your ear canal."

Lendar grimaced. "I'll try this once we're inside. I'm not sure I can manage rolling and squishing while carrying Max." He offered a self-deprecating grin, as he often seemed to do when he attempted to use the common vernacular.

Max tried to open Lendar's hand. "Ret me rook," he said.

Elise patted Max on the back. "Honey, just wait. I've got some for you too."

Max stopped and stared at his mother, then leaned against Lendar's shoulder.

Two security guards smiled and nodded and the greeter offered them a program. "Good evening," he said, "Welcome."

Elise smiled at him. Lendar nodded in the man's direction. He indicated with a sign that she should enter first. She led the way into the auditorium and between the rows of seats to a pair in the center section. Other attendees filed in a few at a time. The worship team appeared on stage.

"Here let me have Max," Elise said after she'd installed her earplugs.

Max opened his arms and stretched her direction.

"Oh, sweetie," Elise murmured and kissed his cheek. She offered him his earplugs, then took one out of his hand. "Ok, honey. I'm going to put these in your ears. You can play with them after the music is over. Ok?"

Max nodded, but tried to stop her from installing the first earplug.

"Honey, no, let me do this."

Max pounded her hand. "No wanna."

"Max, do you want to go to the nursery?"

"No wanna."

"Then let me do this!" Elise managed to place the first earplug and finally the second after a brief tussle. Immediately, she pulled a stuffed animal, specially saved for church services, from her bag and gave it to him. While she grappled with Max, Lendar watched, looking for an opportunity to help, an indulgent smile on his lips. Once Max was settled, he turned his attention to the stage. Two guitarists checked the connections between their instruments and their amplifiers. A keyboardist fiddled with her settings and the drummer slipped on headphones.

I bet he's never been to this kind of church service before! Elise stole a glance at him. *I'm glad he was willing to come!*

The house lights dimmed, the stage lights came on and the lead guitarist strummed the first bars of an updated, old hymn. The words to the song appeared on three different screens and the music began. Lendar attempted to join in, though he clearly did not know the song. By the time they had sung through the verse and chorus, he had the melody.

He has a nice voice, she thought. She raised one hand as she sang. Max copied her, lifting his stuffed animal into the air and wailing. A couple in front of them looked back to check on the noise, then grinned and nodded.

After the music, the local pastor came onto the stage, gave the announcements and prayed. Then he said, "We're watching the pre-recorded message from Sunday. I'm sure it will be a blessing to you."

The sermon opened with a video counting down through the Ten Commandments, Roman numerals that looked as if they'd been cast in metal flashed on the screen. Each commandment followed the numerals accompanied by soaring music that evoked thoughts of a powerful, loving God. The count stopped at VI: "Thou Shalt Not Murder." The images and music faded and the preacher appeared, life size on the center screen sitting on a chair.

His sermon: Four ways to commit murder. First, he made clear murder was not the same as killing, such as during war or in self-defense. Murder included the obvious pre-meditated or rage-driven act of taking a life; it included suicide; verbal abuse and abortion.

Lendar's focus never wavered, but Elise spent much of her time distracted with Max. She produced toy after toy keeping him entertained and near the end, a sippy cup of juice, a rare special treat.

The local pastor returned to the stage, encouraged the group to return Sunday for the next installment and then asked everyone to greet his neighbor on his way out of the building. Elise shook hands with the couple in front of them.

"He's really a good boy," the woman said. She smiled and tweaked Max's hand.

Max pulled away and stuck out his bottom lip.

The husband nodded to Elise and to Lendar. His pained smile seemed to say, "Boy, I'm glad our kids are grown and we don't have to go through all that anymore."

Elise couldn't help but grin at him. They wandered toward the exit while she struggled to dig through her bag for the tithe buried somewhere underneath grocery receipts, diapers, colored pencils and tubes of baby ointment.

Lendar said, "Elise, let me hold Max."

"Oh, thank you, Lendar."

He took Max. She finally found the money. "I'm ready."

"Is this the end of the service?"

"Yes. I know, it feels kind of strange. The service flows better at the main campus, that's why I usually go there," Elise apologized.

Lendar nodded and followed her to the offering box where she stuffed her money through the slot. He fished out his wallet and pushed in his own offering. "Are you hungry?"

"A little bit."

"Would you like to split an entrée? I saw a restaurant I would like to try."

"Great!" Elise grinned. Man, I'm getting spoiled!

Lendar seemed unusually quiet, though no less attentive as they went through the routine of loading into the Escalade and leaving the parking lot. Elise forgot to wonder at her ease in his silence and enjoyed the comfort of the ride.

At the restaurant they discussed what to order and shared their selections with the hostess. "Here you go," she said, handing them a stand with a number stuck in the clip.

Lendar set the stand on the table and helped Max into his high chair. "Elise, do you have an extra copy of your Sacred Text." He made a sign that reminded her of someone warding off a curse or something.

Startled, Elise asked, "What's that sign you just made?"

Lendar looked puzzled. At last he chuckled. "The sign translates, 'The Ten Sacred Words.'"

"The Ten Sacred Words?" Elise scrunched up her lip, then sipped her tea.

"You know them by the name, 'The Ten Commandments.'"

"Oh. Hmn, I think I like your name better." She added a sugar packet to her tea and stirred it with her straw, then helped Max with his drink.

Max sipped and smacked his lips. Elise began to replace his cup to the table when he demanded, "More!"

"Ok, honey, you can have more." Elise held his cup for him again. She eyed Lendar. "So, you have the same commandments where you come from but they have a different name?"

"Yes." Lendar beamed.

Elise looked askance at him. "You're from Andorra. Aren't you mostly Catholic? Doesn't everybody call them the Ten Commandments?"

Lendar shrugged. "Eh. They're the same commands, makes nothing if the list has different names in other locales."

"Well, I admit I don't know much about Catholicism." She zeroed in on Max who'd started blowing air into his cup. "Max, don't do that!" She put his cup in the center of the table and he immediately pounded the polished metal with his fist.

"Wanna! Wanna!"

"No, honey. Not if you're going to blow air into it." She fished through her diaper bag for a toy. "Here, play with this."

Max threw the toy.

Lendar got up, retrieved it, handed it to Elise.

Max screamed, struggling to reach first the toy and then his drink.

Lendar took Max out of his highchair. To Elise he said, "We will return in a moment."

Elise watched them exit and stand outside under the lattice-shielded entry. Lendar pointed at things, as if he were teaching Max their names. Max bobbed up and down on his arm. Lendar plucked a leaf and gave it to the boy. Max studied it, then threw it to the ground.

"Oh well, he was good in church," Elise muttered, then glanced up at the waitress.

"Orange peel beef with white rice and a side of egg rolls. Besides refreshing your tea, will there be anything else?"

"Ah, could we have an extra couple of plates. I'm sharing with my friend and son," Elise pointed to the window.

The waitress looked outside, then back at Elise and nodded. "Sure. I'll be right back."

Lendar returned to the table and slipped Max into his highchair. "Our young master is tiring."

"Yes." Elise answered, then giggled. "Don't you mean,

our young master is very trying?"

Lendar seemed confused, then he grinned.

Their waitress arrived and refilled their glasses.

"Thank you," Lendar said, then added a packet of sugar to his and stirred.

"You're welcome." The waitress set two more plates and additional silverware on the table, then walked away.

"Elise, if you have an extra copy of your Sacred Text, I would like to borrow it." He sipped his tea.

"You already asked me that," Elise said and grinned.

Lendar made a sign she interpreted to mean, "forget it," then he said, "I will purchase a copy for myself. You needn't give up one of yours for my sake."

Elise flung a hand. "No worries. I have three. One I hardly crack open. You can borrow it. I warn you though, it's not my favorite version."

"Version?"

"Ah, well, since the Bible is translated from ancient Hebrew and Greek with a little Aramaic thrown in, people are always in search of more accurate interpretations, so we end up with an almost endless variety of translations."

"Oh, I see." Lendar frowned, then stuck his fork into a piece of beef.

Throughout the meal Elise had the impression he wanted to say more, but he never did. Instead he queried her about her finals and the topic moved on to art history.

Just as they finished eating, Lendar's nifty I-phone sounded. He plucked it from his pocket. "Excuse me," he said, and walked outside.

Elise was busy cleaning Max's hands with a baby wipe when Doreen Macintosh walked up. She wore skinny jeans and a purple, asymmetrical silk blouse that looked like it came from Neiman-Marcus. "So, if it isn't Elise Ramos and her little brat."

"Oh, Doreen, you've come to ruin another perfectly good meal." Elise peeled Max out of the highchair and placed him in her lap, putting the table between them.

Doreen studied her slightly frayed shirt. "I'm surprised to see you here. You don't look like the type who can afford to eat out by yourself. You must be well paid for your services." Her perfectly painted mouth puckered, made a smacking sound, then formed a faint smile.

"If you're referring to the mural I'm planning, I haven't turned in any sketches, so no advance payments yet."

"Oh, I think you know to what I'm referring."

Elise suppressed a scowl. "No, actually I don't. Tell me what you mean. Be explicit." She attempted a withering smile. Internally her heart quailed. Old feelings of low self-esteem buffeted her system.

"Why Lendar Marl, of course, servicing him." Doreen leaned over the table. "You work cheap, you're young, foolish and easy; otherwise a man like Lendar wouldn't give you the time of day."

"You're quite stunning, Doreen."

Doreen straightened. "What on earth do you mean?" Her puzzled look faded to pride. She preened. "My new Michael Kors blouse."

"No, I mean, it takes a lot of talent to insult someone as thoroughly as you've insulted me..."

Lendar strode up. "Elise, please finish. You were saying?"

"I was saying..."

Doreen interrupted, "She was saying that I look quite stunning. She complemented me on my blouse."

Elise's eyes narrowed. "I said you have a stunning talent for thoroughly and utterly insulting a person. It's clear you know absolutely nothing about Lendar Marl. How you can claim to love him while you know so little of his character, I'll never understand."

I may not have the strength to defend myself against this hussy, but I'm sure not going to let her bad mouth Lendar!

"Well! You little twit!" Doreen hissed. "How dare you!"

Elise challenged. "Go ahead, tell Lendar exactly what you were saying before he walked up."

"I don't have time for this. I'm late."

Elise's heart pounded and beads of sweat broke out in her hairline and under the waistband of her skirt. "Ha! You don't want him to hear it, you want him to try and get it out of me. Meanwhile, you'll invent something and then call me a liar next time it comes up. So, guess what, Doreen, you can rush off if you want, but if you don't tell Lendar what you said right now, he's not going to believe you later. I'm calling your hand."

"Well!" Doreen sniffed. Looking to Lendar she said, "I told this little piece of white trash that I couldn't imagine why you would spend any time with her, unless of course, she satisfies some physical need, that's what I said!" She gave Lendar a look best reserved for the bedroom. "Lendar, I had no idea you were such a sex pot," she purred. In a slightly louder voice she said, "When you've finished sowing your wild oats and tire of this little uneducated plaything, give me a call."

Elise's eyes watered. She coughed.

Lendar stood and reached for Max. "Elise, allow me to drive you home."

Numbly Elise let Max go to Lendar and scooted back her chair.

Max rested his body against Lendar's chest and stuck his thumb into his mouth.

To Doreen Lendar said, "Do not call me; I will not call you."

"Bye." Doreen chuckled, "Oh, you'll be calling me when you're ready for a real woman."

Lendar's hand rested on Elise's hip with a pleasant jolt. It communicated protection, possession and constancy. She threw a glance at Doreen who had already turned and was stalking away. Unconsciously she wiped her nose with the back of her hand. Lendar looked down at Elise, one eyebrow cocked.

Elise swallowed. "I lied to Doreen. I guess it was my pride kicking up." She looked down and then back up, abashed. "I implied I had a commission to do a mural, which I don't." She winced.

Lendar chuckled softly. "The woman insults you, behaves in the most hateful manner possible in a public setting and you are sorry for having lied. You are a wonder."

Elise gasped. Every pore of his face, every wrinkle around his eyes, the very shape of his mouth announced in no uncertain terms that he found her absolutely and utterly desirable. Something warm and soothing flowed into her battered heart. She blinked and a tentative, trembling smile formed on her lips.

13

Late Friday afternoon Elise fed Max an early supper. He alternately jabbered and nibbled. She helped him with his cup and spoon, admiring his lovely skin and pleasant, childish voice. "Oh, Max, I love you," she cooed. She fluffed his hair and kissed his forehead.

He tried to stuff a piece of food into her mouth, missed and smeared it on her upper lip. He giggled. "Mama messy."

"Ha, thanks to you!" Elise wiped her face. "You adorable imp."

"I imp," he said, happily picking apart his meal.

"Off to Andorra today. Off to Andorra today," Elise sang. Too nervous to feed herself, her mind soon buzzed with unfinished thoughts. Summer semester is over. Thank You God. Need to collect work on Tuesday. Wonder why the prof didn't say anything about my painting? Is that a bad sign? My essay was good, I think. I'm sure I did well on the test.

There'll be leftovers in the fridge, wonder if I should put them in the freezer so they won't be ruined by the time we get back? Do I really want to eat them later anyway? Ugh. I should cook things I want to eat as leftovers.

How many hours does it take to fly to Europe? I should have looked that up on Google when I had the chance. Somebody said TSA people are grouchy.

Andorra sounds so romantic, all mountains and rustic loveliness.

Lendar will be here soon. When the picture of Lendar entered her mind, the fizzing in her brain ceased. Ahhh.

She pictured him parking outside and walking up to her door with that sexy, confident walk of his. He'll be coming up to my door, to fetch me and my son. And Doreen can go take a swim in the Atlantic. She chafed her arms, gentle delight oozing through her being. Memories of the previous days when he had met her for lunch bubbled to the surface. Lunch with Lendar every day for the past four blissful days except Thursday when he'd joined her for church and supper sure made the final week of school real nice. She sighed.

Max snorted and threw his food on the floor. "Mama!"

"Ok," Elise muttered. "I can take a hint." She washed his hands and face in the kitchen sink.

When she set him on the floor, he toddled across the room to empty the box of cars Gabriel had given him for his birthday. "Crash," he cried and plopped down to play. She checked on him periodically, glancing over her shoulder as she cleaned the kitchen. That done, she packed, unpacked and started over again.

Her great-grandmother's hard-sided suitcase held just enough clothes for a weekend. "If it doesn't fit, you don't need it," she repeated.

She liked the suitcase's brass corner protectors and the two catches on either side of the handle that snapped up with a pleasing clacking noise when nearby buttons were pushed. She loved its stuffy smell and stretchy pockets on the inside walls.

On Monday she'd found a fifty-dollar bill in her diaper bag. No idea where that came from, but she wasn't going to argue with a blessing. Wonder if Lendar snuck that in there? When could he have done it? No clue. "Thank You, Lord." She raised clasped hands toward the ceiling.

With the money, she'd purchased paint (two tubes) at the university bookstore, a summer sale blouse and some food, but completely forgot small-sized shampoo, conditioner and body wash. Not one single, sample-sized bottle of anything lurked anywhere in the house. She'd been through the medicine cabinet and the under-sink storage twice to check.

"Supposed to have sample sized stuff when you fly," Elise groused, throwing a packet of facial tissues into her diaper bag. "I wonder if TSA allows regular sized toiletries in checked bags? Assuming we'll fly."

She glanced at Max who drove a station wagon a few inches on the floor then lifted it, "Whoosshhh," to sail, ramping over another vehicle lying on its side.

She muttered, "Well, duh, how else can a person get to Andorra for the weekend except by flying."

Lendar hadn't mentioned flying, but what other options did they have? How about driving to Galveston and boarding a cruise ship? Ah, yes. Lovely. White beaches, cerulean blue seas…wouldn't that be romantic? A couple at church did that last winter. A seven-day Caribbean cruise. While you're dreaming of things you can't do, why settle for a seven-day cruise, how about a month to the Mediterranean on a yacht, how about that? No homework. No cooking. No laundry. No cleaning. And all that lovely, historical scenery!

Silly Dreamer. Andorra is landlocked!

She packed her regular sized toiletries into a gallon-sized zipper bag. That bag went into a grocery store plastic sack along with a pair of sandals. She stuffed the sack into a backpack. She paused, tapping her lip thoughtfully. "No, I should put the shampoo and stuff in my suitcase and some clothes in the back pack. It can be my carry-on." Elise emptied everything on the desk and started over.

Do planes land in Andorra? I don't know. I have no clue where European airports are.

She was savvy enough to realize summer time in the mountains might require a light jacket. She packed that. And one for Max. Her canvas shoes would have to do for hiking. "I hope baggage handlers don't destroy my old suitcase."

Elise stared, trying to think of something she'd forgotten. "No, haven't forgotten anything. Ok, that's done."

Standing on the toilet lid so she could see her full figure in the mirror she decided to change her clothes, again. What about the hair?

No, forget it. It's the best you've managed in awhile and if you mess with it, it'll be worse. Just leave it.

Ok. What else needs done? Except for picking up Max's toys, I'm ready. Thirty minutes early. Still time to try to fix the hair.

No! Quit fussing with it. Just relax.

Are you kidding me? I've never been farther east then Amarillo!

Max seemed to understand something out of the ordinary was about to happen. He staged a massive car wreck on the floor. He made whirring noises and "shosh" sounds as he crashed toys into one another. "Kerboom..." he said by way of sound effects as a semi-tractor trailer smacked into a mid-sized car.

Elise paced, dodging flying trucks and sidestepping wreckage. "Oh, Lord, take care of Lolly and Bruce, Mama and Frank, and Uncle Wilbur, Grammy and Grandpa. Thank you Lord."

Lendar's here! She could hear him speaking to Bruce through the wall. She stood at the door, hand on the knob, waiting for him to knock. At the first sound of his knuckles rapping, she flung it open. "Hello," she breathed.

"Hello." He grinned. He wore jeans and a sage green shirt, the usual long sleeves rolled up to just below the elbows.

Max turned to look over his shoulder, then stood and rushed to cling to Elise's leg. "'Endar 'ear."

Elise laughed. "He's been out of sorts all day." She pointed at the mess on the floor. "Kinda took it out on his cars. Let me scoop all this up and we'll be ready." She unclasped Max's fingers, took the pick-up he held and pushed the toys into a pile with her foot.

Max scampered about trying to put the miniature vehicles back where they'd been. "No! No," he repeated glaring at her.

Elise ignored him, placing the toys in his car box.

Max cried, "Mama, not do that!" Frowning, he struggled to peel a Corvette from Elise's fingers.

Lendar crouched. "Max, we can't leave these on the floor while we're gone. Let's help Momma."

Frustrated, Max flung cars at the box.

"Don't throw them so hard," Elise warned. "You'll break them."

Lendar grasped his wrist. "Max, not so violent," he said, then released it.

Max flung one last dump truck, noticed Lendar's look of disapproval, then carefully placed the rest. His bottom lip stuck out in protest.

The job finished, Lendar picked him up. "Good work, Max. You're a big man."

Max buried his face in Lendar's shoulder.

Elise closed the kitchen window, checked the back door and gathered her backpack. When she reached for the suitcase Lendar extended his free hand.

"Let me have that one," he said. "I'll carry it." He smiled at her, took the suitcase then turned to Max. "We're going on a little trip, Max. Are you ready?"

Max lifted his head to expose his pout. He shook it. "No, not 'eady."

Elise went to him, touching his arm gently. "Are you ok, Max?"

Max stuck his tongue out at her.

"Max! Why did you do that?" Elise demanded. She wanted to swat his little bottom. "You're a toot today. A rip-roaring toot!"

"Toot, Toot, Tooty." Max said pointing at himself, at Elise and then at Lendar. He snickered.

Lendar looked bemused. "What is a 'toot'?"

Blushing, Elise hunched her shoulders and lifted up-turned palms. "Oh, I don't know…just an endearment."

Lendar eyed her, his brow cocked as if to say, "Come on tell me the full story."

"Ah, well, 'toot' is a word describing the noise a horn makes. It can also refer to passing gas." She covered her embarrassed grin with her fingertips.

Lendar turned his attention to Max. "Oh, I see. So, Mr. Max, you've made your mother think of some unpleasant things. Not good."

Max patted Lendar's cheek, with almost enough force to qualify as slapping. "'Endar toot."

Lendar daubed the end of Max's nose. "And you are a darling whelp," he said affectionately. "Hopefully a little ride will improve your mood." Glancing at Elise, he asked, "Are we ready?"

Elise scanned the apartment, the blinds were down; the toys were cleaned up; the toilet had been flushed. "Yep. Ready."

Bruce sat outside his apartment, the Stanton Friedman book about flying saucers in his hands. "Well. You three heading out for the weekend?"

Elise reddened. "Lendar is showing me where he's from." Her voice became firm. "Just so you'll know Bruce, Max and I will have a separate suite."

Bruce nodded. "Uh, ah, yeah." He attempted a smile, then winked. "Have a nice time."

"Thanks for the resume, Bruce," Lendar said. He pointed to his shirt pocket where he'd stuck the folded paper. "I'll let you know something by Monday or Tuesday."

Bruce raised a hand. "That'll be fine. Hopefully good news. As of Sunday I'll be out of cash."

A slight frown touched Lendar's lips. "I'll do what I can."

Bruce said, "Take good care of Elise and Max."

Lendar bowed. "You can count on it." To Elise he said, "Shall we go?"

Elise paused, eyeing Bruce. Bruce stared back, a faint smile on his lips. "I'll be fine," he said.

Elise nodded. "Ok. I'm glad you're not so crabby today. I hate leaving when those I leave behind are crabby."

Bruce hunched his shoulders. "Gets depressing to be

out of work."

Elise nodded again and gave Bruce a hug. "I'll see you Sunday or Monday if I'm back late." She started down the sidewalk, her gaze sweeping over Javier's house. The place seemed shut, the north wall dark in shadow. The Pontiac was gone. She sighed happily. At least Gabriel wouldn't know she'd left for the weekend with Lendar. She smiled at Lendar and crossed the street.

Colors and edges were soft in the gloaming; even the air temperature was mild. She glanced back at Bruce and waved. His expression verged between hope and worry. Elise frowned, suddenly wishing she'd taken a few more minutes to chat with him before Lendar had arrived.

Standing beside the Escalade, she clutched her diaper bag with both hands. "I should have called, but I didn't. Are we flying? I don't have any small shampoo bottles suitable for TSA."

"That won't be an issue," Lendar replied. He opened the door for her, then went around the back where he stashed the suitcase.

Oh, we're flying by private plane, Elise decided. Cool!

Max straddled his hip, his arms around Lendar's neck. They look so adorable. The pair of them, a matched set with their wavy, dark hair and olive skin. Lendar loaded Max into his car seat. Max jabbered and punched his fingers through Lendar's curls as if he imagined the ringlets were tunnels. He giggled. Lendar paused to tweak Max's cheek then backed out of the passenger seat. He climbed in the driver's side. "Are we ready?" He asked, plugging the key into the ignition.

"Yes. No! I just realized…Lendar, I don't have a passport!" A rush of anguish washed through her body leaving grief in its wake. "I can't go to Andorra!"

"Don't worry, Elise. We're not going to Andorra."

"We're not. I thought you said you were from Andorra."

Lendar started the motor and checked for approaching

cars. He made a u-turn and they were rolling. "That's just a cover."

"Oh." Elise felt her stomach drop. "A cover?"

"Yes, a story you tell when you can't tell the truth." Lendar's expression was calm, but deadly serious as his eyes met hers.

"What?" Elise grimaced and shook her head. "What do you mean? Are you saying you *lied* to me?" Her face scrunched up in a ball of hurt. "Bruce said you were lying, but I didn't want to believe him."

"I'm sorry, Elise." He dipped his chin, then stared through the windshield. "Yes, I lied." A quick look her direction held earnest, heartfelt appeal that would have set her aflutter yesterday, but didn't now. He stopped at the stop sign. Turning to face her he said flatly, "I lied because the truth is strange, what is the saying, 'stranger than fiction.' I lied for security reasons. And I lied because I'm afraid. I'm afraid that when you find out where I'm really from you won't want to be with me." He paused, then said, "Fear is a powerful force. Love drives out fear, so I've heard…" He swallowed and seemed about to add more. After a moment, his lips firmed into a hard line. "I need to know if you'll accept me…"

Elise snorted. "Lendar! That's absurd…me not accepting you." She almost blurted, "I love you," but stopped herself. "Wait, are you from the Middle East, like Saudi Arabia or something?"

"No." He edged the Escalade onto Lead Avenue and continued toward Carlisle.

"Oh, well, that's the only place I can think of…no, I mean, Muslim countries are the only places I can think of where I might hesitate to be with you. They're not very nice to women there."

"No, they're not."

"Where are you really from then?"

"A planet called Minan." Lendar uttered the statement

then glanced away from the road to look at her. He made none of the revealing body language signs Bruce had said liars inadvertently made.

Elise swallowed. "What?" A strange coldness crept over the surface of her skin and her fingers went numb.

Not a hint of levity appeared around his eyes or mouth. They stopped at a traffic light. Staring directly into her eyes, he said, "Elise, a little over four thousand years ago aliens kidnapped my ancestors and took them to a planet about 20 light years from here. I'm an earthling, but this is my first visit to planet earth."

Squinching up her face, Elise shook her head. "Say again…"

"I live on Minan near the city of Ponichar in the foothills of the Ulesim Mountains. Well, I would live there if I didn't spend so much time in space. That's why I said my folks' place was remote."

Elise worked the door handle, but with the vehicle in drive, the door was locked. She tried the unlock button. The light changed and they were rolling again.

"Elise, you don't want to get out while we're moving. At least, I wouldn't recommend it."

"You're insane," Elise said.

A corner of his mouth curled in a half-smirk. "You're attempting to exit a moving vehicle and you call me insane." He chuckled. After a brief pause his tone turned sober. "I'm not insane, Elise. If you like, we can go back and get Bruce. He would enjoy the trip."

"Get Bruce?"

"Yes, we can do that if you would like."

The afternoon before, while they'd watched Max playing in the gravel, Bruce had discussed the Stanton Friedman book with her. He tried to explain why Stanton Friedman, a retired nuclear physicist, believed space aliens existed and why they'd be so sneaky. She'd said she found the idea of space aliens implausible, but Bruce hadn't backed down.

Oh, fun, go get Bruce so he can confirm I am a complete ninny. Aloud she said, "Oh great."

"What?"

"I told Bruce that I didn't believe in space aliens."

Lendar chuckled again.

Elise squinted at him. "Who are you anyway?"

"I am Lendar Marl, Retainer."

"What's a retainer? I thought you were a butler."

Lendar shrugged. "I am. A retainer is like a butler, except a retainer is also a soldier sworn to protect his sovereign…with his life, if necessary."

"What are you talking about? Sovereign? Nobody has sovereigns anymore."

"Minan does. My immediate sovereign is Crown Prince Anwic Dzula Berylin, over him serves Emperor Gartan Cultus Berylin, his father."

Elise's attempt at a chortle morphed into gagging. She waved her hands back and forth. "No, this isn't happening. This is too much." She coughed. Waved her hand in front of her face as if clearing away gnats and squawked, "Space emperor? Gak!"

Lendar raised a hand, made a sign and said, "I'm not making this up, Elise. If you allow me, I'll prove it to you, right now, this very evening."

Elise's scornful smirk fell away to be replaced by a look of blank dismay. "What have I gotten myself into?"

"You haven't had anything to do with it, Elise. The Most High has done this."

Her brows furrowed. "The Most High? I know who *I* think is the Most High, but who do *you* think is the Most High?"

"The Creator of the Universe."

"You think He put us together."

Lendar nodded. "Absolutely. I saw you in a dream over twenty years ago, before you were even born."

"But you're only, what? Thirty? That would make you a little kid, like maybe a toddler, when you saw the dream."

"No, I was about twenty-eight, I think. Maybe I was thirty. Actually, I don't know how old I am." He shrugged, as if uncertainty about one's age were no big deal.

Elise shook her head, wriggling her index finger in a "no, no bad boy" sign. "That's not believable. How can a person such as yourself not know how old he is?"

"Simple. I spend a lot of time in space traveling really fast. Alfred Einstein explained it, the faster a person travels the slower time passes for the traveler. Speed up to travel, slow down to arrive, speed up again to go somewhere else, time passes at varying rates. I haven't kept track."

"Oh, yeah. I vaguely remember something about that." Elise contemplated his words for a moment, then said, "So, now you're going to tell me you can travel at light speed?"

"We can, but I don't think anyone has. For one thing, all ships registered with the Federated Planets have regulators to control speed so that law enforcement has a chance to catch up. Once a person achieves light speed, nothing can catch him."

Elise stared.

Lendar looked at her, then turned his attention back to the traffic. "Nobody knows for sure what happens if someone were to make light speed. He might enter another dimension; he might not be able to slow down. We don't know. So far, nobody that I know of has tried it."

Elise licked her lips and swallowed. "I thought nobody could go light speed anyway. Isn't there some kind of weight restriction, like things get heavier the faster they go?"

Lendar nodded. "Yes, but we use gravitational drives which convert that into energy."

Elise tried to observe the passing landscape, but found her eyes refused to focus. "That's sort of like a perpetual motion machine and those things aren't possible."

Lendar grinned. "It's not a perpetual motion machine,

Elise. The gravitational drive and the other power systems we employ are a little more complex than I am able to explain at the moment."

"Ha, likely excuse." Elise groused and shivered.

"I'm no engineer or mechanic, but I can give it a try, if you insist."

"No, that's ok. I wouldn't understand it anyway." Elise studied this man who called himself Lendar Marl. He's cute; he's polite; he's generous, but that's not enough is it? She fanned herself. The rules aren't enough. They won't protect me after all! Arrggghh.

Just look at those muscles ripple inside his shirtsleeves. Not a body builder's physique, his is more like a cowboy's physique, all sinew and ripcord, a man who works hard and eats right. Probably a martial arts physique, no, his body is like those Marines' returning from Iraq, a military man's physique.

Never thought about adding, "don't date an insane man," to the list.

Kinda goes without saying, don't you think?

It's not like insane people wear warning signs! Aarrgghh!

Meanwhile, buildings on Carlisle Avenue whipped past. The homes lining this section looked besieged by renters and whizzing cars.

Elise blurted, "Ok, let's go back and get Bruce." A chill hit her spine and worked its way through her nerves. Her stomach felt as though it were filled with rocks.

Lendar made a right turn into a residential neighborhood and another right back to Lomas. They waited at the stop sign for a chance to enter traffic and head west to Carlisle.

Elise sighed. She patted his forearm. "Lendar, I'm sorry. I think you've finally gone off your nut. Maybe you're delusional."

Lendar's eyes flicked her direction for a second. He

cocked his eyebrow. "If you give me a chance, I'll show you where I've lived most of my adult life, the ship, my quarters…"

Interrupting him, Elise snorted, then blushed. "Those things you said, they're just not believable."

"If I were in your place, I'd feel the exact same way."

"You'd be scared too? Then why are you telling me this stuff?"

Lendar seemed amused. "Because it's the truth." He pursed his lips. "Elise, I'm sorry, but I just don't know how the truth can be softened." He turned onto Lomas, met the light at just the right moment to take a left, south on Carlisle, retracing their path. "We'll go get Bruce and then you can relax."

"You're really going to get Bruce, aren't you?"

Lendar shot her a small frown. "Of course, that's what you want, isn't it?"

Elise bit her lip. "Well, no, not exactly." She stared out the window. God help me, I don't know what I want!

I know what you want, Miss Smarty Pants with her ten rules! You want to take a private plane to Andorra and be married to an Andorran butler, that's what you want.

No, that's what I thought I was getting.

What if Lendar isn't crazy? What if Bruce is right and there are aliens out there?

She looked back at him, her mouth twisted with an embarrassed grimace. "If we get Bruce we won't be alone."

Lendar laughed. "You are a wonder."

Elise drew a bead on Lendar, angling his direction and touching his sleeve. "You're just kidding. You're not really from outer space, are you?"

"Elise, my Lord, Prince Anwic, gave me one year and five hundred thousand US dollars. I've used five of those months trying to find you. He might grant me an extension, if I can prove I need it, but I can't count on that."

Lendar gripped the steering wheel. "We can put this

off, but in a few months I will have no more time and I must leave." He frowned, looked her in the eye, then back at traffic. "Most people have plenty of time to get to know one another. We don't. Maybe I'm asking more than you can give, but I'm feeling the pressure." When he looked back at her, his eyes shot clean through her like bullets. "You said you wanted to know who I am and I'm trying to show you. Do you really want to know?"

"Yes," Elise squeaked. Oh, God, is he truly from outer space? Oh God. Oh, my God. Are You really in on this? Give me a sign!

Lendar had been right about Max's attitude improving once he went for a ride. Happily oblivious to his mother's upset, Max pointed at passing vehicles, jabbered, pointed and jabbered again as if he were addressing each car or counting and lecturing. That child is perfectly content for once today. Grr. He's always happy as he can be when Lendar's around.

Well, aren't you?

Shut up, I'm panicking.

Elise patted her chest and fanned herself again. She turned the air conditioner vent so the cold air blasted her in the face. Ooooh, focus on that new car smell--that alien new car smell. Arrggghhh.

"Is this car an actual Cadillac Escalade?"

Lendar shook his head. "No, it's a...how do you say...oh, yes...it's a knock-off."

Elise's shriek came out strangled like the sound a mouse might make if someone stepped on it. Oh, gak, it really is an alien Escalade! "Ok, where did it come from then?"

"The artificer aboard the *Lalf* built it with the help of robot assistants and a very fine artificing computer." Lendar answered, as if he read a brochure from a Cadillac dealer. He drove through the intersection at Central. "It's rather amusing, but this vehicle would fit right in back on Minan, though there it would be equipped with hover. So many people spend enough time in space that when they return home and withdraw their vehicles from long-term storage, we end up with quite an assortment of motor conveyance on the roadways and in the airways."

Oh, my, oh, help. She snatched her checkbook from her diaper bag and began fanning herself. It is an alien Escalade! It'll probably turn into something weird, like a Transformer. It'll probably eat me. Maybe Lendar's a hologram, like the one inside that police car in the movie, one of those evil Transformers, what did they call those…oh yes, Decepticons, that's right. Gak. You're losing it. Well, why shouldn't I lose it, I'm inside a Decepticon!

Elise croaked, "So, you people built it from scratch aboard your space ship…the *Lalf*?"

"That's correct. A deep space vessel like the *Lalf* is virtually self-sufficient, that's what qualifies it for deep space-- the ability to survive and thrive indefinitely, far from civilization." He made one of those weird signs, like his hand was a ship's sail.

Elise coughed. "It all sounds so reasonable."

Lendar grinned at her. "That's because it's the truth."

Elise gazed out the window. I don't really want to get Bruce; what I really want is to not be scared.

So, don't be scared, just don't do it.

Of all the things I was afraid of, I never thought of this! Fat lot of good all this worrying has done me! He's not a serial killer; he's a space alien!

Suddenly she recognized the weird feeling that preceded a fainting spell. Elise dropped her head between her knees. Breathe, Elise, breathe.

Lendar asked, "Elise, are you all right?"

She lifted her head a few inches and rotated it to face his direction. "Is that why you can't contact your parents? Radio signals take too long to reach them?"

"Yes. Back home we have boosters that warp radio transmissions into another dimension so that the recipient, who may be light years away, can, what is the term, ah, download the transmission almost instantly from receivers. There aren't any boosters around here to warp a message into the proper dimension, so no purpose in sending any." He looked like he might add something, but instead returned his attention to driving.

Elise felt her pulse thump. Ok, heart's still working, it's the brain that's malfunctioning. Good thing the organs are on an automatic system. Gak. I'm losing it.

Flying cars and messages warped into another dimension? This can't be real. God please help!

She resisted the urge to work the door handle again. Breathe…

Lendar spoke. "Elise, I want to tell you everything. I hate keeping anything from you, but it's up to you. Do you want to do this or not?" His look of disappointment was unmistakable.

Elise's heart didn't like that look. Now it felt full of rocks.

He'd rather I did this. He wants me to do this. He wants me! Just look at his face, that disappointment, that longing. He wants me! A space alien wants me! Oh gak.

Head between her knees, images of Lendar's bravery when confronting Kendall and the way he flipped Gabriel on his back with such simple elegance, making a jackass out of him with complete and utter politeness floated before her mind's eye. Ah, delightful. My knight in shining armor!

Can a girl swoon and have a panic attack simultaneously?

Yes, I think I can. Watch me!

Lendar gave her a side-long glance. "We're fetching Bruce, Elise. Everything will be all right."

Elise sat up and tried opening her mouth, but nothing came out. She clapped it shut and clutched the edge where the window rolled down into the door. Oh my goodness, I'm falling apart. I want to run away and stay right here simultaneously! God are You there? Are You really in on this!?

At her apartment building, Lendar parked the Escalade and walked across the street. Late evening gave way to full night. Crickets chirped and dogs barked, as usual. A familiar mini-van rolled up the hill to park in the usual driveway.

Why did the rest of the universe have to keep on going as if nothing was out of the norm? I mean, really, God, is that fair?

Is Bruce home? She leaned forward hoping for a better view.

His porch light is off. Lendar did screw the bulb back in, didn't he?

Lendar walked back, hands in his pockets. He stopped outside the Escalade's door. The window rolled down as if on its own accord. "Bruce isn't here. You want to go find Lolly?"

Elise shook her head. "No, she's at her Aunt's house in Las Cruces. In fact, she might not be back for months!" She folded into a slumped bundle of shattered nerves.

"Oh, yes, I recall her mentioning that now." Lendar muttered. He folded his arms on the opened window frame.

Trust Lendar or not? Ok, what if I tell him to forget it, that I can't ever go see his spaceship or whatever it is he's planning to show me. Can I stand to end this?

The black ache in her bowels and the rocks in her heart and stomach let her know this choice was not an option.

Ok, so that leaves do this now or do it later. Will it be easier later?

No, don't think so. Same scenario, only more advance freak-out time.

Lendar scanned the neighborhood. Waiting.

She suspected he was looking for threats, like Javier or Gabriel, for instance. But, thankfully, Javier hadn't returned and Gabriel's noisy pick-up hadn't announced his presence. Wonder why I haven't seen them all week? That's kind of strange, especially given the fact that Gabriel didn't scare Lendar away.

Lendar seemed to do that frequently, sort of

thoughtfully observe his surroundings. That's why he turned around in Javier's driveway, he noticed him standing there watching...

Lendar asked, "Anybody else you want to find?"

"No." Elise's voice sounded squished. "Lendar, I don't know if you're telling the truth or not, but Bruce thinks space aliens are real. I thought the whole business was crazy, but maybe I just didn't want to believe it."

Max interrupted. "Dink. Wanna dink."

Lendar opened the passenger door and fished a water bottle from an ice chest on the floor behind the driver's seat. "Water for young Master Max," he said, unscrewing the cap, the little safety ring made its characteristic miniature clacking noise. He handed the bottle to Max.

Max glugged the water. "'iscious," he said, trying to pronounce "delicious" and failing. He wiped his face with the back of his hand and grinned. "Tanks."

Lendar smiled. "You're very welcome, Master Max."

Elise laughed, glad for something ordinary to focus on. Not that a man who bowed on a regular basis and called little boys 'young master' in the United States of America was all that ordinary. "Max, do you need your diaper changed?"

Max shook his head, his bottom lip protruding in a pout. "No, not 'et."

Lendar stuck his finger in the top of Max's pants. "Feels damp to me." He proceeded to unbuckle Max.

Elise climbed into the middle seat. "Thanks, Lendar." She took the water bottle from Max, set it in the cup holder and removed a diaper from her bag. She gulped.

Ok, here goes! Decide. If I'm not willing to end this relationship I'd better let Lendar show me whatever it is he's planning to show me. She glanced up at him, a hot, wet diaper in her hand. He'd turned his attention outside, his body shielding the opening.

He's protecting us.

She rolled up the diaper, stuck the tape around it and

shoved it into her bag. "Lendar, the truth is, I am scared out of my wits. But I've been scared out of my wits now for quite awhile, even before we met, so that's nothing new. The freaky thing is, everything I worry about, that never happens. The things that actually happen, I never worry about. I guess that should tell me something about how useful worrying is…"

Lendar gazed at her, waiting for her to say more.

He didn't look like a space alien with his lean, muscular body clothed in the cotton shirt, the dark hairs on his tanned arms inviting her touch and his carefully creased blue jeans. All bright in the light from the overhead bulbs.

She bit her lip and affixed the sticky tape on Max's clean diaper. His tummy was so soft and wonderful. He reached to pull her hair.

Trust God or not? That's what it comes down to.

She let herself tip forward so that her forehead rested on the seat back. Ok, do this or not do this? What's your decision?

Well, if I don't do this, I'll regret it.

Taking a deep breath she said, "Let's go find your spaceship." She hoisted Max into his seat.

Lendar clapped his hands together and grinned. "Elise, you are a wonder."

"Ruv Mama," Max said and smeared her ear with a wet kiss.

Elise looked into his large, brown eyes. "I love you too honey." At least two of the three of us are happy. Her heart and bowels lightened; now only her stomach felt rocky. God, I'm obeying rule number ten, now it's Your gig. She buckled Max into his car seat and crawled into the front.

Lendar shut the passenger door, returned to the driver's seat and started the motor. He made a u-turn, a repeat of the evening's earlier false start.

Human efforts to push back the darkness that blanketed the city were evident everywhere: streetlights, headlights, solar powered walkway lights, porch lights… We fear the darkness. We fear the unknown. Lord, you are the Solid Rock, but why do you expect us to walk in such dim light?

Duh, I guess that's what You call faith!

Oh Lord, I'm terrified.

Lendar didn't speak. Reeser Peland's Spaceman's Fugues started on its own. Things around Lendar seemed to happen without his having to do anything. She remembered the time Lendar's car had rolled up the hill past Javier's house seemingly of its own accord. Men from outer space should have advanced technology, shouldn't they?

"How do you do that? Make things happen without doing anything?" Elise asked.

"Mind control. When my lord gifted me this Escalade, he also fitted me with a device that allows…"

"Oh, I've heard about those things. I saw a magazine article about a paralyzed guy who uses a computer linked to his brain to control robotic arms." Elise relaxed a little.

Max kicked his sandaled feet and patted the car seat arms making up his own song in accompaniment to the music. A search for Reeser Peland, composer, on Google at Zimmerman Library had netted nothing. Reeser Peland must be from outer space, too. Wake up girl: Spaceman's Fugues, duh!

She asked, "Do you know anything about your ancestors or the aliens who abducted them?"

"Don't know much, most has been forgotten. We only discovered recently--well, recent from a space traveler's perspective--that we are earthlings. Before that, people had assumed the old stories were just myths." Lendar offered a small smile and turned his eyes back to his driving.

"How did you find out?" Her voice sounded tiny. Given the tightness in her throat she was surprised she could speak at all.

Lendar cleared his throat. "Er, well, there are other aliens. Marsupial humanoids." She noted his knuckles tightening on the steering wheel, but he didn't rub his face. His glance her direction was serious in its intensity, the side of his face suddenly edged with a car's light.

"People with pouches?" Elise asked, incredulous. A cold sweat broke out on her forehead. Now the air conditioner was too cold. She turned the vent to point away from her toward Lendar.

"Yes." Lendar grinned, seemingly glad she caught on so quickly. "This is their third time coming to earth to conduct remote research."

Elise rubbed her forehead. "What? Ah, you mean, they're around here somewhere right now?"

"Yes, they are, as Providence would have it."

"Oh." Elise tried to catch her breath. "Gak." She swallowed. "Here? Right now?"

Lendar nodded. "Well, not in person, they observe remotely."

Elise's head ached. She choked. "That's like Star Trek, no interference."

Lendar continued. "It was from one of them, one of the marsupial scientists, a Placental Physiologist, who tested our blood and compared it to humans left here on earth, that we learned that the ancient stories were true: we Minans are transplanted earthlings."

Black spots floated before Elise's eyes. "You mean they take blood samples from humans?" She dropped her head between her knees again. Oh God, aliens who spy on us and conduct research on us. It's all true! All those UFO nutcases are not really nutcases after all. Gak! She murmured toward the floor, "Are these marsupial humanoids gray or green skinned or thin, tall, white skinned things with large blank eyes."

"No, not at all."

"Oh, so where do the gray, green and white aliens come from?"

"I don't know Elise. It's possible that they're the ones

who originally kidnapped my ancestors, I just don't know." Lendar hit the steering wheel with the heel of his hand. "The truth is locked up in the temple in the city of Ponichar. The priests have kept it secret for centuries." She felt rather than saw the concerned glance he shot her direction. "Sorry, a little too much information."

Elise lifted her head and stared at him, her mouth hanging open, pretty certain slobber dribbled from her slack lips. "Do you believe in God or not? You know, the God Who created the universe…that One."

"Yes, Elise, I believe in Him with all my heart."

"Ok. Well, that's a plus." Deciding she might not faint after all, she lifted her head high enough to scan the terrain. They'd already reached Carnuel with its odd mix of ramshackle and middle class housing just outside Albuquerque. "Where are we going?"

"We're rendezvousing with a space jet a few miles south of Clines Corners."

Elise's brain went staticky. "You're just going to drive out there and the jet will be waiting? Like what, in the middle of 285?"

"Yes." He smiled, seemingly happy she had so quickly guessed his plans. "Precisely."

Elise swallowed. "I don't know what I expected. Maybe I thought we'd go to the space port over by Hatch, though, now that you mention it, we're going the wrong way." The rocky butterflies were still busy in her stomach. I think I'm going to throw up.

Lendar smiled. "We Minans are not official, Elise. We're strictly clandestine."

"Clandestine? Why? Why don't you announce yourselves and meet the President and stuff like that?"

"Because we don't want to meet the President. We don't care about the President. We're not trying to establish diplomatic relations, Elise, we just want women."

Elise screeched. "Women?! You want women? What,

are there, like a thousand of you Lendars running around romancing ninnies like me and taking them off to your space ship? This is like those shows on the Discovery channel where aliens abduct people and do experiments on them!" Elise covered her face with her hands. "Oh my God, oh my God!"

"Elise, it's not like that. We're not going to kidnap anybody. We're only taking women, and some men too, if they want to come. I promise you, I won't force you to come back to Minan with me. Why would we force any person when so many are so willing?"

Elise narrowed her eyes at him.

His face was open, as if he hid nothing.

Suddenly angry, Elise blurted, "You won't have to force me. You'll inject me with some drug and I'll lose my will power. I read about that in a science fiction short story one time."

"Elise!" Lendar snapped.

"Mama silly," Max said.

"I am not silly, Max."

"Elise, if we don't find willing women and men to bring back, human life on my planet will go extinct!" Lendar's face, revealed in a sudden flash from automobiles in the westbound lanes, expressed nothing but grief.

"You're kidding me? You have superior science and technology, how can you be going extinct?"

"It's a genetic mutation cause by a virus, probably cross species from the aliens who abducted us. According to the legends, they used to come back every few years and check on us, but they haven't been back for centuries. It was about the same time this virus swept Minan that they stopped coming. By the time we realized that the virus not only made a person ill, but had a devastating side effect, it was too late, virtually every person on the planet had been affected."

He lifted a hand and made a sign, some kind of swirling movement, like a cyclone. "The side effect is the mutation I was telling you about. It affects the x-chromosome.

If a woman conceives a female, she can carry the baby to term, but after that she's sterile.

"There's the theoretical possibility of a tribe hiding in some jungle somewhere that hasn't been affected, but we haven't discovered them."

Elise asked, "If there's a virus, what good will it do for you to kidnap women? Won't they get sick too?"

"We've eradicated the virus and developed a vaccine. Nobody gets it anymore." He paused. "I'm not kidnapping you, Elise, this whole thing was your idea."

"My idea?"

"Yes, you said you wanted to know where I come from." Lendar seemed irritated, but for once Elise didn't care.

She snorted. "Oh great. I'm a breeding cow. You want me for a breeding cow."

Suddenly Lendar took the Tijeras exit and pulled over in the Molly's Bar parking lot. "Elise. We don't have to go. We can turn around right now and I'll take you and Max home."

"What?"

Lendar blew an exasperated blast from his nose and mouth. He lifted his hand from the steering wheel and made a sign, like rolling up a stream of paper. "Elise, I'm sorry. Maybe I should have kept the information about the aliens and how my people are going extinct for later." He glanced away and gathered his breath.

When he looked back at her his eyes seemed filled with anguish. "I know this is completely bizarre, nothing remotely similar to what you expected, but I hate keeping anything from you. If I've failed now, it's been on the side of offering excessive information rather than withholding it." He sighed. "It's obvious that the truth about me is too much for you. I'll take you home." A muscle in his jaw twitched and he checked his blind-spot preparing to leave the parking lot.

"What?"

Lendar threw up his hands. "If you don't want to come to visit the *Lalf*, where I've lived most of my adult life, then we won't go."

She thought he might be trembling. He put the Escalade in park and stared sightless at the instrument panel. Finally he looked at her. His face was craggy, like an unforgiving cliff, his fabulous eyes crinkled with grief. "Elise, I've dreaded this moment since before I met you because I knew it had to come…"

He shook his head, spent a few moments staring out the window, then sighed. Looking back at her, he said, "I'd say, no worries, we can put this off and try again later, but in seven months I have to return to my duties. It took me five months to find you. I'm running out of time.

"My lord, Prince Anwic, has given me a gift beyond any even the Emperor has ever gifted, the chance to find my own wife. I have taken time off, left the mission team and been allowed to search by myself, for myself. Nobody else has been given that kind of a chance. If you are not the woman the Most High intends for me, then I must continue my search elsewhere."

Elise patted her chest. "There are other Lendars wandering around looking for women?"

He nodded. "About three hundred of us, male and female, starting temporary employment services, dating web sites…other ventures… Human life here on planet earth is cheap, Elise. Very cheap." He cleared his throat and wiped his nose with the back of his hand before fishing his handkerchief from his pocket and wiping it properly.

"What are you talking about?"

"China aborts babies for the purpose of limiting a family to only one child…Americans abort babies because they're inconvenient. Indians starve their baby girls because they only want boys. You can buy a child for a few hundred dollars, Elise." The grief in his voice was unmistakable. "If I wanted a "breeding cow" I could buy a hundred of them. It grieves her highness, Empress Jaizem, but she's already bought a hundred of them. Thai girls whose families think selling their daughters will help their finances. African girls. Girls from the former Soviet."

"Oh." Suddenly she felt very small and petty. She looked down at her hands. "Yes, you're right. It's terrible."

"I could give it all up for you, my hereditary lands, my wealth and position, stay here on earth with you, but if I were to do that after what I've told you tonight, you'd always wonder if I really were from outer space and you'd never quite trust me. You'd always have this kernel of a notion that I might actually be insane. That is a situation I could not live with.

"You see, Elise, tonight is all or nothing for me." He glanced her direction, then stared out the windshield. Lights from passing vehicles flashed on his face while Spaceman's Fugues played. He looked tired, broken, devastated.

"Who is Reeser Peland anyway?"

"He's a spaceship captain who is also a composer." He pointed skyward, making one of his fascinating signs. "He's up there, not far away. He's the captain of the Somainai ship."

"You mean somewhere near earth?"

"Yes."

"Oh. What's he doing here?"

"He's the Captain of the research ship. He's one of those marsupial humanoids I was telling you about." Lendar stared at her.

Elise coughed. "Ah, how many, ah, marsupial humanoids are with him?"

Lendar paused. "About six thousand."

"Six thousand?"

Lendar shrugged. "He flies a full-sized deep space vessel. He has the room and the authorities chose to send that many."

"Gak." Elise held her face in her hands. Now what?

"Elise, you said you'd give me a chance. I'm asking, are you able to keep that promise?" Lendar waited.

After a moment, he turned his attention outward, once

again doing that thing he always seemed to do: assess the environment. That incredible patience of his apparently kicked in once again. A vehicle's headlamps arced as it turned into the parking lot illuminating his profile.

Oh God, he's so handsome!

He turned to stare at her.

Max wriggled his fingers trying to reach his water bottle. "Dink," he said.

Absently Elise handed him his bottle. Go or not go? She tried to remember what he'd said, but her ears roared, distracting her.

This is just like those people in burning buildings who can't move when they really ought to be running for the exit. They sit there trying to process the information and their brains crash. My brain is crashing. That's what's wrong with me. I have blue screen of the brain.

Max patted his knee and sang. He pointed at a fire truck rolling past. "Fire 'ruck." He said and clapped his hands. "Rook, fire 'ruck."

Elise turned her eyes to gaze at the fire truck. It rolled down the road and out of sight. Not far away, three men holding beer bottles and leaning against a pick-up bed talked, the light from the bar grazing their faces. Experimentally, she tried opening the door. With the vehicle now in park, it swung open easily. Music and chatter from the bar drifted on the wind accompanied by the roar of traffic on Interstate 40.

If I don't go to his spaceship, it's over. No part of her liked that thought. The idea that she might never see Lendar again made her whole body feel as if it were at death's door. Tears collected in her eyes. She sniffed. "If I'm going to see this spaceship of yours tonight, we'd better get going."

Lendar's frown did not disappear. "Elise, are you sure?"

"Yes, Lendar, I'm sure. I think. I hope. I reserve the right to freak out again at any moment." She attempted a smile and closed the door.

He almost smiled, but the grin died stillborn. He turned his attention to driving and put the Escalade in gear.

Max repeated. "Gro! Time to gro!" He emphasized his statements by pounding his fist on the car seat arm.

"Very well, Master Max." Lendar checked for traffic and entered the travel lane. Soon they merged onto Interstate 40 heading east. Spaceman's Fugues still the soundtrack for the evening.

Gently Lendar said, "Everything will be fine, Elise. Just relax and enjoy the ride." Tijeras Canyon was dark except for madly rushing vehicles.

"'Ruck," Max called and pointed.

Suddenly Elise realized the Escalade was surrounded on all sides by trucks. She felt a new panic attack coming on. "Yes, honey," she whispered, "trucks. Lots of them."

Lendar seemed as calm as ever. He eyed her. "They're doing fine. I've been monitoring them." He punched a button and the video screen popped up, the same one he'd used to show her the church ladies walking to their car. The screen split into four sections, each one pictured a driver with his eyes on the road.

"Oh." Elise murmured. "Lendar, you do have mini-cams all over the place!"

"Robotic eyes, about baseball sized, hover mechanisms inside, can travel over a hundred miles per hour," Lendar answered and winked. "They're covered with a film that makes them invisible."

Oh gak. This just doesn't let up does it.

They came out of Tijeras Canyon. Yard lights dotted the landscape on either side of the interstate. Traffic that had pressed in ominously through the canyon sorted itself out, the downhill run easing the trucks from slow hazard to speed equal with the cars.

Moriarty, Edgewood. Opportunities to turn around were slipping by. Where was he taking them? What were his intentions? Were they really going to a spaceship? Why hadn't

Bruce been there the one time she needed him!?

Pictures of cattle mutilations, inexplicable crop circles and little green men holding surgical tools and peering at hapless victims rolled through her mind like a bad "B" movie. His words about viruses and searching for women meshed with droning accounts of kidnapped humans she'd heard at some point in her life. Little bits of metal inserted under the skin and inexplicable pains after forgotten encounters sometimes only remembered under hypnosis. I can't do this. I'm a coward after all. "Stop. Lendar, just stop!" Elise clutched the dashboard, panting. "I can't do this. Stop. Please! Stop!"

Lendar pulled over onto the shoulder.

Elise opened the door and ran to the fence. She looked back at the Escalade. Lendar stared after her, his wrist on the steering wheel, his hand hanging loose. The dome lights went out. The Escalade's headlamps created sharp shadows of pebbles and road debris. Vehicles rushed past, the sound of their passing like waves crashing on the shore.

"Oh, God, tell me what to do? Tell me!" Elise turned her face toward the field where juniper trees stood dark against the night-gray grass. Insects sang, semi-tractor trailers rumbled. "Lord, please, tell me what to do." She rested her arm on the fence, heedless of the barbed wire. Her forehead clammy against the flesh, she stared at the ground. Her white canvas shoes appeared blue against the dirt. "I'm going to throw up."

Daughter, where is Max?

He's in the Escalade with Lendar.

Elise spun around. There stood the Escalade, the door open, the light on the inside panel a white spot against it's black shape, the headlamps and taillights parenthesis containing the most important person in the world…and she'd left him in the vehicle…alone…with…a space alien…a stranger…the most handsome man in the universe who at this moment had complete possession of her son…Max, the only ordinary mortal in the world she'd ever truly loved with all her being, besides her Dad, in her entire lifetime…alone in that alien car with that man from outer space…

Elise gulped the evening air, her hands trembling.

Stars peered down from above. They seemed to ask, "Well?"

"You know God, that's a really good question."

Lendar had turned down the music. She watched his silhouette as he leaned to speak to Max. Max's black form bobbed forward, his delight in Lendar evident even from here.

"Oh, Lord, tell me what to do," Elise whispered and let go of every thought. Her mind cleared and joy slowly filtered in. Before she could change her mind, she strode toward the vehicle, climbed in and pulled the door shut.

Lights from the instrument panel glowed like the cockpit of an airplane.

"Why haven't I seen all those lights on the dashboard before?" Elise asked.

"Usually they're hidden behind a panel so the Escalade looks normal to most people," Lendar answered.

"Oh."

"Momma cry baby," Max announced.

Elise whirled to glare at him. "Max! I am not a cry baby."

Max sucked the bottle, then slammed it down next to his leg splashing water over himself and the car seat.

Lendar used his handkerchief and wiped up what he could. She studied his manly wrist as it rested on the steering wheel, the hand hanging from it elegant and strong, the long line of his body, one arm stretched into the middle seat, his chest broad.

There's that watch, with its slide show. Same nice house from before only at night, must be his house in Albuquerque; same view of Javier's place, only tonight nobody's there; a new view of some place…ah, look there's Gabriel's mother sitting outside the front door, must be her house… Those invisible robotic eyes…

Faith is believing in something you can't see. Faith is knowing that sometimes the things you can't see are more real than the things you can.

He's telling the truth. He's from outer space. He wants me to marry him. He wants me to go to his planet. Oh, God. Now I'm really freaking out. Elise fainted.

When she awoke, Lendar held her in his lap in the front passenger seat. A damp cloth rested on her forehead and a funny baseball sized thing whizzed around her. Lendar studied her visage, searching every centimeter as if he wanted to memorize it.

His face was so close she could see the slight imperfections in his skin, a faint scar and a tiny mole. So wonderful. Sharp cheekbones like shallow cliffs over the plains of his cheeks; a generous, friendly mouth; long lashes. Oh those long, thick, eye lashes. Fabulous, aquamarine eyes with striations of thin gold. Gorgeous. His eyes invited her trust, the pupils like openings to a whole 'nother world.

I think I'd like to be in that world. Yes, I think I would.

Lendar's hand edged upward, cupping her jaw in his palm, the skin dry and warm. His breath washed over her. "Are you all right?" he asked. "My diagnostic team thinks you've only had a fainting spell; they can't find anything wrong with you." He pointed to a second robotic baseball, its single lens peering at her with unabashed interest.

"Oh. Yes, I think I'm fine."

His lips approached, his teeth straight and pearly in the light from the instrument panel. "Elise…" he whispered, as if her name were a magic word, as if each letter were worth a million dollars. His fabulous, otherworldly scent enveloped her. Her flesh gave way, only remaining erect because her bones had not yet crumpled. But they vibrated like power lines carrying a heavy load, threatening to explode. His lips hovered so near…

Max coughed. "Gro! Time gro." He splashed more water. Droplets landed in her hair and on her skin.

Lendar's eyes smoldered, his mouth parted for a kiss, his lips so clearly longing for hers. She watched them move. "Elise..."

His voice flowed over her like chocolate music, like rose scents solidified into letters, like starlight captured and released as cologne. His arms encased her in an embrace of ecstasy, his chest rose and fell, his breathing generating a thrill with each subtle exhalation, his thighs supporting her the most solid and secure place of rest. Time seemed stalled. Forced to a stand-still in the music of now.

At last Lendar whispered, "Master Max reminds me that I am a gentleman and a gentleman never takes advantage of a lady."

Time restarted with an unpleasant jerk, even as his words reshaped in her mind as chocolate rose petals. Elise laughed, suddenly unnerved.

Lendar smiled at Max, then at Elise. "Ready?"

She nodded, then shook her head. "No..." I'll never be ready as long as you hold me like this! Half-heartedly she said to Max, "Honey, stop that splashing." She should clean up his mess, but a languid peace permeated her so that she didn't care anymore about the splashed water or the lights on the instrument panel or anything except to be in this man's arms. Just let me stay right here, she thought.

Only a few moments earlier she'd felt as if her stomach were filled with rocks and her head about to explode. Now, she felt like cotton candy, all airy and floaty. Like a dandelion seed head, one puff and she'd drift away in a cloud of ecstasy. Let Max dump the whole bottle, just so long as I can stay right here. Ahhh....

Finally she murmured. "Can I just stay here, like this, in your lap?"

Lendar shook his head. "Eventually one of us will need something." He gently tugged a tendril of her hair, then traced curve of her cheek, then her lips. "Can't make time stand still Elise, just slow it down." His blue-green eyes fixed on hers like gem stone lasers.

Darn. "Ok, in that case, I guess I'm ready."

Lendar got out, still holding her. Careful of her head, he set her back in her seat.

His body heat radiated pure delightfulness. She tried to suck in a little extra, to memorize how this moment felt to hold it in readiness for the future when something weird was bound to happen and scare her out of her mind.

Lendar buckled her in himself, checked to see if her feet were inside and shut the door. She watched him walk around the front of the Escalade. He stepped into the vehicle and put it into gear. His profile, framed in the window. How to describe it? Noble and faithful? Wow, noble and faithful. Could it be true? Oh, God…please make it true. Thank You.

14

Clines Corners Travel Center's tall, digital sign announced special deals on t-shirts, moccasins and fudge. Lendar took the exit, curving south, away from the store. To the right communications towers flashed red. To the left, gently rolling hills obscured Interstate Forty, except for one small dell that allowed a glimpse of rushing trucks decorated with yellow travel lights. Ahead, Highway 285 stretched south into darkness.

A "Road Closed" sign blocked their path. Lendar winked and drove right through it! Elise shrieked, raising her arms to protect her face, but nothing happened. When she looked back, the sign still stood.

"Hologram." Lendar grinned.

Elise punched him in the arm.

Lendar laughed.

Ahead a red "x" seemed to glow on the pavement. "Are they going to beam us up or something?" Elise asked.

Lendar shook his head. "No. That's the spot where we'll stop."

"Ok." A weird thing happened on the way to the "x," they entered a cargo bay that hadn't existed…no, hadn't been visible before.

Lendar put the Escalade in park and turned off the motor. The compartment reminded Elise of the insides of cargo planes with its metal ribs and floor. Cables and various types of catches and hooks were secured against the walls. Strange machines wandered around securing the Escalade. The compartment was large enough for two vehicles to park side by side with plenty of room to open their doors. Pot lights on the ceiling illuminated the space.

Elise gasped, fanned herself and patted her chest. "Lendar, what just happened? A minute ago there was nothing here!"

"This space jet is equipped with chameleon battle skin. When it's activated, the jet is invisible." His aquamarine eyes seemed to glow, his brows relaxed and friendly.

"Oh. Romulan cloaking device." Elise muttered. "It really does exist!" Ok, here we go! Strange stuff coming at'cha. Ugh.

Lendar laughed. "Romulan cloaking device?"

"Star Trek, science fiction." She gulped and pressed herself into the seat. Yes, it was still there, the leather same as ever. "Ah, where did this leather come from?"

"It came from Minan. We carry stocks of all sorts of things so we can build anything we need in the Artificer's lab." He cleared his throat. "Although, actually, we can either tan new hides or create acceptable copies with our facsimile machines." He eyed her through his brows, one corner of his mouth curling with humor.

He doesn't even try and he's completely sexy, Elise thought, her mouth forming an "o." "Copies, not synthetic or something?"

Lendar nodded. His hand clutched the door handle, but he didn't tug it. He watched her intently for a moment, then scanned his surroundings, which seemed to be his habit anytime he had waiting to do.

Elise bounced her folded hands in her lap and asked, "What's an artificer?"

Those blue-green eyes fixed on her, his affection obvious. "The artificer is the officer in charge of fabricating things. He uses artificing computers, facsimile machines, lathes, saws, kilns," he shrugged. "He uses all types of equipment assisted by a staff of robots to create whatever we need and much of what we want." He cocked his head, as if waiting for her to ask another question. When she didn't, he stepped out, his boots clattering on the metal floor. He opened her door and went to retrieve Max.

Max held up his arms and hugged Lendar's neck, his

eyes wide.

Elise started to ask another question, but a dark haired man walking through an opening doorway into the cargo bay distracted her. He wore a moss green tunic with matching pants edged with black piping and a black cap. A small gold pin decorated his chest.

He raised his hand and said, "Ho, Lendar…"

The rest of his speech might as well have been in Apache for all Elise knew. She got out of the Escalade and stood next to Lendar.

Lendar answered the fellow, his incomprehensible, rich baritone flowing into her ears like Kahlua. He gestured to Elise. "Elise Ramos, gi Max." He pointed at the man and said to Elise, "Ty Criter, Pilot."

Wonder if they do handshakes? Elise thought, offering her hand.

Ty slapped her palm then clutched it firmly. "Meet you pleasure," he said in peculiarly accented English. He bowed. "Please *Lalf* joy visit."

Elise copied his bow. "Thank you."

He grinned, then faced Lendar and spoke, once again in that language. Had to be Minan-ish, or whatever they called it. Lendar answered him, nodding his head and looking serious. Then Ty exited the bay, the doors opening for him as he approached.

Lendar made a sign that seemed to indicate they follow Ty.

Must have motion detectors, like at the grocery store. With a giggle, Elise quipped, "Be funny if that door made the same sound when it opened as the ones on Star Trek make."

Lendar offered an indulgent smile.

The luxurious passenger compartment had large windows and wide, high-back seats facing one another in groups of four or six. Elise suspected a hidden table could be raised from the floor or dropped from the wall or ceiling between the seat groupings. The walls were paneled and upholstered with a comforting velour-type material, white with subtle, gold swirly shapes. The royal blue, crimson red and daffodil yellow carpeting reminded her of fancy hotels. Diffused light emanated from panel strips in the translucent ceiling.

Outside Highway 285 stretched north and south in the New Mexico darkness. A vehicle appeared and hesitated at the southern "road closed" sign. After a moment, its headlights arced around the sign, then approached.

"Time to buckle up." Pointing, Lendar said, "Please, take the window seat."

Elise said, "On Star Trek nobody buckles up."

"Elise, we're not making a movie, we're flying in a space jet."

"Yeah." All the sudden she felt fluttery and a bit nauseous.

Lendar buckled Max beside her. "Not very safety conscious on Star Trek, are they," he finally added.

Ignoring her stomach, Elise flicked a hand. "I don't know. It seems amusing. High tech stuff everywhere and we have to buckle up." She winced.

Lendar seemed unimpressed. "Some things are universal, Elise."

Ty made an announcement over the intercom, which Max promptly repeated.

Elise shot him a quizzical eye, then turned a questioning glance on Lendar.

He translated. "Commencing take-off."

Elise gazed out the window. I'm glad my stomach settled down again.

The jet hardly made a sound, though the characteristic jet noise was vaguely present. Maybe all that means is that this passenger cabin is practically sound proofed, she decided. She watched the approaching vehicle, a pick-up. The jet lifted and it rolled out of sight underneath. "That was close."

Lendar shrugged. "If Ty were worried about it, he

could have taken measures."

"Measures?"

With gentle tones more appropriate to "Darling sweetheart," Lendar said, "Oh, temporarily stalled the motor, caused an electrical glitch...any number of things." He toyed with her hair, a soft smile playing at his lips.

Elise's face felt thin and worn. She looked out the window again, trying to put off that growing feeling that she must throw all sense aside and ravish Lendar as soon as possible. At last she said, "I'm glad he didn't have to do that."

The cabin lights dimmed, soft music played somewhere like distant tunes through someone's opened window, gentle, jazzy comfort.

Clines Corners, with its signs and busy parking lot, appeared in view through windows on the opposite side of the cabin. The jet rose, mostly upward, angling to the northwest.

Interstate 40 became a ribbon of white and red. Albuquerque and its metropolitan area spread brightness across the dark land. National forests, ranch land and Indian reservations were notable for their lack of streets and lights-- except casinos. The casinos were as glaringly gauche as ever.

The land shrank away, the lights signifying human habitation less easily identifiable, perhaps that bright spot was Las Vegas, perhaps that large spot was Los Angeles; it certainly was big enough. Suddenly Elise realized they were higher than anyone could possibly achieve in a normal jet. "We're in space, aren't we?"

Lendar nodded.

Max rested his head on Elise's thigh.

"Past your bed time isn't it honey," she murmured, stroking his hair.

Max made a couple of attempts to pop his thumb into his mouth before succeeding, then fell asleep.

What if this window is just one of those high definition screens pretending to be a window? What if this is all a hoax?

Forget that! What if it isn't!? That fluttery feeling in her stomach returned.

Oh, gak, what if it isn't?

Elise gasped. "We're flying in a space jet? We're going to outer space?"

Lendar took her hand and squeezed. "That's right. We are in outer space." He cocked his head, then said, "Breathe, Elise. Ten deep breaths."

"Ok, I'll try that."

One. Oh, God, I'm in space! I'm in outer space and I'm not even a millionaire.

Two. Lendar looks like he's only about thirty, but he said it took twenty light years to come here, how old is he really or more important, how long ago did he start traveling in space? Hundreds of years? Could hundreds of years of real time have passed since he started flying around? If time is variable according to speed, what is real time? Gak!

Three. Oh, God, did I mention, I'm in outer space and I don't understand this variable time thing. It's making my head hurt.

Four. Eventually I'll have to meet the prince!

Five. When You answer prayer, You really answer prayer.

Six. How am I, a dumb ranch girl from New Mexico, going to fit in with a bunch of aliens?

Seven. Oh, God, what terrifying things have You planned for me next!?

Eight. Lendar said aliens abducted his ancestors. Does that mean little green men are in my future!?

Nine. Aloud, Elise exclaimed, "Lendar, this deep breathing thing is not working!"

Lendar chuckled. He gestured toward the window. "Isn't it a spectacular view?"

Elise glanced outside. The earth's albumen, like a halo, glowed at the edge of blackness, the planet, a luminous jewel. "Is that a satellite over there? Look at that."

"Yes, it is."

"Cool. I've actually seen a sure-enough, real satellite." Elise's eyes rounded. I'm in outer space! A sudden flash of heat rose from her hips and shot into her head.

Lendar was speaking. She focused on the sound of his voice. How to describe it? It's like in those commercials where the chocolate ribbon flows over the model. Elise licked her lips, unconsciously leaning closer to his wonderfulness. He was saying, "…a closer look at Jupiter tonight? We can fly over there, it will only take about an hour."

"What?" Elise blinked. "Take a closer look at Jupiter? You can do that? Just zip over there and have a nice little tour?"

Lendar winked. "Sure, it's only a few million miles, no big deal for a space jet capable of near light speeds." He waved his flattened hands back and forth. "We wouldn't be getting out of the jet, Elise. But truly, I think we'd better save that for another time and stick to our original itinerary."

"Oh." Her giggle came out strangled. "Aren't you funny."

Lendar stroked her cheek as if it were finest porcelain requiring the most delicate touch. "We'll be at the *Lalf* in about fifteen minutes." He studied her expression for a moment, looked thoughtful, then said, "If you'd like to see Jupiter, we can do that. I don't want to offer something and then not deliver."

"Oh my…just go see Jupiter like we're driving over to Jemez Springs or something." Elise choked and coughed.

"It's something we can save for later." Lendar shrugged. "For now, I'd really like to show you where I live."

"The *Lalf*? What kind of a name is that?"

"It's just a name."

"A strange name."

The corner of Lendar's mouth edged up slightly. "Well, it is a Minan name. I suppose you could call it the "mother ship" if you want."

Elise gagged. "Little green men and mother ships."

"Well, I don't know about little green men, but yes, mother ships we have." Lendar scooted closer, unbuckling Max and lifting him onto his lap.

"I thought you said we had to be buckled," Elise asked.

"Just like an airplane, Elise. We can unbuckle once we achieve cruising state."

Elise laughed. "Cruising state, how funny."

Lendar cocked his brow at her. "Funny?"

"Oh, it's just that this is all so very, very weird. I thought we were going to Andorra. I was fantasizing about a cruise to the Caribbean or in the Mediterranean, I never expected this!"

Max settled across their legs, happily sucking his thumb in light slumber.

Elise stroked his hair, enjoying the delicate feel of the strands.

Lendar's body edged hers, thigh to thigh. Oooh, wonderful. Her woozy stomach relaxed. That sensation of oneness comes back every time we touch. I could live in that forever. Elise sighed and lay her head on Lendar's shoulder.

He draped his free arm around her and drew her close. His wonderful, male smell mingled with cologne enveloped her. I could give it all up, yes, I could give it all up in a heartbeat if you truly are everything you seem to be, Mr. Lendar Marl.

Aloud she asked, "So, Lendar, can I do a space-walk?"

Lendar shook his head. "No, not at this time." With his fingertips, he followed a curling tendril of her hair to its end then chose another and repeated the caress.

Elise bit her lip. "That's because we're not really in a spaceship, are we?"

Lendar sighed. He leaned across her to touch the wall under the window and a control panel brightened into life. Strange, curvy cuneiform-style lettering glowed green in a display window. He punched a button.

"Ho, Lendar." The voice sounded like Ty.

"Ho, Ty…" Lendar talked. Ty responded. Lendar nodded and blathered some more. Ty blithered at him.

Elise watched Lendar, her mind a complete blank. She didn't know enough about linguistics to even begin to analyze their noises. "What do you call your language? Minan-ish?"

"Like the English who call their language English, we just call our language Minan." Lendar gave her that sexy, cocked brow expression with intense, I'm-totally-fixated-on-you eyes that turned her knees to putty. "Elise, in a few minutes Ty will shut down the gravitational field. Do you understand?"

"Well, of course I understand. You're speaking English now. Well, English with that cute Castilian Spanish accent of yours." Elise licked her lips. "Wait. You're going to turn off the gravity?"

Lendar lifted his upturned palm toward the window. "If you won't believe the evidence before your eyes, maybe you'll believe weightlessness. I'm going to place Max back on the seat and buckle him in again. After that, you and I will unbuckle. Do you understand?"

Elise nodded. Duh, what does he think I am, a nitwit? Don't answer that.

Lendar did exactly as he had explained. A couple of seconds after he unbuckled, a blue light glowed on the ceiling. He pointed upward. "That light indicates the gravitational field has been turned off. Now, unbuckle."

Elise didn't move.

"When you're ready, unbuckle. But don't make any sudden motions. Every move will bring unexpected results. To begin, slowly stand." Lendar stood and drifted upward at the same rate of motion at which he had risen from his seat.

Elise licked her lips. "Ok. So maybe this is real." She wanted to add, I don't have to do the space-walk thing. I believe you.

"Try it."

Elise unbuckled, suddenly aware of the fact that when she didn't place her hand on the armrest and hold it there, the hand tended to drift a little. She glanced at Max. His entire left arm floated upward. *God help me, I'm scared. My hair is all floaty.* Her heart rate accelerated and her skin turned clammy. *Girl, when will you stop asking for trouble? Gak!*

Instead of simply standing, she rotated and clung to the armrest. Her hips' swinging movement carried her bottom toward the ceiling. If she hadn't been clinging to the armrest, she would have risen until she bumped into the light panel. She let go and pushed with her index finger. Slowly she floated upward and as suspected, her bottom bumped the ceiling. She twisted, trying to look at Lendar and ended up spinning. "Lendar! I think I'm going to throw up!"

Lendar gave himself a tiny push from the ceiling and hooked his feet in the armrest. He reached for her, snatching hold of an arm and stopping her, but not without ending up at a 45-degree angle to the seat.

His grip cut into her forearms. Elise gasped, "Thank you, thank you. This looks more fun on TV when they show those astronauts in the space shuttle." Elise coughed. "Right now, I'm not liking it."

"Astronauts train for this, Elise." Lendar pulled her to himself and wrapped his arms around her, the strength within their muscles comforting her. "You have no training."

"Yeah. And apparently I don't listen very well either." Elise tried to relax and enjoy his protection--from herself. *Oh, gak, you are a total nitwit.* "You know, I appreciate the opportunity to float around thinking I might vomit, but if you don't mind, could we have the gravity back? I think I need a few no-gravity lessons before I attempt this again." She covered her mouth and suppressed a cough.

Pictures of stomach bile floating around this luxurious cabin appeared unbidden in her mind. *Oh, Lord, please, keep me from throwing up!* She nearly strangled on her next sentence, "I had no idea gravity was so important!"

Lendar grinned. "No. I think we'll just float here awhile. I'm enjoying this. How do you say, yes, enjoying this way too much." He nuzzled the crook of her neck, his breath wafting over her flesh.

Elise pushed against him so she could look him in the eye. She felt the drift her movement created, but tried to ignore it. "Lendar, I think I'm going to be sick. Could we please sit down with gravity, please?"

Lendar shrugged. "As you wish." He bent his knees, bringing them closer to the seat, reached with one hand, grasped the seat back and tugged gently. They landed in the spot where he'd sat moments earlier. He kept his arms around her. "Hang on." He clutched the armrest next to the window and they bobbed over Max into her seat. "How's that." His embrace had kept her firmly pressed against him, the fabric of his shirt rubbing her cheek and his calm heartbeat in her ear.

"Believe we're in space now, my silly Elise?" His lips grazed her ear and a tingle shot through her body like a static charge. He loosened the strap and buckled it over her hip, the two of them now held in the same seat belt.

Elise swallowed. "Silly? I'd argue with you, but then I'd look stupid and silly." She pressed against him, reveling in the feel of his ribs next to hers, his collarbone edging her face and the firm muscles of his arm. She sighed. "Ok, you win, we're in space. I'm sorry I ever doubted." Despite his comforting presence, her skin still felt clammy and her belly in turmoil. Droplets of sweat collected, cooling too rapidly. "That was kind of fun. If you don't mind the nausea." She coughed. "Maybe I shouldn't have said that; you'll get the idea I liked it."

Lendar smiled softly. "You're doing fine, Elise." He rested his chin on the top of her head and she gazed out the window at the stars. The cabin smelled clean and fresh, the vent above blew a gentle flow over their heads.

I wish he'd kiss me.

Ty interrupted with some kind of announcement.

Lendar translated. "We've arrived at the moon."

And there it was, after only a few minutes flying time. "Amazing," she breathed. The white and black landscape spread below them, stark and beautiful. "Somewhere, down there, Neil Armstrong's footprints remain in the dust." She sighed.

"Would you like to see them?"

Elise's eyes widened. Before she could answer, the space jet crossed the line into darkness. An almost spherical thing, more like a gigantic, platinum, Faberge egg, visible only because it was lit up and decorated with tiny colored light-baubles. "That's it, isn't it? That's the *Lalf*. It's huge! How big is it?"

Lendar leaned toward the window. "Oh, yes, that's the *Lalf*. It's a little over a two miles at its widest point and about eleven hundred and fifty feet tall." His bemused expression was soon replaced with pleasure. "Prince Anwic has turned off the chameleon battle skin and activated all the lights in recognition of your visit." He glanced at her, as if checking to see if she understood the honor Prince Anwic did her.

Elise's voice came out pinched. "It's wonderful! It's amazing." Her brow squinched with worry. "Oh. I won't see him. Will I? It's…I'm not a snob or anything, but…it's just…I don't know anything about royal etiquette or any of that stuff. Ah, I don't have to see him this time do I?"

Lendar shook his head. "No, you won't see him this time. Perhaps next time."

Elise nodded, simultaneously relieved and disappointed.

The *Lalf* was small compared to the moon, but it was not a tiny thing. It makes the Apollo spacecrafts look like little tin cans. Reminds me of the Death Star, she thought, except the Death Star was a sphere with a funny divot. She stifled a giggle. "What's the funny bubble on the side?"

"That's the cockpit window. It's man-made diamond."

"Diamond? How big a diamond are we talking?"

Lendar shrugged. "Oh, I don't know for certain, probably fifty feet wide and thirty feet high."

"That's some diamond!"

Ty made another announcement.

Elise glanced at Lendar for a translation.

"He's just advising us to buckle up. He's reactivating the gravity."

Elise covered her wincing, nervous smile with her fingers. Her heart thwacked against her rib cage and her stomach churned. Oh! Help. "We're about to land in the, er, *Lalf*?"

"Yes, that's right." He paused. "It won't be dramatic Elise, Ty is a very good pilot."

It won't be dramatic! Whose definition of 'dramatic' are we using?

As the jet neared the ship, a huge camera shutter-looking thing opened, revealing a brilliantly lit interior: a gigantic room where peculiar, wide bellied planes with weird wings were parked in a tidy row.

Elise asked, "Is that what this jet looks like?"

Lendar nodded. "Yes. And that glassed-in wall to the right is the control booth."

"Oh."

Max stirred, his hand falling free of his mouth.

Elise traced the line of his brow before turning her attention back to the *Lalf*'s interior. The jet seemed to have slowed almost to the point of stopping. They glided through the opening into the light. A soft thud announced their landing.

Ty said something through the intercom that brought a chuckle to Lendar's lips.

"What did he say?" Elise asked.

Lendar shook his head. "Too hard to explain." He pointed toward the control booth. "Watch that sign. While it's flashing red, the oxygen level is too low to support life. When it turns green, we'll be able to breathe."

"Oh." Elise sniggered. "That's crazy. Just like something I'd expect on earth."

Lendar shrugged. "Red for danger, green for life. Pretty much universal for all carbon based life forms."

"Do you know any life forms that aren't carbon based?"

"Not sentient ones." He frowned. "But there's always a possibility, isn't there?"

Elise watched the sign. "Why a man-made diamond for a cockpit window?"

"A man-made diamond has no flaws, therefore it is utterly transparent. Diamond can withstand whatever comes without change, except contact with another diamond. If it is cut or shaped properly it can help protect from harmful radiation. Add a gold shield as needed and you have a fine cockpit dome."

It didn't take long before the warning light's flashing ceased and a placid green glow replaced the glaring red. Lendar unbuckled them and released Max from his straps. Awkwardly Elise rose to her feet and watched Lendar gather Max into his arms.

A hatch opened on the side of the cabin where one row of seats had so obviously been missing before. Light from the bay entered the compartment.

Lendar asked, "Shall we go?"

Elise hesitated. She clutched Lendar's arm. "You go first." She released him.

"Very well." He took a couple of steps then paused. "Elise, it's not so different from leaving a plane on the tarmac at an airport. Just take my arm and we'll go together."

"You think it's not so different? The fact that we're on the back side of the moon in a very large space ship doesn't really make any difference?"

"Let's find out."

"After you."

Lendar sighed, strolled toward the hatch, glanced back

at her and walked out.

Ok, that's not better. Now I can't even see him. He's out there, with Max…Gak! Aren't you brilliant. Elise hesitated, then followed. She stopped at the opening, her hand griping the frame.

Ty stood on the polished floor chatting with another person over a thing that looked remarkably similar to an I-book. Lendar waited at the bottom of the ramp. A machine rolled past him.

"What's that machine?"

Lendar glanced at it. "Robot."

"Oh."

"We have many robots Elise, most of them too small to see."

"They don't eat people do they?"

Lendar chuckled. "No, they do not."

Elise took a deep breath and a step down the ramp. The ramp seemed real enough. It was carpeted with a clingy sort of stuff that tried to grip her shoes. Ugh, this stuff is nasty. Oh my. Elise patted her chest. Don't faint again! Don't do it. Breathe. Elise stumbled, then sat down. Sitting on the creepy stuff was worse. "Just need to catch my breath."

The space jet docking bay ceiling disappeared above into darkness. The docking bay stretched into the distance toward the interior of the ship. It was divided into areas that looked like repair stations, workshops and storage rooms.

I'm in a spaceship. Oh Lord, help me! I'm in a spaceship. Elise dropped her head between her knees again, only the odor from the carpet made her ill. Oh, gak. I'm going to throw up.

A noise caught her attention. Looking up she noted a robot carrying her suitcase, backpack, diaper bag, some other luggage and Lendar's ice chest from the Escalade. Lendar hadn't seemed to notice her most recent panic attack. He spoke to the thing and it whirred away toward the control booth, through a now opened doorway and into its darkened interior.

Robot servants. Lendar has robot servants. Don't start, don't think, you'll just freak out. Just get up and follow Lendar. Ok. I can do this. Aloud she asked, "Now what?"

Lendar gestured toward the same doorway where the robot had disappeared. "We go through there."

Max was deep asleep, completely unaware and totally at ease in Lendar's arms.

Elise sighed. Good thing I'm almost to the bottom of this creepy ramp. She edged down the ramp with her hands, found the polished floor then worked her knees in that direction. Ty and the other fellow watched, their mouths hanging open, then spun to turn their backs to her. She noted how their shoulders shook with suppressed laughter. Great. A laughingstock on two planets, I bet that's a first for a citizen of the United States.

At last she could place her feet on the floor and stood up. "This floor is amazingly clean," she remarked.

"Nanobots keep most everything shipboard, except the gardens, ah, what is the phrase? Yes. White room clean." Lendar grinned. "Can't have any stray bacteria, insects or lint mucking things up."

"Oh. Well, I don't know what I'd do if my apartment was that clean. The place might literally fall down." She managed to walk the three or four steps to his side without fainting. A small accomplishment, but she felt proud of herself. "Ok, maybe I can do this now that I'm not walking on that nasty boarding ramp."

Lendar cocked his brow and looked back at it. "What's wrong with it?"

"Didn't you feel how it wanted to take hold of your feet, like Velcro or something?" Elise shivered. "Eeew."

Lendar smiled. "Oh, that." He shrugged. "Never thought about it before. Low gravity aid so a person doesn't drift off into space when he disembarks."

Elise parked a fist on her hip. "In that case, what does a

body do when he leaves the ramp?"

Lendar gave her a pointed glance. "Underneath that nasty surface, the ramp is metal. Metal creates a more dramatic reaction to a person's footfalls--remember action/reaction?" He jagged a hand to one side then the other. "If you're walking on dust, like the moon, less impact, less reaction. You'd have to work harder to get a bounce."

"Well, all this space stuff may be old news to you, but it's all new to me!" Elise snorted, folding her arms across her chest. "Nanobots. Robot servants. Chameleon battle skin…it's enough to make a girl go bonkers!"

Lendar bowed. "Madame, of course you are correct." His eyes glowed, amusement bouncing around inside them like happy beams of sunlight.

Elise offered an affectionate smile, then narrowed her eyes. "You're so adorable."

Lendar grinned. "Let's go."

He strolled toward the control booth. Ty and the other man stood to her right behind a console covered with buttons, dials, digital displays and various other mechanical and electronic looking things Elise could not label.

They spoke to Lendar. He answered them. Next, he faced another doorway opposite the one where they'd entered. Elise realized what Lendar had called the 'control booth' included the control booth, a storage or utilities room behind it and a passageway on one side. He took her elbow and together they walked through the doorway into a dark hallway that stretched into the distance.

"Good heavens, how far does this corridor go?"

"It's about a mile long. Would you like to walk or would you prefer to ride?"

Elise stared at him, her mouth open. "You people have all this advanced technology and you walk?"

"Why not? We need exercise too."

"I suppose so. I just thought space people would have fancier ways to get it."

Lendar shook his head. "Elise, you are a wonder." He started down the hallway. As he went motion sensing lights came on.

After a few moments, Elise realized she'd better follow.

She concluded that the mural decorating the upper walls on either side probably stretched the corridor's full length, interrupted occasionally by doorways and lighted keypads.

"What does this mural portray?" Elise asked.

"The history of the Berylin Dynasty." Lendar answered.

"Ok," Elise tried to make sense of it. However, except for the obvious things like fight scenes and so on, the mural didn't tell her much, at least not without more study. The architecture was weird and the costumes other-worldly. Duh, you think? "That would be your Prince Anwic's history, right?"

"Yes." Lendar paused.

Elise shrugged and chuckled. "Walk down memory lane."

"Ah, I reckon it is," Lendar replied.

Great. All my silly, culturally relevant jokes will be totally lame in his world, won't they?

If you're going to keep seeing him, you'd better get used to it.

Their shoes clattered dully on the vinyl-clad metal. Elise studied the painting, analyzing the style, color choices and method. At least, this mural gives me something to think about besides the fact that I'm on a spaceship on the backside of the moon with a bunch of aliens from another planet.

Don't start; just don't start.

Lendar didn't speak. And neither did Elise, who was afraid to ask any questions.

At last they reached the end of the hallway and he turned to face her. "Please take Max. I need my hands free."

Elise held her arms open to receive her son. Lendar touched the wall. A control panel appeared with a keypad and a glowing glass screen. He pecked at the keys, then placed his palm on the glass.

"We have those," Elise said as the end of the hallway opened.

Lendar nodded. "Yes. I know." His expression changed from gladness to something less pleasant.

Is that worry?

Yeah, I think he's worried.

You know, that's the first time I've ever seen him worried.

The cold sweat returned and trickled down her back. Elise's hands set to trembling. "What's going on? Is there a problem?"

The sound of distant wind soughed through the corridor's now open, but dark end.

Elise craned her neck to take a look. Maybe we're losing all our oxygen. "We're going to die, aren't we? You just let all the air out."

"No, we're not going to die. Everything's fine." Lendar rubbed the bridge of his nose. "Elise, let me have Max, please. This next part might be rather trying for you."

"What are you talking about? If you say it's going to be trying for me, then by golly, it's going to be a doozie, isn't it?" She gawped at him.

"Ah, possibly. Many people who have no experience with energy elevators find them rather, ah, challenging." Lendar spoke with a calmness and precision that Elise found unintelligible.

He continued. "We're about to enter the energy elevator. We call it the "tube" because it's a hollow cylinder about fifty feet across that stretches over eleven hundred feet from cockpit to engine plants. That sound you hear is the gravitational field thrumming through the tube; it is not escaping oxygen."

He pointed at the dark opening where the terrifying soughing sound originated, he said, "We're going to step through that doorway and onto an invisible gravitational field." Lendar leaned her direction, "Elise, there will be no floor."

She stared at him. What? "No floor?" Did you say "no floor"?"

"That's correct. Are you ready?"

Elise shook her head.

"Elise, I assure you, there is nothing to be afraid of. The gravity flowing through that tube will support any weight that enters it. That gravitational field is the heartbeat of the ship, it's probably the safest place on board."

"Ok, so why do you look so nervous?"

"I'm nervous because the tube is always a challenge for someone who's never entered it before," he repeated patiently.

Elise winced. "You go first then."

"Very well." Lendar walked through the doorway.

Elise suppressed a shriek. Lights came on in the "tube" and she could see Lendar standing not far away. That's not so scary. He just walked through a doorway and now he's standing right there. Max is doing fine, he hasn't even stirred.

She went to the edge, her foot poised over…nothing. Darkness below. Darkness above. Well mostly darkness, there's a sort of orange glow up there like when the moon is about to rise. She stared at Lendar. There he was, standing on thin air, his feet flat. She made a strangled kind of chuckle. Except for the fact he didn't have a looped cord sticking out of his head, he looked like a Christmas ornament. Flat footed hanging in space. Holding a little kid in his arms. Strange ornament!

Elise blurted, "Are you sure there's, like, no chameleon battle skin covered steps or something?"

"None. Just a gravitational field that supports anything that enters it."

"Ok. I can see you out there, it's obvious you're doing fine. Max is doing fine. Heck, Max is totally oblivious. So-o-o-oh, I have no excuse for this irrational fear, do I?"

Lendar's smile was more like a slow burn of desire. "You are a wonder."

"Yeah, right." Under her breath Elise mumbled, "More like 'wonder how she managed to survive this long'!" She turned away. The long hallway was dark except for a light bubble that seemed to contain two figures. Great. Pretty soon I'll have an audience. She spun to check on Lendar and Max.

"Elise, are you coming?" Lendar asked.

Funny, he's not impatient, he's just probably thinking he'll have to come and get me and carry me like a baby. Sigh. Elise pursed her lips, then said, "Yeah. Eventually."

Lord, please give me Your strength. I'm being a total ninny. Lendar's out there, he's doing fine. Lord you led me this far. I want to stop being an idiot.

"Ok, here goes." Elise crouched like a runner, then rushed straight for Lendar, keeping her eyes firmly locked with his. Strangely, the gravitational field didn't feel squishy like a waterbed or a kids' Jolly Jump, it felt firm like a regular floor, only with no clatter of footsteps.

Elise wrapped her arms around Lendar and hid her face in the curve between the humeral head of his arm and his clavicle. "I think I'm having a heart attack."

Max stirred, uncomfortable in the sudden crush, but didn't awaken.

Lendar adjusted Max's position, gently placing his head on his other shoulder, to accommodate Elise. "You're not having a heart attack." His tone was soft, like a breeze.

"How do you know?" Elise didn't look up. She focused on the feel of his arm around her waist.

"Because, if you were, the robo eye I've assigned to monitor your health would have informed me. Now stress, that's different. It's telling me you are very stressed." His exhalation ruffled her hair, bringing tingling delight to her scalp.

Looking up at him, Elise managed a faint smile and

quipped, "So now you have one of your invisible spies watching me, is that it?" Suddenly, apparently, as usual, she felt perfectly safe with Lendar when she quit freaking out and worrying herself into a tizzy. He's like a solid, reliable safe place. So far, for a human, he does that safe, reliable thing pretty well.

"Elise, it's not invisible, it's right there, about a foot above your head." Lendar pointed with his nose and eyes. In the next instant, he studied her face, as if he wanted to memorize every pore.

Elise attempted to glance up, but came close to falling over and decided not to try. "I'll take your word for it."

Lendar muttered something in Minan and they began drifting upward, gradually picking up speed.

So this is walking by faith? Elise asked.

15

Her eyes closed, Elise reveled in the feel of his body under her hands. His heart beat calm and steady in her ear. She breathed his unique Lendar scent mingled with the strange rosemary-like odor that seemed to characterize the energy elevator. The weird soughing sound continued unaccompanied by breeze. It didn't even feel like they were moving.

Lendar rested his chin on the top of her head, its bony point grounding her in reality, blocking the frightening feeling that she'd walked into some kind of surreal, sci fi nightmare. The reprieve ended too quickly. His throat bobbed against her forehead. "We've arrived."

Elise lifted her face from the protection of his shoulder. She felt the tube's hollowness, though she didn't dare look down. The well-lit walls seemed very similar to what she'd seen below, except here a few anachronistic doors made of wood, stained and varnished, perched without landings. Conduits and hoses snaked around their frames like steampunk vines, with rivets and bolts for leaves.

She pointed. "Is that yours?" A large, raku vase with a spray of grasses issuing from its mouth, stood beside the only entry fitted with a balcony.

Lendar smiled, his expression warm and kindly. "Yes. Shall we go in?"

Elise nodded, her eyes widening and her pulse quickening.

His arm tightened reassuringly around her waist and released. When he took her hand, it tingled. The tingling roved up her arm, making her feel they could go anywhere and overcome anything together. If he is the one You've sent, Lord.

"Elise, it's about two ante meridiem back in

Albuquerque. Would you like supper, or would you rather sleep?"

At the mention of "sleep" Elise realized exhaustion edged the bank of her consciousness like a threatening flood. "One thing at a time. First we go in."

As before he pecked at a keypad beside the door and placed his hand on a lighted panel. Elise noted the door's six sections were carved with botanical reliefs and framed by glass tiles that promised a well-lit interior. It swung open revealing a tiled entry hall.

Lendar stood aside, waiting. Elise glanced at him apprehensively. He smiled, sweetness playing about his eyes, but desire held possession of his mouth. A now awakened Max perched on Lendar's arm, sucking his thumb. She stepped inside.

Immediately she was struck by a sense of calm. "It's so clean!"

Lendar followed her inside and the door closed. "Easy to be clean when you have a host of robots doing the work." He winked. He held out his hand and the hovering, baseball size robot that had been floating above her head, whizzed into his waiting palm. He toggled a switch and set the thing on the side table standing near the door. "I don't think we need that anymore."

Elise scanned the room. "I could get used to robots doing all the cleaning real quick." She grinned.

Furniture groupings divided the expansive room into separate areas. The living area was defined by a collection of comfy looking couches and chairs; a credenza stood behind one couch bearing a squat bowl filled with peonies. Small tables stood near the seating, each with its own lamp and a large coffee table made from a limestone slab crouched in the center.

Straight ahead a bank of tall windows, hidden behind translucent sheers, formed the far wall. To the right, beyond the couch group, four tall cabinets with glass doors, rustic red and waxed black, held interesting artifacts, memorabilia, knick-knacks and books. Beside them, on either side, darkened doorways promised more rooms to explore.

To the left, a partition cut by another darkened doorway intruded into the room. Where the partition ended, a chair, its legs just visible, hinted at a dining area just out of sight.

"It's lovely. It's normal."

Lendar cocked his brow at her. "Normal?"

Elise blushed and shrugged. "Well, granted, it looks like one of those places decked out for a home magazine photo shoot, but it looks normal. Like someone really lives here. Not like some futuristic, science fiction place." Her face scrunched into an apologetic grimace as she looked up at him.

Lendar's face expanded with an amused grin. "In that case, I'm glad I didn't install the bubble hover seating and the deluxe, robotic bartender."

Max stretched and smacked his lips. "'Ow-n. Want 'ow-n."

Lendar released Max to the floor and he toddled away searching for something interesting. He soon discovered a box filled with toys and tipped it on its side, spilling the mixture of plastic animals, metal vehicles and wooden blocks to the floor.

Elise laughed. "Do you think of everything?"

Lendar blushed and rubbed his nose. "Simply functioning within my training."

Elise noted his pleased expression. "Is that so? But a man likes to be recognized for a job well done, doesn't he?"

Lendar's smile was wan, his eyes twinkling.

Elise cast a flirty glance over her shoulder at him as she stepped past the couches, toward the windows. She found the hem of a curtain panel and pushed an opening with the back of her hand. A rising hillock, basked in brilliant moonlight and crowned with distant treetops, rose to almost eye level. "Are those really trees out there?"

Lendar joined her. "Yes."

"Full grown trees?"

"Yes."

Elise stared. "You have full grown trees on a spaceship."

Lendar reached high and rested a hand on the window frame, drawing his body into a long line of masculine elegance. His aquamarine eyes seemed to capture silvery light from outside and reflect it back at her: magical allure mingled with affection. "Human beings require nature, whether they're aware of it or not."

Elise swallowed. "You have sky?"

His hand came down to make a series of his peculiar signs. "Not exactly. Together with the magnetic gravitation shield on the outside, this ecosystem includes a sort of limited atmosphere that helps protect us from radiation. The ceiling is lined with high definition wafer panels that mimic sunlight and starlight and daylight blue. It can rain, hail, sleet, snow. Wind is created near the hull, at the horizon. Weather is orchestrated according to whatever environmental program is presently in play."

"Oh my." Her skin felt as if it had absorbed just about all it could handle, her mind balked and her spirit felt bloated with newness. She longed for an opportunity to be still and make sense of what she'd seen. She pushed away a growing feeling of exhaustion.

Lendar looked down at her, his expression full of anticipation and delight. "Would you like to go out?"

"Can we?" Her voice came out hesitant. She noted his eagerness to share this with her. How amazing that this man from outer space would choose me above all other women on planet earth. God has to be in the middle of this somewhere.

The internal argument started. Ha, you think God is in on this? Any minute now the good stuff will end and it will be the same old crap just farther away from home and you with no help at all.

No, why should it be like that? Why do you always

think everything turns bad?

Hrumpf, couldn't have anything to do with your Dad dying young, or your mom disowning you or Gabriel turning out to be a rat, could it?

Well, even if this turns out bad, why ruin the moment wondering when it will be end?

Lendar was speaking, his dreamy baritone pushing at the negative thoughts crowding them, making them squeal in protest. Unconsciously, like a flower straining for the sun, Elise leaned his direction.

All of me, she thought, take all of me and then maybe everything will be ok.

He was saying, "…around the gardens now. We're having a barbecue out there later."

"A barbecue, how funny." Her fears now shoved into the background, Elise basked in the feeling of safety she enjoyed within the bubble that seemed to envelop Lendar and those he favored everywhere he went.

Not like Gabriel whose bubble was one of agony and pain.

That should tell you something! So hush your negative nonsense already.

Lendar cocked his brow again, a knowing look passing through his eyes, as if he'd seen through to every thought as it drifted through her mind, the worry, the reminders of mistakes and things gone from good to bad, maybe even the desire.

Next, affectionate, good humor took hold of his features. All except his mouth. A kissable look overwhelmed his mouth begging her lips to act.

Elise ignored the burning longing that made even her teeth ache. She loosed a twittery laugh. "We don't have anything like these gardens. Last I heard, when they tried to put some people inside a geodesic dome that was supposed to be self-sufficient, it didn't work. They liked to starved to death."

"We operate on a much larger scale. Won't work if you do it small. Even so our gardens require constant monitoring and tweaking." While he spoke, Lendar went to the wall to her left, past a large dining table with eight chairs. "And we don't even try to obtain our food from the ornamental gardens."

She turned and glanced back toward the entry hall. The partition divided the living area from what appeared to be the kitchen; an arched doorway opened into a faintly lit room fitted with cabinets and countertops. Weird. They're normal looking.

Max tugged her pants leg. "Mama, rook."

Lendar had opened the sheers and now the windows telescoped into compartments in the walls, one half to the right, the other half to the left. Insects' nighttime chatter and a soft breeze laden with pine and flower scents floated into the room. It's just like standing on the porch at Inlow. Elise sighed.

Images of the Baptist summer camp's sometimes dry and sometimes wet summers flooded her mind. Nostalgia for those happier times when her father still lived rushed in to join them. Wish Daddy could have met Lendar!

Max ran across the stones, past the flowers and onto the grass. At the hillock's crown, he stopped and pointed. "Mama, rook!"

Elise followed. At the top she gasped. "Amazing." The artificial moonlight bathed the spreading meadow. And on its fringe of black, graceful, sighing trees, a small deer stood at the edge of the copse, gray in the blue light. Its luminous eyes stared at them, wondering at their intentions, before slipping out of sight into the vegetation.

The landscape seemed endless, a tree-strewn grassland stretching to distant, rocky outcroppings and thick forest. Silvery clouds rolled lackadaisically, alternately obscuring and exposing the disc of light that looked so much like a moon. Without realizing she spoke aloud, Elise breathed, "Are those clouds real?"

Lendar's gentle voice floated in the air like a dandelion seed, pleasing and lovely. "Mostly no." He stopped beside her.

"Do you have birds?" She looked up at his moonlit face, Prussian blue in its shadows, his hair blue-black in the faint light.

"Yes. You'll see flocks in the sky during the day." His hands, edged with white where the light struck them, made a beautiful sign that readily brought to mind birds in flight. "Some are real; some are not. The wafer ceiling includes computer generated illusions to add to the impression that one is out of doors."

Elise blinked. "You live here all the time?"

"Most of the time." He grinned, his teeth flashing blue-white. He looked powerful, ethereal, like Elrond or Celeborn.

Elise shivered. "Who are you anyway?"

Lendar bowed. "Lendar Marl, Baronet, if I understand earth's rankings correctly, second son of Vant Marl and Lady Khossie; Retainer to Crown Prince Anwic Dzula Berylin, the rightful heir to the Minan throne."

Elise patted her chest. Her stomach objected to the thunk of suddenly rock heavy butterflies. Baronet. That sounds important. Is that, like a mini-baron? Her face squinched up with questions she felt too terrified to utter. Her head throbbed. Sounds so medieval, like King Arthur or something. "You're totally serious, aren't you."

"If you mean, am I telling the truth, then yes, I'm totally serious." He waved toward the meadow, his hand making a fleeting arc in the air. "Would you like to take a stroll?"

In that movement, Elise saw hints of the postures and gestures she'd seen portrayed in movies set in the times of kings and queens. He's made those kinds of moves all along and I failed to add it all up. Oh gak. I'm just a girl from the dry wastelands of Claunch, New Mexico. I can stumble over a potato chip. I can say the stupidest things. Me? Marry a baronet? She shook her head. "No, thank you. All the sudden I have a headache. I think I'm exhausted."

Lendar bowed again, a formal gesture of resignation. "As you wish." Though utterly formal, the words were totally lacking in coldness; they were filled with affection and a hint of disappointment.

Elise turned toward the opened glass wall. The patio was roofed with terracotta tiles and a second floor loomed above it, the windows dark. The stucco walls and wood frame windows reminded her of Italian villas. Above the building, gently curving metal seemed to pierce the sky. "What's that metal thing?"

"That's the energy elevator's exterior."

"Oh." Elise rubbed her forehead. The Middle Ages meets Star Trek. Gak. That fight or flight feeling pummeled her organs. Only there's nowhere to run and nobody to fight.

Max sat on the ground ripping handfuls of grass and piling the blades into little, haystack-like mounds. His hands and knees were stained black with chlorophyll. He looked tired.

"Max, let's go to bed."

He eyed his mother, then lifted his arms, the mounds of grass forgotten. He stuck his thumb into his mouth, smearing a chlorophyll smudge on his face.

Elise glanced at Lendar expectantly.

Lendar studied her, a slight frown creasing his brow. Something about his expression was intimate, knowing, like a husband concerned for his family. The courtliness she'd observed minutes earlier was gone. Now, he seemed once again familiar, yet, as always, enigmatic. His eyes went to her mouth, then up to meet her gaze.

Before she knew it, his lips neared hers, their firm lines softening with longing. "Elise..." His hands clasped her upper arms, his grip tightening. His brow furrowing, he searched her face. He was so close she could feel emotion emanating from his body like steam from a pot.

Her lips parted in anticipation. In the next instant she knew her body would collapse under the weight of it all. If he would just kiss me, then I would have sweet release, she thought.

"I will show you to your quarters," he said gruffly and took her elbow.

Despite the aborted kiss, the luscious sense of oneness that persisted each time he touched her flooded throughout her being. She started to blurt, "Just forget the separate room thing," but didn't.

He led her back into the apartment, past the couch grouping to the far darkened doorway beyond the red cabinets. They entered an office grounded around a large desk and executive's chair. On the far wall, a high definition screen showed a view from high cliffs of a winding river, verdant farms and distant mountains.

Lendar edged around her and opened a door to her right. His movement created a draft of air. Eddies of his cologne swirled around her, his chest stretched broad and strong before her. Dark, curling hairs peeked from the 'v' of his collar. Inhaling, Elise averted her eyes into the room, her pulse thrumming.

A large, four-poster bed on a platform with gossamer curtains and satiny jewel-tone comforter and pillows, promised pleasing sleep. Elise's bedraggled suitcase, backpack and diaper bag sat on a chest at the foot of the bed. She stepped over the threshold. Lendar hurried in and through another doorway. Curious, she followed him. He had entered a white marble bathroom that reminded her of a palace.

"Oh," she exclaimed, suddenly overwhelmed again.

"Allow me to draw young Master Max's bath," Lendar said with a professional, butler-like tone, that courtliness returning.

Elise giggled nervously. Her wits felt stretched, as if about to snap.

Lendar kneeled beside the tub and turned on the water with a wave of his hand. He uttered a word, presumably in Minan, and a tray bearing a handful of bottles appeared from within the wall. He chose a bottle, "Shampoo." He chose another, "what do you say, yes, body wash." He touched the third, "lotion. Also astringent and ladies' perfume." He glanced at her. "Ah, please take the perfume home. I chose it especially for you."

Elise shook her head. "Oh my, better than a five-star hotel. They never give people free bottles of perfume!"

Lendar stood. "I shall retire. Sleep well, Elise." He bowed, then strode out.

Elise turned to watch him, then looked back to the filling bath, a large, squarish thing that reminded her of a hot-tub only somehow more comfortable and rich-looking.

She stepped into the bedroom to retrieve her suitcase and bags. On the wall beside the door another high definition screen. Within it trees trembled as if in a breeze and birds flitted about. A handful of leaves drifted lazily to the ground and evening sunlight's long rays stretched below their branches to give the view its romantic, heightened hues.

"Oh, the tub." Elise scurried into the bathroom fearing the water might have overflowed onto the floor, but it hadn't. It had stopped automatically several inches below the rim. "Where's the towels I wonder."

A compartment automatically opened in a nearby wall and a heated towel rack rolled out.

"Oh." Elise exclaimed, a hot flash of anxiety briefly assaulting her. When she'd regained her composure, she undressed Max, then undressed herself and carried him into the water. "Plenty of room for both of us, we might as well not waste all this water."

Pictures of the old, enameled, cast iron tub at the ranch and Grammy helping her with the water while admonishing her not to waste it came to mind. Wish you were here, Elise thought wistfully, her eyes hot and watery.

Lethargic, Max allowed himself to be washed. While he wove his opened hand through the water, Elise quickly shampooed her hair and scrubbed her face before climbing out, Max clutched tight against her side. The bathroom seemed to sense that they'd exited the tub: a warm draft helped them dry and kept them comfortable.

"Oh, this is like heaven," Elise mumbled. "Thank you Lord." She dried herself and Max, slipped on her nightgown and tugged Max's arms and legs into his sleeping t-shirt and short pants.

Together they climbed under the covers and the room lights faded. The picture at the foot of the bed, where setting sun's rays had emphasized the scene's lovely hues turned to night, hints of stars winking through gaps between dark trees. Elise fell asleep to the sound of insect song and gentle breeze sighs.

16

Elise awoke. The room seemed bright though the lamp near the bed wasn't on, nor the floor lamp beside the armchair. Blinking and smacking her lips, she sat up and folded her hands in her lap.

Dawn played on the screen across the room. Long rays from a newly risen sun plucked the trees' fresh greens, vibrant yellows and flecks of orange. Gray ground fog shimmered pink on the edges and roiled between the dew-blackened trunks.

Elise sighed. That screen all by itself is simply amazing.

She peered down at Max, his sleeping face smooth and peaceful; his lashes an endearing sweep along the rosy curves of his cheeks. She longed to touch his tender skin and trace the delicate line of his eyebrows. But knowing she would wake him, she resisted. Instead, she crept slowly out of bed and walked toward the landscape.

The screen was even more amazing up close. Individual leaves, blades of grass and insects were clearly defined, as if she were actually there. Wherever "there" was. A bird flew directly at her. Elise jumped, worried it would crash into the ceiling.

Following the bird's trajectory, her eyes drifted upward where patterns that reminded her of paisley combined with compass roses spread. At the ceiling's center, a crystal chandelier clung like a squat, perfectly round beetle latched to the plaster.

She stared at the screen again, suddenly wondering if someone were in it, watching her. Nope, nobody stood among the trees or walked there. On impulse she reached for the screen, but chickened out and ended up touching the wall instead. The wall was covered with ochre-hued silk. Before she could change her mind on the side of caution or in favor of getting permission, she touched the picture. "Plastic. Feels like plastic. What did Lendar call it, wafer? Yes, wafer, whatever that is."

She paused another moment, admiring the view. It seemed that either the video loop was hours long or its programming contained no loops at all. Every movement, change in lighting and hue seemed unique, fresh. Within the picture, day took over from dawn, color and shadow altering with the light, the birds' song shifting from morning praises to daytime discussion in the search for food.

Elise went to her suitcase and dressed. Blue jeans and a plain t-shirt, barefoot. She sat down beside her things and fished her travel Bible from her diaper bag and read the next portion in her trek through the New Testament.

Max stirred.

She glanced his direction. He didn't awaken. She rested her hand on the Bible's pages, closed her eyes and thought about the words. Several moments later she murmured, "Oh Lord, guide me and give me strength." Quietly she put away the book.

Standing, she checked on Max. Then, leaving the door open, Elise ventured into the office.

Lendar reclined in his executive's chair, intent on an I-book sitting in his lap. He wore a pale gold shirt that emphasized his olive skin tones.

He swung his bare feet to the floor and set the I-book on the desk, still seemingly unaware of her presence. He spoke Minan and referred to a desktop screen standing on a side table. There, the strange cuneiform symbols she'd seen elsewhere rambled in jumbled ranks, responding to his voice and realigning themselves into new configurations. He pecked at the I-book's surface, then glanced at his watch. He seemed so professional, so competent. This was a side of him she had not seen before, the man at work.

At last, he looked up. "Elise!" Lendar smiled and stood. "Did you sleep well?"

"Wonderful. How about you?"

"Refreshing." He edged around the corner of the desk. "Would you like some breakfast?"

Elise nodded, suddenly shy, she murmured, "Yes, please." She pointed at the opened bedroom door. "Max is asleep, ah, at least he was when I left."

Lendar went to the opening and peered in. His attention returned to her, then he stepped her way, pausing within arm's length. She felt his warmth filling the space between them. He said, "He's still asleep." His whole body seemed wound tight like a spring; he raised a hand, it hovered, then fell. His expression was unreadable, his aquamarine eyes startlingly brilliant in his tanned face.

Elise stepped closer until she stood inches from him. He was so handsome, so comfortable in his skin, so self-assured. Led by her longing, she leaned into his space, her lips parting and her face softening with hope. She wanted to say, 'Kiss me, you fool,' but didn't.

Lendar's scent surrounded her, thrilling her and bringing tingling excitement to her skin. She came close enough to feel the expansion of his lungs, his shirt fabric brushing against her breasts. At last his arms encircled her, his heart beat against her cheek.

She asked, "What is a gentleman?"

Lendar attempted to look her in the eye, but she kept her face pressed to his chest. His heart thumped a little faster. Instinctively, her hands clutched his shirt, wanting to grasp that elusive Lendar-ness he held in reserve, always just out of reach. The Lendar-ness that might be released with a kiss…

When he began speaking she gazed up at the underside of his chin.

He said, "A gentleman loves others as he loves himself; he fulfills his duties with enthusiasm and he comports himself with honor. A gentleman exercises his courage, never allowing fear to overcome him." Straining to look down at her, he cocked his head, an awkward effort at such close quarters, reminding her of a bird eyeing a worm. He added, "A full description is rather lengthy. Would you like me to continue?"

Plucking at an imaginary slub in the fabric of his shirt, she asked, "Oh. Well. Does a gentleman ever kiss a lady?" She looked up.

A crease appeared between his brows. "A kiss seals a promise, a kiss begins the joining of two lives into one. A kiss is no casual thing." His eyes were hard, like pewter; his muscles tensed under the shirt and veins in his neck throbbed.

Elise shivered. "May a lady kiss a gentleman?"

"Does she also promise to join her life with his?" If it were possible, he seemed even more tightly wound than before, as if he were about to explode in a sudden release of energy.

Elise backed away slightly and smiled tentatively, peering at him through her brows. "You know, back on earth, that kind of thinking is considered quite quaint and old fashioned." Remembering the Apostle Paul's writing about the believer's body being the temple of God, she dropped her eyes. Her face turned hot. *Oh my, more Christian than me. Oh Lord, help me honor You and grow in You and not embarrass You.*

Lendar replied. "Ah, yes, and so it is with much of the populace of Minan, but we Protectors hold ourselves to a different standard. We are set apart..." He stopped short, leaving the sentence unfinished.

Humor crinkled her face. "Oh my, a knightly order. If Bruce only knew. You see, he worries about me." *Lord, is it wrong to kiss a man before marriage?* She searched his face, her gaze roving over its plains like the beams from a lighthouse.

Lendar rubbed the bridge of his nose, a smile plying his lips. "Bruce may come to know me quite well since I am considering hiring him."

"Are you now?" Elise grinned. *I think that rubbing the*

nose could be lying, but isn't always. I don't think he's lying when he does it.

"Why yes." Lendar paused, tensed, then launched the next phrase. "I am hoping to acquire a ready-made family. And we might be in need of help." He observed her intently, gauging her reaction.

Elise kept her face blank and then felt that, not only did she border on behaving like a hussy with her lusty desire for his kiss, but now she'd abused his trust. His words, spoken days earlier, revealing how much he admired her lack of guile burned in her brain like a branding iron.

"If I, personally, am not needing help, someone with his skills can be very useful to the mission team." As Lendar spoke, his eyes eased into the familiar blue-green she loved. "Before I make my final decision, I intend to speak to her highness, Empress Jaizem, as she is the captain general and must, ah, what is the term, "ok" any such additions." Courtly, reserved humor prevailed, his edgy desire was once again smoored by force of will.

Elise pretended to straighten his already perfect button placket. "Have you asked this ready-made family if they're willing to join you in your life?" Her pulse quickened, arteries in her neck and wrists throbbed and fear filled the pockets within her that desire had left empty.

"I have not formally done so. I am waiting for the appropriate moment," his voice went tender, "would that moment be now?" He fell silent and she looked up. Lendar's lips parted, his head bent her direction, anticipation fairly emanating from him like a heat wave. He does want to kiss me! Just look at him, he can hardly contain himself.

Instead of answering, Elise rested her cheek on his chest, her eyes wide. Am I ready for him to ask me? Oh my, if I say "yes" he'll ask me to marry him right now! Could I live here on this ship and give up everything on earth? She swallowed. Aloud she murmured, "That moment may be nearing, but I don't think it has yet arrived."

Tension reached a peak, snapping through Lendar's body. She could feel it through his shirt, in the way he trembled, struggling to maintain control. When she finally looked up at him again, she saw an odd mix of tenderness, desire and...anger?

In the next moment, the tension eased and dissipated until she wondered if it had ever been there. And though the desire also faded, it hadn't disappeared, she could still discern it in the edges of his mouth and the glint of his eyes.

He retreats into formality, like it's some kind of safe haven. I guess, for him, it is.

His expression returned to its customary, neutral friendliness.

Elise covered her mouth. It's that sort of hiding one's emotions he talked about. It's like putting on a mask. What kind of a culture does he live in where people have to do that all the time? Fear pummeled her heart. It couldn't be a very nice one!

Lendar's voice resumed its pleasing tone devoid of everything but the most polite and impersonal kindness. "Breakfast then? I have acquired some green chile and a recipe for a green chile omelet from the, ah, internet. Does that sound appealing?" He made a sign that she could not begin to interpret, but somehow it made a bad feeling well up into her heart.

Elise's eyes teared. "A green chile omelet sounds awesome," she murmured. Shaking her head, she looked away. Ugh, that ended up feeling awful.

Duh! You think? You backed away. Now you're scared he won't ask.

Well, I've only known him a week for crying out loud!

The verse, "Perfect love drives out all fear," came to mind. Whose perfect love, Yours or his, God? He's only a man; he's not perfect.

Nevertheless, he loves.

But I know little of his character.

Do you really know little of his character? In one short week you've had more opportunities to see the real Lendar than many women get in a month of dating. How many men, besides Bruce, have even tried to stand up to Gabriel for even ten minutes? How many men would think of getting a car seat on the first date? And without your mentioning it? How many men would cut short a date to spend the rest of the afternoon helping you work? How many men would slip a 50 dollar bill into your diaper bag when you weren't looking? Or put a guy in his place in a restaurant? A week and the list of wonderful Lendar deeds was already pretty long. Elise sighed internally.

Lendar took her hand, about to lead her to the other room, when Max toddled toward them, dragging the comforter.

Seeing Elise, he held up his arms. "Mama."

She picked him up while Lendar returned the comforter to the bedroom. "Good morning, Max," she muttered, nuzzling his cheek. "Oh, baby, I love you."

"Ruv Mama," Max said, placing his hands on either side of her head. He kissed her cheek, a slobbery patch of sweetness.

Lendar stepped out of the bedroom and Max reached his direction. "'Endar."

Lendar stood very close and spoke that incomprehensible Minan-ish to her son.

Max patted his cheek.

Elise watched, her mind irritated that Max so readily accepted Lendar at face value, determining him worthy of his affection while simultaneously her joyful heart basked in the growing, mutual devotion the two males shared. Her inner turmoil threatened to break out in a headache or a sour stomach or a crying fit. I'm so overwhelmed!

Cheerfully, Lendar asked, "Breakfast and then a romp in the gardens, how does that sound?" He spoke to Max, then looked at her, a slow smile etching through the plains of his cheeks. Not a mask now, she decided.

Casting aside her worries, Elise grinned, and said, perhaps a little too brightly, "Wonderful! But first Max needs to change out of his pajamas."

Lendar bowed and gestured toward the desk, making another of his signs. "That will allow me to complete my immediate task."

Elise retreated to the bedroom with Max in her arms and gently closed the door. "Well, Max, what do you think? Would you like Lendar to be your new Dad?" Her voice came out wobbly. "It's quite soon to consider such a thing, don't you think?"

Frowning, Max watched her movements: tugging off his pajama pants; slipping the changing pad under his bottom; pulling the sticky tabs free. "'Ike 'Endar," he repeated.

Elise's eyes watered. "Of course you like him, but you don't know what a Dad is. But I suspect you'd be thrilled if he was yours." Isn't that significant? That you and Max both know he'd be thrilled to have Lendar as his father? Think of his attitude toward Max. He's affectionate, reasonable and fun to be with.

But I don't really know him!

"Me, 'Endar t'rilled." He pointed to the door and then at himself.

"You imp," Elise gently pinched his cheek. "Yes, I think the two of you would be thrilled. You've already made up your minds!" She sighed and finished dressing him for the day.

Lendar was sitting at his desk when they emerged. "Let's go cook," he said and took her hand.

She inhaled the clean, lemon grass scent that seemed to permeate the apartment. Her feet reveled in the super-clean soft carpet and cool tiles. Elise smirked. If we were at my apartment there'd be grit or surprise bits of gravel on the floor.

Lendar led the way across the living room through the arch in the partition and into the kitchen. Lights came on.

"What a lovely kitchen," Elise said. "Kinda minimalist."

"Thank you," Lendar replied, giving her a quizzical look.

"No, seriously, it is lovely." Elise ran her fingers along a cabinet door, the cherry wood shown white where the light hit. The counter tops reminded her of gray, artificial stone she'd seen at a home improvement store. Glass tiles filled the wall space under the cabinets. Some of the cabinets were lit inside, the glow shining through the frosted and ribbed panels.

"Do you have motion detector lights everywhere?" Elise asked, her palm making a run over the smooth counter top. She climbed onto a stool on the far side of the kitchen near the bar.

"Not everywhere." His voice came out muffled. Lendar rummaged through the refrigerator removing eggs with a grocery store brand name printed on the carton.

Elise giggled. "You have eggs from Albertsons?"

Lendar glanced at the carton. "Yes. Why not?"

"It's hilarious. What would the store owners think knowing their eggs went to outer space in a knock-off Escalade loaded into a space jet to be served on an alien space ship." Elise laughed. "Delight your extraterrestrial guests with a fresh omelet made from Albertsons brand eggs." She chortled. "The only thing that might make it even more hilarious would be if you served the eggs to some other variety of alien, like maybe the little green men or something. That'd be a wild twist on Dr. Seuss!"

"If you find the eggs amusing, look at this." Lendar lifted a tub of Bueno green chile.

Elise laughed. "Green chile, the choice of little green men everywhere."

Lendar grinned, adding packages of tortillas, bacon and cheese to the growing pile. "Well, if I'm going to become a television commercial celebrity, I'd better wear the proper costume." He winked, slipped on an apron with the words, "Just call me Bobby Flay," printed on the fabric. He set to work.

Max pulled open a cabinet, emptied the pans onto the floor and began practicing his drum routine. Lendar's eyes skimmed the scene, a pleased expression lightening his face. He looked like a father home for the weekend doing the things he loves best with those who matter most.

"What can I do to help?" Elise asked.

"Ah, you might set the table." Lendar suggested.

"Ok, I can do that." Elise hopped off the stool. She paused. "Where's the robots? Don't you have robots in your apartment?"

"Yes, as I mentioned earlier, most are invisible to the naked eye. For cooking, we have a chef robo, which can serve as a trainer for persons who don't know how to cook or as a sous chef. In a pinch it makes a decent meal, though it lacks creativity." He lifted his free hand and made a shooing, finger wriggling kind of sign. "I could use it, but I'd rather not. Sometimes robots just get in the way."

Elise giggled. "Oh my, everybody on earth thinks having robots around would be just awesome."

"Sometimes they are. In my case, the most awesome thing they do for me is cleaning. I really dislike cleaning." The word 'awesome' came out sounding a little off-kilter, as if he weren't quite comfortable using it that way.

Grinning, Elise nodded and changed the subject. "Ok. So, why do you use sign language sometimes?"

He peered at her over his shoulder. "It's mostly unconscious. Happens if a person spends enough time around Somainai."

"Oh yeah. You mentioned them earlier." Elise gulped, then charged on. "Ah, who or what are Somainai?"

Why, oh why did you have to bring that up?

Why not bring it up? I can't avoid it forever, not if I'm going to keep seeing Lendar.

He spoke matter of factly. "They're the marsupial humanoids I was telling you about. The only alien species we have any dealings with--at least for now. The aliens who kidnapped my ancestors haven't returned in centuries."

"Oh-kay." Elise stared. *Of course, none of this is a big deal for him. He's dealt with them his whole life. But how far do I want to take this line of questions?*

Not very!

Coward!

She pursed her lips and clutched her hands together. "Where are the dishes you want me to use?"

Lendar set his spatula on a spoon holder and crossed the room to open a cabinet for her. "Here are the plates." He opened a drawer. "Here is the flatware." His face stopped very close to hers. She could feel his exhalation and it set every cell on the surface of her skin straining to be nearer.

"Thanks." Her voice came out mangled, as if something more urgent stumbled over the innocuous word.

His aquamarine eyes spoke loudly, declaring plainly, 'I want every morning, just like this morning, to be shared with you from now and into eternity.' In the next moment, he backed away, his face turning sober. He bowed and retreated to the stove.

Elise bit her lip. "So, do you have pictures of these marsupial humanoids?"

"I do. Would you like to see them?"

"Yes, I would and pictures is probably all I can stand right now." She turned away just as he looked her direction. She counted plates, enjoying the feel of the smooth, thin edges of fine porcelain. But she didn't take them from the cabinet. She asked, "So, these marsupial humanoids use sign language?"

"Yes. It's due to their physiology. Our brain hemispheres are unified; marsupials' brain hemispheres are not. Both Somainai brain hemispheres have language; the left brain speaks and uses an abstract alphabet, the right brain signs; it uses a hieroglyphs and a kind of Morse Code."

Feeling that avoiding eye contact was a really bad idea, she looked over her shoulder and watched Lendar flip the bacon onto a serving platter, drain the fat and then add eggs. He turned to meet her gaze. "If a person spends enough time with Somainai he eventually finds himself unconsciously signing." He made a sign, then shrugged.

Elise's smile turned to a wince as she removed three plates from the cabinet. She didn't ask what the sign meant. Asking about the signs suddenly seemed too risky.

He must spend a lot of time with them.

Gak. If I married Lendar, I'd probably have to spend a lot of time with them! At the word "married," her heart rate accelerated and her hands went sweaty. She tried to ignore the feeling that the word "married" sounded real nice. No! Are you crazy?

Max followed her into the dining room and went to the sheers. "Gro ourside," he said, pointing at the triangle he'd opened between the curtain panels.

"After breakfast," Elise replied, glad for the distraction. "Aren't you hungry?" She joined him at the windows, marveling that they felt warm as if sunlight actually pelted the glass. To Lendar she called, "How long do days out there last?"

Lendar answered from the kitchen. "Average Minan days," he paused, "about 20 of your hours, I think; about ten hours daylight and about ten hours night depending on location and season."

Elise grunted. Time is relative isn't it? And that whole concept just makes my head hurt. "Shorter day, but not too different from us." She started to ask how he made the calculation of Minan time compared to earth time, but balked. She rubbed her temples. You just can't seem to stop piling it on can you?

Max rubbed his belly. "'Ungry, now."

"You are in luck, Master Max, breakfast is served."

Lendar arrived, carrying a tray with the omelet, bacon and a tortilla warmer.

"You bought a tortilla warmer?" Elise exclaimed.

"Yes."

Elise grinned. "Are you going to start growing chiles?"

Lendar nodded. "Either grow them or have them grown. Robot gardeners, you know." He winked. "I've already begun research into what it takes to produce quality chile. Incidentally, my research may require a trip to Las Cruces."

"Oh my goodness, you are hooked." Elise collected the flatware and brought it to the table. "Ha, yeah. I got a text from Lolly yesterday. She's already working in her aunt's hair salon."

Lendar fetched the glasses. He returned with a pitcher of juice and filled them. For Max, he produced a booster chair from a huntboard standing next to the wall near the windows' storage compartment. Above the huntboard hung a large landscape painting depicting a bucolic farm scene that might have been found on earth except for the strange architecture and a peculiar, bovine-type beast standing in the foreground.

Elise averted her eyes. Oh gak. What if that picture isn't surrealism or fantasy art?

Can I irrevocably leave earth and everything I know to share my life with this man? Her heart thumped, every other beat filled with anticipation, the rest with dread.

Will you quit thinking about that? One thing at time; just survive this visit; then think about it.

Lifting Max and placing him in the booster, Lendar's voice turned firm. "Master Max, today you will endeavor to desist from throwing food on the floor."

Max glanced up at Lendar. "'Ungry now," he said and pounded the table with his fist.

Lendar frowned. "Patience, Master Max. A gentleman practices patience. First we pray."

Max shook his head, his bottom lip protruding. "Eat

prease."

Elise stated firmly. "We will honey, after we pray!"

Max's bottom lip stuck out even further and he folded his arms across his chest.

Elise bowed her head.

Lendar mumbled in Minan-ish, then said in English. "Praise you Most High for this repast. Amen." He winked at Max.

Max beat the table with his fist.

"Max, you won't die of starvation. Stop it!" Elise snapped.

Max simply stared.

Elise opened the tortilla warmer.

Max reached for a tortilla, his hand opening and closing eloquently. "Prease. Give, prease."

Elise handed him one. "Please is good Max. Good boy." She forked a bite into her mouth and savored the flavors. "This tastes great!"

Lendar bowed at the waist. "Thank you." He placed some food on Max's plate and cut it for him.

Elise tore a piece of tortilla, her face pensive. "You said it took you twenty light years to get here. I still can't get used to this idea that you can cover that much territory and not age."

"It's an unpleasant side effect." His joyful expression faded.

Elise shot him a quizzical look. "Unpleasant side effect? I'd think not aging would be a good thing. American women spend a fortune trying to look young."

"Oh, we age, we just do it at a different rate. Meanwhile, everyone else we know, unless they, too, spend a lot of time traveling in space, ages normally. Friends grow old and die, whole cities transform into unrecognizable entities. Space travelers, unless they travel together, age at different rates because we're spending dissimilar amounts of time traveling at varying rates. The youngest sibling can end up being the oldest or die of old age before his brother born before him returns. The experience can be rather unpleasant, actually."

"I suppose. Especially if a loved one was dead when you returned, but that could happen anyway."

"True enough."

Thoughtful, Elise chewed. "Good heavens, this whole business of aging at different rates probably creates all sorts of legal problems!"

"Indeed."

She watched Lendar help Max with his cup. At last she said, "You gave up your last days with your parents to come here, didn't you?"

"Yes, but wherever my lord, Prince Anwic, goes, I too must go." His smoldering, aquamarine orbs met her gaze. He seemed to be thinking that he had other, more personal reasons for coming this far. Her fingers longed to touch the shallow ridges of his check bones.

Elise looked down at her half-eaten plate. Wow, I get the impression he would have come all this way just for me, if he could! She muttered, "You will eventually return to Minan, but if I go with you, I will never return to earth, will I?" Her appetite ebbed.

"Not likely."

"If I don't leave earth, I will lose you, won't I?"

Lendar didn't answer her question; instead he asked another. "Would you leave earth to come with me?"

"I don't know. We've only known one another a week…and I've just now begun to realize…what…" she cleared her throat, "ah…the cost." Blinking rapidly, she daubed her lips with her napkin.

Lendar's shielding mask seemed to have edged back into place, banking hope behind it. "Unless we go our separate ways, one of us will have to make that decision."

"One of us? You would leave all of this to stay with me?" Elise's eyes widened, her hand went to her throat.

"If my lord, Prince Anwic, released me from my bond, and I think he would, if I asked." Lendar's expression was gentle, but with a hardness underneath that unnerved her. His eyes had that same pewter-like appearance as before. "I'd prefer you join me, Elise." His voice sounded metallic. No chocolate or creaminess now.

She looked away. *He's so certain, so confident that we are meant for one another. After only one week! Lord, I know I'm being silly, but show me again if this is Your will. He has a job and a prince who loves him very much, I love my family, but lately we haven't been very close. In all fairness, I can hardly argue with him. I'm the one who should leave, that is if we're meant to be together.*

I can't believe I'm even entertaining the thought! After a moment, she toyed with her food and resumed eating.

While they'd talked, Max had struggled to please Lendar, his stubby fingers working to make proper use of the fork. He'd managed a few bites, but now he gave up, plucked a bite size chunk of omelet and stuffed it into his mouth. Grinning, he looked up at Lendar, green chile smeared on his cheek. Lendar smiled indulgently and held his cup for him.

Max smacked his lips and kept eating with his hands. When his plate was empty, he said, "'Inished."

Lendar clapped his hands. "Very good, Master Max. Not one morsel on the floor."

Max raised his arms. "Down. Want down."

"Just a moment." Lendar hurried to the kitchen and returned with a damp cloth. "Allow me."

Max tried to pull his hands away, but gave up when it became clear Lendar had no intention of letting him on the floor until he was clean. Hands and face free of food, Lendar set him on his feet. He immediately toddled to the bank of windows and pointed. "Gro ourside."

"Honey, Mama needs to go into the bedroom for a few minutes before we do that." Elise rose from her chair and wriggled her fingers inviting him to come along. Reluctantly,

Max clasped her hand, then tugged the seat of his pants. "Ok," Elise laughed. "You need some serious attention, too. Then we'll go outside."

She knew Lendar watched with a satisfied smile playing on his lips, but she didn't look at him. She didn't want to think any more about either of them having to give up his or her world. And yes, it would be giving up an entire world, wouldn't it!? And I haven't even really seen mine yet!

Elise entered the bedroom. A robot was busy making the bed.

"Oh," she exclaimed.

The robot whirred. "Just be a moment, ma'am." It hummed a few bars of some tune, then whizzed toward the door. "Your toilet is tidy," it said and disappeared into the office.

"Oh, my goodness. And it speaks English." Elise patted her chest. She took Max and the diaper bag into the bathroom and closed the door. "Hhmn, wonder where the trash can is?" A container popped out of the cabinet under the sink. "Oh, thanks," she said without thinking and blushed.

"You're welcome," a voice answered.

"Who is that?" Elise demanded.

"Your bathroom valet, ma'am. May I be of service?"

"Oh. Ah, I don't think I need anything right now."

"Always ready to serve."

Elise shivered and scanned the room looking for anything that might be responsible for the voice. "Well, as long as you're not watching me. I hate to be watched."

"Voice command only, my lady. No visual programming included for general purposes."

"Oh, well, that's a relief." Elise wiped Max's bottom a little too vigorously.

Max whined.

"Oh, honey, I'm sorry. I think I'm a little freaked out." She looked around the room again. "Bathroom valet, where's your voice box anyway?"

"My transducer is beside the mirror over the sink. I am also equipped with health diagnostic equipment, a complete massage unit and full facial and cosmetic services. Naturally, for the facial and cosmetic services visual capabilities exist."

"Oh my goodness."

"Ma'am?"

"Never mind. I won't be needing any of those at the moment."

"Very well, ma'am."

Max lay still, waiting patiently, also apparently wondering who his mother was talking to. He twisted to scan the room.

Elise looked at him and winced a smile.

Max stared at his mother. "Gro ourside."

"Yes, honey. I haven't forgotten." Elise slipped a new diaper under his bottom and peeled the sticky tabs. "Bathroom valet, you have anything suitable for a small child to play with?"

A cabinet popped open and a box of bath toys appeared. "Will these do, ma'am?"

"Those are fine." She turned to Max. "Honey, look!"

Max examined the box and shook his head. "Gro ourside."

"Yes, I know but mama needs to use the bathroom." Oh gak! What if it's watching me? "Bath towels please." The heated bath towel compartment opened and the unit rolled out draped with fresh towels. "Thanks."

"Ma'am, it is not necessary to thank me."

"Oh." Elise blushed, shook one of the towels to release some of the heat and draped it over herself before sitting on the toilet. Oh gak. I can't even talk to myself or it will answer me! Ok, I get it. Robots may not be so cool.

Max leaned over the box of toys, obviously tempted, but he refused to touch them. "Gro ourside," he repeated.

Elise buried her face in her hands. Who would have thought a bathroom this luxurious could turn out to be this stressful!

Max opened the door and toddled out of the room.

"Max!" Elise groaned. Lendar's out there somewhere. I hope he finds Max before he does something I'll regret. "Max!" Arrggh!

Once she finished in the bathroom, Elise entered the bedroom, hesitating just inside the door. Nervously she collected her canvas shoes from the foot of the bed. She stepped to the office threshold. Max stood at a glassed-in cabinet studying the contents.

Elise stuck her feet into her shoes, then hurried to Max who now stood at Lendar's desktop computer prepared to punch buttons. She gripped his hand and dragged him into the living room.

Lendar stood, arms folded across his chest, at the wide-open maw where windows had been closed minutes earlier. Light bounced off the patio and the green grass silhouetted his manly stance. Bird song floated in.

"Walls around here have a lot to say," Elise stated. "You know they give new meaning to the phrase, 'if walls could talk'." Her heart pounded and beads of sweat formed on her skin. She felt as if her breakfast had turned into a ball of indigestible clay. "I'd go back in there and throw up, but I don't think I can take the commentary."

Lendar chuckled. "If you order them to be silent, they will be silent."

"Is every room, like, a robot?"

Lendar faced her and shrugged. "Yes. I didn't utilize the kitchen. I didn't want to alarm you, but for some reason the bathroom seems to have a more independent attitude." He frowned. "It was told it to keep quiet unless spoken to."

Elise's eyes widened. "I guess I did speak to it. I wondered out loud where to find the trash can." She blinked. "Can robots get out of control?"

Lendar laughed and shook his head. "No, not exactly out of control. I mean, they function according to their programming and it depends on how they were programmed. Some programmers build in a little more, eh, how to say it, ah, personality than others."

"Oh, good grief." Elise hid behind her hand. "Personality."

Lendar frowned. "That is, of course, assuming grief can be good, and I suppose it might be, but exactly what is meant by the phrase "good grief" and how does it have any relevance to the topic?"

Elise's hands dropped and she hung her head. This would be funny if it weren't so scary! Think of the cultural differences between us! She wandered to the couch and plopped down. "I'm feeling a little overwhelmed, Lendar. Yeah, a little overwhelmed. And a little sick to my stomach."

"Oh, so the phrase "good grief" is used in the context of feeling overwhelmed." He walked to the seating area. "Would you like some medication for your stomach?"

Elise sighed, swallowed and considered lying on the floor. Medication? What I need is the next new thing to not happen for a few years! "What do the robots in the rooms do?"

Lendar settled on the edge of a love seat opposite her. Parked his elbows on his knees and clapped his hands together. "They inventory the room's contents, keep the room at the occupant's preferred temperature..."

"...give people massages, and facials and what the heck is a health diagnostic?"

"Remember the hover robos in the Escalade?"

"Yes."

"Well, they were doing a health diagnostic."

"Oh." She felt a flu-like flush roil through her body. Gak. Great time to be sick! "You said, "keep an inventory," does that mean, like what, it can read the paper you're writing on and knows how to file it or where you put it? Like, it knows everything about you and becomes, like, your best friend. Someone can just come in and pick its brains and find out whatever they want to know?" She dropped her head between her knees. Oh God, are You there? Do You intend for me to marry this man and live here? Oh God…it's so…why does everything have to be so hard? A weird noise somewhere between a sob and a shriek escaped her lips.

Lendar was beside her in an instant. "Elise, aren't you over-reacting?" He rubbed her back.

His attempt to soothe only infuriated her. Elise suppressed a snarl and raised her face high enough to look Lendar in the eye. "Yeah. And I reserve the right to over-react at any moment in the future." She lowered her head again and stared at the carpet. "And don't you forget it either!"

With Max's fingers entwined with hers, both hands were soon sweaty. She sat up and pulled Max into her lap. It felt like the inside of her head spun. Ugh. I'm going to be sick!

Lendar's hand fell away. He replied. "The room valet is your servant. It will not gossip about you or release your personal information to an unauthorized person."

"Ok." Elise gulped. Get a grip. Remember that show on TV about the house of the future? "Ok, I admit I'm being unreasonable. I saw a show on TV about the house of the future and those houses talk. They keep track of your groceries and stuff. And I saw this article on the internet about a guy who programmed his house to have a personality and talk to him and his family. Ok, I get it."

Face it, Elise Ramos, what you're really freaking out about is this idea of marrying Lendar and leaving earth forever.

Or not marrying Lendar. Take your pick!

Ok, what if marrying Lendar is a mistake? I'd never be able to come home. Never! And never is such a dang, long time!

But what if not marrying Lendar is a mistake? That would last forever too!

Lendar asked, "Shall we go outside?"

Elise stared. "I'm about to throw up and you want to go outside."

Lendar shrugged and stroked her back again. "Fresh air might help."

Elise shook her head. "How does the bathroom speak English anyway?"

Lendar seemed taken aback. "I programmed all the rooms to speak English. I recorded your voice and fed it to the apartment's master computer. My quarters know who you are and will obey you. All the robots that work for me will obey you."

Elise kept one arm around Max who diligently sucked his thumb and snuggled against her shoulder. "Why did you do that?"

Lendar waved his hands. "I wanted you to have everything you needed."

Clueless. He's clueless. Elise gave him an anguished look. "You did that and you didn't breathe a word about it to me. Lendar Marl, sometimes you are a little creepy." She turned her face away from him and hugged Max tight.

Lendar seemed at a loss as to what to do next. "Elise, I...."

A woman's voice from the opened windows interrupted.

"Lendar, are you at home?"

Lendar hurried to the opening and out onto the patio.

Elise could see him looking up toward the top of the rise, but nothing more. She listened to Max's diligent sucking. Wonder if it would help me if I sucked my thumb, she thought.

Lendar talked to the woman in Minan, though oddly she'd initially spoken to him in English. Wonder who it is?

Lendar climbed the hillock and disappeared from view.

Elise sighed and tried to release her anxiety. "Cast all your cares on the Lord, for He cares for you," she repeated in her mind. I know that verse is found is Psalms and in Peter, but I never can remember the specific chapter and verse number.

Aloud she murmured, "Cast your cares on the Lord, for He cares for you." She glanced about the room, challenging it to disagree with her.

Nothing spoke.

Seeking distraction, Elise's attention drifted. Some of the books in the cabinets had English titles on the spines, others bore titles in languages she recognized, like French and Spanish, still others bore that weird cuneiform style she'd seen on the ship's control panels and Lendar's desktop monitor. The odds and ends mingled with the books included a bird's nest, of all things, a handful of figurines, almost Chinese looking with their long robes and gowns, and some photographs.

With Max perched on her hip, Elise left the couch and studied the photographs. Wither her fingertip she touched the glass in front of a picture of a middle-aged couple. This one has to be his parents; he looks like a combination of their features. The couple smiled, both wearing a proud expression as if a child had just graduated college summa cum laude or something like that.

Max pointed and giggled. "Rook, Mama." The item that caught his eye was the dolphin statue Lendar had purchased at the Albuquerque Aquarium.

"Yes, dolphin," Elise said, smiling at him. At once she was relieved to see the familiar object and then thrown into another disorientation loop that manifested in freshly tensed shoulders and neck. A statue from Albuquerque Aquarium on a space ship!

"'Olpin," Max repeated. He tapped her on the lip, then tapped the glass. "'Olpin."

Elise nuzzled his neck. "Yes, it's a dolphin. We're going to be fine, aren't we honey."

"'Olpin." Max repeated and nodded.

"Silly." Elise gently pinched his cheek.

"Mama silly," Max replied.

Elise returned to the photos. Upon closer examination, the landscape proved to be a holographic image portraying large, graceful trees and distant mountains, background for a house that reminded her of the one Lendar had described. It had a flat front with a small arched porch over the doorway and windows at regular intervals on both floors. A glassed in breezeway jutted from the back to one side linking another building to the main structure. When she moved her head side to side, she could see more details through the windows and hints of things behind trees. "It's lovely," she breathed.

Lendar's voice intruded. "Elise, we have a guest."

The woman who strolled into the living room wore a flowing caftan in white silk with hints of lavender blossoms, pink flowers and sage hued leaves. Her white hair was glossy and thick, but her face was youthful and open.

Lendar performed an extravagant bow. "Empress Jaizem, I present, Elise Ramos and her son, Maxfield."

Elise attempted an awkward curtsy, her face burning like flames.

Empress Jaizem clapped her hands together. "What a handsome boy." Her voice was a melodious contralto. "Lovely Elise, welcome to the *Lalf*. I hope you are enjoying yourself?" She came to Elise and offered her hand.

"I am, thank you." Elise took the hand, hoping she'd applied the right amount of strength in her grip, and shook it.

Empress Jaizem turned to Lendar. "Lendar, you are taking good care of Elise and her son, I hope."

"I'm doing my best, highness, but our technology has proven a challenge for her."

Empress Jaizem's smile was kindly and gentle. "Yes, I expect it has." She looked to Elise, "I assure you, my dear, when I first came aboard this ship I found it quite daunting. But, you know, we humans seem to be designed to adapt. After a while one grows accustomed." She paused, then said, "Oh please, let's sit down and order some tea. I've had a trying morning and I'm ready for a little conversation and relaxation. Elise, won't you join us?"

Elise hesitated, then went to the couch not sure what to do next. Empress Jaizem sat down so gracefully that Elise felt like a cow when she settled on the cushions.

Jaizem waved at Lendar, her hand smooth and the skin lovely. "These men, they mean well, but frankly, sometimes they are a bit incompetent, don't you think?" She leaned in Elise's direction, smiled and winked. "Yet, I suppose, it's not easy to explain everything well enough to put one at ease. Sometimes one must simply be immersed."

Elise looked at Lendar. He seemed embarrassed, yet totally lacking in defensiveness. His demeanor was of a man whose great love for this woman made him eager to please her and ashamed when he failed. Wow. She looked back at the older woman. Her blue eyes twinkled. This empress doesn't miss a thing, Elise thought.

Lendar was speaking. "...my Empress, you know us quite well. You always bring out the best in us." He bowed. "Excuse me, I will fetch the tea."

"He is a wonderful man, Lendar. Yes. I quite admire him," Jaizem spoke in a low voice for Elise's ears only. "He's been such a boon to my son, Anwic. He's a blessing to everyone he meets, as I'm sure you're aware." She seemed thoughtful for a moment before saying, "Please, will you tell me about yourself? I hear you are an artist."

"Yes, ma'am, I'm studying art at the University of New Mexico. Specializing in painting. Er, highness."

Jaizem leaned closer, as in a conspiratorial fashion. "Between you and me, I can do without the title 'highness.' Ma'am will do. Or nothing but Jaizem. I hope you will call me Jaizem and that we may become fast friends. I do long for feminine companionship." She stretched her fingers in Elise's direction in appeal. A touch of sadness passed through her face. "I'm not actually an empress anymore. Though, given what you hear aboard this ship, you might think otherwise."

She offered an impish smile.

Elise had no idea what to say. She's obviously not one of those women who hide their emotions that Lendar was talking about.

Max had relaxed enough that he reached from the safety of her lap for a decorative object on the coffee table. Since he wasn't willing to leave her arms, he couldn't touch it so he gave up and stared at the Empress, his thumb back in his mouth.

Jaizem continued speaking. "Art provides comfort and brings illumination to the soul, don't you think?"

"Yes. I believe it can. I would like to make a difference for the better through my art, though I'm not sure I can pull it off."

Jaizem smiled. "Oh, my dear, you can and you will, if you don't give up. It's amazing how many gifted people give up right on the verge of success. Of course, when one is the person struggling to achieve and better one's self, it's difficult to see beyond the hardship of a moment." She paused a moment, looking pensive, then seemed to remember where she was and brightened. "Oh, yes, but don't give up dear. I'm told you are quite talented. You would enjoy seeing my collection, I think. I brought my best pieces, the ones that delight me the most."

"That would be wonderful." Elise gulped.

"What is required for a marriage to last?" Jaizem asked.

"Pardon me?"

"What do a man and a woman need in order to make a good marriage?"

"They need love, commitment and respect," Elise answered, her eyes wide.

"Yes, I agree."

Lendar appeared with a tea set on a tray. He set it on the limestone slab that was the coffee table's surface.

"Lendar, where is your robot?" Jaizem tapped his hand and took over tea serving duties. "You should have your robot doing this."

Lendar perched on the edge of one of the armchairs. "Empress, I am quite capable of serving acceptable tea. Please, allow me."

"Bah." Jaizem's eyes twinkled. "I enjoy it. Let me bless you."

"Yes, highness," Lendar replied, but maintained his ready-to-act pose.

Jaizem poured tea. "Elise, my dear, have you noticed that our beloved Lendar does not make full use of robot assistants?"

Elise covered her face with her hands, then lowered them before speaking. "To tell you the truth, I'm kind of glad. Every room in this place is a robot, apparently. It's completely freaky if you ask me."

"Sugar?"

"No, thank you."

"Lemon?"

"No, thank you. Plain is very nice."

An eyebrow climbed Jaizem's forehead. "Plain? How can a tea be a proper indulgence if you take it plain?"

Elise giggled.

Empress Jaizem smiled and turned to Lendar. "And you, dear Lendar, sugar?"

"My empress, sugar and lemon, please." He blushed, covered his mouth and coughed. Obviously having the empress serve him completely blew his cool. He couldn't seem to stop himself from trying to take over the job. Every so often his hands edged toward the tray and he had to keep pulling them back.

Jaizem lifted a striped cloth Lendar had draped over a large bowl. "Oh, Lendar, what an excellent choice. You have brought us some of those lovely tea cakes Alma makes." To Elise she said, "They're Kabelian, made with honey and plenty of chopped nuts. Simply fabulous." Jaizem placed one each on small plates. "And for you, young Master Maxfield?"

Max turned away, looking over Elise's shoulder toward the office.

"If there's juice or milk, that would be nice," Elise answered.

"Very good then." Jaizem poured milk into one of the delicate teacups.

"Oh, Empress Jaizem, he shouldn't have one of those." Elise blushed. "Er, ah, well, he'll break it!"

"Bah, what good is it if it can't be used?"

Elise winced, then loosed a nervous, twittery kind of laugh.

Empress Jaizem distributed the drinks and cakes, then sipped her tea. "Yes, this is exactly what I needed. Fine companions, delicious cakes. You do make a fabulous tea, Lendar, the best. And I quite agree with you, the robot would have done an acceptable job, but not to your caliber."

Lendar's visage wrinkled with pleasure at her compliment.

"Now, what were we talking about? Yes. You are an artist, Elise. And has Lendar acquired any of your work for me yet?"

"No, ma'am." Elise felt stunned.

"An oversight, I'm sure. Something he will rectify at his first opportunity, no doubt. I'm sure your paintings are quite lovely, yes? How do I know this? I know it because you are such a charming young woman and if Lendar had thought your work insignificant, he would not have even mentioned it to me."

Elise stared at Lendar.

Lendar muttered. "Highness, I will choose a piece for you as soon as we return to earth."

"Very well! I can tell you Elise, I'm reasonably certain that our Lendar has completely forgotten to photograph any of your work. I will have to trust to his ability to pick one I'll find to my liking." She drank from her cup, her posture perfect. "I tease him, it's true, but he is one of the most thoughtful men I know. I have every confidence in his abilities."

Unconsciously Elise sat a little straighter. She drank from her cup. Max felt her movements and turned to look. She replaced her cup to the table and helped him with his.

"'Iscious," he said and smacked his lips. He wriggled his fingers at the pastry and Elise held it for him while he took a bite.

Jaizem offered her a napkin. "How old is your son, Elise?"

"He's two."

Jaizem folded her hands in her lap. "He's very well behaved for two!"

"I can take little credit. He's a good boy," Elise mumbled.

Jaizem made a sign. It looked like she drew loops back and forth. "A good boy will respond well to loving discipline. It's a synergy, don't you think?"

Elise nodded.

"Lendar, your tea is delicious, but if you don't mind, will you wrap my pastry so that I may take it with me? I'll nibble it while I continue my walk." Jaizem's smile was small, but not lacking in affection. It was regal, like a queen's smile. Oh my. She really is an empress, isn't she? Gak.

"Highness, I would be delighted." Lendar took her plate and hurried to the kitchen.

Elise swallowed.

Jaizem reached in Elise's direction. "I congratulate you on your upcoming marriage! I wish you joy."

"Ma'am?"

Jaizem squared her shoulders. "My dear, it's clear. If you will have him, Lendar has chosen you. You can hardly do better and you certainly can do worse. I've never seen him look at anyone the way he looks at you and I've known him all his life. Lendar is loyal, industrious and well-respected. If a person earns his affection, it cannot be easily lost. I advise you to accept his suit."

Elise's face burned while her heart pounded. "Yes, ma'am. But ma'am, we've only known one another a week or so." Her face burned anew.

"A week you say. Well, then, what characteristics do you seek in a husband and father?" Jaizem sipped her tea, watching Elise over the rim of the cup.

"Ah, hardworking, loyal, trustworthy, kind…" Elise stopped. Lendar is all of those things. Elise hid her unsettled feelings behind her tea cup. "But, after only one week, how does a girl know she's found those things in a man?"

Jaizem's smile was gentle. "Has he been tested? Unpleasantness? Some men side-step. Responsibility? Some men shirk."

"Oh, yes, he's passed some pretty serious tests."

Jaizem's eyes twinkled. "But in the end, dear Elise, regardless of how long a woman has known a man, when she accepts a man's proposal she does so, joining her life to his, by faith. It's an act of faith, whether it be done one week after introduction or one year."

"And faith is the substance of things hoped for, the evidence of things not seen," Elise finished.

Lendar returned with a small paper box.

Jaizem stood up and accepted it from his hand. "Thank you, dear Lendar." She cupped his cheek in her hand.

Lendar bowed, that extravagant bow again. Nervously, Elise curtsied, as before, not an easy task with Max on her hip.

Jaizem smiled benevolently, including each of them in her favor. "I hope you three will join me for dinner soon. Lendar, I have promised Elise a viewing of my collection. You will remember this."

He bowed again. "Yes, highness."

"Good day." She strolled toward the patio, Lendar following behind.

Elise fell into the couch, letting Max stand at the limestone coffee table and finish his treats.

17

Several moments later a breathless Lendar returned.

"She's really an empress, er, I mean, an ex-empress?" Elise asked.

"Yes. And as far was I'm concerned, she will always be empress." He made a sign Elise took as indicating something final and irrevocable.

"You really love her."

"Yes. I'd give my life for her and for my lord, prince Anwic."

"Not the emperor?"

Lendar cleared his throat. "My feelings about him are more complicated and difficult to explain. But, if needed I'd give my life for him too." He made another sign.

Elise shrugged, wondering if the feeling she got from the sign--that somehow the Emperor was a traitor--was what the sign truly meant. "Well, I barely understand that kind of stuff. I read a book about Queen Elisabeth once, how she rallied her men before their battle against the Spanish Armada. They really loved her a lot. She was like the embodiment of their whole nation."

"Precisely." Lendar sat down opposite her. He soon began gathering tea items onto the tray.

Elise watched him work. "She seems real nice."

Lendar hesitated. He stared at Elise for a second then said, "Yes, Empress Jaizem is, ah, 'real nice'."

Elise gave him a flinty look. "Well, how would you describe her?"

Lendar sighed. "I would not use the word 'nice,' but then I have lived under her reign with Emperor Cultus all my life." He paused, hung his head, then glanced at her. "It's not that 'nice' is inaccurate, it's that it is so utterly inadequate...and common. It doesn't do her justice." He collected the napkins, then paused. "You are correct, Elise, you don't know what it's like to have an empress or a queen, which is neither good or bad, it is just the state of things." He stood and took the tray to the kitchen.

Elise stuck out her tongue at his retreating back and sighed. Is this room watching me? She bit her lip and scanned the vicinity.

Lendar returned with a damp cloth. "Empress Jaizem has asked me to tend to some details in Andorra on Monday. Would you be willing to go to Andorra before returning to Albuquerque?"

"You really have offices in Andorra?" Elise's mouth hung open.

"Yes and in Antwerp; Sydney; Singapore; Miami," he shrugged, "and a few other places."

"You people get around."

"We have a mission." He signed again and sat down. Suddenly he seemed vulnerable, as if the veneer of butler/retainer had fallen away and she was seeing pure Lendar. He clasped and unclasped his hands together. At last he asked, "Elise, how did you feel while Empress Jaizem was here?"

"What?"

Lendar reached for Max who tried to run to the other side of the table. "How did you feel?"

Elise spluttered her lips. A slight furrow appeared between her brows. "To start with it was kind of nerve-wracking, but after a little while I felt comfortable with her. Why?" Did I completely misread him? Confused, she cocked her head to one side and studied him.

Lendar wiped Max's face and hands. "Elise, all in her own right Jaizem is a Duchess, the hereditary governess and mistress of a province twice the size of Texas. Alongside her husband, Cultus, she ruled an entire planet. Yet, when she came in here, she immediately put you at your ease. That is more than nice, it is grace." He made a sign that reminded

Elise of leaping gazelles.

Elise dropped her gaze to the limestone table edge. When she looked back at Lendar her face burned. Something inside snapped. "Just one more thing I know nothing about!"

Lendar leaned across the table, his eyes that steely hue again. He lifted her chin. "Ignorance is not the equivalent of stupid! Many more cognizant of Jaizem's standing and rank have behaved far worse. Besides, I'd think her visit should reveal that you are entirely capable of functioning in my world." He made a boxy sort of sign.

Elise groused. "Oh well, good for me then. I'm really on a roll here." She shook her head. It used to be cute, but that stupid signing is really starting to irritate me. She wanted to blurt, 'And I don't want to learn sign language either,' but decided she'd sound even more childish and didn't.

Lendar's face reddened with annoyance. He opened his mouth to speak, but Elise interrupted him.

"I'm feeling a little overwhelmed here, Lendar. I don't think I can handle this. I just woke up a little while ago and all I want to do now is go back to bed and hide, except I'd probably have to listen to commentary!" She bit her lip, as if it would help hold her emotions in. "Listen." She tamped one fist into the other hand. "I don't know if you can think about this from my point of view, but try.

"I'm an ordinary ranch girl who made a stupid mistake and married a guy who turned out to be an abusive drug addict. I'm divorced, I have a kid and I'm trying to finish my art degree. Ok? That's my world. My reality.

"Now, in a matter of a few hours, I'm behind the moon in a space ship with a man who I thought was a butler from Andorra. That alone is plenty enough cause for upset, if you ask me. I went from normal to surreal science fiction in the span of a few hours. Not only that, I came here with a liar.

"You're a liar. Lendar, lying about your identity is huge. Huge." Elise bit her lip and blinked to clear her eyes.

She waved her hands back and forth. "I'm riding in

floorless elevators; having conversations with rooms. Never mind failed space walks and invisible space jets. And an empress from a planet I have never heard of before walks in for tea and a nice chat. Hello. Nice to meet you. Please come over for dinner and view my art collection. And when I say she's 'nice' that word isn't descriptive enough for you!"

She paused and glared at him. "In case you hadn't noticed, this is totally freaking me out!"

Lendar squeezed her hand, but his sympathetic gaze infuriated her.

Elise narrowed her eyes at him. "Furthermore, I don't know beans about robots and I'm not sure I want to! You didn't tell me that the apartment already knew who I was and would obey me. You let me walk in here clueless, like, maybe it was just another opportunity for a sick joke. During the past week I've been the brunt of a lot of sick jokes, if you ask me. I think you're being a jerk!" She pursed her lips and yanked her fingers from his grasp. One hand bobbed like a blade up and down ticking off the remainder of her list. "There was a robot in the bedroom making the bed. It said, "Your toilet is tidy!" I've never had a maid, not as a child, not any time, never mind robot maids!

"I've hardly been in any kind of a house that wasn't about to fall down. Nothing about this is anything like what I know except, so far, the food. I know a green chile omelet when I see one."

She hung her head, her anger spent. "How pathetic is that?" Her eyes felt hot, then blurred.

Lendar stroked her cheek with the back of his index finger. "You are a wonder."

Elise snapped. "And what does that mean?" She eyed him, fierce with fear.

"It means I delight in you every moment." He leaned toward her, leading with his face. His expression was laced with happy expectation, as if the place where he wished to land was the most wonderful spot in the universe.

Elise sniffed. "Ha, you delight in freaking me out every chance you get!"

"No, not in freaking you out. I delight in how you rise to every challenge. True, you have moments when you struggle, as now, but then you gather yourself up and proceed. I can think of no one I'd rather have beside me for the rest of my days."

Ignoring the tenderness, the sincerity in his voice and the adoration in his face, Elise choked a laugh. "Oh, yeah, I'm a wonder. Everyone wonders when I'll screw up! And when I'll fall for the next lie."

She sat up straight, then looked all over the room, searching the ceiling and upper walls. "Are these nosy rooms recording or filming me?" She stopped and squinted at him. "And if you say they're not, how do I know you're telling me the truth?"

"No, they're not recording or filming you. And you can't know whether I'm telling the truth. You'll have to trust me."

What a peculiar expression. Odd how his sincere, anguished look seems mingled with humor, like the romantic hero in a Jane Austen drama. Like Darcy or the Scarlet Pimpernel! Gak. Both of whom seemed one way but were in actuality completely different. Darcy seemed to be mean and hard hearted, but wasn't. The Scarlet Pimpernel seemed a fop, but wasn't.

You're not going to distract me, buddy. I'm busy being annoyed!

Elise stabbed the air pointing in his direction. "Trust you! Ha! You lied. And you recorded me without telling me."

Lendar's face turned rigid, like he was about to lose his temper. "I recorded you because, as far as I'm concerned, you're mistress here and without voice command, you'd be restricted. I don't want you restricted.

"I intended to explain the room robots, but I felt that you were too overwhelmed to deal with another new influx of information. Instead, I commanded them to be silent until spoken to and waited for an opportunity to inform you of their willingness to serve."

A vein pulsed at his temple. "And, Elise, if I'd told you the truth about my identity the moment you asked, would you have believed me?"

Elise's head throbbed. "Oh, really, because I'm 'mistress' here. Well, I think if I were a mistress here, I'd be involved in the whole process. I think you'd have been telling me what you were doing and showing me the thing you recorded me with and stuff like that right from the start. You're not treating me like mistress of anything. You're just barreling along, doing your thing, without including me, hoping I'll go all gaga over it and forgive you for being a totally selfish, lying jerk!"

Lendar grimaced. "I'm sorry you feel that way."

Suddenly it occurred to Elise that if Empress Jaizem had been the person who'd been recorded and given command of room robots, whether anybody had explained it all to her or not, she'd take it as a matter of course, in this case, as part of Lendar's duties as retainer/butler, whatever he was. Her shoulders slumped.

You wouldn't have believed Lendar if he'd told you his identity; you would have thought he was completely off his nut and furthermore, you wouldn't have agreed to come here and find out the truth.

Elise Ramos, face it, you're the selfish jerk. She buried her face in her hands.

Max wandered away and found the box of toys he'd discovered on the first day. He dumped it on the floor and threw a couple of blocks across the room.

Lendar spoke. "Elise. I apologize. I have no excuse. I'm used to taking care of all the details for those I serve and, I, I, just didn't think."

She wiped her nose with the back of her wrist and hacked a laugh. "Now I see your point about robots not being so cool. I don't want robots. I don't want rooms that talk or inventory my stuff. I don't want energy elevators and… and…or…or…" Elise trembled, clapped her mouth shut and covered her face again. She'd started to add, 'I don't want to ride around in spaceships and be trained on how to do a space walk or learn Minan or speak to marsupial aliens. Or have butler service,' but she knew if she uttered all those words, especially the ones about 'butler service,' she'd regret it for the rest of her life.

At last she spoke through her fingers. "What I really want right now is to see Grammy and sit in her lap." The emotions she'd held at bay swamped through her makeshift levees and burst through her tear ducts.

Bawling like a baby is going to ruin your make-up and make your eyes red. Besides that, you're going to have a completely awful headache. And, when you finally stop carrying on, you'll still be a total basket case because as soon as the next new thing hits you'll have a complete nervous breakdown. Ugh! Some relaxing weekend this has turned out to be!

Ever helpful, Lendar said, "You have a few weeks before the fall semester begins. We can visit your Grammy Wednesday."

Elise gawped at him, tears pouring down her face. The name "Grammy" sounded strange issuing from his mouth. She didn't know whether to punch him in the arm or hug him. Maybe she should do both.

His head tilted and a funny look took over his face, a mixture of compassion, desire, adoration, determination and something she couldn't immediately identity. He glanced down at the floor for a second, then kneeled before her and took her hands. The earnestness in his face took her breath away. His posture spoke humility and supplication.

"Elise Ramos," he cleared his throat and that vulnerable look he'd exhibited earlier returned. "Long ago I saw you in a dream. I woke from the dream where I'd spent what seemed were hours with you and Max. I didn't want to wake up. I couldn't bear to leave you. It took me several minutes to remember that I was lying in my bed in my quarters here aboard the *Lalf*.

"I rushed up to the cockpit and examined Prince Anwic's holographic globe of the earth the Somainai created during their previous visit. I found Albuquerque on the globe, but it was only a dusty village filled with donkey carts and sun-baked adobe.

"I wanted to see the University of New Mexico, find the street where I'd seen you in my dream, but of course, the dream was a vision of the future and the globe could not show me such things.

"When my lord, prince Anwic, asked me if I'd come up to the cockpit to work or to gawk at his globe, my mind turned from my quest. My immediate duty was to serve my lord, Prince Anwic. Your presence had already been fading. The clarity of the dream gradually slipping from my mind, I laid aside my own longing to focus on my duties and forgot the vision.

"At the restaurant when you borrowed my links unit, the image on the screen was of you standing in front of that store, Max in his stroller pointing at me. I saved the scene my own eyes beheld to my links unit.

"When I saw that picture at the restaurant for the first time in your presence, with your ebullient essence surrounding me, your personality influencing me with its unique optimism and creativity, I remembered my dream. I remembered it as if I'd dreamed it only a moment before. And I knew that the feeling that had assaulted me that day on the hot sidewalk when I first saw you in the flesh was real and true: you are the woman the Most High has selected for me. You are, quite literally, the woman of my dreams.

"You are the woman I've come millions of miles to find; the one woman in the entire universe chosen for me before you were even born. And conversely, I have been chosen for you, because the Most High does not bless one without blessing another. He always showers blessings like rain, splashing them over anyone standing near." One hand added arcing movements as if he drew splashes in the air.

"You have only known me for a short time, I have known you for years, more than I've attempted to count. I have dreamed about you and woken to find myself alone aching with loneliness. Even when I had no conscious memory of my dreams, I still carried them in the core of my being where they joined with my spirit and merged with my identity." His hand went to his chest where it involuntarily clutched at some invisible thing.

"I love you. I have loved you across light years of time and distance. One kiss and I will endow you with my worldly goods and worship you with my body. And our hearts will be joined into eternity.

"If you cannot bear to leave earth, if you cannot bear to enter my world, but yet, you will have me, then I'll renounce my ancestral lands, my titles and my position and live with you in Albuquerque or wherever you prefer."

"Awwwww…" Elise bawled, her heart breaking. I'm not worthy! I'm just a stupid ranch girl turned urban dweller. As soon as I screw up something, and I will screw up something, he's going to be sorry!

He's a professional in a field I know nothing about dealing with the sort of people I've never encountered before in my life. I can't handle that. I'm a clueless ninny.

I can't marry him either here or in Albuquerque. I can't marry him at all! I'll never be able to adapt to this life and it wouldn't be fair for me to expect him to give up his!

She dropped her face into her hands again. It's all over.

Her entire body felt as if it were being crushed under a mountain of heavy and sharp stones. Her mind felt numb as if it suffered hypothermia. Tears flowed until her hands were sopping. Her body and heart were devastated by her mind's confident declarations.

His arms enfolded her and that sense of oneness they shared enveloped her. Embraced in his comfort, confidence and peace, ease felt accessible, readily possible. Her heart and body wanted to give up the anguish that came with doubt and choose to believe, but her mind refused. It argued that those sensations of comfort, confidence and peace weren't real, but rather figments of foolish imaginings.

Her mind argued: What's real are the problems of differing cultures and adapting to his advanced technology; the sacrifice of leaving earth behind and the agony of knowing that his embrace is unintentionally deceitful. Rather than forever warm and committed, it will eventually turn cold and empty, just like Gabriel's, because one or both of you will fail. And that's the hard and unforgiving truth.

Elise trembled, her whole body now feeling hypothermic and crushed with grief. She wanted to speak. Her jaw worked, but no sound emerged.

"Ourside," Max said and ran through the open maw into the garden.

Lendar stuffed his handkerchief into her hands and hurried after Max.

Elise blew her nose. After a moment, she followed them. Her tears spent, only her eyeballs felt dry. Her energy was gone. Climbing even the tiny hill outside Lendar's quarters seemed overwhelming. Nevertheless, she slogged up to the top. She stopped and lifted a hand to shade her protesting eyes.

A living meadow, quietly murmuring of waning summer and approaching autumn, lay at her feet. Peace spread to the horizon in blue and green with occasional splotches of yellow, red and purple. Insects' rhythmic thrumming lulled her uneasy mind, inviting relaxation, even sleep.

Max and Lendar were nowhere to be seen. How can a small boy and a grown man disappear so thoroughly in such a short time?!

Birdsong; soft, floral scents and a gentle breeze played through the atmosphere. In that moment, Elise felt she might be the only person within miles. She strained her ears for some sound indicating where they'd gone. Nothing. Nothing but the sighing of grasses; the somnolent talk of insects and bird-sung lullabies.

She stared at the grass, hoping bent blades might show her the way, but the short leaves gave no clue. She stared in fascination at the grasses' summer seed heads nodding when fingers of air touched them.

Elise clasped her hands together. "God, you know where they are. What should I do?" She looked up at the sky. Only it wasn't a sky, not really. Yet standing here on this hill, it seemed real.

Directly above her, deep blue offered the same promise of stars waiting for nightfall and Heaven above where angels sang eternal praises to their King just like a real sky. Heaven where the King sat on His throne and His beloved Son interceded for her, reminding His Father that she was frail and lowly and desperately in need of His Mercy. She, Elise Adele (nee Trujillo) Ramos, an insignificant, incompetent child, who still, though one of billions of other incompetent children, remained His precious daughter, a daughter He loved with all His heart.

Peace flooded her being. Oh God, You are here, just like in real nature. The light felt warm, warning her that she might sunburn. When she glanced up at its brilliant disc, she was forced to squint, just as she would if she were foolish enough to look at the sun back on earth.

Max's voice came to her through the trees straight ahead. She walked toward the sound, bushes and grasses rustling as she went, summer flowers bobbing in welcome. Lendar's discussion with Max about some insect floated in the air. She passed through intermittent splotches of shade and flashes of light. A butterfly flitted past. She stopped. "Lord, what do you want me to do?"

"Trust Me."

Lendar's words, "the Most High has done this," resounded in her mind.

"Have You done this, Lord?" Elise shook with fear. "Oh no, Lord. No. This is too much." She swallowed. Ugh, what if it is God's will I marry Lendar?

She'd disobeyed God before when He'd advised her not to marry Gabriel. But, at the time, she hadn't felt herself capable of resisting Gabriel's wild beauty. Yes, back then, at least in her eyes, he'd been a beautiful man, thrilling, dangerous. Yes, dangerous. Hazardous. Deadly. And God had proved right. Duh! You think!? He's God! What made you think you were smarter than Him?

Elise sat down on a large rock that seemed fashioned for the purpose. She remembered the last time Gabriel had come to her apartment for his weekly visit. The same day she'd met Lendar. What was it really only a little over a week earlier? She rubbed her forehead. No wonder Lendar doesn't seem to think much of time. A second can contain more than an hour. This past week has had held more than the previous month, maybe even year!

She clasped her hands together around a knee. Coldness from the stone seeped through her jeans, a sharp contrast between the balmy air and the spots of warm brightness.

What if you don't marry Lendar and that ends up being you disobeying God again? Ugh. The consequences for that would be very bad. You'd miss your destiny forever.

Her shoulders hunched. Elise changed the subject.

The problem with Gabriel is he's a coward, she thought. In so many ways, a total coward.

Her heart wanted to address the issue of missing her destiny forever and not think of Gabriel. Gabriel is in the past, ancient history. Let's move forward. Urgency pressed from deep within pushing through to her skin. Discover God's will and do it, the urgency demanded. Sweat sheen broke out on her forehead.

Her mind observed, 'A coward is often more dangerous than a brave man because he doesn't know when he's beaten. And that's because he starts out feeling beaten.' Gabriel'll come, maybe an hour, a day after I return to Albuquerque and make me pay for this weekend. He'll come hunting Lendar and try to stab him in the back since attacking at the front didn't work. She trembled, suddenly cold. Lord, You've protected me and Lendar so far, please, protect us again.

Don't you love Lendar?

But God, it won't work! We're from different cultures; different planets! Oh, God, You said, 'Trust Me,' what do You mean?

Lendar and Max appeared, Max sprinting her direction with Lendar in pursuit, both laughing.

Max is never quite as happy as he is when Lendar is around, Elise thought. They look like father and son. Can a boy be born of one man and really belong to someone else?

Max climbed onto the rock and tackled her.

She rolled to the ground, a smile playing on her lips.

"Mama," he said.

"Max, my darling." She ran her fingers through his hair as he lay on her chest. She stared up at the wafer ceiling hundreds of feet away. "It looks so real," she muttered, remembering her first sight of it moments earlier.

Lendar lay down beside her, his forearm beneath his head. "Yes, it does."

Elise turned to look at him.

He met her gaze, his expression steady and calm, though unspoken questions roamed there. Finally he said, "Tell me about Gabriel."

"Oh." Elise looked back at the sky/ceiling. She enjoyed the feel of Max's wriggling body under her arm and Lendar's hand around hers. Tension and anxiety seemed to leave her body and seep into the ground beneath her. "Funny, I was just thinking about him." She swallowed.

She began. "Well, he's supposed to come see Max every other week, though he can't take him anywhere. He's supposed to come on Friday and call first, though usually he doesn't…come, I mean, though, yeah, he forgets to call too…but especially when he's behind on child support, he doesn't come."

Elise winced, glanced at Lendar who watched her intently, his features smooth, his eyes soft like pools of still water. She continued. "Eh, well, Bruce always waits in the backyard, just outside the door, ready to burst in if necessary. Gabriel came that day I met you even though he's behind on his payments. He arrived more or less on time, about 9, with three, cold, Sonic breakfast burritos.

"You know, Sonic breakfast burritos are pretty good, well, for fast food, but cold, they're just nasty. Gabriel acted like he'd brought us caviar or something. He crouched on the floor and offered Max one of the burritos. Max just stood there, stiff, like a tin soldier. He wouldn't take it.

"Gabriel jabbed the foil wrapped burrito under his nose. 'Aren't you hungry, Buddy?' Max said, 'No. Not 'ungry.' Gabriel was ticked. 'Nothing I do is good enough for you, is it Mr. Maxfield High and Mighty.' He snarled, threw the burrito on the floor and smashed it with his foot. Then he said, 'What kind of an ass are you raising here, Elise?'

"There was an ass in the room that morning, but it wasn't Max!" Elise covered her mouth and stifled the sound that threatened to erupt, a sound somewhere between a chuckle and a moan. "I thought about telling him that, but if I had, it would have just given him an excuse to hit me, so I didn't say anything. Then, Gabriel announced. 'Well, I'm taking the kid with me today. It's time he learned some stuff.' I told him, 'You can't. You're not allowed.' Then I realized I wasn't close enough, he could snatch Max into his arms and run before I could do anything and way before Bruce could help.

"Good thing Gabriel hesitated. Finally, he said, 'To hell with the court orders.' He reached for Max, but Bruce walked in.

"I was so relieved, you know, that Bruce was paying close attention. Oh, Lendar, it's so wonderful you're going to give him a job. This whole ship and everything will be a dream come true for him!" Elise smiled at him, happy in knowing warmth and joy filled her eyes.

"I am gratified." He pushed a tendril of hair out of her face. "What happened next?"

Elise stared back up at the sky/ceiling. "Well, Bruce walked in and opened the refrigerator. He said, 'Say, Elise, can I borrow some milk.' I said, 'Sure.' Bruce took the milk from the refrigerator, poured himself a glass and sat down at the kitchen table. 'Do you have any bread?' I said, 'Yeah, there's a few slices in there, somewhere.' He said, 'Cool,' and rummaged through the cabinets deliberately looking in all the wrong places. Of course, he knows where most everything is in my kitchen.

"When Gabriel's really mad, his jaw kind of jerks and the artery in his temple pulses like a snake. He was really mad. But, he didn't want to mess with Bruce and most of the reason for saying he wanted to take Max was to make me miserable, he didn't really want Max with him, so he said, 'F- - - you!' and stormed out of the apartment." Elise paused. Her voice came out small. "He's a coward. I was just thinking about that, how a coward fights dirty and doesn't know when to quit." She knew her eyes were opened wide, but droopy in the bottom lids like some pitiful cartoon.

Meanwhile, Lendar's dry palm sent tingles up her arm, reminding her of that feeling of oneness. Her heart pulsed with the realization she'd really hate to give up that feeling forever. He said, "Gabriel had a camp-out with friends last night."

"Really!?" Elise stared at him. "Do you know what he's

doing all the time?"

"Every word he says, every place he goes. I record it."

"Oh." There are definite plus sides to this snazzy technology. "Well, what was he doing?"

Lendar's troubled look was unmistakable. "They grilled some meat, drank some beer, ah, what is the term, shot some bull, and…" He made a sign.

"And?"

"I don't know. That's the problem. I don't know what he was doing." The next sign he made seemed coupled with frustration.

"Maybe they weren't doing anything except shooting bull." Elise couldn't help but smile at his attempts to use slang.

"They were doing other things, but…"

"It's ok, Lendar, I don't want to know. My imagination can fill in the blanks."

Lendar smoothed her hair. "No, I don't mean anything by that except I…I'm overlooking something, I'm missing something. Elise, I don't know what he's plotting, but I'm certain he's managed some way to evade me."

Her heart lumbered with a sudden sharp pain. "What are you going to do about it?"

Lendar released her hand and perched his torso over an elbow resting on the grass. "I am asking permission to, ah, what is the phrase, ah, to have you followed. The person would not enter your apartment. You would retain complete privacy there." As usual, sign language punctuated his words.

"Oh. Ok." Have me followed. Elise squinted at him. "Followed by whom?"

"An elite marine, ah, one of Empress Jaizem's personal guards. That's one reason why she came this morning. She wanted to speak to me about it."

"Oh. Hmn. Well. I suppose having an alien marine who won't bother me is better than putting up with whatever nonsense Gabriel is plotting." She frowned, not looking totally convinced.

Max squirmed loose and toddled toward a thicket of berry bushes.

Elise pointed. "Are those berries eatable?"

"Yes, they're wild; I believe they're very much like blueberries, though I don't know if they're actually the same species or not."

"Ok." Elise bit her lip and glanced at him through her eyelashes. "So is this guy going to introduce himself?"

"Would you like to meet him?"

Oh gak. Do I want to meet him? "Sure. I think it would be nice to know the fellow who's going to be following me around." Elise swallowed. You just can't seem to keep from adding new stuff can you?

Lendar pulled his I-phone from his pocket and spoke into it.

Not understanding a word he said, Elise studied his profile. Handsome. He'd look good on a coin. A strong, but not overbearing brow and nose, well-shaped, firm mouth. The light enhanced his skin tones.

Lendar ended his conversation. "Retief will be here soon."

"Do you know what part of earth your ancestors came from?"

Lendar replied. "No."

"Hmn, well, I'd say you were Greek, except you have blue-green eyes. Wait, do you know if the ancient Greeks had blue-green eyes?"

Lendar chuckled. "As a matter of fact, they did."

"How long you people been spying on us poor unsuspecting backwoods types anyway?"

"For the Somainai this will be the third trip. The last one occurred during your 1860's."

"Wow." Elise paused to think of what had been going on in the 1860's, then pursed her lips. "Do you know what they're doing now?"

Lendar shrugged. "They observe human society. Other than that I don't really know. In the past they have studied geology, plant life. Each trip has a specific focus. I'm not involved with their efforts."

"Oh."

"They have made their research available to the public. We have much of it on board here. If you like I can show you."

"Yes, but at the moment...no. Let's do that later." Elise bit her lip again. I hope there will be a later.

Really? You hope there will be a later? Didn't you just decide you could never marry him?

Oh, shut up. I think if he'd kiss me, I'd know whether I should marry him or not.

You know he can't kiss you. If he did, it'd be the same as saying 'I do.'

Elise closed her lids again.

Seriously, you think a kiss would really tell you anything? Like people thinking living together is practice marriage? Most couples who live together and then marry end up divorced.

Yeah, but we're talking a kiss, that's not the same thing.

She licked her lips, thinking of his kiss, the kiss he might give her if he would.

Aloud she said, "This garden part is real nice, Lendar."

She listened to Max smacking his lips and tugging on the bush while Lendar's soft breathing provided rhythmic background music. "Hmmn."

She prayed: Lord, I'm asking You to make what You want me to do so painfully obvious that I can't ignore it, because if this isn't Your will...

"What are you thinking?" Lendar asked.

"I'm thinking I want to do God's will," Elise answered, her eyes popping open.

"Do you know what He wills?"

"I'm afraid I do, but I want to be sure beyond a

reasonable shadow of a doubt."

Lendar traced the bridge of her nose. "Does He ever remove all shadow of a doubt? Especially if one is determined to have doubt."

Elise stared. "How can you know God and not know Jesus?"

"Who is Jesus?"

"He is the Son of God."

"What does that mean?"

"Well, it's complicated. Do you want to hear about it all right now?" *He looks like he'd rather kiss me! If he'd just kiss me, then I'd know what to do.*

"I want to hear about it as you feel comfortable."

Elise explained how Jesus was God's Word made flesh, begotten because He was born of a woman by the power of the Holy Spirit, a God/Human. She explained how He came to pay for sin and rose from the dead. This led into questions about the Holy Spirit and how could the Word be a Being. Valiantly Elise tried to answer his questions.

Lendar listened intently. Finally he said, "I have begun reading your Sacred Text. Where does one discover Jesus in them?"

"He's all the way through, but not obvious until the book of Matthew." Elise licked her lips.

"The book of Matthew," Lendar repeated.

While she'd been speaking, he'd been unconsciously leaning ever closer. Closer and closer until, now, his face hovered inches above hers. His lips parted, the pearlescent sheen of his teeth just visible between the pink. She lifted her head, straining her neck to close the distance. His breath washed over her mouth and chin. His eyes were so close she could see the thin gold strands within the blue-green of his irises and each, individual, precious lash.

"Elise," he paused, his brow gently furrowed with desire, his eyes searching, "will you marry me?"

"Lendar!" *Her heart cried, "Say 'yes,' say 'yes!'"*

Instead, she asked, "Ah, do you really think that's a good idea?"

Lendar frowned. He settled back on his elbow and then lay flat on his back, his hands folded over his chest.

The balmy air had suddenly turned cold. Elise rushed to fill the unpleasant chasm now open between them. "I've only known you a week…I made a mistake before marrying Gabriel…It would be worse than awful if it didn't work out, at least for me, because I'd be giving up everything…I couldn't come back home…"

After a moment, he turned to her. "Elise, I'm sorry. Please forgive me. I was far too forward. My behavior is completely inappropriate. Inconsiderate. I apologize." Lendar bent a knee, folded himself toward it, then stood. "Master Max has wandered off."

Elise sat up. Max's yellow and blue shirt winked through the leaves. She followed Lendar who trailed him. Max took his time, choosing a pebble, pulling up a flower, trying to capture a butterfly.

For the first time Elise realized that she'd heard no motor or mechanical noises of any kind since leaving the tube what seemed ages ago. These gardens were as perfect as any remote forest on planet earth. Evergreens, mingled with handfuls of deciduous trees, stretched tens of feet into the air. They creaked and sighed with the wind; they were filled with birds just like forests she'd hiked through on earth. The same sorts of animals she might expect to see on earth occupied the terrain. And the air smelled fabulous! She breathed in like a woman who had just now been allowed to smell anything for the first time in her life. This garden seemed to suck anxiety and worry from her like a poultice cleanses a wound.

Max moved on and she followed, Lendar nearby. It wasn't long before the noise of babbling brook lured Max to its banks. Wild irises greeted her from the opposite shore.

Elise grinned. "Wow, you have a brook! And it looks real!"

"It is real. What is a brook made of, Elise? Soil, gravel, running water, the correct types of plants, animals and micro-organisms, they're all here."

"Nobody on planet earth, that I know of, has been able to create an enclosed eco-system like this!"

Lendar shrugged. "The Somainai did it." He made a sign, one hand kind of hopping over the other like leapfrog. "We just, ah, what is the term, ripped off their technology." He grinned and rubbed the bridge of his nose.

Elise laughed.

Max splashed in the stream, sat down in the water and was soon thoroughly soaked. Fortunately, he'd chosen a patch of warm light for his impromptu bath and he wouldn't be cold, yet. Elise crouched on the water's edge and ran her fingers through the water. "It's real nice here." The water was clear and beautiful, promising a sweet drink to any who might bend to taste of it. I could get used to this very easily.

Lendar stood beside her, arms folded across his chest, a look on his face similar to one she'd seen on Uncle Wilbur's face when he was analyzing whether it was time to plow out the alfalfa or let it go another year.

"Max, come here," Elise said, wriggling her fingers in his direction.

For once, he obeyed without dawdling.

Crouching, she tugged off his clothes, diaper, socks and shoes. "Might as well go feral for awhile," she muttered. "It's warm enough." She straightened.

Max giggled and returned to his spot in the stream. He splashed and looked up at his mother, a broad, open mouthed grin spread over his face.

Lendar took her hand. His strong fingers encased hers and that reassuring sense of oneness returned. She squeezed the fingers and released them. But Lendar would have none of that. He took her hand more firmly this time, his face hardening with resolve. As if he had no intention of going through life alone any longer.

She glared at him, thinking she might just yank her hand free and jump across the stream leaving him by himself. But something vulnerable and pained in his expression and in the set of his face made her reconsider. Her eyes widened in surprise. Maybe he needs me, she thought and swallowed. His body seemed to say: We are one; shoulder to shoulder, hand in hand we can get through anything together. Can't you see that Elise?

Can we get through anything together? I don't know. I think I'm the weak link, but alternately, what are his character flaws? I mean, besides occasional cluelessness? I don't know what they are. Elise swallowed.

Her emotions felt like beads on the surface of her skin, some filled with joy, some filled with anxiety, all easily popped. Marry him? Lord, should I?

Elise blurted, "What time is it in Albuquerque?"

"Why?"

Elise shrugged. "Just like to know."

"I have no idea."

"I'm supposed to pick up my art work on Tuesday."

"Right now, time is irrelevant, Elise." He looked down at her. Enigmatic, yet demanding. "There is only now."

"So what time is it in Albuquerque?"

"Elise, we're on ship's time. We are in now. Don't worry about Albuquerque."

"What?"

"Relax. I'll make sure you're home as promised."

She watched Max for a moment, then said, "Funny, I was raised on a ranch. Spent a lot of time in the mountains hunting with my Dad; hiking with my cousins. But Max," she gestured in her son's direction, "he's never really been outside like that. He's an urban kid."

"Time we fixed that problem, don't you think?"

Elise looked up at him. "What do you have in mind?"

"Camping. You have a few weeks before the fall semester starts. After we visit your Grammy, don't you think a vacation doing whatever strikes your fancy sounds pleasant?"

Elise stared. "Really?" A slow smile grew on her face. "Oh, yeah. You can do that, you're already on vacation." She laughed.

Lendar's arm wound around her waist easily, as if it belonged there. And she didn't resist.

18

Elise lay relaxing on a cushioned chaise, drowsy in the warmth that radiated from the patio paving blocks and reflected light. The delicious smell of Lendar's marinade mixture wafted from the grill side-table to mingle with the spiky floral scent from the flowerbeds bordering the patio.

Max played nearby with a set of strange vehicles Lendar had given him, each with its own set of sound effects and special features like lights, holograms and weird hover capabilities that kept certain of the vehicles floating a few inches off the bricks.

She felt rather than heard or saw a change. She opened her eyes a crack, just enough to note a tall, dark stranger standing at the patio's edge, his arms folded over his chest. He wore moss green slacks with black piping and a white t-shirt, as if he'd left the rest of his uniform behind. She sat up.

"Elise Ramos meet Retief Urkay." Lendar made one of his creative signs.

Elise didn't know whether to bow or offer her hand. She decided to offer her hand. "Hello."

"Greetings." Taking the hand, Retief bowed and kissed her knuckles. His lips were soft surrounded by bristly whiskers.

Elise managed to squelch the giggle that strained to burst from her lips. "It's nice to meet you." Oh my, Lolly would fall for you in a heartbeat.

"Likewise delighted," he said, his strangely blue eyes were set in a chocolate brown face. His voice was deep, as if it came up from a fascinating cavern.

"Oh my, what striking eyes you have," Elise exclaimed.

"Family trait." His face was pleasantly cheerful and his manner amiable.

Lolly will definitely like you, Elise thought, tapping her

index finger to her lips.

"Retief will you join us for dinner?" Lendar asked.

"I'd be honored, sir." He bowed.

"Fetch yourself a chair." Lendar pointed to the closet at his left. He studied Retief speculatively, then his face broke into a mischievous grin. "Once we've dealt with whatever Gabriel Ramos has planned for us, I'd like you to meet a young lady I discovered during my stay in Albuquerque." With one glance, he included Elise in his plan.

Elise's face brightened in anticipation.

Retief paused, the folding lawn chair in hand. He seemed hesitant, but hopeful. "What is her name?"

Lendar winked at Elise. "Lolly Lang. She's a friend of Elise's"

Retief bowed to Elise. "An unexpected bonus. Given your beauty and grace, I'm certain she will also prove a beautiful and gracious lady."

Elise smiled. "Gracious, maybe, beautiful, certainly, but spicy." Her lips curled with delight at the thought of Lolly laying eyes on this man.

Retief beamed. "Intriguing." He snapped open the chair. "I like spicy." He paused, as if about to ask for more information, then turned to Lendar. "How may I be of service?"

"Ah, well, in a moment I may request help, but at present I have no needs."

Retief sat down. "Lady Elise, have you found your stay aboard the *Lalf* agreeable?"

Lady Elise? Interesting. "Well, to tell you the truth, up until today I found it very stressful." She perched on the edge of the chaise.

Retief nodded. "Ah, yes. That is to be expected for your first time in space. And presently?"

"Presently I am completely relaxed and enjoying myself." Elise smiled. She glanced at Max who had not stopped playing with the Minan toy set since the moment

Lendar had gifted it to him.

"Your son?" Retief asked.

Lendar breezed into the apartment to fetch something.

"Yes, his name is Maxfield," Elise replied.

"A fine name."

Elise relaxed into the chaise seat back, wishing she had a pair of sunglasses to hide behind so she could study and compare the two men. She reclined and settled for narrowing her eyes to slits, as if she were once again drowsy.

Lendar strode to the grill and began cleaning it.

He was lithe and lean while Retief was brawny, wide shouldered and narrow hipped, the stereotypical, heroic build. He had a strong nose, thin mouth and powerful jaw. Lolly will find him irresistible. Oh boy, Lolly has no idea what she's in for! Elise smiled. The light on her eyelids felt good. She breathed deeply, savoring the moment.

Retief clasped his hands together with a loud clap.

Elise's eyes popped open.

He leaned her direction, his elbows resting on his knees. "Ma'am, Lendar has explained that I will be your close protection detail for the next period of time until the matter of Gabriel Ramos has been closed."

"Yes, that's what he told me too."

"I will be wearing chameleon battle skin which will render me effectively invisible. Most of the time you will be unable to see me, but I will be within fifty feet of you at all times. Please, do not allow my presence to interfere with your normal activities. Forget about me. In fact, it is preferred you forget about me. Forgetting about me allows you to behave normally and permits our suspect to imagine himself free to act as he wills."

"Ok." Elise squinted at him. Might be a good thing having a guy like you following me around. She relaxed, her face easing into friendly openness again.

"I have brought a electronic communications ear bud which operates in conjunction with the unit I will be wearing.

It will allow me to offer instructions or in the case you must speak to me you may contact me, but only if absolutely necessary. Please keep in mind: I won't be far away. I'll be able to observe whatever is happening around you at all times."

"Ok." Elise wanted to get up and walk away. Wander off into the gardens and escape. *Just when I'm finally enjoying myself real life has to intrude.*

Retief fished into his pocket and handed Elise a tiny button. "This device is water proof and safe under all conditions. Place it in your least useful ear, in the canal. It will not transmit until you first say, "Retief," then it will transmit whatever you say until you finish with the words "complay." 'Complay' is Minan for 'complete.' I won't be eavesdropping on you and you won't be able to eavesdrop on me either." He lifted his hand, ready to help as she plugged the thing into her left ear. He offered a faint smile. "Because the device will be powered off most of the time, it will be very difficult to detect."

"Cool." Elise smiled.

Retief looked uncomfortable. Finally, he braved a question. "What is meant by 'cool'?"

"It means that I find what you've told me and this little gadget quite interesting, useful and nice." She put on her best face.

Retief nodded and rubbed his hands together. "Yes, like you, we also have slang terms and words with strange origins. Very well then…" He paused. "Our objective is to deal with Gabriel Ramos and end his intimidation, for that we may need to allow events to transpire until the appropriate moment in which to act."

Elise nodded, hesitant. "Ok…"

Retief grinned, then pointed at her. "The term 'ok' is an old one first used in a Boston newspaper in 1838 as an acronym for 'oll right,' meaning 'all right.'"

Elise grinned. "Cool."

"Do you have any questions?"

Elise shook her head.

Retief left his seat and joined Max on the ground.

Elise closed her eyes again, pushing real life out of her mind and basking in the happy sound of males busy around her.

Are you sure you can't marry Lendar? Are you sure this won't work? Once you get past the advanced technology, how bad could it be? I mean really? Her brain lolled in a pleasant stupor of warm light and delicious food odors. I can't remember the last time I've eaten so well. Fat and happy. Inwardly Elise chuckled.

She'd already set the table, a glass topped, iron thing to her right surrounded by outdoor furniture in white with antiqued turquoise cushions. Lendar had a bottle of wine waiting to one side on a stand and he'd promised a pitcher of iced tea, the kind Lolly would have appreciated: sweet tea with lemons.

Ok, I could definitely get used to this part, lovely back yard, happy males and good food. But, is that enough to balance the other stuff? Face it, you have one lazy afternoon, or whatever time of day this is, and you think it's lazy afternoons forever. Is this enough to balance the other stuff? Elise swallowed, ignoring the cold sweat that suddenly dotted her forehead and made her shiver.

If I agree to marry Lendar I'll have to meet the prince, see the Somainai and maybe actually speak to one. Ugh. Probably deal with them all the time and start signing without realizing it just like he does. But on the other hand, would that really be so bad? Couldn't you get used to it? Jaizem wasn't so threatening, was she?

I wish he could kiss me, then I'd know.

No, the real question is: do you love him or not?

Well, how am I supposed to know the answer to that after less than a month hanging with him?

Ah, but you do know, don't you?

Delightful sizzling of moist slab hitting the grill followed by fabulous seared smell of deliciousness broke into her reverie causing her to forget her internal argument. Her mouth prepared itself for another grand meal.

Lendar interrupted, "Retief is also a space jet pilot."

Elise opened her eyes.

Lendar looked at her over his shoulder and winked.

Retief nodded. "Yes. First in my unit. And in a pinch, I can function as engineer, but have to be a real tight pinch." He chuckled, probably at his use of the word 'pinch.' "Unlike Marl here who is capable of flying this vessel, should the need arise."

"Flying the *Lalf*?" Elise turned from Retief to gape at Lendar.

Lendar blushed. "My lord, Prince Anwic, trained me at a time when we operated his previous vessel by ourselves. And then updated my training to this vessel." He bowed. "Though I am technically qualified, I think the 'pinch' warranting my taking the *Lalf*'s helm must of needs be most extreme."

"What was that other ship called?" Elise asked.

"The *Ola*." Lendar turned his back to them to focus on the smoking meat.

"Retief, you ever fly with the *Ola*?" Elise asked.

Retief shook his head. "No, I did not. This is my first time in far space."

"Far space?"

"Yes, outside one's sun system."

Elise nodded. Travels in a different world, don't he. "So what is your age compared to Lendar's age?"

"I don't know." He opened his palms, separating them a short distance before bringing them back together again.

Elise frowned. "I find that time thing gives me a headache. How do you keep it all straight?"

Retief seemed bemused. "Often we don't and usually we don't try." He winced. "Rather, I should say, those who travel in space don't try."

Elise pressed on. "What do you know about the Somainai?"

Retief glanced at Lendar who looked over his shoulder with a smirk, but didn't say anything. Retief's expression seemed to say, "Thanks for nothing." He glanced at Max, collecting his thoughts then looked up to Elise. "I've never had any dealings with them. My empress has not left Minan since I came into her employ. This is my first journey away from Minan and near space. The Somainai are not allowed to step foot on our planet."

Elise's mouth fell open. "They're not allowed to step foot on your planet? Is there something wrong with them?"

Retief shook his head, straightened his posture and jagged one shoulder uncomfortably. He and Lendar exchanged a look, Lendar at first seeming to display disapproval, then only humor. Retief shrugged and said, "It's a long story that began hundreds of years ago."

"Oh." In that case, don't tell me, Elise thought and swung her feet to the floor. They have enough dealings with the Somainai that they end up unconsciously signing, but Somainai aren't allowed on their planet? That just doesn't make sense. "Lendar, I need some of that iced tea you promised."

Lendar snapped his fingers and a robot rolled out of the apartment. "Elise would like a glass of iced tea."

"Yes sir," it replied. It opened a compartment and lifted a glass of sparkling iced tea with lemon to Elise's hand.

"Oh, good grief, that's just like Futurama!"

Retief looked to Lendar for an explanation. Lendar shrugged.

"You guys need some DVD's of Futurama." Elise tasted the tea, then giggled. "Pretty good tea. I guess you figured a robot could handle iced tea, but not hot tea for the empress...is that it?"

Lendar blushed. "Ran out of time to do it all."

Elise waved her hand. "No worries."

Retief, who sat cross-legged on the patio, parked his fist on his knee. "What is "good grief" and what is "Futurama"?"

Lendar eyed her quizzically. "I'd like to know that myself."

"Ah, 'good grief' is an expression used to express dismay. Futurama is a cartoon television show. Haven't you guys been watching our television and listening to our radio?"

Retief nodded. "We have, though of the recent offerings, there are too many to assimilate in such a short time. I assume, from your remark, that Futurama features robots?"

Elise nodded. "Yep. It's hilarious."

Retief stood. "Sir, may I have a beer?"

Lendar pointed in the general direction of the kitchen with his tongs. "In there, help yourself." His eyes twinkled. "Forgive me, I neglected to add beer serving to the robot's duties."

Elise watched Retief walk into the apartment. "Do you people really listen to our radio and watch our television?"

"Yes, but that doesn't mean we've made sense of it all. Elise, you earth people produce vast quantities of broadcast material. Takes time to gather and analyze it."

Elise sipped her tea. "So, I kinda pick up on a hint of disapproval there. What? You don't broadcast anything?"

Lendar shook his head. "No disapproval. Just worry. All that noise and you don't know for certain all who intercept it."

Elise made a slight frown. "No, we don't. I don't think we've collectively given it much thought." She chuckled. "On the other hand, I heard the other day that the UN has a person ready to play ambassador to extraterrestrial aliens should any announce themselves."

Lendar flipped the meat. "Name this person so that I may avoid him!"

Elise chuckled. "I don't know, I forget. You can

probably google it."

Lendar glanced her direction, an eyebrow cocked. "I assure you, we have no intention of announcing ourselves."

"Thank God!" Elise giggled. "Meeting him would probably entail a slew of boring meetings loaded with drivel."

One corner of Lendar's mouth curled. "No doubt you are correct." He bowed. "Now explain "google it"."

After the meal the men attempted to teach Elise how to play a board game popular back in the Federated Planets while Max watched a holographic movie on Lendar's holo unit. Elise found it difficult to concentrate on the game.

The holographic movie, apparently made by the Somainai, gave the viewer the sensation of swimming with earth's whales through all sorts of waters. The movie showed more about whales in their environment than anything Elise had ever seen in her entire lifetime.

What scientists wouldn't give to have that holographic movie, she thought. Max found it entirely engrossing and sat gape mouthed on the couch watching every second. Wonder if I can sit in the middle of that hologram and, like, be immersed, Elise thought.

"Now, Elise, it is your turn. I recommend you move your wolf," Retief said, pointing at the board.

Lendar frowned, an index finger pressed to his lips. "I disagree. A strategic slip through the storm at this point would prove most beneficial for her game."

Elise sighed.

By the time Retief left, the artificial moon had risen in the gardens.

"An evening stroll is in order, I believe," Lendar announced. He scooped up Max and carried him on one arm while offering Elise the other. The window wall had remained open throughout the day and into the night, yet somehow the apartment hadn't filled with insects. Yellow light from the interior bathed the patio and tinged the edge of the rise. They climbed the hillock and paused at its crest. The blue-gray light seemed to soak through her skin, producing tingling in her retina that penetrated to her brain. Amazing. Her hand on Lendar's arm, the sensation of oneness returned. The grass felt cool, soft and moist under her feet. The gentle air stroked her exposed skin with songs of new wonders just ahead.

A few minutes into the walk and Lendar wrapped his arm around her waist, his stride perfectly matching hers. She watched his boots appearing within her vision and disappearing as they walked, gray against the black grass. She gazed at her environment, an idyllic setting any self-respecting French king or queen would have found delightful. Even the mosquitoes were carefully managed here.

Soothing nighttime sounds mixed with evergreen and floral scents to create a synthesis of mental deliciousness. And all of this aboard a spaceship! I could get used to this. Maybe I can handle all this advanced technology. Maybe Lendar and I are meant to be together.

19

A large space jet waited in the docking bay. Robots and human crew scurried about filling opened compartments or tinkering with machinery.

Elise cast a glance at Lendar. "Is this jet safe?"

Lendar nodded. "Yes, perfectly." He pointed to the rear of the two boarding ramps. "We'll board there."

This passenger compartment reminded Elise of a well-designed four-person travel trailer. It had a tiny galley kitchen, compact bathroom and u-shaped couch that could serve triple duty as seating, dining and sleeping. She went to the door opposite the entry and pushed open the curtain. A narrow passage stretched as far as she could see; across the hall, she could see the space jet docking bay wall through a large window. *Reminds me of a passenger rail car compartment.*

Elise glanced over her shoulder at Lendar remembering he'd offered a trip to Jupiter. *Maybe this thing is like a touring space jet or something.*

Lendar placed Max on the couch and handed him a toy. "Master Max, we'll be taking off soon."

Max looked up at Lendar. "Reave?"

"Yes, we're leaving."

"No wanna reave."

"Mama has things she has to do in Albuquerque."

Max shook his head. "No wanna reave." He lifted his arms in appeal, then flung his hands down to pound the cushions. "No wanna reave!"

"I'm sorry, Master Max, but we must." Lendar's tone was firm, but nevertheless communicated empathy.

Elise's faced creased with a tired smile. *Lendar has definitely met the criteria of rule #8 for politeness. The rules seemed silly now, especially since Lendar had proved capable* of challenging her in ways the rules didn't cover.

She joined Max on the couch and flipped the tag on the back of his shirt out of sight where it belonged. Her fingers lingered over the sweet skin at the top of his collar. She kissed the little knob his vertebra made at the base of his neck.

Max brushed the kiss away.

"Excuse me, I'll return in a moment." Lendar bowed and disappeared into the passageway.

"Well, Max, what should I do? Should I marry Lendar?"

Max eyed his mother, his expression sour.

Elise smiled again. Fatigue from the previous night spent fretting instead of sleeping glittered in her eyes. The moonlit stroll had passed like an idyll from some romantic poem. She'd retired to her room, relaxed and at ease. But after she'd gotten Max ready for bed, she'd lain awake for hours, staring at the moving picture at the foot of the bed, trying to make up her mind. You are such a loser, she thought. She touched a tendril of Max's hair.

Max stuck his tongue out at her and pushed her hand away.

Elise allowed her hand to drop. Well, if Max were deciding he'd just forget earth completely!

Max marched a toy figurine over her leg, then stuffed it between cushions. In the next instant, he yanked it out and stabbed in her direction. "'Ungry. Eat now!"

"We'll eat in a minute." Elise promised, patting his head. "Oh honey, I'm such an idiot."

"Mama ijiot." Max grinned and crammed the figurine back between the cushions.

"Oh Max!" Elise rubbed her throbbing forehead.

Max rooted for the toy he'd just buried. Triumphantly he pulled it out and began marching it along the top of the cushion, then rock climbing it down the precipitous drop from the top of the seat to the bottom.

Meanwhile, the boarding ramp closed. Elise watched

activity in the bay through the large window facing her. The oxygen sign remained placid green, its weird cuneiform letters as unintelligible as ever. "I'd have to learn that language," she muttered, knowing that problem was one of the most trivial, but the idea made her feel exhausted. "So much to learn."

Lendar returned, smiling from ear to ear. "We'll be taking off in about ten minutes." He settled beside her, one arm around her shoulders, fingers of his free hand stroking her hair. "I hope you enjoyed your weekend," he said, his breath touching her flesh, bringing tingling delight to the surface. His face wore hope and a question.

Elise relaxed. Her skin sang everywhere his fingers brushed. Desire flooded through her body washing away the acid stomach feeling and headachy grouchiness. Oh Lord God, forgive me. I want Lendar. With effort she replied, "At first it was terrifying, but it got better." An armless hug, she pressed her cheek into his and ran her fingers through curls on the side of his head.

When she pulled away to look, humor danced on Lendar's face. "You won't have any more success than Master Max with my recalcitrant locks."

"I know it." Elise winced, offered a wan smile and let her hand drop. Her whole body ached despite his comforting presence. Anxiety fatigue, that's what I've got, she decided.

Lendar touched her cheek with the backs of his fingers, a gentle caress that did not match the flare in his eyes, a flare that demanded possession and submission.

Elise's heart pounded. Oh, just kiss me. Just kiss me! Then I'll know. Her skin felt prickly, burning from the inside out. Her hands trembled.

If you'd say, 'Lendar, yes, I'll marry you,' then he'd kiss you.

Why don't you say it?

Elise's mouth opened and the words rolled to the tip of her tongue.

But what if that's a mistake?

I don't care! I don't care if everything goes to hell in a hand basket later. Besides, It's not a mistake. Just say it!

Just as she was about to speak, Ty interrupted, making an announcement through the intercom. When she tried again, it was as if someone had taken her tongue and tied it into a knot.

Unconsciously Lendar edged nearer. His smoldering eyes flamed in a face marked by yearning, each line and plane opened, exposing his inner being.

He's a good man! It's so hard to find a good man! You can make a life with a good man!

Elise licked her lips. He wants to kiss me; he wants it bad. Her heart thumped loudly in her ears. She felt her caryatid arteries pulse in her neck. Her skin glistened.

When Lendar spoke, his lips hovered only a few inches from hers. "We are about to take off," he murmured, but his whole body screamed a completely different message. It said, 'I want you; I desperately want you.' Heat roiled at her in waves luring her ever closer. His eyes were dark, the pupils dilated and deep. His face went hard, etched with hunger.

Elise threw herself at him, clinging to his neck and pressing her body against his. "Oh Lendar…" she breathed, knowing every ounce of desire and longing she'd held tight within her filled each letter of his name as it whispered from her lips. "Oh Lendar…"

His arms crushed her, but she didn't care, she only wanted more. Absorb me, she thought, consume me. His breathing changed from calm and steady to ragged sucking, as if he could not catch his breath. She tasted his neck and felt a new rush of craving rising from her loins. "Oh Lendar," she gasped, "won't you kiss me? If you'd kiss me, then I'd know."

His body stiffened and he pushed. By force of will, he turned the deluge of passion aside.

Elise's heart broke within her, emptying grief and bewilderment into her body.

Lendar's breathing became even more ragged. The

hands that had only an instant before entangled themselves in her hair, now clasped her upper arms. The face that only a moment early had been thrilling her neck with soft kisses, burying itself in her hair and murmuring strange endearments in Minan, hung low. His body shook. He placed his forehead on her shoulder. She felt his exhalations pouring heat over her breasts.

"I have forgotten myself," he whispered huskily, his voice hoarse.

And with what appeared great effort he drew away. He sat, eyes closed, his hands and arms trembling, the arteries in his neck throbbing. His face was red and puffy as if it were about to burst.

Elise leaned into the couch back, her eyes staring sightless at the ceiling. I feel as if I've just been turned inside out, she thought. Every nerve was raw and painful, every inch of her flesh felt as if she'd just been flayed. Oh, Lord, God help me, I'm such a fool.

With effort she righted her head and caught sight of Max, now at the window ogling the proceedings outside. Oh my, what if that had really gotten out of hand...right in front of Max. She gulped. "I'm sorry, Lendar. It's my fault. I'm truly sorry."

Lendar disappeared into the bathroom. Elise heard water running, then splashing.

Max jabbered and pointed.

Elise scooted to sit behind him and look over his shoulder. She struggled to focus, to see what had captured Max's attention, but her mind didn't seemed capable of co-operating. Her body ached as if she'd just experienced the most severe work-out of her life. It demanded to be one with Lendar. Now! And how!

She blinked and shook her head to clear it. Outside, something had gone wrong. The contents of a container had spilled a mountain of little, pill-like, pink things onto the pristine floor. "Oh, look at that Max. Did you see what happened?" Her voice came out funny, mangled by strangled desire.

"Crash," he replied and brought his fists together, "Boom." He giggled.

Elise studied his expression. Oh, Lord, Max is so beautiful. But the joy had a weight attached to it: the heavy, radioactive question: why not marry Lendar? At the moment, her body knew the answer, her heart knew the answer, but her mind refused to agree. It's too soon; it's too risky; you don't know him well enough.

She turned as Lendar plopped into the couch. She wanted to hold his hand, to comfort him, but she knew the only comfort he wanted was to hear her say, "Yes, I'll marry you." And I can't say it. She hung her head, her nose suddenly burning with unshed tears, her head instantly spiked with pain. Oh Lord, I wish You'd make it perfectly and utterly clear to me what I should do!

"Time to buckle up," Lendar mumbled.

Elise buckled Max again, and then herself, the pair of them now facing Lendar across the open place within the "u." They stared at one another like zombies.

After the space jet had achieved cruising speed, a robot arrived to serve breakfast. A table lowered from the ceiling and was soon set. The cabin filled with the delicious odors of baking and a freshly opened container of jam. Soothing, synthesized music wafted through the sound system. The robot was efficient, precise and unobtrusive. They breakfasted on soft-boiled eggs and crusty bread.

"Soon we'll be arriving in Andorra. We'll land on a mountaintop near the villa which I purchased for the mission last spring, then we'll hike down to the guesthouse in the rear..." It was obvious Lendar gained control of himself by forcing his mind to deal with practical matters.

Elise barely heard a word. Her whole being felt scattered, as if bits of her were in limbo and other bits were spread in different places in time. Maybe I'm scattered between here and the moon. She tasted her beverage. She had no idea what they drank. It wasn't coffee. It was some kind of Minan drink that Lendar had said didn't exist on earth. He called it, "co-fay-nee." She couldn't decide whether she liked it or not. It reminded her of coffee, but not really; too chalky and caramel-like in flavor for coffee.

Lendar's hand rose up from the table. "…Minan space jets make virtually silent vertical landings and take-offs from any location with a relatively flat surface of about thirty by thirty feet. One of our construction teams has created just such a field on the spot where we're landing. They have replanted the newly flattened area with tough, native grasses and strategically placed a handful of boulders to make the landing field look natural. Can't tell anything particular about it from satellite. I doubt anyone could identify it as a landing pad."

Elise stared out the window. I don't like this separation from him. I don't like it. I want to sit beside him, feel his thigh pressed against mine, his hand brushing against mine while he eats. Her whole body ached as if she'd been run over by a Mack truck; her heart felt as if it had been pierced and now strove bravely to do its duty while impaled; her bones thrummed. Each pulse brought a new stab of agony to her head.

End the agony: make a bold declaration of love, "Yes, I'll marry you," and kiss him!

I can't! What if things don't work out? I'll be abandoned on a distant planet.

All you want is safety and the comfort of the known, so you think. But when you get to the bottom, there is no safety, nowhere, no how, that idea is an illusion. Only God can keep you safe. And He's not limited by time, space or place.

God, what do You want me to do?!

Lendar kept talking. "…meeting at the villa. About fifty people attending, some of the first women and men serious about venturing to another planet, ready to take the risk…"

Funny. As soon as I decided I couldn't marry Lendar, the battle inside of me only escalated.

"…we decided to include a few men to better balance the genetics. Male fertility can make a huge difference, even if the earth men marry Minan women…"

What if Lendar turns into some kind of an abusive monster? Eh? What about that?

Lendar waved his hand through the air mimicking the flight of some bird or plane, now resuming his talk about the space jet. Now he's all relaxed and at ease again. He looks like a kid playing. "…carry a few hundred people at a time up to the *Lalf*…" He has that same happy look Max gets when he's enjoying himself.

Elise sighed. Really? You think he can turn into a monster. Remember how he blushed when you teased him about the tea? Sheesh.

Max watched, sipping juice from the Minan-designed space cup a mother aboard the *Lalf* had sent him as a welcome aboard gift. It was meant for use in no-gravity situations, but it worked great for a kid who liked to pour out his drinks. Max stuffed bread into his mouth, his eyes following Lendar's every move. He grinned and mimicked his flight pattern.

Lendar beamed, just like a proud father. "…we take this load of passengers up to the *Lalf* for a visit and then they must make their final decision whether to come with us or not to come with us…"

Look at those two, especially Max; he really likes Lendar. Who was it said that most kids have a sort of sixth sense about adults, they can tell when they're lying and they usually know who to trust?

"…don't worry about what those who reject our offer say when they return to earth. Few will believe them. But, these have already, what is the slang, ah, yes, jumped through the hoops and it's not likely any will turn aside our offer." Lendar puckered his lips. "Perhaps one or two theoretical possibilities…" He shrugged and continued.

Elise frowned and spread butter on a fresh piece of bread, then daubed some jam on top of that. Earlier Lendar had said the jam was made from Minan berries grown in the hydroponics gardens aboard the *Lalf* where they produced most of their food. The jam was definitely tasty. He'd said robots ran the hydroponics garden with a little oversight from some guy named Kip Hooting, princess Alma's brother. Elise savored the jam.

Truth be told, Empress Jaizem was right, you could get used to it, you could adapt. You've already been adapting. She squinted at Lendar who was now busy wiping Max's face and jabbering pleasantly at him. What was it she'd said, it would be hard for me to do better and I could certainly do worse…yeah.

All well and good, but at least if Lendar were an earthling I wouldn't be giving up my entire planet!

You know what, that old saw is starting to get old.

Oh yeah, well, have you really thought about it?

Well, what about him living on earth? He'd do it, he said he would and you know he would, he's that certain you're the woman of his dreams.

Elise exhaled. I can't ask him to do that. He obviously has a fulfilling life already. And I'd be asking him to do something I'm unwilling to do! Yeah, but he's willing!

She shook her head. You're just hacking over the same old stuff!

Ty made some kind of an announcement.

She caught Lendar eyeing her.

With her mouth full she said, "I'm sorry. Did you just ask me something? By the way, I love this bread!"

"Are you finished?" Lendar grinned. "You like the bread, but do you like the company?" He cocked his head. Unconsciously giving a come-hither look that suddenly irritated her.

"Yeah, I'm about finished." She bit the bread. He's not going to kiss me! That look is all flirt and no action.

Oh, just listen to you, you sound like one of those octopus boys from high school: all hands and no heart.

Ugh! Elise put down the bread and wiped her fingers.

Irritably she snapped, "Yes, I like the company." She attempted a smile and felt like a hypocrite. You know that smile didn't make it into your eyes at all.

Her gaze dropped. Ok, I came a little too close to losing my temper.

Want to try bursting into tears?

Oh, Lord, help me; I am such a ninny! She stuffed the last of the bread into her mouth.

Lendar merely gazed at her, studying her intently.

The robot returned and set to work cleaning the table. Elise gulped the rest of her cofaynee and handed her cup to the thing. The table ascended into the ceiling and Ty made another announcement.

"Time to buckle up," Lendar translated. He lifted Max from the booster seat. Oddly enough, the seat was a model Elise recognized from a department store in Albuquerque. He buckled Max in next to her. The robot put away the booster seat in a nearby closet and departed, presumably to stow itself somewhere.

Max slapped his palms on his thighs. "Dah, dah, dah." He giggled and grinned at her. He jabbered at Lendar who smiled indulgently and said something in Minan to him. Max answered by waving his hands around and making airplane noises.

Can you really tell Lendar "no" when Max loves him so much? Can you really do that?

Well, if it's the best thing for both of us, sure.

But is it?

Lendar turned to meet her gaze head-on. His smile faded, replaced with sober intensity. He watched her until she looked away.

Outside the edge of earth's atmosphere glowed, the heat of re-entry. Tears dribbled unheeded down her cheeks. I wish I knew what I am supposed to do! You've spent years not giving in to fear, now look at you! Elise glanced back at Lendar, his expression thoughtful and patient. Her voice barely audible, she said, "Lendar."

His undivided attention weighed the air between them. "Yes," he said, the word carefully neutral.

Elise swallowed. She had been about to say, "I'm sorry," but decided against it. Instead she began the sentence in a different place, "Ah, I haven't said 'no'...yet..." She squinted and winced, one lip curled with dismay. Words from the unfinished part of the sentence rattled in her brain like ball bearings. She blurted, "Will you please be patient with me a little longer?"

The corners of Lendar's mouth edged upward, but his eyes did not smile. His mouth firmed into a hard, curved line, his jaw appeared as a solid immobile object. "I am a patient man, Elise, and I will win your heart."

Her heart leapt. Think of the solidity of his will, the certainty of his resolve, the constancy of his character--why do you have to put him and yourself through this torturous waiting?

She attempted a smile, but it died stillborn. Oh, buddy, you have no idea how much you've won, two against one: my heart and body are all yours; it's my brain that's holding out. Nervousness hit her like a flash flood and she felt all twitchy and itchy. Oh, I want out of here!

Outside, a tree-packed landscape filled the view; inside desolation. Lord, forgive me, right now I can't tell for sure if I'm letting fear dictate or if I'm being smart. It isn't smart to marry a man you've only known for a week, is it?

The space jet touched down. They waited while another group disembarked from the forward cabin. Elise imagined she saw Empress Jaizem among the ten or so people walking away.

Yeah, but people, especially in the old days, used to marry people they never even met before. And they made it work.

While her attention was directed outside, watching the group amble away, Lendar said, "I have to go into Andorra la Vella for a few hours and then we'll fly to Albuquerque." She looked at him. He cocked his head, a hint of regret marking his face. "Unfortunately, I also have duties which require my attention on Tuesday, but I will again be free on Wednesday."

"Ok." She returned to the window. It felt good to be back on planet earth, even if she were in a foreign country. Elise laughed. "In Andorra after all, and me with no passport."

"I apologize, it won't be much of a visit. You must stay at the guesthouse while I'm gone. You may walk in the forest behind, but, please, do not go down to the main residence." He looked askance at her.

"Ok…" She stared at him, hoping he'd explain, but he said nothing more. Maybe he already explained and you weren't listening! Maybe that's why he's giving you that look. Ugh. You are a double-barreled jerk.

They disembarked, this time with Lendar carrying her things and Max in her arms. Fresh forest scents filled her nostrils. She inhaled deeply. At the edge of the landing field, Elise glanced back. The jet was invisible, though she imagined she could make out a few faint, white lines against the dark evergreens. Ty and another man appeared out of nowhere. A section of machinery was suddenly visible and they set to tinkering and discussing. Weird, Elise thought, noting how the panel where they worked seemed to float in mid-air.

High mountains and narrow river valleys characterized Andorra. Turning her attention to the well-constructed trail she followed Lendar down its gentle switchbacks. Soon, the guesthouse loomed through the trees. It was a large, modern construction of stone, steel and glass.

Lendar opened the door for her. "The kitchen," he pointed to the left, "and just ahead the living area." He placed her diaper bag on the low table between couches and set her suitcase and backpack on the floor.

Stairs made of stone blocks with steel banisters and a polished wood rail climbed to the second floor. The balcony stretched across one entire side, topping the living room wall. The living area was open to the ceiling twenty feet above where a huge chandelier hung at its center. The furniture was boxy, with an almost industrial feel.

"I don't think you decorated this place," Elise commented.

"No, I didn't." Lendar stroked her cheek. She leaned his direction hoping for more, but he breezed to the door, paused long enough to say "Good-bye" and was gone.

She helped Max climb the stairs. Together they explored the bedrooms. All decorated with the same impersonal attitude, but every window provided lovely views. She monitored Max's stair climbing for almost twenty minutes before he tired. In the kitchen they found some juice and unfamiliar snacks labeled in French and Spanish. She discovered a blanket in a closet and spread it on the living room's single attempt at luxury, a luscious sheepskin rug. She lay down with Max and sang to him softly until he slept.

Elise's curiosity nearly overwhelmed her. She dragged a leather and steel armchair to the front window and watched the main house. Figures moved past the windows. After awhile, a handful of workers set up folding chairs and a podium on the patio, a few minutes later the chairs filled with people. Someone came out of the main house and gave a talk. Even with the front door open, Elise couldn't hear the speaker. She might have disobeyed Lendar if she hadn't been painfully aware of the fact that she had no passport, no visa, nothing to legitimize her presence in Andorra.

Bored with the meeting, Elise fished her Bible from her backpack and read it for a while. Lord, I'm sorry. I've been fretting and making myself crazy when I should just cast all this care on You. Oh, Lord, help me cast it all on You. I'm going to wait and expect You to make it painfully clear what I should do. Then, please, just cause me to do it. Amen.

When Lendar returned he brought a cabbage, potato and pork stew in a ceramic pot. They ate in companionable silence, cleaned up the kitchen like an old married couple who'd done it a million times, then hiked up to the waiting space jet, its opened hatch the only sign it even existed.

Ty swooped low over Paris and circled it once, giving Elise her first glimpse of the Eiffel Tower, the Arch de Triumph and other fabulous landmarks.

"Oh, please tell Ty thank you for me," Elise breathed.

Lendar smiled indulgently and touched a button on the wall before speaking in Minan.

After Paris, the jet picked up speed, entering earth's thermosphere for what seemed only one brief moment.

Before she knew it, they landed on a rancher's road just off Highway 285, in the state of New Mexico, United States of America. It was late Monday morning. Ok, never mind the space time thing, going instantly from evening in Andorra to morning in Albuquerque is kind of freaky all by itself, Elise thought as she followed Lendar down the passageway to the cargo bay. A crewman released the Escalade from its moorings. They climbed in. Lendar backed the Escalade into the New Mexico summer heat and drove to Albuquerque.

20

Late Tuesday morning, Elise opened her door and backed out, pulling the stroller with Max buckled in the seat. The sun bore down onto the gravel yard and bounced under the porch disrupting perfectly good shade with enthusiastic brilliance.

Bruce sat outside his door in his rusted lawn chair. He grinned. "Morning, Elise."

"Morning, Bruce. How are you?"

"Doing great! Lendar offered me a job."

Elise beamed. "Cool!"

"Listen, he's coming over later to pick me up." He stared down at his hands, then squinted at Elise. "Is Lendar from Andorra or what?"

Elise answered cautiously, a glint of humor playing in her face. "He has a place there."

"Really." Bruce clasped his hands together, his elbows on his knees. He cleared his throat. "So he wasn't lying?"

"Well, not really…but, he wasn't telling the whole truth either."

"Hmn. So what's the "whole" truth?" Bruce made quotation marks in the air, his face wearing a sarcastic grimace. "Why'd he lie?"

Elise cocked her head. "Bruce, he has a really good reason and I think you'll understand once he shows you."

Bruce pursed his lips and frowned. "Well, o-k-a-y." Elbows still on his knees, he clapped one fist into the other palm, once, twice. His eyes shifted around the yard, then back to her. "So you're not going to tell me."

"Nope." Elise's mouth twisted into a grin. "Wouldn't ruin it for you, not for the world."

"Hmn." He grimaced and straightened. "Fine then."

She winked. "Yep. Did he tell you what you'll be doing,

like, will you be cooking for him personally or what?"

"I'll either be his personal chef or work for his corporation."

Elise sighed contentedly. "It's what you've always wanted!"

"He's coming over tonight," Bruce glanced at his watch, "er, about 7 p.m., to show me what I'm getting myself into."

"Well, there, you said it yourself. You'll find out tonight." Elise grinned and gently rested her arm on his shoulder, the beginnings of a hug. "Oh man, this is so amazing! Really. Bruce, you have no idea, how amazing." Her eyes twinkled. Her arm fell to her side.

Bruce smirked good-naturedly. "Ha, ha. Leave the poor fool in the dark; the last to know."

Elise's lips curled mischievously. She winked. "That's right."

Bruce eyed her, obviously longing to pump her for information. After a moment he asked, "Where you headed?"

"I'm supposed to pick up my work from my painting professor between 9 and 11." A slight frown creased her brow. "I guess I'm sort of pushing the deadline."

He glanced at his watch again. "Yeah, you're pushing it. It's 10:15, you'd better get moving. By the way, I didn't see Javier or Gabriel all weekend, hopefully they never realized you've been gone."

"That would be better," Elise replied. "How about we have lunch?"

"Ok, I'll fix you this new recipe I dreamed up. You'll be my tester. If it seems appropriate--we'll have to see--I might cook it for Lendar and his crowd." Bruce looked daunted, his eyes rounder than usual. "I'm supposed to meet his superiors tonight. Maybe fix a meal for them." He coughed. "He gave me an advance on my salary. A nice one too. Real nice. Like, more than I've seen in a year." He grinned and coughed again.

Elise knew her smile made it into her eyes. "I'm sure

your recipe will be great. I've been your guinea pig before and I've never been disappointed."

"Always the flattery…"

"Never flattery, simply stating the facts." Elise cocked her head like an inquisitive, friendly bird. "Really Bruce. Believe people when they tell you good things. Disbelieve them when they tell you bad things. You'll enjoy life a whole lot more."

"Oh, you mean flip the way I normally do it." He illustrated by turning his hand over. One corner of his mouth angled upward in a self-deprecating smirk.

"Yep. Besides, that way's usually more accurate." She chuckled. "Or at least, it ought'a be." She winked.

Bruce grunted and fell into an awkward silence.

She offered an impish grin. "Well, I'll see you in a couple of hours or less."

"Ok, later." He cleared his throat, rubbed his palms on his khaki pants and stood. "Should I go buy a chef's outfit, you think?"

"Yeah, you should. You'd feel more comfortable if you looked professional, I think. At least I would." She winked again. "You are a professional, aren't you? At least, I always think of you that way." She smiled.

Glowering, Bruce nodded. "Well, see you in a bit."

"Ok." Elise repositioned the empty cardboard portfolio with duct tape shoulder straps she wore on her back. She'd fabricated it at the beginning of the summer term to protect her work during transport to and from school. It allowed her to keep her hands free instead of trying to juggle the stroller and cranky paintings that always seemed to find the slightest breeze and turn into sails.

At the corner of the apartment building, she muttered, "Duct tape and cardboard." She blushed, then firmed her lips. "Who cares if you look squirrelly?"

"Squirrelly 'uc' 'ape," Max repeated. "Quack, quack." He giggled.

Elise mussed his hair. "Silly."

Max shook his head. "Wha's Up 'uck, quack, quack." He flapped his hands like wings, then lifted the sippy cup she'd stuck in the seat next to his hip and drank.

"You really like that book, don't you?"

Max's reply hardly qualified as language, his thoughts had already moved on.

Elise checked Javier's house. Faint music drifted through the opened and screened front door. The swamp cooler on the roof rumbled softly. Javier might be over there. Ugh. Hopefully not. Maybe it's just his girlfriend. His car is gone. Oh Lord, protect us please. She sighed and made a tight smile. "Thank you."

Elise tucked her chin, checked for traffic and followed the stroller across the street. "Retief, you around here, somewhere, complay?"

"Yes, ma'am."

"Retief. It's good to hear your voice. I have to admit, Bruce's not seeing Javier or Gabriel all weekend is pretty creepy." Her skin crawled. She cast an anxious glance at her surroundings. Defiant, she thought, I refuse to cower in my apartment and live in fear. Ha, what a joke, just listen to yourself. "Ah, complay."

"Trust me, Elise, I'm right here."

An idea, that the routine Gabriel had observed since the divorce might be thrown out in favor of ratcheting up the bullying a notch, maybe into something more violent and less predictable, pressed into her consciousness. That would explain why he hadn't been at her apartment door that morning ready for a confrontation.

You do love me, don't You Lord Jesus?

Yes, You love me, that's why You sent Lendar…the man of my dreams…the one I've been praying for…the one who wants me to move to a planet I've never seen and live on a space ship where the rooms talk…and eventually I'll have to meet the royal family and those Somainai, marsupial, humanoid-creature, things. Gak.

A bead of sweat popped on her brow. Absently, she wiped it away with the back of her hand. Ok, that isn't working. Let's try something else. How about instead of agonizing about myself in his world, imagine what it'd be like if I took Lendar to my high school class reunion. Drive up to the high school in his Escalade; walk into the cafeteria with him on my arm, all crisp and manly. Sweet revenge on that snotty Pam Johnson.

Stubbing her toe on the edge of a section of jutting sidewalk brought her back to reality. "Ouch!" She swallowed and cast furtive glances at the neighborhood.

I heard Gabriel's pickup. He's never tried to pick us up on the street before.

There's always a first time, isn't there?

Oh, Lord, please keep us safe! "Retief, you there? Complay."

"Yes, I am here. Please not to talk unless absolutely necessary."

"Ok," Elise said, then continued her inner dialogue. Wonder what Gabriel's plotting. A chill shot through her. I can't imagine him giving up yet. Actually, I can't imagine him knowing when to give up! A spike of fear pierced her heart.

Lendar's done something no one else had ever been willing to try: beat Gabriel in a fight. Gabriel probably has a special hatred for Lendar. He's probably plotting something especially dastardly! Gak. Absently Elise wiped her suddenly, extra damp forehead, soggy and not just from the heat.

Lord, I'm counting on You! Oh Lord, please get me and Max through this and keep us in Your will. Er, cause me to do Your will 'cause it's obvious that I'm a total, freaked-out ninny and I can't do anything by myself. Ugh.

While she walked, her eyes searched the terrain for any hint of Retief's presence. No unexplained noises, no weird blurry edges, nothing. Not that she knew what to look for anyway.

Retief probably thinks I'm a complete idiot muttering to myself and carrying around a ridiculous cardboard contraption on my back. Sigh.

She bent down and looked Max in the eye. "Max, we're going to be fine."

Max gave her a look as if to say, 'Well, duh, of course we'll be fine.'

A breeze dashing under the trees blew welcome moisture from a sprinkler swooshing over someone's bedraggled lawn as she walked past the run-down, college student rentals. In moments they arrived at Central Avenue buzzing with speeding cars and fumes. They crossed the street. Only a handful of vehicles occupied spaces in the normally packed parking lots. The asphalt blasted heat through her sandals. It even seemed a bit melted. The campus is so empty!

She met a fellow painting student as he came out the door of the art building. He lifted his hand in greeting, his black, nylon portfolio tucked under his arm. She watched him hurry away. No smile, no nothing. Hmn.

The art building felt cold with no warm student bodies rushing through its halls. Elise shivered. It's always spooky when no one's around. I don't even hear Retief puttering along. Well, duh, he wouldn't be very effective if you could hear him, would he?

Max attempted to splash water from the sippy cup, but it refused to co-operate. Experimentally he began working his fingers around the base of the lid.

"Oh, no you don't," Elise muttered, pushing his hand away. "No!"

Max made a whining noise, jerked the cup up and down, then drank.

Elise's sandals clattered on the polished concrete floor. A student came striding out of her painting professor's office, a canvas wrapped in Kraft paper clutched in his hand. He thumbed toward the open door and mouthed, "Bad mood."

Cautiously, Elise approached. She eased a glance around the door molding.

The professor sat brooding over an opened journal. She knocked on the doorframe.

"Elise Ramos." He scowled.

"Hello. How are you today?"

"I've been better."

"I'm sorry."

He clapped the journal shut. "Elise, my agent was in here over the weekend. He saw your work and he wants to represent you."

"What?"

Her professor stood and parked his knuckles on the desktop. "He wants to represent you." His frown cut through his face like a scar. "In all my twenty years teaching painting, this has never happened!" He made a dramatic downward slash with his hand as if he sliced through some ugly goo.

"Oh, wow! That's wonderful!"

"Like hell it is." He glared. "Excuse me, Elise, if I'm not exactly thrilled one of my students will be showing work in the gallery that represents me in New York." Though Elise hadn't thought it possible, his frown deepened. He snarled, "Never mention my name. If you ever do I will disavow any relationship with you or knowledge of your existence."

She didn't know whether to shriek with joy or snark at him, so she did neither. Instead she folded her arms over her chest and said, "I should think you'd be delighted seeing as how I am your student."

"Delighted, after you've graduated, maybe with a Masters, and paid your dues struggling through the requisite contests, juried shows and what have you. Not when you leap over the whole process."

Elise shrugged. In the next instant she felt swamped by fear of the unknown and an unpleasant conviction that her own inexperience and incompetence would destroy everything. She lifted her chin, defiant. "Well, how does that work? I mean, me and the agent thing…ah, that kind of relationship…" She drew a circle in the air with her index finger.

The crease between his brows deepened. "He was so anxious to get started, he took your piece to get it framed. Which frankly is utterly unprofessional, if you ask me. The man has lost his mind. He wants to see more like it." Angrily her professor yanked his wallet from his back pocket and snapped a business card from one if its sleeves. He leaned her direction, his nose leading the rest of him like a tomahawk. "Here's his card. Call him. You two work it out." He paused. "I don't want to see your face around here again, Elise Ramos."

"I'm sorry you feel that way. I've enjoyed your class." Mostly, mostly enjoyed your class. Well, sort of enjoyed your class. Well actually, no, you were pretty much a jerk. She winced at her lie.

He waved his hand. "Go, go, get on with your life…"

"I intend to finish my degree, I'm almost there."

Her professor stared. "Really? When you have a chance to skip all the rigmarole?" He shook his head. "Whatever, I don't care, just go." He waved his hand, shooing her away. "And don't sign up for any more of my classes." He reopened the journal and sat down, ignoring her.

Back in the freezing, echoing hallway Elise giggled. "This is so amazing! Thank You, Lord." She pulled her cell phone from her diaper bag and texted Lolly and Bruce the good news, then punched Lendar's number. She'd never texted Lendar or even called him before. Come to think of it, they'd hardly been apart since the day they'd met. Elise warmed at the thought.

Lendar answered, "Ho."

"Lendar, you won't believe this: my art professor's agent wants to represent me!"

"Good, but ah, what exactly does that mean?"

"My work will be shown, for sale, in a New York City

art gallery. He'll promote me as an artist. Sell my work. Manage my career." Elise indulged in another giggle this time coupled with a silly dance. "I need to get busy painting. He wants more!" She felt as if her feet suddenly had springs built into them, or as if she were Mercury, able to fly wherever she pleased. "If I can just paint more like the one he liked, I'm home free. You know, more like the one with the rocks morphed into figures."

"Oh, yes, that one is delightful. I intended to purchase it for her highness." Lendar cleared his throat. "That's wonderful, Elise."

Elise bit her lip, then asked, "Can you front me some cash to buy supplies?"

"I can. Today I have some duties to tend to, among them taking Bruce to the *Lalf* for a tour..." Lendar chuckled. "Will tomorrow be soon enough? We'll revise our plans, postpone our trip a day, drive to Langell's instead and purchase everything you need."

"Oh, Lendar. Thank you! How many paintings do you think I can finish in five months or however long it is you have before your vacation runs out?"

He chuckled. "I don't know, Elise. I suppose it will depend on inspiration and perspiration--that's, ah, Thomas Edison." He seemed pleased to know a catchy, earth phrase and the name of the person who'd uttered it. "Does this mean you'll marry me?"

"I'm still considering it." Elise swallowed. Oh gak. Did you really just say that?

"I'll call you in the morning."

"Ok, bye." Elise swallowed. A little of the joy fluttered away like a fickle butterfly. Lord, this is not an obvious message--unless You don't want me to marry Lendar! Or maybe You mean he should stay here. Arrgghh, what am I supposed to do?

Vincent Paulson, a guy who used to work for Gabriel, stepped from a recessed doorway right into her path. He looked like he'd been working out at a gym lifting weights since the last time she'd seen him. He was summer tanned and wore a Raiders baseball cap.

"Oh, Vince, hi. What are you doing here? You know someone in the art program?" Elise stopped, struggling to put on a friendly face and behave like a Christian toward this man she did not like or trust.

Vince folded his arms over his chest. "Yeah, you."

"Oh." A twittery laugh escaped Elise's lips. "How are you?"

"Pretty good."

"That's great! Well, I gotta go. I'm glad I got to see you. Talk to you later." Elise tried to arc the stroller around him, but he blocked her.

"What's going on, Vince?"

A different voice from behind interjected, "You're coming with us, Elise."

Elise spun to identify the new voice. "Ah, Tony Natividad. I haven't seen you in ages." She gulped. She knew of Tony as a guy Gabriel had run around with growing up in Deming. Coincidentally, Tony had showed up in Albuquerque about the same time Gabriel started doing drugs. "Well, I gotta go." She made another attempt to pass Vince and failed.

Tony stepped closer and kneeled beside Max. "Yeah, well." He squinted up at Elise. "Don't want to talk to you either." His teeth looked terrible.

"Then you won't mind if I go home now."

Tony shook his head. "You not going home, puta."

Her face reddening, Elise gulped. "Why not?"

Tony's small, pig-like eyes drew a bead on her. "Gabriel. He wants to see his kid."

"The court sets the rules. He can't see Max anywhere except my apartment or public places where we both agree to meet in advance. And I don't agree to this."

Tony snorted, his face set like granite and about as

mottled. "I don't give a crap. No judges here, no cops either. Just you, me, Vince and Max." He crouched beside Max. "Niño. Yeah. See this?" He slipped an unopened switchblade from his sleeve and rubbed it along Max's jaw line. "Yeah, how's that? Eh? Nice and cool and smooth." He grinned. "Nobody here on this entire floor. How long you think before somebody get up here if Mommy scream, eh? How long? 'Bout ten minutes, maybe five…oh, you think maybe three? Plenty of time to do whatever I want. Yeah. How about that?"

Max watched the shiny metal, his eyes round like saucers, his chin scrunched into his neck trying to put distance between himself and the blade.

Tony looked up, a rotten-toothed grin spreading across his face. He held the deadly weapon high for Elise to see. The unmistakable swish of the blade snapping from its casing filled the hallway. He lowered it to within a few centimeters of Max's delicate skin.

Max's nostrils flared and the whites of his eyes showed.

Tony whispered. "You think I cut him, Elise?"

Elise stared. A drop of sweat seared her hairline. Her waistband felt suddenly hot and damp. Oh God, help! She swallowed and squawked, "No, I don't think you will."

Vince cleared his throat, then looked up and down the hall, his brows furrowed.

Tony muttered, "Elise, you love this cabeza hueca more than anything in the world, no?" He looked up at her, a sneer spreading like disease. "You don't want him cut? Keep your fucking mouth shut and do what I say."

Vince's bravado had faded now Tony had exposed his blade. His expression verged between apologetic and tough. He seemed to steel himself, then spoke. "Your professor walked out of his office and headed the other way a few minutes ago, Elise. There's nobody on this floor except us." His expression bespoke earnest appeal. "Come on, Elise, keep quiet and nobody will get hurt."

Elise clutched the stroller's handles, her knuckles

whitening. "Ok. If you remove that knife from Max's neck." Her hands felt slick and her feet soggy.

"All right." Tony smirked. "But you're not pushing niño. I'm gonna carry him. Yeah, Max, you and I go for a walk together with your puta mama, yeah." He unbuckled the boy and tried to lift him from the stroller, but Max clung to the metal. "Oh, you don't want to, well too bad, little mierda la cabeza." Tony peeled Max's fingers loose.

Max wailed.

Tony snarled, "Let's go."

His face contorted with fear, Max leaned Elise's direction, his arms opened in futile appeal.

Elise clutched his hand. "I'll carry him."

Tony said, "And me risk you running off? Naw, naw, we don't go there."

Elise's skin burned with useless fury and anxiety. She ground her teeth. In the next instant, her skin felt icy, her fingers numb and her head loose on her neck, as if it were barely attached. Her hand went up to steady it, sending a jolt of unpleasant sensation through her body. Ugh, I think I'm going to throw up!

Vince took the stroller from her, snapped it closed and clutched it in one hand. Max's cup cracked on the floor and rolled, leaving a trail of water.

Elise murmured, "You wouldn't cut Max anyway; Gabriel wouldn't like it." Fear almost sealed her trachea. Black dots danced before her eyes. Where is Retief and why isn't he doing something?

Tony's eyes narrowed, then he grinned. "You probably right about that. But you know what, Gabriel, eh, I can take him any time I want. You know what else, I like for you to do what I want; I threaten Max, you do what I want." He chuckled. "If I have to cut him, eh, you still do what I want." He drew the flat of his knife blade along her chin. "You make this hard for me, eh, your little mierda la cabeza will be bleeding and it would be your fault. Just go for drama, you'll see."

Elise winced at the foulness of his breath and struggled to collect her wits and strength from the internal hiding places into which they had fled. I can do all things through Christ who strengthens me, she reminded herself. She hissed. "Whatever you think you're going to get out of Gabriel, you won't get it if you cut Max."

Tony smirked. "Estúpido, Gabriel's a scared, little, baby-dog." He spread an opened palm in a semi-circle and shrugged. "I'd just say you gave me a hard time and he'd believe me. He'd believe me in a heartbeat because he knows I can take him any time I want."

Elise swallowed, a fresh sheen appearing on her brow. "He has to be offering you something..."

Tony laughed, ripped her makeshift portfolio from her back and threw it down the hall. "It's none of your damn business, but I'll tell you since it probably make you cry. He has a '55 Chevy..."

Elise interrupted, "His grandpa gave him that car!"

"Yeah, and he's going to give it to me when I deliver you and Max." Tony pointed at his own chest and loosed a cackle. His evil expression made Elise's stomach churn. Gabriel was supposed to let Max have that car! Tony's doing meth, she thought. He's about 3/4ths out of his mind. He won't be able to do anything with that car but sell it to feed his habit. Sure enough, her eyes watered. She felt like someone had taken her soul out of her body and stomped on it for a few hours.

Tony grinned.

Vince pointed at the exit down the hall. "Let's go." He led the way. Elise slogged in his footsteps. Tony fell in behind her.

Elise passed through the door and stumbled down the stairs. "Now which way?"

Tony pointed. "Toward Central."

Numbly, Elise obeyed. With Max pinned tightly in

Tony's arms, she felt she had no choice. She thought about screaming or running into a store; kicking Vince in the shins and making a scene, but Tony could cut Max before anybody could do anything to help. And being in a hurry, he might do serious damage. Besides, he could flee clutching Max in his arms, be far away before anyone could catch him.

Where's Retief? Why isn't he doing something? Panic hit like a hot, blasting gale. Elise struggled to breathe. Together with the sun, it burned her flesh like a furnace. The street reflected blinding glare and released acid-like, fiery turbulence. Exhaust fumes nauseated her. Just when she thought she couldn't take another step, the men pointed to a midnight blue Chevrolet Blazer a few cars beyond the Post Office parking lot. It wavered in the vaporous flux like a mirage. Fixing her eyes on the vehicle, Elise stumbled toward it.

Vince unlocked the doors, opened the driver's side and pushed the seat forward, out of the way. She hesitated.

"Get in," Tony commanded. "And give me your cell phone."

Elise hauled herself into the passenger seat. She pretended difficulty finding her cell phone. Her fingers fumbling in the diaper bag, she found the "send" button and pressed it before reluctantly handing the phone to Tony. Lendar was the last person she'd called, it would automatically ring him. Hopefully he'd answer and listen for a while instead of simply deciding it was an accidental call.

Vince tossed the stroller in the back and hopped into the driver's seat. He cranked the engine.

Tony stuffed the cell phone into his jacket. She hadn't given it a thought before, but Elise realized he probably wore the jacket, despite the heat, to hide other implements, like maybe a gun. She swallowed the bitter fear taste that suddenly hit her throat.

"Where are you taking me?" Elise shouted for the benefit of the cell phone now in Tony's pocket. Oh Lendar, please already be listening.

"You find out soon enough, puta."

Tony settled in the front passenger seat, then handed Max to her. Gleefully he snarked, "I get bored later, I read your texts; get your numbers." He chuckled. "Ha, Elise, where's your high tech boyfriend now? Eh? He abandon you?" His laugh turned derisive. "Probably out looking for some other easy open legs." He made a suggestive gesture with his hands that set Elise's stomach agitating with fresh bile.

Vince smirked. "Gabriel saw your boyfriend's little spy drone in the barbecue smoke the other night. Ha, get this, Elise, your idiot boyfriend doesn't get texting." He made slicing gestures with a flat hand. "Totally doesn't get it. Do they not text where he comes from? No sexting?" He leered and shook his head. "Lame. Totally lame."

Tony chortled. "Yeah. Burro idiota. So Gabriel texted us and set this up." His exhalation reminded Elise of a foraging pig. "You won't be messing with that estiércol comer idiota any more, not after we get through with him." He chuckled. "Things are going Gabriel's way from here on out--unless he screws up!" He threw back his head and laughed derisively. "Cabeza de pene. But hell, I don' care. As long as I get that car."

Elise clutched Max in her arms. "How do you know I'm not wearing a bug?"

Vince hooked his thumb through the air. "You're not wearing a bug. Three hundred dollars and we got a bug detector off the internet."

Max nuzzled Elise in the neck. Absently, she patted his back and asked, "When did you use it?" She kissed the top of Max's head.

Vince glanced at her in the rear view mirror. "When you were sitting in the professor's office."

Tony sneered. "Yeah, we walk up and down the hall and check you out." He bobbed his head in time to his words.

He chuckled. "You don't got no spy drone following you around neither."

How does he know I don't have a spy drone following me? An icy shard of fear stabbed through her being. Never mind that, how's Retief going to follow me? Unconsciously, Elise continued patting Max's back while rocking back and forth.

Thankfully, Max hadn't thrown a fit or said anything after his initial wail. He just sucked his thumb, his eyes wide and his heart rate fast.

Oh Lord, we're counting on You! Ok, Elise, think…at least Retief knows these guys have you and he'll do something. And maybe Lendar is listening right now. Don't panic! You can't afford to panic and leave Max with nobody looking after him, even for a minute. Just calm down and take regular breaths. You must be strong for Max. The Lord is with you; everything will work out fine. Eventually.

She trembled and stared out the window, trying to count cars or take note of the businesses, anything but focus on her situation.

Vince took Central Avenue west to Interstate 25, headed north to the interchange then took Interstate 40 east. The afternoon traffic ran quickly, people on their way somewhere--oblivious to a kidnapped woman and child. Just after the Tramway exit, one man stared in dismay. He drove alongside for a few miles before taking the Carnuel exit. Oh Lord, please protect us, Elise prayed.

Vince turned on the radio and Rush Limbaugh's voice blasted into the vehicle.

"What kind of crap does your uncle listen to anyway? Find something else." Tony griped.

Vince played with the knobs. "How about this?"

"Classic rock. Sounds good to me."

Vince turned up the volume.

Tony rapped on the dashboard along with the beat. He yanked his head and rolled his shoulders in time to the music.

His singing voice turned out to be a screechy tenor.

Elise sighed. In her mind's eye, she could see Grandpa Ramos' barn with its collection of old cars he'd bought through the years in the hopes he could fix them up one day, or at least pass them down to appreciative grandkids. He even had a beat up, 1960 Triumph Italia he'd mortgaged his house to purchase and ship to Deming.

Man, how stupid can you get, Elise decided. Is Gabriel really bartering all those cars for this fiasco? Another sigh escaped her lips. What on earth does he hope to accomplish? Her heart thumped uncomfortably and her skin felt clammy, but at least her ears weren't roaring with pre-fainting din. Maybe I can keep my wits for a change.

Vince took the Tijeras exit and drove south along 337 toward Chilili where old Mexican land grants with their ancient homesteads and, in between, attempts at modern, high-end, mini-ranches made for an odd mix in the foothills of the Manzano Mountains.

Tony rolled a joint one handed and lit up, still singing along with the radio. Smoke filled the vehicle and Elise pushed the window's control button trying to get some air.

"Oh, no you don't," Vince snapped. He pushed the driver's control and the window rolled up most of the way. "Now it's locked."

Elise met his eyes in the mirror. Her anguish clearly reflected back at her. Vince's expression seemed apologetic before it hardened and he returned his attention to the road.

The winding pavement snaked through dry forest meadows with views of dusty homesteads spreading toward the horizon on the east with the forested Monzanos rising on the west. Perhaps an hour south of Tijeras, Vince chose a right turn onto a red dirt road. Dust billowed up behind them, obscuring the view to the rear. Elise swallowed. Piñón and juniper occupied the terrain except for the swath of road and its shoulders. Miles ahead, the road disappeared behind a rise. The mountains loomed blue in the distance.

Vince had driven about five miles when he stopped beside an aluminum gate. An old, white horse eyed them with interest. Vince opened the door and barked, "Get out."

Elise held Max's head against her chest and scrambled through the door.

Tony fetched the stroller and opened the gate. "We walk." With Vince taking the rear, Tony led the way.

Elise adjusted her diaper bag and plodded behind Tony. Dust puffed at her heels. They passed a small camping trailer, then stopped at a shed made of corrugated steel. "In there."

Elise hurriedly scanned the area. Where is Retief? Why doesn't he do something? Trembling, she fought down a new wave of panic.

Tony held the door for her, a mean smirk on his face. "You got shade. Good thing it's not too hot or this shed cook you like an oven." He set the stroller just inside the door. He chortled.

Elise shot him a foul look and entered the gloomy building. The dirt floor was powder, but at least it didn't stink. Instead, the scent of freshly oiled riding tack reminded her of happier days. Once her vision adjusted to the darkened cell, she noted a saddle perched on a wooden sawhorse just inside the door and bridles and other gear hanging on hooks nearby. Twenty or thirty small hay bales were stacked at the rear. Light peered through nail holes and under the ridges of the roof, dust motes dancing through its thin beams. A chair and a bale of hay with some water bottles set on its surface stood in one corner. A cot occupied a wall.

Tony shut the door. Metal scraped on metal, then a lock clicked. Elise sat down, still clutching Max to her chest. Max sucked his thumb. She murmured, almost under her breath. "Retief. Where are you? Complay."

"Standing right outside your luxurious accommodations."

Elise sighed with relief. "Retief, by luxurious

accommodations you mean this sheet metal shed near a red dirt road off 337. Complay."

"Yes, ma'am, that one precisely. Just waiting for Gabriel and Lendar to arrive. No more talking for now, Elise. You're doing fine."

Elise kissed the crown of Max's head. "I guess Lendar and Retief have a plan." She opened a bottle of water, glad for the crackle of its breaking seal as she unscrewed the cap. "Might as well take it easy."

"Dink, prease," Max said holding out his hands.

Elise held the bottle for him. When he had drunk his fill, Elise said, "We'd better check your diaper." She laid him on the cot and changed him. Then she decided to take off his clothes. After she'd finished, she lay him on his tummy, patted his back and sang to him, "Jesus loves me, He Who died, heaven's gates to open wide…" Peeling a clean cloth diaper from her bag, Elise wiped her face and neck, then sponged Max. Man, it's hot in here. She dampened the diaper then daubed them both again.

With no more excitement, Max finally dozed in the drowsy heat. When his body sprawled in sleep, Elise left the cot and wandered around checking each of the nail holes and rips in the sheet metal for any interesting sights. Most gave views of piñón, cactus and rocky terrain. Through one, on the far eastern corner of the shed, she saw the small camping trailer where Vince and Tony lolled on folding chairs by its door.

Javier appeared, walking through the trees carrying a sack of charcoal and lighter fluid. He spoke to the two men, then opened the trailer door and went in. Gabriel's noisy pickup rumble caught her attention. Hurrying to a different rip in the metal, she caught a glimpse of the pickup's side before it disappeared behind a juniper. A cloud of red dust mixed with gray smoke rolled through the camp. After a few more moments heading north, the pickup rumble seemed to veer east. Must be an entrance down there that circles back or something Elise concluded.

She glanced at Max. He still slept soundly. Good. The better he rested, the less trouble he'd be later. She gently sponged him again, then scurried back to the spot where she could watch the men.

Javier had stepped out of the camping trailer with a shoulder-holstered pistol strapped to his body. He stood next to Tony and handed each man a beer, yammering and chortling.

While she watched, his pistol lifted from its holster and disappeared. After a moment, the gun floated back into its slot. She covered her mouth and sniggered. I bet Retief just emptied his bullets.

Tony parked his beer and removed a handgun from inside his jacket, checked the bullets and stuck it into his pants' waistband. He commented to Javier, chuckled, then removed another gun and checked it.

Oh wow, two guns. Elise swallowed.

Meanwhile, Vince seemed more nervous than ever, he rapped his fingernails on the chair arms, his head wobbling on his neck as he eyed the terrain one side and then the other. Javier tapped him on the shoulder, pointed at the camping trailer and spoke. Vince grimaced, got up and went inside. After a moment he returned, a shotgun in his hand. Javier pointed at the trees south of the dirt track, behind the trailer. His beer forgotten, Vince wandered in the indicated direction, his eyes roaming. She soon lost sight of him. Smoke now filled the space between the road and the trailer. Green wood fire.

Javier took Vince's seat. He made some remark and Tony laughed. Then he stood and shambled in an arc to the north. Both men apparently assigned as the front line guards. Elise caught a glimpse of Lendar striding in Javier's direction.

For a moment, the smoke cleared and Elise could see Javier. He apparently caught sight of Lendar. He raised his gun, an evil smirk spreading over his face like algae bloom. Elise held her breath, watching his trigger finger twitch. He stared at the pistol in shock, turned and ran, the useless weapon clutched in his hand.

A shotgun blast took Elise to the other side of the shed, but she could see nothing. The smoke had again thickened, the trailer was now barely visible. She coughed and gnawed her lip, then remembered she was thirsty and drank from the bottle she'd been clutching in her hand.

Max stirred and whined, then went back to sleep.

A brief gust of fresh air cleared the air in the middle distance revealing Vince slipping soundlessly through the piñon and mesquite, an apparition in the haze, his weapon ready. He raised his gun to shoot again. But before he could pull the trigger, he loosed a pained squeal and dropped it. He bent to pick up the shotgun and toppled face down to the ground.

On the alert, Tony edged toward one end of the camping trailer, trying to get a look without being seen. Smoke roiled through the forest, obscuring everything from Elise's sight.

The sound of panting and snapping twigs took Elise to the north side of the shed where she caught a glimpse of Vince running as if his life depended on it.

Lendar's voice sounded in her ear. Retief's communication link. "Elise…" He spoke in that quiet, not a whisper voice he'd used outside her apartment the night he'd defeated Gabriel the first time.

"Retief? Lendar. Complay."

"How are you?"

"Retief. Doing fine, I suppose. Complay."

A slight pause, then Lendar muttered. "I'm sorry you and Max had to go through this. I had no idea what he was planning."

"Retief. Yeah, Vince said that they realized you didn't know about texting. Complay."

Grief laced Lendar's voice. "He's right, I didn't. A foolish mistake; unforgivable."

Elise gushed. "I forgive you. Ah, Retief. I forgive you. Complay."

A tense moment passed, the air fairly crackling.

She gasped. "Lendar..." Her mouth felt over full. So many words pressed against her lips jockeying for an opportunity to be spoken. She started to say, "I love you," but the sounds did not come out. They ended up tangled in her throat.

Lendar spoke. "Retief and I will soon release you. Meanwhile, remember I love you." His words carried such an air of finality that Elise shrieked.

Elise licked her lips and swallowed. "Oh, Lendar." Desire and fatigue; longing and desperation over flowed into her voice. Then she realized he hadn't heard and it would be unwise to interrupt him now. The conversation was over and he was back on task.

Do you really have to kiss him? I mean, really, when he's willing to fight Gabriel not once, but twice and the second time when Gabriel's collected his posse and they're armed?

Elise peered at the trailer. At that moment, Gabriel walked out of the underbrush and spoke to Tony. It was obvious from his ugly expression Tony had no respect for Gabriel. They both looked at the shed, then scanned the area behind them. At last their eyes turned upward and they drew their weapons, firing into the air and releasing loud guffaws.

"Look-ee there," Tony chortled loudly, pointing with his gun. He fired again.

Gabriel shouted, "That idiot, he never dreamed we'd out smart him!"

Six, seven, eight robo eyes crashed to the ground and disintegrated leaving black circular patches where they fell.

Gabriel's shooting spree ended when he ran out of bullets. It seemed a multitude of robo eyes had fallen from the sky. Tony clicked an empty magazine, then dug through his pockets preparing to reload. Lendar walked out of the trees. He stopped a short distance away from the men, his legs planted firmly in an aggressive stance. The two men stared, their bodies immediately ready for action.

Gabriel squawked. "Well, if it isn't my wife's high-tech, idiot boyfriend, who as it turns out, doesn't know about texting." He smirked at Tony. "Guess that means he's never sexted my wife." He loosed a lewd snicker.

Tony stowed his gun in his pants, chuckled and flipped open the switchblade he'd just yanked from his sleeve. His reply came thin on the breeze. "So this is the estiércol encabezada novio."

Elise swallowed, her hands unconsciously clamped into fists.

Lendar folded his arms across his chest. He projected his voice loud and clear. "This fight is between me and Gabriel Ramos. Tony, you may leave now with no loss of face."

Tony puffed his chest and barked. "Not happening. I don't come here to turn pussy and run."

Lendar gestured. Elise knew he commanded one of his invisible robo eyes.

Tony dropped his blade with a shriek. "What the hell!?" Enraged he charged Lendar, bellowing like a bull. His fist came up, about to punch Lendar in the side of the head. But, Lendar deflected his arm and chopped Tony in the ribs. Tony moaned in pain and turned to strike again. Lendar grabbed his fist, twisted his arm and flipped him to the ground pinning him. Tony snarled with ferocious futility. Lendar whacked him solidly below the ear knocking him senseless.

Gabriel dropped his useless gun to the ground. A knife appeared in his hand. He lunged at Lendar. Again, Lendar deflected the aggressive arm. He punched Gabriel in the head and kicked him in the groin. He fell to the ground immobilized in pain.

Now Tony had regained his wits. He leapt to his feet and reached for one of his guns. The arm began its upward arc, his hand level with his waistband. Lendar flicked his fingers and a brilliant flash momentarily blinded everyone in the vicinity. At the same instant, a weapon fired. Elise shrieked. She blinked her eyes trying to bring back her sight.

Tony screamed, "My pants are on fire. You burned my dick. My dick…Arrrgghhh."

Finally, Elise's vision cleared. Tony's zipper was charred black, the fabric surrounding it gone. Of the front of his pants, only the center seam and the lining of one pocket remained, though a few burn holes marked the spot where his coins had once rested. The remnants of his underwear were exposed and long, oval shaped burn hole circled around the zipper and the empty gun in his belt. His skin was red and peeling, his pubic hairs were singed and his penis bore a deep, ugly welt. Another likely existed under the emptied gun.

Elise shivered in sympathy, tears dampening her face. Oh Lord, I didn't want anyone to get hurt.

Tony's howling faded, his face turned chalky and he collapsed to the ground in a heap. While she'd been blinded by the flash Gabriel had revived and had gotten to his feet. But until Tony had dropped to the ground, Gabriel had been partially hidden. He looked dazed, his mouth hanging loose. A blood-red hole shed scarlet drops under his eye, the eye weird with strange mottling, purpling like a sick plum.

Elise gasped. He's been shot! "No!"

Gabriel pointed a small gun at Lendar, but crumpled as his finger twitched on the trigger. The bullet went high. Lendar caught him as he toppled and gently laid him on the ground. Silence fell. Not even birds made a sound. Soon, two robo eyes came into view and zipped around Gabriel and Tony. Health diagnosticians. Tony moaned, oblivious to everything but his pain, then passed out.

Lendar walked toward the shed and soon had the door open. Elise rushed into his arms.

She looked up at him, tears running from the corners of her eyes. He's not hurt! Praise God.

Gently, he smoothed a tendril of her hair, watching the light play in the strands. His hard expression did not match his delicate touch. He stopped. "Elise, Gabriel is dead."

Elise trembled. "I never wanted him dead, Lendar."

"I didn't shoot him. It was an accident."

"I just wanted him to stop harassing us."

Lendar resumed stroking her hair. "Elise, it's not your fault. You didn't bring this upon him, he did it himself."

Elise laid her head on Lendar's chest. "I know what happened. I saw the whole thing. Tony accidentally killed him." His comforting embrace surrounded her, easing her agony. "I've never seen anyone die before. Lendar, I didn't want anyone to get hurt." Pain filled every vein in her body, she wanted to fold up and weep.

Gently Lendar tilted her head so that he could again look her in the eyes. Love pooled in his blue-green irises; tender concern crested his brow. "Elise, you didn't do this-- nothing about this is your doing. Gabriel and Tony did this all by themselves. This evil was in them, not in you."

Elise blinked. "But I didn't want Gabriel to die. I just wanted him to leave us alone. Or better yet, get to know Jesus." She whimpering increased into an agonized wail.

From the cot Max cried out. Lendar lifted Elise into his arms and carried her. He sat next to Max, hoisted her son into her lap and embraced mother and son together. Max had no idea why his mother wept, but he felt her grief keenly and howled along with her.

Retief entered the shed, a strange bodiless head floating in the air. He spoke to Lendar in Minan, bowed and exited.

A strange, pained numbness replaced the agony. Her sinuses were clogged, her eyes dry and throat raw. She felt as though she had fallen into a black hole where the afternoon's horrid proceedings played repeatedly on some viewing screen in her mind's eye. Gabriel's wound, Gabriel lifting the gun, Gabriel dead.

Elise whispered. "What about Tony?"

"He's receiving an antibiotic salve and an anodyne. Firemen are gathering right now to check on the smoke here. When they find Tony, they'll call paramedics from Estancia to take him to the hospital." The back of his finger brushed her cheek. "Elise, we cannot do more for either Gabriel or Tony at present, but Bruce has been waiting in the Escalade. We can do much for him. The best for him lies ahead. We must not allow this incident to rob him of his opportunity to shine." Lendar's voice penetrated Elise's pounding head, piercing the swirling awfulness like a light saber shattering darkness.

"Bruce is in the Escalade?" Elise lifted her super-heavy, throbbing head from Lendar's damp shoulder. Visual shards of the awful scenes she'd witnessed ripped her consciousness. But Lendar's words gave her cause to look away, to think on something hopeful here and now.

Lendar nodded. He brushed her forehead with his lips. "He's probably wondering what became of me."

Elise blinked and licked her lips. Her mouth was so dry. "Bruce is in the Escalade?"

Lendar replied, "Yes. He's waiting for us." She studied Lendar's neck where his Adam's apple jogged as he spoke and dark hairs, shaved that morning, prepared to leap into view. Her fingers longed to touch the little divot where his clavicle met his sternum, that spot suddenly seemed so precious and dear.

Max rubbed his face back and forth wiping his snotty nose on Elise's shirt.

"Max!" Elise groaned and choked a sob. Max will never know his father. She rested her face against Lendar's chest.

Lendar stroked her hair. "Elise, I can provide fresh garments for you aboard the *Lalf*." She listened to his heartbeat, the rhythmic sound calming her. His voice rumbled in her ear. "Elise, I cannot legitimately duck my obligations to my empress or to our friend, Bruce, not when Retief and his men are perfectly capable of dealing with this situation without me. You will be a great comfort to me if you will accompany us. And Bruce will appreciate your presence at his triumph. Will you not come with us?"

Elise sniffed and ran the back of her index finger under her eye to remove the collected moisture. "Ok. I guess I'd better since I don't want to go home." Another wave of emotion spiked and expressed itself with a fresh round of bawling. "Lendar, Gabriel's dead."

Lendar drew her into his embrace. She buried her face in his neck and Max sucked his thumb.

21

Max hugged Lendar and kissed his cheek with a slobbery smack. "'Endar," he said, one hand on each side of his face.

"Maxfield," Lendar murmured. His eyes watered, he blinked and cleared his throat.

Max was damp with sweat from his nap in the stuffy shed, but rather than turning stinky as an adult would, his sweet, childish scent was released as the moisture dried. He wrapped his arm around Lendar's neck and looked at his mother as if to say, 'Well, we've had a good cry, can we leave now?'

Elise untangled herself from the two males and sat on the edge of the cot struggling to collect her wits. She retrieved the damp diaper she'd used to cool herself and Max and daubed her face, doing her best to clean away her smeared make-up. She scrunched up her nose and upper lip, peered at Lendar and asked, "Do I look like a raccoon?"

A brief smiled touched Lendar's lips. He took the diaper and dabbed. "Do you have any oil?"

"Well, I have some lotion."

"That will do."

Elise handed him the tube, then sat bolt upright, her hands in her lap and her face uplifted while Lendar carefully dotted her skin with the cream. She closed her eyes. He began wiping it away. The tugging on her skin translated into sparks of happiness in her brain, but those fizzled away when an image from the afternoon's events appeared unbidden in her mind's eye.

Gabriel is dead. Oh Lord, Gabriel is dead, his talents and better qualities gone forever. A tear squeezed free to run down the side of her face.

Maybe, when you really get to the bottom of it, maybe

it was already too late a long time ago. Maybe in the long run it's better this way. He won't be able to influence Max for the worst instead of the better. Elise sniffed. I wish things could have been different.

Nothing new about grieving over Gabriel; she'd begun grieving years ago when she'd first comprehended she must divorce him. With grief came shame and regret joining forces to form a trio of constant companions that seldom left her alone. They had colored and shaped her from the core outward, influencing almost everything she did.

Forget that other stuff for the moment. Elise tried to ignore her throbbing forehead and concentrate on Lendar's breathing. A handsome, brave man is doing something tender and sweet for you. He doesn't think you're a failure; he's not ashamed of you, even though you're divorced!

Lendar's exhalations rippled over her face. Soothing waves of promise. Somewhere from deep within an odd sense of weightlessness came stealthily into her consciousness. Inwardly, Elise gasped.

Lord, I've been asking you to heal me for years, but You couldn't because I was feeding that awful trio and keeping it like a pet. Why? Why did I do that? Are they like some kind of sick security blanket?

Lord, I've been grounding my life on the fact that I'm a failure instead of my identity in You! Your Word says I'm more than a conqueror; that I'm a queen and priestess. Why didn't I understand that before?

Have you sent Lendar to help make those facts real to me? Elise sniffed again. I'm letting go, right now. I'm not keeping those three around full time anymore. Be gone in Jesus' Name.

The weightlessness expanded, as if someone had removed a heavy backpack from her shoulders. Meanwhile, the delicious feeling of oneness with Lendar bubbled along the edges of her consciousness. Her heart quickened. Something new; something wonderful waited just ahead.

She opened her eyes and blinked.

Lendar's brow creased. The diaper hovered near her cheek, then lowered into his lap. "I hope my efforts have been sufficient." His baritone washed over her and into her ears like a rejuvenating splash of love.

Elise bit her lip and nodded. "I'm sure you did fine." Desire flooded her, but the flavor was different. Her eyes widened, her face opening like a flower. She watched him stash the diaper in her bag.

She gulped. What's going on inside of me? What is happening?

Something is different within me. I don't need Lendar's kiss to validate me. I don't need a kiss to know I'm worthy or to know whether love is real. Their eyes locked. I don't want the kind of "love" people write about in modern romance novels where all that's really happening is lust in search of physical satiation. Physical satiation doesn't mean a person is valued.

I want the kind of love people used to talk about when they said words like "amiable" and "brave" and "trustworthy" to describe their beloved not "hot" or "rich" or "wild."

I want to gaze into Lendar's eyes, without concern that anything else at all should happen next; the kind of gazing where I might loose myself for hours while listening to him read poetry or ramble on about how to prepare landing fields for space jets.

Her cheeks burned at the realization she'd had such opportunities and wasted them. Wasted them focusing on things she didn't have! Wasted them worrying! Wasted them listening to the grief trio.

Lendar cocked his head and gave her a quizzical look. Something deep within him flared in his eyes.

In that moment she understood his passion received its energy from a steadfastness of spirit that sustained him through all adversity. It was passion born in resolve and fortitude. He knew what he wanted. He didn't need more time. And he was willing to do whatever it took to earn her trust. This was all hers and she'd been looking somewhere else at other things, the wrong things all this time.

For her he would spend every ounce of his strength; devote every penny of his resources; give every available moment of his time. This passion was fueled by, dare she think it, dare she entertain the idea, respect for her; admiration for her; commitment to her. Love transcending physical need.

I was so blind.

Hope surged within her like thundering waters suddenly released from some deep well she'd never known existed.

Lendar loves me. He loves me as no other human has ever loved me. Her inner self felt more vital and alive than it had in a long time. Fresh tears collected, blurring her vision.

The pad of Lendar's thumb followed the ridge of her cheekbone leaving a streak of wetness. "Ready?" he asked. His forehead tilted her direction, leaning into her space.

Elise shook her head, but in the next instant, she nodded. She bit her lip.

With Max perched on his arm, Lendar collected the stroller and Elise's diaper bag and stepped outside. Retrieving Max's clothes, Elise followed, pausing in the doorway. Her hand went up to shield her eyes from the sun's harsh rays.

Late afternoon heat blasted with a final, whelming hurrah and insects talked about oncoming evening in contented whirring, cricks and chirps oblivious of human drama. Two blue-jean clad bodies one in a jacket, the other in a t-shirt, lay on the ground outside the camping trailer.

Elise asked, "Er, what's that strange stuff on the side of the trailer?"

Lendar muttered. "Gabriel's blood and brain."

Elise gulped, then coughed. If anything, the smoke had thickened, oddly enough, everywhere except immediately around the trailer. She gagged and swallowed the burning liquid that suddenly seared her throat. Thankfully, in the next instant, a puff of gray obscured the trailer.

Elise jumped when Retief's head suddenly appeared. He spoke to Lendar.

Lendar nodded gravely. "Tony will recover. At present he is unconscious." He glanced at her. He asked, his voice barely audible, "Would you like to view Gabriel's body?"

Elise's eyes narrowed, damming her tears. She lowered her chin and stared at the dirt. Leaves, tiny plants, flowers struggling to grow despite the drought. One drop of moisture hit the ground and made a dark spot. She lifted face to gaze at Lendar. She shook her head. "No, thank you. And it would be better if Max didn't."

Lendar nodded and spoke to Retief.

Retief saluted, turned to Elise and bowed. "Ma'am. Pleasure to serve you." He clapped his fist to his chest then disappeared again.

Elise gulped. If she'd had a moment to think she might have said something appropriate. Lendar breezed past. She turned her attention toward the road following him first with her eyes, then with her feet. The aluminum gate swung easily on its hinges. The horse crowded near hoping to escape his smoky environs. Some invisible hand led him away.

The Escalade stood on the opposite side of the road, pointed toward the highway. Lendar opened the driver's side, passenger door for her and helped her climb in.

22

Elise fell gracelessly into the seat. I've had that kind of love all this time, from the moment he laid eyes on Max and me. She blushed. Face it, Elise: you've confused lust with love; you've confused lots of things. Oh Lord, forgive me. She trembled and sighed, then turned to speak to Lendar, but the door was already closing. To the closed door she muttered, "Thanks, Lendar."

The Escalade's window glass was flat, pale gray like the backside of a mirror. When she tried the handle, the door was locked. Bruce watched her over his shoulder, his face full of questions.

Elise tugged some thoughtfulness and energy from deep within and said, "Hi Bruce."

Bruce's hair looked professionally trimmed. When did he have time for a haircut? Maybe he just decided to take a little pride in his appearance.

Elise offered him a tired smile. "Your new chef's outfit looks great." His outfit was black with discreet red chile peppers embroidered on the collar, cuffs and breast. Pinned on his chest was a white, resin nametag.

Bruce said, "Thanks, Elise. Hey, am I glad to see you!" He paused. Watched her for moment then asked, "What gives? Lendar hasn't told me squat! He called, asked if he could pick me up early. I said fine. I told him you hadn't showed up for lunch. He said something vague, like he'd look into it. Actually, he kinda snarled at me--not at me, but in my direction. I guess he was annoyed about whatever it is that's been going on."

Bruce took a breath. "What is going on?" He squinted at Elise, waiting.

She lowered her gaze and rubbed her throbbing forehead.

He asked, "Why are you all the way out here? What happened to our lunch date? I hate to say it, but, Elise, you look terrible! Not that I'm complaining; it's real good to see you."

Elise offered a faint smile, then closed her eyes, suddenly very tired.

"Elise, what's been going on?" Bruce repeated.

In the next instant, Lendar opened the passenger side rear door and carefully placed Max, buckling him into the car seat. The door closed.

"Mama," Max said. He pointed at Bruce, "'Uce." He grinned.

"Howdy Max," Bruce said, took his hand and shook it. "Looks like you're doing fine."

Max nodded. "Me frine. You frine?"

Bruce winked. "Yep, I'm doing fine now, that's for sure. For a while there I was kinda freaking out. What have you been doing? Where's your clothes?"

Max made a spluttering sound with his lips, saliva spattering in all directions. "Hot."

Bruce nodded. "Yeah. It is hot. But you're doing all right now, aren't you?"

"Me frine. Mama frine."

Elise rubbed her aching temples. Haven't drank enough water. Noting the ice chest at her feet, she fished out a bottle and opened it. Max's clothes lay in her lap. "Oh, here are Max's clothes," she said.

Bruce took the clothes and unbuckled Max. Soon he was busy dressing the boy. Surreptitiously, he peered at Elise.

Elise thought, Oh yeah, Bruce asked me a question. Now what was it? I remember. Elise cleared her throat. Her voice came out reedy. "Ah, well, two of Gabriel's friends kidnapped me and Max from the university," she shrugged. "Happened right after I talked to my painting professor."

Bruce's mouth formed an "o" and he nodded. "So, that's why Gabriel hasn't been coming around to engage in his usual low level torture; he saved it all up for one, big doozie."

"Yep." Elise closed her eyes. Her shoulders drooped.

Bruce growled. At last he blurted, "So what's Lendar doing about it? He's been acting like a cross between an enraged tiger and Chuck Norris."

Absently Elise offered Max a toy from her diaper bag. "Oh he's out there dealing with it."

Bruce glowered. "Yeah, but what is going on, Elise?"

"Tanks, mama," Max said. Standing on the floor, he drove the little car over the car seat arms and lifted it into the air making a "shooshing" sound. "Ace get."

Elise made a tired smile. "Space jet, honey. Sp, sp, Max, sp-ace juh-et. Juh, say juh."

"Ace get," Max repeated and giggled.

Bruce rubbed his chin and muttered under his breath.

Elise pursed her lips and allowed weariness to take her. She covered her face with her hands. Oh my goodness, that'll start a whole new string of questions.

Bruce interrupted her attempt at a nap. "Max said, "space jet." Wonder where he got an idea like that?" He exhaled loudly, waited a second for an answer, then tried a slightly different tack. "I can only imagine what you've been through."

His words entered her brain and she thought maybe she should answer him, but she couldn't seem to muster the energy.

Bruce chopped the air with one flat hand. "Lendar didn't tell me where we were going, what we were doing. Nada." He frowned. "What do you suppose is going on now?"

Elise shook her head. "I have no idea." She hugged herself, somehow suddenly cold.

Bruce wouldn't let up. "Have you noticed, not only can we see nothing outside, we can't even hear anything either? It's like being in some kind of hermetically sealed compartment or something. Until you showed up I was starting to get the creeps.

"I can imagine." Elise shivered.

Bruce shot her a sympathetic look. "Sorry Elise, I'm doing all this whining when you're the one who's had a terrible day." He frowned. "What is going on out there?"

Elise waved her hand. "I'm sure we'll be safe in here. Nothing short of a nuclear bomb can hurt this Escalade." For some reason her vision blurred.

"Aw, Elise, I'm sorry." Bruce tried to look sympathetic, but she could tell he desperately wanted information.

Elise sniffled. It's not fair to leave him in the dark. "Bruce," she paused. Is it really a good idea to tell Bruce about Gabriel? Doesn't matter, he'll find out eventually. "Gabriel is dead."

"What!?" Bruce exclaimed.

Elise pressed her fingertips to her forehead, then flung her fingers. "Gabriel planned to ambush Lendar. I think he promised his buddies the classic cars his grandpa has stored back in Deming."

She held up a hand, mentally ticking off the conspirators' names. Tony, Vince, Javier and Gabriel. Only four. "There were four guys, counting Gabriel. Apparently, Gabriel had this idea that since Lendar didn't know about texting they'd have the edge on him." Elise stopped and decided not to mention Retief. "When Tony, that's one of the guys who kidnapped me, when he asked for my cell phone I pressed send so it would call Lendar. That's how he knew where to find me." Half-truth. Elise grimaced. Ugh.

Bruce fell back into his seat. "Wow."

"Anyway, after he left you in the Escalade, he managed to run off two of the guys, Javier and Vince. Vince is the other guy who kidnapped me."

"Ok." Anger etched Bruce's face. "They didn't hurt you did they, I mean physically?"

"No. They didn't." She sniffed and shook her head. "They had water bottles waiting for Max and me in the shed.

Though right now I could use a bathroom. But, never mind. That's not critical yet."

Bruce waited.

Elise sighed. "Well. Like I was telling you, Lendar managed to get two of the guys to run off without a fight, but Gabriel and Tony attacked him. They both had knives and guns." She swallowed, her eyes rounding as she recalled the scene.

"Those guys weren't too bright."

"No, not too bright." Elise wiped her nose with the back of her hand. "During the course of the fight Tony pulled a gun. Lendar was trying to defend himself. Tony's aim went bad, the gun went off and the bullet hit Gabriel right under the eye." She pointed to the lower edge of her eye socket. "Right there. And blew out the back of his head." She touched the upper part of the parietal bone behind the opposite eye. "Nice small hole in the front, somewhat uglier hole in the back." Suddenly nauseous, she dropped her head between her knees. "I think I'm going to throw up."

Bruce whipped his chef's cap into place below her face. "It's ok, Elise. I can get another one. And I'm sure Lendar will understand."

She swallowed. "No, I'm better now. I guess I'll be fine if I don't think about what I saw." A flash of the uglier parts ricocheted through her mind's eye. "Oh, ugh, here we go again!"

Bruce hadn't moved his cap, but the idea of ruining it brought Elise back from the brink. She heard Bruce say, "You and Max are fine, that's the part that matters."

To the floor, she said, "I guess. But I don't think Gabriel ever met Jesus." A sob escaped her lips. "I tried to tell him about Jesus, but he wouldn't listen." Fresh waves of grief washed over her, convulsing her body and forcing tears through her spent tear ducts. Elise wailed, "And now it's toooo laaate."

"Aw." Bruce cleared his throat. "That sucks."

"Yeah. It sucks." She sniffed, choking back sobs and sat up.

"So, wonder why we're sitting here waiting. What is going on out there?"

"I don't know Bruce." Elise fished through her diaper bag and found the damp diaper. She searched for a clean corner and blew her nose. Her water works seemed to have slowed. "And, on top of that, I've been an unmitigated jerk to Lendar." She fought another wave of nausea: the image of blood and gray matter spattered on the side of the camping trailer a little too clear.

Bruce's face darkened and shook his head. "No! You've never been an unmitigated jerk to anybody. Never."

"Oh, yes I have." Elise whispered. She honed in on the idea of being a jerk, preferring it to the replay of Tony's burned body and Gabriel's exploded brains. Her emotions, already gearing up, shifted in this new direction, without slowing down. New sobs wracked her body.

"It'll do you good to have a good cry. At least that's what I've always heard." Bruce frowned. "Lendar's got to have some tissues in here somewhere." He began punching buttons, trying to open the console or any compartment.

The Escalade beeped and said something threatening in Minan. Red warning lights flashed for several seconds then stopped.

"What the…" Bruce gasped.

Elise struggled to speak. "It's, uh, the Escalade, uh, talking." She buried her face in her hands and the floodgates opened. Oh Lord, God, I'm so sorry Gabriel is dead.

"Aw, Elise." Bruce's face twisted with helpless sympathy.

Max jabbered and pointed, then snickered.

Bruce grimaced. "Oh great, Max, thanks for the helpful advice. Try talking in English."

Max wiped the grin from his face with the back of his hand, focused his eyes like lasers and pointed again.

Bruce punched the button Max had targeted and a box of tissue appeared. "Ok, kid, now you're creeping me out." He plucked a couple of tissues from the box and offered them to Elise. "Wow, these are nice, like silk or something."

Elise cried. "Oh Bruce! I have too been an unmitigated jerk!"

"What? That's absurd."

She wiped her nose. "No, uh, it's not."

Bruce snorted. "Bull."

"You don't know the half of it." Her voice came out whiny, then broke with gulping bawls. "But what's worse is, uh, I don't know, uh, what to do about it." Elise took the silken tissues and blew her nose with gusto. "I...I'm...such a ninny."

"About what, Elise. Exactly what are you talking about?" Bruce sounded exasperated.

Elise dabbed her eyes. "Oh, Bruce." She blew her nose and did her best to stop crying. Before she could interrupt herself with more wailing or lose her nerve to confess her sins, she blurted, "I wanted Lendar to kiss me and I thought it was important, but really, it's not because it's just like when people live together, it doesn't prove anything, it just proves you're, uh, hot for someone and that's not good because, uh, lust and, uh, love are not the same thing." A new rush of tears and bawling overtopped her efforts to dam them.

Bruce stared.

"Lendar, uh, wants me to marry him, uh, and, uh, I thought if he kissed me I'd know if I should, uh, but really, a kiss doesn't prove anything." Elise covered her face with the tissue in her hands and bawled.

Bruce snapped. "I think he's being the jerk. You've known him less than a month. How long exactly? A week? And he expects you to marry him? That's beyond the pale, if you ask me! It's selfish." He shook his head. "He's a bully to expect you to answer a question like that so soon!"

"Bruce, it's not what...I'm..."

Lendar opened the driver's door. The Escalade tilted slightly as he swung into the driver's seat and wobbled when he threw himself into the cushion. "Elise…" He stopped, swallowed, then finally said, "Elise. I'm sorry. Such a failure is inexcusable."

A disgusted look on his face, Lendar flicked his wrist and the windows cleared. "I should have been more thorough. I made assumptions. I was blinded by pride in my equipment and training. If Gabriel had been a little more devious, if he'd been a little more competent…" He left the sentence unfinished, his complexion darkened. "If I'd been doing my job nobody would have died today."

Elise sniffed. "It's not your fault you didn't know about texting."

Bruce's eyes narrowed. "I know I'm kinda in the dark here, but I gather you promised to protect Elise from Gabriel?"

Lendar's face was etched with pain. "That is correct."

Bruce chortled. "And Gabriel was able to do this because you didn't know about *texting*?"

Storm clouds struck Lendar, lightning flashed in his eyes, then passed leaving the ridges and plains of his cheeks hard, as if wind swept. "Elise is safe. She was never in any real danger."

Bruce leaned in Lendar's direction, suddenly fierce. "She was safe? How do you figure that?"

Lendar sighed. "I'm sorry, Bruce, I'm not at liberty to discuss the details at present."

"That's a crap answer, Lendar, and you know it." Bruce glared out the window, then turned to study Elise.

Her emotion spent, Elise spoke, her voice flat. "Lendar assigned a body guard to follow me. And he's right Bruce, Max and I weren't in any real danger."

"What? Do you have some kind of weird Stockholm Syndrome?"

"No, Bruce, it's not that," Elise insisted.

Bruce shook his head, then raised his hands as if in defeat. "Well, that puts me in my place doesn't it?" He scowled.

Lendar turned to Elise. His look held an appeal for clemency in the set of the brow and mouth, though it was mingled with an advancing edge of determination. "My conduct has been less than professional. I am mortified and beg your forgiveness."

Bruce glared, then his expression softened. "Dude, Elise is fine, or she will be, and Max seems to be doing great. It sucks that Gabriel's dead, but that's not your fault. So, hell, let's forget all this drama and get out of here."

"Oh Lendar. You're apologizing, but I'm the one who's been a jerk," Elise wailed.

Bruce lifted his hands, looked out the window with his mouth open for a moment, then turned on Lendar. "You know what, scratch that. Elise is overwrought. Gabriel is dead. And you are responsible. What are you going to do about it?"

Lendar stared through the windshield where the dirt road ran due east for miles, a red slash through yellow grassland. Finally, he eyed Bruce coldly. "The firemen and police will arrive shortly, they'll investigate and make their conclusions."

Bruce snapped, "Well, duh, you think? And where will that leave Max and Elise with you in jail? Eh? And me?"

Lendar's frostiness exceeded anything Elise had ever seen before.

She wiped her eyes and gulped. Please, don't you two fight!

Bruce didn't flinch. He kept staring at Lendar.

Who's going to blink first, Elise wondered, glancing from one man to the other and back.

Outside, long, cobalt blue, late afternoon shadows stretched across the alizarin-orange soil, reaching for evening and nightfall.

At last Lendar spoke, his voice even and measured. "I

assure you, Mr. Bruce Keaghan, I have resources about which you know nothing. This entire incident will not be traced back to me, it cannot be traced back to me and will be closed when the police determine Tony killed Gabriel."

Bruce laughed. "Well, yeah, I suppose, since Tony is the one who pulled the trigger, yeah, that's plausible, but I bet you somebody saw this Escalade drive in here."

Lendar used a commanding tone that surprised Elise. "Bruce, get out of the vehicle, close the door and walk east 30 paces. Stop and turn around. At that moment, tell us what you see. We'll be listening for your observations."

Bruce grimaced. "Aw nuts, that's crazy." He rubbed his brow, glanced at Elise to see if she agreed he should do it, then opened the door and got out. Elise watched him walk, his skater-dude style of walking so out of place with his professional chef's outfit.

Lendar checked on Elise, then stared after Bruce.

Bruce slowly rotated. His eyes widened. He craned his neck as if that would help. His mouth fell open. "What the hell?"

"We are still here. We haven't moved. Can you see us?" Lendar's tone was matter of fact.

Bruce looked up at the sky, at the ground, at the trees on either side, his head swiveling in all directions. "No, I don't see an Escalade anywhere. Where did you go?! I can't see a thing except New Mexico countryside, smoke and sky. Wait! How can I hear you?!"

"I assure you, we are precisely where you left us." Lendar flipped a switch.

"What the…?" Bruce gasped. "You're right there! What…what…what the hell!?"

"Chameleon battle skin, Minan manufacture, exclusive Minan technology, never to be offered to any other species in the universe. Ours alone. Perhaps the only edge we've got in the space race of survival."

Bruce looked fidgety. "Space race of survival? Are you

kidding me?"

Elise giggled, then burst out laughing. Suddenly the conversation between two angry men, one standing all alone on a dirt road in rural, 21st century America wearing a chef's outfit and the other sitting in a high-tech, alien manufactured, Cadillac Escalade knock-off seemed ludicrously funny.

Max laughed. "'Uce funny."

Bruce's head dropped. "Great, Max and Elise are laughing at me." His chin popped up. He scowled. "Elise, you're the one who said there wasn't any such thing as space aliens."

Elise leaned forward, as if she needed to be closer to a microphone. "I'm sorry. It's just that you standing there wearing a chef's outfit in the middle of nowhere is hilarious. Bruce, why don't you come back and finish this conversation inside the car."

Bruce grunted. "Besides 'last to know' I can add 'ridiculous' to the list." He smirked, as if pleased he'd broken through her gloom, even if it were accidental. He slouched back toward the car, dust dogging his heels. He climbed in. Apparently the walk had given him time to think. "Man, oh man. Ok, so they don't do texting on your planet, is that what you're saying?"

Lendar shook his head, amused. "Nope." He said the word as if delighted to use a new slang term. He pulled his I-phone from his pocket and handed it to Bruce. "Slightly different technology arc; completely skipped the texting aspect you earthlings apparently have exploited to great effect."

"Earthlings. Never thought I'd hear that outside of some silly 'B' movie!" Bruce took the device and studied it. "Curious-er and curious-er." He chuckled. "Man oh man." He grinned, all his annoyance forgotten, and settled back in his seat to try and master Lendar's I-phone.

Lendar relaxed, his wrists resting on the steering wheel, staring straight ahead, thinking. It didn't take long for his pleasant expression to give way to scowling. He started the motor and the Escalade moved slowly down the road.

He's probably driving real slow to keep the dust down, Elise decided. Aloud, she asked, "What about your tire tracks and Bruce's footprints?" She touched Lendar gently on the shoulder.

He glanced over his shoulder at her. "Soon be gone. We have robots working on that presently."

"Oh."

He continued. "And your fingerprints in the shed, any stray hairs, all evidence of everyone except Gabriel and Tony-- eliminated." Lendar glanced back at her again. "Retief will bring your cell phone up to the *Lalf*."

"Oh." Elise held out her hand for more tissues. "Could I have a few more tissues, please?" Bruce obliged. She blew her nose. "I, I just feel so sorry. Gabriel's mother, she's alone now."

Bruce quipped. "You think she wasn't alone before?"

"Well, when Gabriel was alive, there was a chance." Elise daubed the corners of her eyes. "Lendar, what about the antibiotic ointment and pain killer you gave Tony?"

Lendar smiled darkly, then his face emptied of even faint humor. Sadness and, what was it, maybe rage, edged his countenance. "That will be a puzzle, won't it."

Bruce chuckled and resumed pecking at Lendar's I-phone.

Max giggled and pointed, "'Uce play."

Bruce had rotated to give Max a silly looking frown. "Upstart scamp," he muttered, winked, then turned back to the I-phone like it held the secrets of the universe. Which it actually might.

"Elise, please buckle Max into his car seat," Lendar said.

"Oh, sorry." Elise placed Max in his car seat and buckled him. In the next moment, an Estancia city brush truck whizzed past them covering the vehicle in a cloud of red dust.

Won't the dust reveal us? On the other hand, maybe there's so much dust billowing all around that won't matter. Lendar didn't seem worried.

"'ungry," Max said. "'ungry, prease." He stretched one hand each toward Elise and Lendar, his fingers wriggling.

Lendar gave Max a kindly smile. "Bruce, I have some snacks for Max in the ice chest behind my seat, would you please help him?"

"Sure." He unbuckled and leaned between seats to open it. He selected some cheese chunks and apple sections and placed them on a silken tissue in Max's lap.

Lendar stopped at the stop sign on the corner with highway 337.

Elise looked over her shoulder at the road behind where their tracks were quickly disappearing, as if dissolved. Robots, invisible and busy.

Lendar glanced at Elise in the rear view mirror. Though his face seemed hard, his eyes sparkled. "I'd planned to show Bruce the places where he'll be working, Elise. Would you like to go home or would you prefer to go with us?"

"I don't have any clean clothes. I don't have enough diapers…"

"We can easily resolve those problems. What would you like to do?"

Elise swallowed. "I'd like to go with you guys." Her voice almost broke. "I really don't want to be alone right now."

"Very well then," Lendar turned right and headed south.

Another brush truck approached and rumbled down the road they'd just vacated.

Elise watched as it make the corner and speed away, soon lost in the trees, the only evidence of its passing: a billowing dust cloud mingled with fading smoke.

I guess Lendar has some way to deal with all the dust on the Escalade. She settled into her seat, watching the road rolling toward them. Her former life lay dead on the ground outside a camping trailer in the Manzano Mountain foothills.

23

Estancia far behind, not a soul approached or followed. Heat pooled in puddles on the asphalt, illusions of water. The brown countryside seemed devoid of life. It reminded her of some post-apocalyptic movie scene: barren and dry, dotted with lonely, abandoned houses, landscaped with lifeless grasses and topped with dust blown sadness. The horizon stretched into the distance, hazy with dust and smoke. Storm clouds gathered in the southwest, lightning flashing. Change in the air.

Bruce eyed Lendar. "Back there you mentioned something about 'Minan'? What's Minan?"

"My planet. It's about 20 light years out there." Lendar pointed upward and signed. Somehow the sign made her think of space ships and long distances. "I'm a descendant of earthlings captured by aliens and transplanted there thousands of years ago."

Bruce guffawed. "Nuts!"

Lendar rapped the steering wheel with his knuckles. "Truth."

Bruce looked askance at Lendar. "You're originally from earth? I mean your ancestors are originally from earth?"

Lendar nodded. "Human, just like you."

Bruce's gaze shifted to the outside, his eyes moving back and forth tracking the white lines on the road. He frowned, then fixed Lendar with a penetrating gaze. "What's it like on Minan?"

"We're ruled by a planetary emperor who governs through regional kings, queens and governors and works alongside two bodies of planetary representatives, one house is elected, the other is appointed…"

Bruce waved his hand, "No, no, not what form of government do you have, though that's kind of weird you have an emperor and all that. I woulda thought advanced science and technology would sort of preclude that kind of ruler. But never mind. What I want to know is, what's it like on Minan compared to here? I mean lifestyle and culture and stuff like that."

Lendar nodded. "Take awhile to answer that question. How about I show you some holos instead."

"Holos? what's that?"

"Holographic movies." Lendar's lips curled in a faint smile, but his aquamarine eyes twinkled with humor.

Bruce scrunched his face while his head bobbed. "All-righty then."

Elise bit her lip, turning her attention to the roadside. Her brain fizzed like an electric motor on the fritz, all spark and no function. She blinked and sighed.

Music began playing, soothing sounds that eased her heart. Drowsy, she propped her head on her hand and closed her eyes. Her mind drifted toward sleep. White noise: Bruce pelted Lendar with questions; Lendar answered politely.

Just as she was about to give up consciousness, Max threw a half an apple section into her lap. "'Inished!"

Elise started, then took away the napkin with the remaining bits of food and folded it into a tidy package. A trash compartment opened under Bruce's seat and announced, "Insert refuse here."

One eyebrow cocked, Bruce eyed Max over his shoulder and chuckled. "Talking trash cans. Hilarious." In the next instant, he exclaimed. "Say, Lendar, you just drove over that road closed sign! What gives?!"

"Hologram. Embedded road unit."

"Cool. I could have a lot of fun with a gadget like that." Bruce nodded and rubbed his hands together.

The things that make men go woozy, Elise thought, shaking her head.

Max jabbered and ramped his car over the car seat arms.

Lendar pointed. "See that red "x" up there?"

Bruce's eyes narrowed, first at the road, then at Lendar. One corner of his mouth pulled up in a smirk. "Yeah, that's strange. Usually they mark roads with silver or white."

"'X' marks the spot." Lendar winked.

"O...k....a....y." Bruce laughed. In the next instant, he fell back, gape mouthed. They'd entered the jet's cargo bay. A Hummer-like vehicle covered with red, New Mexico dust was already parked in front of them. Several men stood around it wearing camo, fiddling with their equipment. A helmeted crewman in moss green stood by to secure the Escalade.

"'Tief," Max exclaimed and pointed.

Lendar grinned at the boy. "Yes, that's Retief. We'll see him later, Max, right now those men just want to be debriefed and get cleaned up."

Bruce said, "So those guys helped, eh? Coolness. You got your own SWAT team." He smirked. "Chameleon battle skin is awesome!"

Lendar smiled. He looked a little smug; delighted Bruce was enjoying himself.

Elise remembered the sign, 'I am pleased if you are pleased,' and the other one, what was it? The one that meant draw everyone into a big hug, or something like that.

Her eyes rounded and her shoulders straightened. A big hug, like family.

It was as if her head suddenly cleared. Family.

I know what I need to help me make up my mind.

Lord, if you want me to marry Lendar, make him Your son! Make him a Christian. If You did that, it would settle the whole thing. Her heart quickened. Oh, Lord, if Lendar became a Christian, then we'd really have a chance. Oh Lord, please make it so.

Unconsciously she clasped her hands together and lifted her eyes toward the Escalade's ceiling. Joy welled up from deep within to join that feeling of weightlessness that hadn't totally gone away despite her grief and exhaustion. Her face brightened, a gentle smile transforming her creased brow.

Lendar's reflection peered at her in the rear view mirror. After a moment, he looked back over his shoulder at her, one eyebrow raised in question.

Elise lowered her eyes and gazing at him through her lashes, suddenly shy.

Lendar's quizzical brow eased. He looked to Bruce.

Bruce thwacked the Escalade's dashboard and shouted. "Lendar, this is way cool!" He shot Elise a gleeful glance. "It finally clicked in my mind. Romulan cloaking device! It really does exist!"

Elise smiled. "Yep. Turns out you were right: aliens are for real."

Bruce loosed a loud, delighted guffaw.

Max laughed and pounded his car seat arms. "'Uce space alien."

Bruce replied. "Naw, not me buddy. At least, not yet." He winked.

Now, standing outside the Escalade, Lendar opened her door and took her hand as she stepped into the cargo bay. Reluctantly she gave up his fingers when he turned to greet Ty. Bruce climbed out and fetched Max.

No panic this time. At ease, even. Like she was returning home. Imagine that. Amazement dashed through her. Maybe I can get used to all this advanced technology. Maybe, with a smidgen of patience, it won't be that hard.

Ty bowed to Lendar, then took her hand and kissed it muttering a greeting in Minan. He listened as Bruce was introduced, then bowed to him. And finally, he welcomed Max with a tweak to his cheek and a teasing phrase. Max giggled in response. Though she didn't understand a word he'd said, Elise felt honored and cherished.

Bruce looked like he was about to jump out of his skin.

He mouthed at Elise, "More real aliens!" He pointed at Ty, his eyebrows bobbing ridiculously.

Leaving earth behind feels real good right now, she thought. Happier than she'd been in what seemed like ages, Elise followed Lendar and Ty through the door into the passenger compartment. Ty continued through another hatch. She caught a glimpse of the cockpit with its buttons, lights, monitors, levers and a view of New Mexico highway stretching toward the horizon. Lendar passed in front of her, drawing her attention to the seats.

There's the window where I lay in Lendar's arms.

She sat opposite Lendar and buckled Max at her side. Bruce parked beside the window for the prime view, eager to see whatever he could, hands fidgety on the armrests. Lendar took the seat next to him.

While he listened to Bruce, Lendar occasionally looked her direction, his mouth firm, his eyes full of speculation. Diligently staring out the window, she pretended she didn't notice. She clutched Max's hand. Oh, Lord, thank You for keeping us safe back there. Please transform Vince and Javier and Tony, if he'll let You.

Thank You.

Ty made an announcement, apparently of their take-off, for in the next moment, the land fell away. Bruce yammered about the ugly swatch of burned terrain and smoke, a brush fire separate from the forest fire Javier had tried to set. Brush trucks scrambled like beetles.

Soon that scene was behind them. Albuquerque shimmered in the distance, but New Mexico receded quickly. Within minutes they passed through earth's albumen.

Bruce gasped with delight. "This is so amazing! I'm floored. Simply floored. Flabbergasted." He chuckled happily, pounding the chair arms. "Good-bye Virgin Galatic, great knowing you. Not!" He chortled gleefully.

Max wriggled his hand free of Elise's grip and picked at the seat belt buckle.

"No honey," Elise said, pushing his fingers away from the clasp.

"We're cruising now, he may unbuckle for a short time," Lendar said.

She gazed at Lendar, that old longing overtaking her. What use is such longing? It's emptiness. Like empty calories. Like an addiction. She cocked her head. Funny how when your paradigm changes it affects how you think about everything. It would still be nice to kiss him, to be swept along in a gush of emotion, but that's not enough.

Lendar spoke to Bruce, his body angled toward the window, his hand making those fascinating signs. It was a beautiful hand, broad through the knuckles, well shaped. The black hairs edging up his arm.

She could detect no signs of the day's earlier fracas, no sweat stains, no smudges, except the hair on his head seemed a little more mussed than usual. Adorably mussed, free of his futile attempts to fix it. Deltoid muscles moved under his cotton shirt, the bicep an attractive bump as he pointed at something outside.

Watching him, she felt her pulse quicken and soothing warmth well up within her. It wasn't like the heat she'd experienced earlier. The sexual flare was altered, transmuted into something deeper and richer. Her eyes widened. Then it hit her. I admire him; I truly admire him. That's why he's so attractive. He's literally my hero! He's my knight in shining armor!

Moisture threatened to overflow her eyelids. Her heart thumped, straining to reach Lendar, to be near him, pressed against him, but more, to be wherever he went. Embraced. Enveloped. One.

Max twisted, struggling to be free. Elise released him and he clambered to the floor to toddle about the cabin examining everything within reach. She watched him enjoying himself, climbing in and out of seats and pecking at windows. Meanwhile, she allowed these new revelations to brew.

The two men discussed food and cooking. And Elise's mind wandered back to meals she'd shared with Lendar. Bruce spoke to her and she answered him. He went on at length about food preparations and cooking methods. But a moment later she couldn't remember what he'd said. Oh well, no matter.

All too soon the moon dominated her view. As before, it took her breath away. She stared, again wanting to memorize the sight. Maybe I can do a moonwalk! Wouldn't that be amazing! Actually see Neil Armstrong's footprints with my own eyes!

Bruce gawped out the window, goggle-eyed. "Wow."

Before she was ready, they rounded moon's shoulder and entered its shadow. The *Lalf* glittered in the darkness. Same as before. Beautiful. Amazing. A Fabergé egg.

Lendar left his seat to fetch Max. "Time to buckle up, Master Max. We're almost there." He sat down, Max in his lap. With evident pride, he said, "Ahead is my lord, Prince Anwic's ship, the *Lalf*." He placed Max on the open seat beside him and buckled him in.

Bruce queried. "How big?"

Lendar explained, the same figures he'd used when describing the *Lalf* to Elise, his hands adding illustrations.

Ty made an announcement. Lendar translated. "We're about to dock."

Bruce couldn't peel his eyes from the view.

Max jabbered happily.

"Yep, we're about to dock," Elise repeated.

24

Bruce took in everything with eager equanimity. Standing in the space jet docking bay, he enthusiastically greeted any crew who would stop to shake his hand. He repeated their names and bowed like a well-practiced courtier.

Wow, he's not freaking out at all, Elise concluded. He's like a kid in a candy store. Lendar, watched Bruce, occasionally glancing her direction with a pleased brow. Including her, as if she were a member of the household and should be as delighted as he was to see Bruce happy. Well, imagine that.

When Bruce seemed to have exhausted his available options, short of running through the docking bay like a kid at Christmas, Lendar gestured toward the control booth and led the way. Elise, with Max in her arms, followed. Reluctantly Bruce took up the rear. He hesitated in the control booth, gawking. Lendar didn't even look back to see if his entourage tagged along. He forged onward, making the turn into the long passageway that led to the tube entrance. Elise waited for Bruce at the threshold. One glance and she could keep tabs on Lendar who strode down the passageway and with another observe Bruce itching to query the operators or get his hands on the control booth's equipment.

"Come on, Bruce, Lendar's leaving us behind," Elise said.

He tore himself away and rounded the corner. He gawped, "Would you take a look at this mural! How long is it?"

"It's about a mile long, two miles if you consider how it's painted on both sides of the hall."

"Nice." He began trying doors. The only unlocked door opened into a spacious parlor decorated in autumn hues with couches and chairs that reminded Elise of furniture popular in the '60's.

When Bruce disappeared inside, Lendar retraced his steps and stood in the parlor doorway, arms folded across his chest. He looked like a man who wanted to point out that it was impolite for a person to go exploring in another man's house without permission.

Bruce was undaunted. He asked, "What's this room for? You got a kitchen in there, a bathroom and this living room. What do you do in here?"

Lendar rubbed his nose, his face easing back into its customary neutral friendliness. "We use this parlor for greeting guests or holding meetings." He pointed. "Through that door is a hall leading to the space jet docking bay."

Bruce nodded and tried to open it, but it was locked. He shrugged. "All righty then." He rubbed his hands together. "What's next?" He grinned sheepishly.

Lendar's smile was slow to start, but warmed as it curved into shape. "Shall we continue?"

"Yep." Walking beside Lendar, Bruce interrogated him about everything he saw, the mural, the keypads on the walls, the robot that meandered past them, everything. At last they reached the hall's end where Lendar began keying in the code to open the tube entrance.

"What'cha doing?" Bruce asked.

"I'm opening the entrance into the energy elevator."

Bruce bobbed his head. "Nice. What's an energy elevator?"

Lendar only had to explain the thing once. The hall's end opened. As before, the same sound of distant, rushing wind filled the space. And, as before, Elise felt her stomach drop into her hips. Dismayed, Elise observed Bruce walk right out as if he stepped from his own apartment into the Albuquerque sun.

Poised in the middle, Bruce shouted and danced.

Lendar left her side, striding with that confident, sexy walk of his, then turned to look back at her.

Elise gulped. The two men waited, watching her expectantly. "Ok," she muttered under her breath, talking to herself, "you've done this before. You can do it again." By force of will she placed one foot in front of the other, keeping her eyes on Lendar. Her body trembled and a thin sheen of sweat glistened on her brow. "Ok, I made it," she whispered when she stood close enough to touch Lendar's arm.

Max jabbered happily.

Lendar's hand went to her elbow, a look of delighted approval on his face. She thought he might kiss her right there and then, but of course that wasn't going to happen.

Elise grimaced, then smiled faintly. "Maybe I'll get used to this, like maybe the fiftieth time."

Lendar shook his head. "Won't take that long." He kissed her cheek. The spot where his lips met her skin felt cool and relaxed. When she closed her eyes, that feeling spread through her flesh into her bones.

Max wriggled, striving to fling himself free of her arms.

Elise opened her eyes.

Max pointed downward, toward the darkness below, wiggling his fingers. "'Ow'n. Want 'ow'n."

Her stomach flipped, but she set Max down anyway. She covered her mouth and swallowed. "Nope, we're both wrong. It'll be more like, maybe, the hundred-thousandth time."

Lendar's eyes glittered with soft humor; the look and smile for her alone.

She stared at that smile until her stomach eased.

Lendar spoke and they drifted downward. The walls, encrusted with snaking conduit, piping and hoses slipped by, motion detector lights flicking on as they went. Doors, some with small balconies, some with wide thresholds and others with no surface where a foot might gain purchase appeared periodically like knotholes in wood. She noted oval shaped hatches with wheels in their centers and lighted keypads. Operation lights glowed here and there like someone's misbegotten Christmas lights. Occasionally a bank of futuristic lockers ringed the tube.

First stop, the Minan version of a commercial kitchen complete with sous chef robots and strange gadgets all busy preparing the next meal. In the cafeteria, five or six men and women lounged in the dining area taking a break. They looked forlorn in the room large enough to seat a few hundred people.

Lendar explained, "Up to now we've used robot cooks exclusively. At present, this cafeteria only serves about one hundred fifty people when operating at peak, but we expect this number to begin increasing on a daily basis."

Bruce nodded. "So, you'll be wanting me to manage the cafeteria."

Lendar replied, "We're looking for a person to manage all food preparation in a number of venues, not just here."

Bruce cleared his throat. "I need a crash course in robot management."

"Not a problem. We have a holographic teaching program you will find useful. Meanwhile, I'll see that all food service robots are programmed to understand English, after that, you command and they will obey."

Apprehension laced Bruce's smile. "Well, fifty diners I can handle, a thousand, haven't done that before, not even with help."

Lendar's grin exuded confidence and assurance. "I believe you're equal to the task."

"Really?" Bruce looked like a lost boy for a moment, scanning his new territory. In the next instant, he gaped at Lendar. "You certainly have a high opinion of me."

"I believe you will rise to the challenge. That's why I selected you." Lendar shrugged. "Besides, you won't face that number immediately and you will have help. Robots have done the work up to now, producing eatable meals, you can gradually work into the job. Even if you only take on the dessert menu, that will be an improvement."

Bruce stared at Lendar, then coughed. "Great. Opportunity to succeed big time or go for a gigantic fail." He grunted, hung his head, then scanned the rooms again.

Lendar replied. "Success is your accomplishment, if you fail, the failure will be all mine."

Bruce looked askance at Lendar then said, "You're taking earth people back to your planet, aren't you."

Lendar nodded. "That is correct."

"Why? Some kind of genetic catastrophe back home? Like some sci fi cliché?"

Lendar sobered, though his eyes retained a glint of humor. "Precisely."

Shaking his head, Bruce chuckled.

Next, Lendar led them through an airlock and a moisture seal door into a huge hydroponics garden producing a dizzying array of colorful vegetables and fruits. He explained that the facility was just beginning to gear up to full production. It smelled of moisture and happy plant life.

After clambering through another airlock and moisture seal door, they wended their way down a spiral staircase and toured rooms set in ring around the tube. One room was lined with rows of small freezer and refrigerator drawers storing seeds and animal gametes. Another contained cryogenic freezers where muscle cells waited to be cloned. Another the meat production vats where robots tended passengers' future steaks, chops and roasts growing in nutrient rich baths. Another contained freshwater fishponds, simulated streams and sea tanks where all sorts of odd fish-things and aquatic plants waiting to be eaten thrived.

"You got any humans involved in this work?" Bruce asked.

"Normally, the *Lalf* only retains two deckhands, but for this trip we have fifteen."

"Only two?"

Lendar made a sign. "We have never carried passengers before, hence no need for such an extensive hydroponics garden or labor to tend to it."

Elise watched and listened, but her mind was already full. Most of their discussion bounced off her ears. Interesting. At the moment she didn't have any of the unpleasant physical symptoms of feeling overwhelmed and out of her element she'd suffered before. Odd you should feel that way, she told herself. Maybe it's because you're better at blocking it out. Ugh.

Now in a different section Lendar continued his commentary. "Here we have quality control. These foodstuffs are ready to be transported to the cafeteria kitchen or delivered to persons who do their own cooking. Would you like to taste our produce?" Lendar asked.

"Yes, sir, I believe I would." Bruce rubbed his hands together, then went to the sink where he washed up.

A robot guide arrived to take over Bruce's tour.

Lendar bowed. "Bruce, this robot will take over for a time while I tend to Elise. Please to understand that it is quite capable of keeping you from doing wrong."

Bruce chortled. "That's rich and I love it. Well, you two have a nice time."

Elise, Max and Lendar left him sampling Minan fruits and vegetables and drifted down to the artificer's lab.

The distant soughing continued as background music to engines' thrumming that grew louder as they dropped.

"We needn't bother the artificer to make you a couple of outfits," Lendar said as he palmed the lock and began punching in numbers. The carbon steel, double doors where they stood were wide with thick steel molding and a substantial, industrial looking balcony.

Grateful they were alone, she looped her arm through his. "Really? I thought you'd just borrow some from one of the women on board. You're going to make me some clothes?" Elise smiled. "I haven't had any new clothes in ages." The doors opened.

Straight ahead, door one, next to a frosted window,

seemed to lead to an office. Door two, a larger door, between a pair of huge windows, opened into a gigantic shop filled with machinery of all sizes, some in shapes vaguely familiar, others not. Door 3, on her right and door 4 on her left seemed insignificant in comparison.

Lendar chose the far left door. "Through here," he said, keying in a numerical code. In any other setting she would have called the room large. But compared to the space jet docking bay or the shop she'd seen through the windows a moment before it was only moderate in size. He pointed toward a raised platform in the center of the room ringed by computerized machines, some obviously designed for sewing. "If you'd please stand just there."

"Wow. So this is where you make your clothes. How long from start to finish?"

Lendar paused to consider. "Eh, for a simple garment, about ten minutes for something more elaborate, hours. Depends on the garment. What did you have in mind?"

Elise's face wrinkled with amusement. "Well, since I'm in a hurry, something simple."

"Very well. Allow me to hold Max," he pointed at the platform again and repeated himself. "If you would stand there we may begin."

She placed Max in his arms and walked to the platform. Lendar pressed a few buttons and every machine in the room came to life buzzing, humming, clacking and flashing. Six robo eyes, exiting from below the platform, zipped into position around her.

Lendar stepped her direction with Max perched on his hip. "Ok, now Elise. Put on these glasses. They'll allow you to see each available option, if you like something look at it and use your eyes to drag it to your avatar on the screen and say "ok"."

"All right." Elise took the glasses from Lendar's hand. They were green tortoise shell frames with silvery lenses laced with strange striations. The glasses adjusted automatically to her face and flickered to life, a strange blue light superimposed over her view of the room.

Yellow, pinpoint beams emerged from the robo eyes, circling around her, as if drawing a grid. When they ceased, a 3-D image of Elise Ramos appeared before her eyes. Wow, my figure is actually pretty nice, she thought with surprised satisfaction.

Lendar worked the keyboard. Shirt and pant options appeared beside her avatar.

She soon realized that when she looked at something for a certain period of time it was the same as clicking on it with a mouse and by moving her eyes, she could drag the thing over to her image and place it. The shirt bodice, the type of collar she wanted, the type of sleeves…choices, choices, choices each saved to her image.

"This is so cool!" Elise breathed. She loved selecting the qualities she'd always longed for in a shirt and pants ensemble but had never seen in exactly that combination or could afford before. "Ok, finished."

Lendar said, "Need to choose fabrics."

"Oh. I don't know how to do that."

"I suppose you missed it, it was one of the first choices you were given."

"Oh, in that case, cotton. I want cotton. Cotton for the shirt and denim for the pants."

"Very well, I can enter that information here." Lendar adjusted Max's position on his hip and typed in the data with one hand. "A dress would be nice, don't you think?"

Elise licked her lips. "Yes, that would be nice." Dress options appeared on the screen and the procedure repeated. The weird cuneiform lettering was present, but with Lendar operating the keyboard, understanding them was irrelevant.

At last, Lendar came to her and stopped beside the platform.

Max held his I-phone, pecking at the screen. He lifted it up for Elise to see. "Rook mama, elefink."

Elise took the I-phone and studied his electronic painting. The blue blob he'd created had a pointy, snout-like protrusion and stubby legs. "That's pretty good, Max," she said. "I like your color choices."

Max smiled. "Make it red." He dragged his finger over the screen.

Round-eyed, Elise swallowed. Max was already adapting to Lendar's technology.

Lendar said, "Elise, we're finished. Please let me have the glasses and I'll put them away." He took the frames and helped her to the floor. The touch of his hand brought tingling up her arm.

Elise smiled. "If a person wanted to design clothes from scratch, or that is to say, from sketches, could she?"

"Oh, yes."

Elise followed Lendar to the screen where he'd been directing her selections. A finger skimmed over the monitor and he brought up a new menu and work pad. "Here we have the designer program, I can import your figure from the seamstress menu and…there." He pointed at her image. "You have the same avatar we used with the glasses."

He touched another key. "Here you have the drawing tools. You may use the light pen or draw with your finger, employ virtual implements in the menu bar or these." He withdrew an actual pen and brush from a drawer. "This pen and brush function just like ordinary pens and brushes. You treat the screen as both your palette and your canvas. Here are your colors, your palette for mixing."

At the top of the screen he dragged the position bar to the right and blocks of colors and a white area appeared. He gnawed his lip while he combined two hues. "And you paint them like this." He toggled the bar back to its original position and daubed with the brush at her image, creating an awkward smock. "I'm not any good at it, but I'm sure you could make something quite lovely." He made an intriguing sign. "We can place your avatar on a different screen or reduce the size of the images and options here so they all fit in one screen."

Elise quipped, "It'd probably be easier if you didn't have Max parked on your hip."

He smiled. Turning back to the computer he said, "You have a menu here with the fabric selections currently available, er, that is already manufactured. But you can also use this," he minimized the program and opened a different one. "Starting from, er, what do you say, scratch, with fabric manufacture." He grinned, seemingly pleased to remember a slang term. "Import your own paintings, drawings or sketches and create your own fabric designs."

He made another sign, his face seemed to say, 'I hope you really like it. Do you like it?' Seeing she was intrigued, a satisfied expression took hold. He continued. "And, if you prefer," he touched a button and a three-dimensional Elise appeared over the monitor, "you can use this program to create garments in three dimensions."

Elise bit her lip. Softly she murmured, "This is amazing!" With this machine she could make all sorts of way-cool garments. Possibilities instantly began popping into her mind's eye and her heart settled into a joyful beat.

Meanwhile, the machines hummed adjusting their settings, aligning parts, then went to work, buzzing and clattering. Within minutes a pair of jeans, then a shirt appeared in a tray near the door.

"It's like magic!" Elise exclaimed, dancing over to inspect the garments.

"I'll just save this information for future reference." Lendar muttered.

Elise picked up the clothing and fingered it. She glanced his direction. "Lendar, these machines do great work!"

"There's a dressing room just there," Lendar pointed. He grinned, again clearly pleased. He wrapped both arms around Max whose lower lip stuck out in concentration, his stubby fingers pecking and rubbing across the surface of

Lendar's I-phone.

"Ok." Elise crossed to the door he'd indicated and entered a room smelling of citrus and fresh with cool air. The dressing room contained everything she needed: a shower, a toilet and a tote bag for her sweaty, smoky garments. She stuffed her diaper bag into the tote, along with her old clothes and took advantage of the facilities, showering and changing into her new duds in record time of twenty minutes.

Of course, the clothes fit better than anything she'd ever owned. The full-length mirror showed a relaxed, attractive young lady every bit as well attired as Doreen Macintosh had been back at the restaurant. Except her hair was a little mussy. Elise stuck out her tongue at the figure in the mirror.

Man, Doreen Macintosh seems ages ago, Elise reflected. Ancient history! Exuding happiness, she left the dressing room, the tote on her arm.

Max now sat in the operator's chair, still intent on the I-phone.

Lendar stood at the monitor working. When he caught sight of her, he exclaimed, "Beautiful!" His voice sounded husky. His hand lifted, as if he intended to pull her into his embrace.

Elise blushed, clutching the tote, she muttered, "Thanks."

Deliberately and with effort, Lendar turned away and went to the finished garment tray. "Your dress." He held it by the shoulders.

"Oh, it's lovely," Elise breathed.

Wait, I just realized! It's similar to the one in the window at Buffalo Exchange, but brand new and a way better color! She chuckled. I wasn't even thinking about that. Funny: you were certain you'd never own anything like this.

She clasped the dress to her body and twisted from side to side imagining the fabric swishing around her legs. Beaming, she looked at Lendar. "Does this gizmo make shoes too?"

Lendar tapped his forehead. "I didn't think of shoes. Naturally, you need shoes to go with the dress."

"How about leather sandals in magenta with 3 inch heels and, like, six, 1/8th inch wide straps over the feet and one around the back of the heel."

"Coming right up," Lendar said. "Buckle or elasticized; synthetic leather or authentic cow hide, maybe goat hide?"

"Hhmn, synthetic." Elise picked up Max and joined Lendar at the monitor where she could watch how he used the computer to design the shoes and set the robots to work making them. "Make the straps more evenly spaced."

"Yes, ma'am."

Elise punched him in the arm.

Lendar grinned. "These will take longer. How about I have them delivered to you once they're finished, Lady Elise?"

Lady Elise! Oh my goodness. "You're a brat," Elise muttered, her breath quickly going ragged. His face was so close, the plains of his cheeks topped by the hill of his cheekbone upon which rested the lovely aquamarine eyes she adored.

Elise gasped for air. That face. What if I could never see that face again? Have you considered that, Miss Priss? I don't think I could bear it! Sweat sheen burst on her forehead and she almost blurted, "I love you." Her eyes searched his while she chewed her lip, the words pressing for release. At last she blurted, "Wow. Cool. Robot delivery. Sweet."

Her heart thundered in protest, pounding until her ears roared. You're an idiot. A full-blown, nut-case idiot! What a loser!

Lendar's watch sounded a soft alarm. "We'd better collect Bruce. We're expected elsewhere."

"Ok." Elise sighed.

With Bruce, they skimmed past Lendar's balcony

without comment. Elise stared at it, a twinge of nostalgia washing over her. *We're not stopping at his place. This can't be good.*

Bruce commented on the scent that permeated the tube and asked questions about the conduits, hoses and keypads hugging the walls. He wanted to know everything, but Elise could hardly hear a word, her brain buzzed with fresh anxiety. *Why can't there be some medium ground between total freak-out and boredom?*

After answering many of his questions, Lendar laughed and told Bruce, "Enough for one day; save something for later."

Bruce threw back his head and laughed.

Elise blinked, chewed her lip and smiled.

25

Apparently, they arrived because they stopped. Five elaborate balconies (compared to the unassuming thresholds she'd seen below), each completely different from the others, ringed the spot where they stood. On an invisible floor. A gravitational field. Yeah, I guess I've sort of gotten used to that, haven't I. Elise looked up. The orange glow at the top of the tube seemed much closer here, only 3 to five stories away.

"This is the main crew quarters deck," Lendar explained. "My lord, Prince Anwic and his wife hold court there," he gestured, pointing first at one and then at each balcony in turn. "Our engineer lives there, our navigator there, our security master and our captain general, Empress Jaizem, here." He rotated until he'd made full circle, each time he named an entrance he added a unique sign.

Elise's brow furrowed. This is bad, very bad. I'm not ready for this! "Could I just go back down to your place, Lendar, and stay there until you two are finished?"

Bruce gave her a withering look.

"Ok, well, never mind," Elise muttered, feeling her stomach flop like a fish out of water. "This is the moment of your triumph, I guess it would be kind of jerky of me to duck out on you, wouldn't it."

Bruce didn't reply.

Lendar strode toward Empress Jaizem's balcony: a stainless steel construction, urban and minimalist in style, with a glass floor. He rang the bell at an ultra-modern, brushed metal door surrounded by green-tinted, glass blocks.

How funny, ringing a bell in a place like this, Elise thought, following Bruce, not even noticing she had forgotten to feel terrified when walking on an invisible gravity field.

"At least I've already met Empress Jaizem." Elise mumbled.

Bruce rewarded her with a slight smile. "Lucky you."

Elise grunted. "Yeah, well, you've been sort of preparing for this aliens and space stuff, reading all the UFO junk. I've tried to remain in denial."

Bruce's smiled edged up in one corner more than in the other. "There is that, but at the moment, I have a lot riding on a meal."

A human butler opened the door and bowed. "Empress Jaizem is not in at the moment," he said in perfect, British English.

"You just learn that? That accent?" Elise asked. Though he behaved like a stereotypical, aged butler anybody might read about or see in a movie, he was young, probably in his mid-twenties, with blonde hair, blue eyes and an athlete's physique.

"Ma'am, I am from London, planet earth. I've been with Empress Jaizem for the past nine months. I trained at the International Butler Academy in Valkenburg, completing my studies with top honors." He stared down his nose at her.

Elise teased, "Oh, well, you might be all that, but I bet they didn't have a course in robot management."

"Quite." He frowned and bowed. "Sirs, ma'am, if you will follow me. I've been instructed to guide you to the kitchen."

Elise blushed. Well, I guess that puts me in my place.

"Excuse me, I will return in a moment," Lendar said. He bowed and crossed the limestone foyer, disappearing down a dark hallway to the right. Wistfully, Elise watched him go, admiring his purposeful, masculine stride.

The foyer where they stood was domed, circular and gave the impression of an outdoor pavilion with its limestone columns and large amphoras spilling with flowers between the columns. Their fragrance filled the refreshingly cool apartment.

Empress Jaizem's floor plan seemed remarkably similar to Lendar's, except the dining room was situated on the opposite side, in the far right corner, caddy cornered from the entry pavilion. Her dining room was at once ultra-modern and classic with its glass and steel table, Georgian-style, comfy looking chairs and mercury vases all basking in neon blue light emanating from diodes embedded in the glass wall. Outside, tree branches, made surreal by the blue light, waved in a gentle breeze.

In the living area, jewel-toned fabrics in upholstery, curtain and pillow screamed luxury and good taste. Everywhere her eyes looked she saw a strange conglomeration of styles. Fabulous art works glowed, each under it's own spotlight. However, unlike Lendar's place, the apartment was not bright, but romantically dim, deep with color, hinting mysteries and inviting exploration.

The butler led Bruce and Elise to the left through an automatic, translucent door framed in brushed steel into a well-lit, Capri-blue kitchen outfitted with stainless steel and chrome and accented in white. The butler bowed and strode out.

"This apartment is gorgeous!" Elise exclaimed.

"Yep," Bruce replied abstractedly. He seemed anxious all of a sudden.

She studied his expression. "What are we doing, Bruce?"

A faint layer of humor overlaid his worried expression. "I knew you weren't listening on the way over."

Elise shook her head. "What are you talking about?"

Bruce leaned her direction, repeating the words as if she were incredibly dense. "I'm talking about the whole, long, drawn-out explanation of what's going on from this point forward while we were traveling here in the space jet."

"Oh." Elise pressed her fingers to her lips, her eyes crinkling with apology. "Ah, yeah. I guess I was kinda distracted. I hardly remember anything you guys were saying."

Bruce's smile was wan. He folded his arms across his

chest. His voice came out flat. "You're my sous chef today, Elise. You agreed to do this."

"I did?" She gulped.

"Yep. Don't you remember at all?" Bruce stared, incredulous.

"No, I don't remember." She shook her head. "Bruce! Cut me some slack! The past, er, week, month, has been crazy!" Her eyes widened. "Has it only been a week?"

He frowned. "I guess you have a right to be kind of distracted."

Elise gulped and winced. "How can time be so messed up?"

Bruce replied, "I read somewhere that your brain makes time feel slower when its processing a lot of stuff."

"It's so true!" Elise paced. "I've been asking God to make it clear what I should do, instead He keeps giving me more choices! I'd begun to think God was, like, maybe even sort of indifferent to me, like yeah, He loves me, but from a safe distance. And now, wham! I meet Lendar and an art agent wants to represent me to a New York gallery and well," Elise blushed, then whispered, "Lendar asked me to marry him!"

Bruce shook his head. "You can't be serious?"

"What do you mean?"

"You can't seriously think that being represented in a New York gallery compares with the chance to live in outer space?" He spluttered his lips and frowned. "Besides, with friends like these--I mean, Elise, does your successful art career have to happen on earth? Seriously? I mean, duh! Earth is such a small market."

Elise choked on a laugh. Who, but Bruce, would think that the entire planet earth is a small market? "Er, when you put it that way…" She blushed. "I'm sorry, but I don't think I've been operating on all cylinders today. Maybe I've thrown a rod." She gave him a sidelong glance.

Bruce held up his hands. "Look, you're right. You've

been under a lot more pressure than usual. You saw a man shot to death today! Not a shock if you're a little discombobulated."

Elise rubbed her forehead. "You know how you were worried if Lendar was a liar? You were right, he wasn't being entirely truthful with me, but it's also true that I would have told him to get lost if he'd explained straight up he lives here on this space ship! I would have said, "You're a nutcase," and avoided him like the plague." She chuckled. "It's funny though, he really has a place in Andorra."

Bruce pointed at her. "Wait, you went to Andorra?"

Elise shrugged. "Well, it wasn't much of a visit. Didn't see anything except his guest house and some forest."

"He has a guest house in Andorra." Bruce chortled. He paused to look away, then stared at her. "I still don't get why you're confused about what God wants you to do."

Elise frowned. "Bruce, shut up and listen. I'm trying to tell you."

He held up his hands in surrender. "Yes ma'am."

Elise's frown was mediated in the next instant by a faint smile. "The point is, if Lendar had been a real liar, then I'd have a clearer idea of what God wants me to do. I could just say, "Well, that's obvious: marrying Lendar is a bad choice." Her body angled in Bruce's direction in appeal.

"But Bruce, isn't it like totally awesome. It's a dream come true for me: an agent wants to represent me in New York! He took my final with him when he visited my painting prof. This is exactly what I've been wanting my whole life."

"Wait, did you say he took your painting?"

"Yeah."

"Don't you think that's kind of rude and unprofessional? Like taking advantage of you?"

"Oh." Elise's stomach twisted into a knot.

"He's all the way in New York and you're in New Mexico it will be real hard for you to get it back from him, like, if you don't approve of the contract or you find out he's more than just rude." Bruce paused and scratched his head. "He's manipulating you, taking advantage of the fact that you're a naïve college student with big dreams and not much experience. That painting, in his possession, becomes a bargaining piece to control you, like a carrot to lead you around. At the worst, he could end up effectively stealing it! I hate to rain on your parade and all that, but do you really want to be represented by a jerk like him? Even in New York?"

"Oh." Elise felt deflated and strangely frightened. What if the man kept the picture and no matter how much complaining she did he never gave it back? What if he denied it was even her painting? Her skin went clammy. "Oh, ugh." Her eyes felt hot and wet. She looked at the floor and mumbled, "God hasn't been giving me more choices. He's been clarifying everything and I've been blind." Bruce is here, excited about this great opportunity. Lendar's been so kind and heroic.

Bruce kept on talking, "Look, I have loads of sympathy for you and I wish I could just go on endlessly about this. I get that you've felt confused and you're grieving and all that, but can you put all that trauma on the back burner for a couple of hours, please? Elise, this space ship is real. Empress Jaizem is real. And they really want me to cook for them tonight! I want the job. Can you help me?"

She raised her eyes. "Oh Bruce! I'm such a twit."

Bruce's smile was flavored with chagrin. "Elise, you've never been a twit, not ever. You don't know how to be a twit. Look, I'm sorry it has to be this way, but I can't bring the man back to life or undo any of it. Right now I gotta fix a bunch of food! I need those cylinders in your brain to start firing right now!" He snapped his fingers. "I need a sous chef!"

Max yanked her hair.

Wincing, Elise tugged the strands free, kissed his cheek. "Max, honey, don't do that or I'll spank you."

Max tangled his hand in her hair and yanked again.

Then he slobbered on her ear.

"Oh honey!" Exasperated, Elise set him on the floor, swatted his bottom and snapped, "Max that hurt."

Max stared up at her, his eyes moist.

"I know you're sorry now, but don't pull Mommy's hair!" Elise wagged a finger at him.

Max plopped to a sitting position and folded his arms over his chest.

Elise kneeled beside him, stroking his head. "Sweetie, it's been a rough day, but we can't stop now." She kissed him. "Let me get you something to play with in a minute after I finish talking to Bruce."

Max looked to Bruce, his bottom lip protruding. His expression seemed to say, 'Well, finish already.'

Elise stood, then asked, "Ok, Bruce, what are we doing?"

"We're fixing a meal for Empress Jaizem, her son, his wife, the wife's brother and a couple of other folks."

Elise swallowed. "Ok, but I stay in the kitchen. I'm not up to meeting anybody new right now." She waved a flat hand through the air slicing it. "I'd like nothing strange or terrifying happening for a few hours, please." Her smile twisted.

Bruce nodded, then pointed at her. "Gotcha. Good news is, Lendar's serving, neither of us has to worry about all the protocol and such that goes along with that! Thank God." He formed a brief prayer pose with his hands. "We just have to fix some tasty victuals! Lendar said that the butler has furlough back to London starting the moment we walked into this apartment."

"He ditched us? Mr. Graduate from Valkenburg?" Bruce nodded.

Elise snorted. "Figures."

"No, no, it's ok. If you are able to help me, I'd rather not have that haughty dude around anyway." Bruce grinned. "Everything I requested is supposed to be in this kitchen, somewhere." He opened the refrigerator, then glanced at his watch. "We had two hours from the time we walked in until the guests arrive."

"Oh. I'm sorry Bruce. I've wasted precious time." Elise grimaced.

Bruce's lip curled up more in one corner than the other, "No kidding." He glanced at his phone and added, "To be precise we have one hour and 53 minutes, give or take a minute or two. But we'll be fine if we don't do any more dawdling!"

"Dawdling! So that's what you call it when your friend is having a melt-down!" Elise parked a fist on her hip and pouted.

"You know I didn't mean it that way," Bruce protested.

"Eh, yeah, I do." Elise smiled, then crouched on the floor again next to her son. "I don't want to go out there looking for a bathroom. I guess I have to change Max here. I gotta do that and get him busy first or this whole project is a fail." She fished the changing pad from her diaper bag inside the tote and spread it on the immaculate floor, placed a new diaper on him, washed her hands then found some wooden bowls and a spoon for Max to play with.

Meanwhile, Bruce had his head in the refrigerator. Periodically he came up with containers of vegetables and set them on the cabinet. "Ok, we're gonna make a salad." He placed some grocery store bags of salad greens on the counter. "Here's the bell peppers, they need chunked. Onion needs chunked. Some super thin slices of the red onion for the salad."

Elise found a cutting board and knife. "First the salad."

"Ok, we're going to add dried cranberries and goat cheese to these assorted salad greens." He scooted the food closer to Elise, then pulled a pot from the cabinet, placed it on the stove and spent a few minutes figuring out how to operate it.

Max pounded the bowls with the spoons. "Boom,

boom, boom," he said. For a while, he generated most of the sound heard in the kitchen, his thumping punctuated by Elise's thwacking chops with the knife against the cutting board. Bruce trimmed and cubed chicken breasts, threw the pieces in the pot with a dollop of olive oil. While the chicken cooked, he mixed the salad dressing in a cruet.

The three pursued their activities with little talk. From time to time Elise replaced Max's kitchen playthings with new ones to keep him interested.

After a while, Bruce interrupted their companionable silence. "You know, Elise, the other day when those women showed up with that casserole?"

"Yeah." Elise bit her lip while she lined up strips of bell pepper, then glanced at him.

He grinned. "Well, they stood there yammering like I was a brick instead of a human with ears. They had to be pretty arrogant to think I couldn't understand what they were saying. Maybe they didn't care." He shrugged. "Anyway. They were going on about you, talking about how many Sundays you missed service and how shameful it was you were divorced and how sad it was your son didn't have a father, blah, blah, blah. And I was thinking, 'Wow, these women call themselves Christian!'

"Of course, you didn't answer the door so they stood there trying to decide what to do next."

Bruce used a comical, old hag's voice. "'We have this casserole and I don't want to take it home. And, well, I don't want to come back later, Rob and I have a Canasta party starting in a couple of hours.' The other one said, 'Well, I don't want to come back either, my grandson has a little league play-off game tonight.'

"Then they both looked at me.

"By this time I was mad. I wanted to bite off their heads, the snotty old bags. I mean, where do they get off judging you?"

Elise looked up from her work. "I don't know Bruce.

Everybody who believes in Jesus takes two steps forward and one step back, and sometimes we just fall down."

"Ok, I understand." He nodded. "The point is, it was in that moment I realized something that had totally escaped me before. You've never shoved your Christianity down my throat. You've never bossed me around or judged me, but it's been very clear from the day I met you: you're a Christian. It was abundantly clear that time when you refused to go to bed with me. Remember that? It was a long time ago." His face burned red, but he didn't look away. "I admit, I was out of line. I was drunk, but I was so hot for you I could hardly think straight." He winced.

Bruce shrugged. "Well, that's all old news, the point is: you have done your best to be a Christian and those old bags forced me to finally see it. Criticizing you like that, made me want to pinch off their bony heads and I realized what you do every day. Starting from the moment you met me, continuing right through the moment you turned me down and up until now. You've never treated me like I was a jerk no matter how much I deserved it. And I know I deserved it.

"The big clincher was that time my Dad had a heart attack. You showed up at UNM hospital with a sandwich and sat with me in the waiting room." Bruce shook his head as if he were still dumbfounded by her deeds.

"At first I resented you. I told myself you were a hypocrite, just like all the other Christians in the world. After all, it wasn't like you were a virgin or anything." Bruce's eyes dropped, ostensibly to focus on the food he was preparing. When he looked back, the sorrow and regret peeked through resolve. "I thought I'd just avoid you, but then you brought me the sandwich and waited until we knew Dad was going to be fine.

"I couldn't forget how kind you were and it nagged at me.

"After that I found myself wanting to live up to your expectations; I wanted to deserve your kindness. So I started looking for ways to help you. That's when I discovered what a selfish prick I was ignoring how Gabriel treated you. That's why I started hanging around when he came over."

Bruce squinted at her; his eyes seemed watery. "I hope my pathetic efforts to protect you from Gabriel have helped a little. But, Elise, you love as best you can. From what I gather, that's what a Christian is supposed to do."

Elise's smile was tight, but full of joy. Her eyes welled with drops of moisture. "Oh Bruce..."

He adjusted the setting on the stove, stirred the browning chicken and checked the sauce. "Anyway, those two old bags turned to me and said, 'Would you give this to Elise for us please.' I said, 'Sure, I'll give it to her.' They said, 'Thank you,' and walked away. And while they were walking away I said, 'You know what, Jesus, those women may or may not know You, but Elise does. She's not perfect, but I've always heard You are. I'm kinda floundering around here spinning my wheels. People say You take care of crumbs like me, so if You're real and You can actually hear me, maybe I'll give you my heart.'

"Elise, you showed up pretty soon after that. And when you told me to keep the casserole, it just confirmed everything for me.

"I knew what you had in your refrigerator: practically nothing. You could have kept the casserole for yourself. Other people would have kept it. Other people hang onto things real and tangible, like food when the refrigerator is empty. But you knew I was broke and starting to get real hungry and you gave me your food." Bruce shrugged.

"And I thought, 'You know what, Bruce, she's not living in a mansion or anything, but she never goes hungry or lacks something to wear. She's not worried about what she's going to eat. And you're freaking out all the time with worry. You're a walking anxiety attack!' So, I said to myself, 'Bruce, quit fooling around, just accept Jesus as your Savior. You've heard people say it's what a person's supposed to do, just do it.' So I did. And when I did, I felt this awesome, amazing change. It was like I turned weightless or something. Like Jesus cleaned my guts, my heart, even my brain." He looked at Elise, his face glowing. "And I knew from that moment on, things were going to be ok."

He waved his arms dramatically, like a Greek dancer. "Would you just look around here? Just look! Look what He's done Elise! And so soon!

"I hate to admit it, but at first I was jealous of Mr. Lendar Marl. I thought, the man's a liar and if Elise falls for him, there's no justice--not even in God." He paused. "But, I was wrong about the guy. He's perfect for you, Elise and he's proved he'll do his best to take good care of you. He'd go to the ends of the universe for you.

"If you'd chosen me for your man, we wouldn't be here. So, I guess I'd better just get over this whole idea that I know better than God how anything should pan out." Bruce chuckled softly. "There's someone out there, maybe on a completely different planet, who's the perfect girl for me.

"So, news flash, I finally discovered: God is good, just trust Him." He winked at her, then turned to face the stove, humming tunelessly while he stirred.

Elise dried her cheeks with a towel. Bruce is so wrong. Until today, I've only thought of myself, what I want. How Bruce could help me. Aloud she murmured, "I'm glad for you, Bruce. So glad. Praise God." She dropped her eyes to the bell pepper strips, oblivious to the drops splattering on the wood.

I'm a selfish, whining ninny. How boring and stupid is that!?

Elise looked up in time to see the grin Bruce threw her way before returning his attention to his cooking.

Lendar breezed into the kitchen. "How may I help?"

Max toddled toward him, his hands in the air. "'Endar."

"Max." He lifted Max and hugged him. "How's the cooking business, Master Max?"

"Burning." Max pointed at the stove where Bruce deglazed a pan.

Lendar chuckled. "Looks tasty to me. You know, Master Max, I think you're going to like it." He turned his attention to Bruce. "Bruce, robots have set the table. However, I should check their work. Be back in a moment." He exited with Max in his arms.

Bruce suddenly looked overwhelmed. "Elise. Ah. They'll be here any minute."

Elise bit her lip, then smiled. "Bruce, the Lord is with you. If you ask Him, He'll help you."

Bruce stared, his pupils dilated. "Yeah, good point. Well, I'm new to this whole Christian life thing. So, yeah, I'll ask Him." He bowed his head.

Elise sighed. His simple faith is so pure, he's certain to receive help, no doubt to intrude and muck things up. Lord, thank You. Somehow You actually worked through me even when I was acting like a ninny.

Lendar returned and set Max on the floor. He handed Max a hover toy similar to the ones that had so thoroughly captured his attention during their previous visit.

Elise watched and thought, Ok, maybe Max will be good for a few more minutes. She set to work helping Bruce plate the salad.

Sometime between when he'd left them at the foyer and now, Lendar had changed into a black suit with narrow lapels, moss green piping and a white cravat. A small green emerald flashed in the center of the cravat.

Elise pointed. "Is that a real emerald? And what's the deal with all the green? Ty wears it, other crew members wear it. What gives?"

"Yes, this is an emerald. Moss green and black are my lord, Prince Anwic's, off-world colors. The emerald is his off-world gem."

"Oh. You mean, away from Minan?"

"Yes, that is correct."

"And you mean, like, heraldic colors?"

"Precisely."

Oh, I'd almost forgotten about the royalty thing, Elise thought, her head suddenly pained. Ugh. Just when I imagined I could handle all this. She wiped her forehead with the back of her hand. "Well, as long as I don't have to meet any of them today."

"You won't have to," Lendar said, his voice kindly.

Elise smiled. "By the way, thanks for rescuing me." She blushed.

Lendar's face turned sober and he bowed. "My lady."

My lady. Wow. Elise's heart leapt into her throat and she coughed. Patting her chest she muttered, "Oh my." Look at him! He's gallant, like a knight. Wait, he is a knight or baronet. Yeah, baronet. Oh my goodness. Elise, just don't think about it!

A musical tone caught Lendar's attention. He glanced at his watch. "Empress Jaizem and her party have arrived. Bruce, have you selected a wine?"

Bruce's face turned brilliant red. "Oh…crap…no…ah…"

Lendar bowed. "I will select a suitable vintage. Excuse me." He disappeared into a darkened hallway on the far side of the kitchen and returned with a bottle. "This one will do." He placed bottle and glasses on a tray. "While you finish preparing the plates, I'll serve the wine." He whisked through the door.

Minutes later he returned and took the salad out.

"I've been grazing the whole time and I'm not hungry, but Elise, you'd better eat some of this salad."

"Ok." She leaned against the counter and grabbed a plate. "Bruce, this is really good! This dressing is amazing!"

Bruce grinned.

"Do you mind if I feed Max some of the main course? He's not into salads yet."

"That's fine. I made plenty." He winced.

"Everything's going to be fine! They're going to love every bite!" Elise patted his hand, then crouched on the floor to feed Max.

After that she tried to stay busy, either helping Bruce or keeping Max entertained, but that funny, fizzy brain sensation had returned. I'm so nervous. Oh, Lord, be with me, she begged. Please keep me from screwing this up. Please help Bruce succeed. Oh Lord, I should have prayed that awhile ago, but I know You hear me and You can still help him.

Lendar came in with dirty dishes and left with a tray of loaded plates. Elise played with Max while Bruce added the finishing touches to the dessert.

This time when Lendar returned, he said, "Bruce, Empress Jaizem and her son would like to speak with you before the dessert course is served."

Bruce cast her an anxious glance.

Elise reassured him. "The Lord is with you. You'll be fine, Bruce."

His answering grin seemed hesitant, but he strode out, following Lendar. Moments after Bruce had exited the kitchen, Elise realized Max was gone.

Suddenly sweaty, she rushed down the darkened hallway leading to the wine storage. He wasn't there. He wasn't hiding in the pantry or in the cabinets or under the island. That left only one place to look: the main living quarters.

"Oh Lord, cover me." Elise took several deep breaths, jacked up her nerves and passed through the automatic door. She gasped.

26

Three of the guests were clearly not human. Two were violet eyed, nut-brown, and barrel-chested, with huge heads. One of them wore bangle bracelets and a caftan and the other wore the off-world black and green. The third was a dark-blonde, pale-skinned guy with a small face in an over-large head. He also wore the black and green, but his costume included a sash covered in medals.

Two different types of aliens!? Heads twice the size of Empress Jaizem's?

Somainai. They're Somainai.

Elise swallowed.

Somainai. Right there, staring at me.

Do they have forked tongues? Hidden claws? Weird teeth? Do they cut people up and do experiments on them?

Lord, where's Max?

Elise felt herself hyperventilating.

Where's Max?

If you don't breathe you're going to end up on the floor!

Aliens. Standing right over there! I thought they were all on the other ship.

Breathe, girl, breathe! She struggled to obey her own instructions, but her knees threatened to buckle anyway.

Lendar sprinted toward her. The others stopped and stared.

The room spun, Elise's ears roared and her stomach churned.

Lendar's hand on her elbow stopped her fall.

She blurted, "Erp, I've lost Max."

Lendar's voice seemed to come from some place far away.

She squinted at him. What is he saying?

"Elise, allow me to help you."

Lendar led her back to the kitchen, snatched a chair from against the wall, set her on it then fetched a cold washcloth for her forehead. He pressed the cloth against her skin and placed her hand over it. "I'll find Max. You stay here."

As soon as he left, Elise blacked out.

Voices came to her through the tumultuous noise of frightened blood coursing through her body. Max!? Yes! That's Max. She lifted her head, struggling to make her eyes and brain work together.

"Mama!" Max said. "Mama not frine!" He patted her cheek.

"Mama is better," Elise answered weakly.

Max looked up at Lendar. "Mama frine?"

Lendar pulled a robo eye from his pocket, turned it on and released it. It eyed her, then zipped around doing its inspection tour. In a moment Lendar captured it, glanced at its display window and pocketed it. He helped Elise up from the floor to the chair.

Max struggled to climb into her lap. Elise helped him up. He stroked her forehead, his gentle touch tingling like tiny, electric zaps. She closed her eyes, but when the image of the aliens appeared in her mind's eye, she stopped breathing again.

"Elise. Look at me," Lendar demanded. She opened her eyes. He studied her carefully, his brows furrowed with concern. "Elise, listen: you're safe. You're fine. Max is here; he's fine. All is well."

Elise licked her lips and whispered, "Aliens, the aliens are here, in the next room." Saying the words out loud made her feel sick. The sight of the aliens and Gabriel's death melded into one horrid nightmare in her imagination. She blinked, trying to clear the scene away. "Lendar, I can't take any more. I'm losing my mind."

Lendar's voice sounded firm, yet somehow

sympathetic. "Yes, Elise, two aliens are aboard ship. The other strange person is not an alien, he just resembles one." His smile was gentle. "They're not coming into the kitchen. You're safe."

"You didn't mention aliens were here in Empress Jaizem's apartment!" Agony coursed through her body, battering at her heart. "Oh, Lendar, this is too much for me." Hot drops of liquid fell, coursing down her cheeks. She leaned his direction. He stepped closer and her head landed awkwardly against his belt. His arm looped around her shoulders. She mumbled, "Why didn't I ask you to take me home? Why? Why did I think I could handle this?"

"You didn't want to be alone. And you knew Bruce needed you," Lendar replied. He crouched. "You were a blessing to him, Elise, you helped him achieve success. His dream has come true!"

Elise's eyes widened. "Bruce will be cooking for aliens!"

"He will be cooking for the human beings aboard this ship. Alma and her brother, Kip, are just two of us. They enjoyed Bruce's food very much. You have tasted Alma's pastry. Do you remember?"

"I ate pastry made by an alien?" Suddenly her skin felt cold and her lips felt numb.

"You did. And it was very good." He stroked her hair. "Remember, it was full of honey and chopped nuts. Like baklava."

"Yeah, I remember." She swallowed. "And I've drunk co-fay-nee too, or whatever that stuff was."

"Yes, you did." He continued stroking her hair. "Elise, they're both different from us and not so different. They're created in the image of God, just like you and me."

"They are?" Her eyes narrowed. "How do you know?"

"Art, language, math, all those things that set us apart from animals. And a core law written in the heart that tries to guide us to do good and not evil. The Somainai have those qualities too."

"Oh."

Lendar stopped stroking her hair and stood. "Let's go through the gardens to my apartment and tomorrow we'll go back to earth."

Strange how the "go back to earth" part didn't gladden her heart or cause the anxiety quotient to ease up, but rather she felt that going back to earth was a really bad idea. Oh my, girl, you are a nutcase. Elise hugged Max closer and closer until he pushed.

"Too 'ight, Mama."

"Sorry honey." She kissed his cheek and looked at Lendar. "I should like the idea of going back to earth, but somehow I don't. Things are not going too great there either."

It seemed that time froze for an instant, as if everyone and everything waited for her. Sniffling, she muttered, "Lendar, I don't know what I'm going to do. That guy in New York stole my painting!" She clutched Lendar's hand. "Why did he do that?"

Lendar's face hardened. "It's not certain the painting is stolen. If it is, I will retrieve it."

"I'm supposed to call that agent. I've got his number around here somewhere." Elise's eyes skimmed the room searching for her diaper bag forgetting it was hidden inside the tote from the artificer's lab. "What happened to my diaper bag? I need to call that guy." She gulped air. "Lendar, I've lost my diaper bag! It has all my important stuff in it."

Lendar fetched the tote, pulled the diaper bag out and placed it in her hands. "Your diaper bag, my lady."

"Oh, man, that sounds so absurd: "diaper bag" and "my lady" all in one sentence." Elise giggled, a little hysteria lacing her mirth. She covered her mouth, cleared her throat and asked, "My lady? Why do you call me that?"

"You are 'my lady' because I would give you my troth and serve you all the days of my life, if you allowed it."

Roiling emotion shook her body like a tree in a

hurricane. "Why? Why do you love me? Why do you want to serve me!? I'm just a stupid girl."

Lendar crouched again, one knee on the floor. "I love you because you are transparent and beautiful within and without; I love you because you valiantly forge onward. Today, you agreed to come and help Bruce though you suffered a kidnapping, witnessed a brutal murder and lost a person you once cared about. Your bravery energizes your pursuit of your dreams, despite your fears that it's all for naught." His hand rested on her jaw line for a moment before falling to his side.

Elise wailed and the floodgates opened. "I am not any of those things. I'm a liar and a phony. I'm a failure!"

"No, Elise, you are not a failure." Lendar picked her up, with Max in her lap, and sat in the chair embracing them together, just as he had in the shed. "Far from it, you shine like a star in the heavens."

A grinning Bruce came through the door bearing a tray loaded with dirty glasses. His face fell. "Elise!" He set the tray on the cabinet and rushed to her.

Lendar said, "Bruce, will you please keep Max for a little while? Elise needs a change of scenery."

"Sure. Glad to, but I kinda need to get these desserts served first." Bruce licked his lips. He glanced anxiously toward the counter where the desserts waited to be taken to the diners.

Max fidgeted, struggling to be released, almost throwing himself to the floor. "Wanna go!"

"Max, stop it!" Lendar demanded.

Max came up short. He stared at Lendar as if he were a stranger, then he burst into tears, wailing and carrying on like a banshee.

Bruce patted Max on the back. "Come here, Max."

Snuffling, Max leaned Bruce's direction.

Bruce murmured, "Max, buddy, it's going to be ok. Nobody's mad at you. It's ok."

Max stuck his thumb into his mouth and lay his head on Bruce's chest.

Bruce placed his hand on Elise's shoulder. "I'm definitely no expert on this, but oh well, gotta start some time." He bowed his head. "Lord Jesus, let Elise know You're here and comfort her and make her brain work. Amen."

"Thanks," Elise muttered, "I needed that!"

Bruce cleared his throat. "Well, time to serve the dessert." Holding Max, he moved the dirty dishes off onto the counter, placed the dessert plates on the tray, managed to take hold of the tray with Max still on his arm and left the kitchen.

"Lendar! Bruce just took Max out there!"

"Bruce is very capable of protecting Max." Lendar strained to look at her. "The aliens in the next room are not violent or evil, Elise, they're just different."

"Oh gak." Elise pressed her forehead into Lendar's collarbone. "If you say so and I guess you should know." She swallowed. "And, well, I guess Max isn't scared of them! He was glad to go back out there. Probably tired of all this bawling I've been doing."

She thought about Bruce's words. "Lord Jesus, let Elise know You are here and comfort her..." Bruce wasn't afraid. Max wasn't afraid. Lendar wasn't afraid and neither was Empress Jaizem. I'm the only one. Sigh.

Maybe if I stopped freaking out for ten minutes I could feel Your Presence, Lord.

Lendar's voice filtered into her consciousness, "Elise."

She didn't want to move; she didn't want to think about anything except the Lord Jesus being with her and Lendar's arms around her. She sniffed.

"Elise." A silken handkerchief found its way into her hand.

She daubed her nose. "What?"

"Let's go outside."

"Ok."

Lendar carried her toward a section of wall between the

near corner by the door and some cabinetry. She hadn't realized it was a door until he pushed the panel and it swung open. They entered a dark space where a table and chairs formed black silhouettes against night-gray walls and floor. Yellow light, conversation and tinkling music filtered through a crack under a door to the living room.

This must be a breakfast room, Elise decided, taking the opportunity to distract herself. The Empress does have a dining room in the same spot as the one in Lendar's apartment. She snuffled and blew her nose.

Lendar stretched to touch a lock panel and a section of the glass wall slid open. A brisk breeze and trees' sighing filled her senses. She lifted her head to look at the landscape. Stars covered the indigo-hued wafer sky.

"Feeling better?" Lendar asked, his voice reminding her of another starry night.

It seems like that was a long time ago! Elise clutched his neck, clinging to him as if he were a bastion in a storm. Lendar crushed her and she hung on even more tightly.

She whispered, "Oh, Lendar."

"My Elise." No other man had ever uttered her name the way Lendar Marl uttered it, like each letter was precious, like it were made of expensive jewels needing white glove care. He whispered, "Elise, stay. Stay with me forever."

The pleading and longing in his voice tore her heart. Can you really let this man go? Just to avoid seeing strange aliens? Just to be represented by a jerk for an agent who has probably already stolen your painting? Can you really give up a man who admires you and respects you and would give his life for you just to stay on planet earth?

Are you crazy?

What if tonight were the last night you were to see Lendar, ever? What if he were leaving tomorrow for Minan? Could you let him go? Her lips touched the back of his neck, his hair sticking to the sudden dampness on her face. Being separated from him would be worse than aliens and advanced technology! Way worse.

Girl, it's obvious you can stand more than you thought! Now that you survived the alien thing, what's left? You've already been physically and verbally abused; you've been kidnapped and seen a murder; you've been undervalued by your painting prof and manipulated by a high-powered agent from New York; you've met the empress. What's left? Elise wiped her nose. You're such a ninny.

Lendar's breath washed over her neck warming it. "Elise," he repeated softly, "Elise." His arms, had gradually relaxed, but now tightened once again.

A flash of light in the darkened room behind them caught her eye. Bruce pushed open the swinging door and stood in the bright yellow rectangle. Max sat perched on his arm; he pointed at Elise and jabbered. In the next instant, Bruce let the door swing shut.

"Lendar, I'm sorry I lost it in there."

"Lost it?"

"Ah, had a nervous breakdown."

"No, Elise, it's my fault. I should have been more diligent to keep watch over Max."

"Oh, don't be silly," Elise said, pulling far enough away to look in the eye. She sniffed. "Little boys do that sort of thing."

His face looked gray in the artificial starlight, his hair black and so dear with its unruliness, little tufts of it spiked all around his head. She cupped his cheek, fighting the longing to throw away all caution and commit herself to his kiss. She studied his lips, their firm, noble lines. She watched him speak her name,

"Elise."

Her phone beeped. "Oh, how funny. I have a text." Something so normal! And here!

Lendar set her on her feet and she checked the screen. "It's from Bruce." She glanced at Lendar. "How can we text on our earth service from behind the moon?"

Lendar replied, "We're, eh, what is the term, ah yes, we're piggy-backing our electronic communications off earth's satellites."

"Oh." She giggled and opened the message.

Bruce: "Are you ok?"

Elise: "Yeah. I'm better. Just coming outside helped a lot."

Bruce: "Change of scenery done the trick. ;-)."

Elise: "Yes!"

Bruce: "Lendar took charge & asked me to keep Max, but is it ok with you?"

Elise: "Yes. Please keep Max. I appreciate it."

Bruce: "Good news: I'm hired. The dinner was a success! They loved it. Robots are cleaning everything up!"

Elise: "That's great! Yay! Thanks."

Bruce: "No, thank you. Without your help, I would have bombed."

Elise: "I think my diaper bag is still in the kitchen. It should have everything you need."

Bruce: "Max & I will do fine. In a minute Empress Jaizem is taking me to my new apartment. We'll hang out there. Don't worry about a thing. Max can sleep over. I'm sure I have plenty of room!"

Elise: "Thanks Bruce. Congratulations!"

Bruce: "I'm really excited. I'll give you a tour of my new place when you come to pick up Max."

Elise: "hugs. I'll text you later."

Bruce: "I'm just glad texting works behind the moon. :-)"

Elise: "lol" She pocketed her phone and sighed.

Something normal! Finally! But do you want normal? I mean really? Normal for you includes that dingy apartment and your annoying landlord! And Bruce and Lolly won't be in Albuquerque anymore anyway.

Forgetting everything that is behind, press onward toward the prize.

Wow. Is that You, Lord?

Forgetting everything that is behind me.

Lendar's hand skimmed her hair, his index finger tracing the line of her jaw. "You can live here forever," he murmured, his mouth so close she could feel his lips move, tickling her earlobe. "Share this garden with me; keep house with me; become my wife."

She giggled. Love bloomed in her mind's eye: a flower freshly dotted with dew and soft with life. Oh, let me keep that flower! Unconsciously she inclined her head in Lendar's direction, like plant straining for the sun. "Oh Lendar."

Her heart clenched. The prize. There's only one prize worth everything, a human soul. Lord, will you make him Your son? If You would, then I would know this dream of his is Your will.

Lendar straightened and lifted her chin. He looked into one eye and then the other, back and forth, searching. "Elise, do you believe what you told Bruce?"

"What did I tell him?"

"You told him that the Lord was with him."

"Yes, I believe it."

"Then believe it now, believe it for yourself, not just for him. Believe what he prayed for you."

"I believe. I do. That belief is the only thing that keeps me going. It's in Jesus that I have any strength or beauty at all. It's all because of Him." Elise shivered. Her voice sounded small and tentative. "I can't marry you unless you know Him too. Lendar, our life together won't work unless you become a Christian." She swallowed. Oh, gak. Now, what? Sudden fear chilled her. No Lord, I cast that fear on You. I refuse to fear his answer.

Lendar pulled her close.

She didn't resist, but her arms hung at her side. "Lendar, have you read that Bible you borrowed?"

"I have."

"Well, what do you think?" Her cheek resting against

his chest, she listened to his heartbeat. It sounded steady and peaceful. And his body didn't tense up like it would if he were offended or annoyed. That's a good sign, I hope.

Lendar smoothed her hair, his Adam's apple bobbed as he swallowed.

He smells so nice, she thought. Her fingers rubbed his jacket fabric and sought out the raised muscles of his bicep and the brachiordialis of his forearm. He's so strong and so beautiful! Oh Lord, please make him Your son.

"Let's walk through the garden to my quarters and we'll talk," Lendar suggested.

"That sounds like a great idea." She shivered.

"Excuse me a moment, I'll be right back." Lendar went inside, threading past the table and chairs in the darkened breakfast room. The bright rectangle of the kitchen's swinging door appeared for a moment framing his handsome shape and then the room went dark.

Elise sighed and turned her attention to the landscape. "It's so amazingly like the real outdoors," she breathed in wonder. Treetops swayed in a current of moving air. The landscape seemed to stretch infinitely, just as it did on earth, the horizon always a far off instead of finite and near. It felt as if she were in a vast, open world instead of a spaceship. A bird hooted and some animal snuffled on the ground. She squinted at it, trying to discern what sort of beast it might be, but it remained nothing more than a moving hump. It disappeared into the brush.

Lendar returned with a jacket. "The Empress sends her wishes for a lovely walk." Even in the faint light she could see it was a beautiful, embroidered garment. The buttons and collar reminded her of Mongolian nomads' jackets.

"She's not mad at you for ditching the party?" Elise asked. Lavender wafted in the air as she swung the jacket around her shoulders and slipped it on.

"No, not at all. I explained that you were overcome by the heat in the kitchen and needed the fresh air. It's likely she wasn't fooled by that, er, lame excuse." Lendar rubbed his nose.

"You are the most honest liar I've ever met." Elise laughed softly. "And you always sound so silly when you try to use the common vernacular."

Suddenly, Lendar grabbed her and pressed her body against his. "Elise!" The fire he kept carefully smoored threatened to burst free. His eyes flashed in the faint light, his teeth a sudden brilliance of blue-white. His desire burned through the fabric of their clothing, searing her breasts. She gasped and returned the embrace with all her might. "Elise." Ozone seemed to hang in the air as after a lightning strike. He pulled away, his face etched with effort.

"Let's go." He took her hand and led her down the spiral staircase to the grassy knoll, into the crickets' song and the breezes' rustling whisper. Then he ran, taking her into the night-black forest. At first he pulled her along a little faster than she could manage, and she struggled to keep up, then he found her pace and slowed to match it. He knew the way through the forest, along a trail she could barely see. She was forced to trust him and simply run.

Leaves grazed her face, branches slapped her arms, but the race was exhilarating. With each step a little more anxiety and grief fell away, like droplets of sweat releasing toxins from the body. After several minutes, he sensed she was tiring and slowed again. They trotted down a rocky incline and splashed through a stream, scrambled up the other side, then sprinted down a final slope before the view opened on a starlit meadow. They stopped at its edge.

Elise inhaled the grassy perfume. Somewhere flowers added their bouquet. "Oh, Lendar, it's so beautiful." Treetops tilted in wind, sighing music through the leaves. "Leaving the past behind and pressing toward the goal," Elise repeated. What is the goal?

They skirted the meadow, remaining in the trees'

shadows. They climbed toward the horizon where the sky seemed to meet the ground at a rocky ridge. Quiet as they were, they had made enough noise that animals kept their distance and Elise did not hear another beast.

At the base of the rocky outcropping, Lendar helped her scramble onto the small plateau. At last they sat, side by side. The grassy meadow stretched at their feet to a copse of trees at the foot of the metal tube, the exterior of the energy elevator, at least a mile away. The metal glinted faintly in the artificial starlight.

Elise clutched Lendar's wonderful hand, relishing the feel of it. *If he rejects You, oh Lord, I won't be holding this hand much longer.* She inhaled the pine forest scent and sighed, her eyes stinging with anticipated grief. She breathed, "Yes, I could live here forever. It's so beautiful! The gardens help clear my head and free my heart. I could adjust to the technology. I could overcome my fear of aliens. I could be trained to behave properly when among the nobility." She looked at him, her eyes searching. "But Lendar, unless God is in the center of our lives together, we have no life at all."

At first his expression seemed troubled. His brows were furrowed and a frown played at his lips. Then one eyebrow cocked, as if a sudden realization had come to him. "That is the Protector's way."

"Really." Elise angled her body away from him to better scrutinize him. "Explain."

"A man and his wife become one before the Most High. When He is their center they are a cord of three strands that cannot be broken."

"Ecclesiastes chapter 4," Elise murmured.

"So it is in your Sacred Text. I asked the Most High in my heart, I promised Him that if He was the same Lord you love to cause you to mention that sacred verse, the location where it might be found and the concept it teaches." He kissed her hand and gazed fixedly into her eyes. "That concept is the root of a Protectors' marriage. Three strands, a man, his wife and the Most High." His nostrils flared, his breath steamed in the chill, smoke from the fires of his longing.

Lendar continued, his voice low and resonate. "He is the Same Lord the same King of the Universe, this One we both know and worship. And this Son you call Jesus is His Messiah, the One prophesied to live among the stars." He buried his face in her neck, his voice bringing prickles of joy to her skin with each exhalation of sound. "Oh, Elise. Be my wife."

Her hand went of its own accord to touch the back of his head, the curve of his skull and the texture of his hair delighting her senses. Shivering, she whispered, "But do you receive Jesus as Lord?"

"I do."

"That's it then." She closed her eyes and clung to him. Her heart sang. Every sound: the click of some insect nearby, the rustle of their jackets' fabric, the soft murmur of the breeze; every scent: the pine-sweet perfume, the floral scents from the meadow, Lendar's cologne, all were enhanced and extravagant. She inhaled and sighed.

Well, in that case, forward it is.

27

"Oh, Lendar, I love you, let's get married right now."

"Sounds like a good idea to me." Lendar smiled and smoothed a tendril of her hair. "We can honeymoon anywhere on earth you like."

"Oh my, it's all so sudden."

Lendar chuckled. "Come." He scrambled to his feet and pulled her up.

Hand in hand they walked to the edge of a precipice and looked down. A river rambled through night dark trees and gray grassy meadows in the fields far, far below. The starlight sparkled on the water and the wind rushing up the cliff smelled of farms and pines.

"Now, touch the sky."

Elise stretched forth her fingertips and smacked into the wafer-lined wall. "Wow. That river valley looks so real! I forgot we were in a spaceship."

"That's the idea." Lendar turned to face her and took both of her hands in his. "This is the walk with the Most High. There is a reality more real than what can be seen with the eyes or felt with the fingers. It is the reality of the spirit realm where the Most High holds court and watches over creation."

Elise blinked. "Oh, Lendar. Just kiss me; then I'd know."

He cocked his head. "What would you know, Elise?"

That dear face, she thought. Unconsciously her lips parted in anticipation. "I'd know. I'd just know." She blushed.

He tugged locks of her hair, following the bundle of strands to the ends. "You know, Elise." He looked at her, his eyes penetrating. That look invited her, begging her to take his head in the crook of her arm and kiss him. The look demanded a decision.

Elise's eyes went round. "I do?"

"Yes."

"What do I know?"

He studied her expression, examining her face as if he wanted to memorize it. In the next moment, his eyes closed, he leaned closer until his forehead touched hers. His words became her only reality. "Until I met you it didn't occur to me to even think that maybe our Messiah might be born on earth. I ignored everything but my quest to find you--until I recognized how important the Lord Jesus is to you, the idea never entered my mind.

"Tonight you brought it all into sharp focus. Startled, I recognized that you might reject me if I did not join you in your faith." His eyes opened. The irises were so close, so lovely, like precious gems. "I did not expect that. Reject me because I am from another planet; reject me because aliens are among us, but reject me because I did not receive your Lord as my own? Here was someone whose faith meant more to her than life, just as my faith means more to me than life. Then I fully understood why our Sacred Texts are so similar. The same Mind operates behind them, not only causing them to be written, but enlivening them today.

"Your whole life depends on the Lord Jesus, you spoke of Him only little, but I saw you muttering your prayers to Him and reading your Sacred Text." He blinked. "When I visited you in the painting studio, when you believed yourself alone you, you sang hymns to Him and I felt He was there, listening to you."

Elise gulped. Wow, I had no idea he was paying that good attention! "Well then." She waited for him to say more, but he didn't.

She closed her eyes and allowed herself to drift, to feel the air moving across her body, to smell the various scents and feel his warmth so near. Light seeped through cracks in her soul, bursting them open and joy began to well up from within her bringing color to her interior landscape.

"Now that I see your God and my God are one and the

same, I know your Lord Jesus is our Promised One."

Lendar has received You as Lord! Praise You Lord Jesus.

Words from a hymn her father had loved came to mind, the piano accompaniment and his strong tenor picked up the phrasing. Dust motes floated in light piercing the colored glass: the old church where she'd grown up.

He paused, his hand falling away. He murmured, "I believe Jesus is Lord, Elise. I believe He is the Anointed One, the long promised Son of God who redeems the universe by His Blood."

"Oh." Elise swallowed. "In that case then, you're right. I do know."

Lendar's smile was a slow burn. "What do you know?"

"I love you and I want to marry you."

Lendar's mouth opened ever so slightly. His eyes, almost shut with longing. He breathed, "May I kiss you Elise Ramos?"

The words echoed in her mind, bouncing through her nerves like tiny mallets exciting lovely chords. "Yes."

His lips came closer. Elise tilted her head to meet them. She closed her eyes. His fingers felt warm on her cheek and jaw. At first his lips were tender, tentative, gentle. The flesh tasted spicy-fresh, the softness contrasting with his beard's sharp stubble. Then his lips parted and his kiss turned insistent, demanding more. It was as if he searched her, reaching for her inner, hidden self. And the sensation of oneness she'd felt other times before began to pulse like a growing thing, like a thing being born.

Surprised that the delicious oneness she'd thought so wonderful could be surpassed, she felt herself merging, forming into a new being. This new oneness was deeper than anything she had ever imagined possible. In that moment, she knew that if Lendar were to die, she might also die. If he were to leave her, she would be split into half, bloodied and shattered.

She felt, rather than saw his nostrils flare, hot exhalation burned across her cheeks. No careful smooring now! His mouth pressed hard, his teeth clacking against hers. She met his passion with fire of her own. One hand tangled in her hair at the back of her head, the other hand grasped her waist, his fingers pressing into her flesh, the power in his grasp piercing her body. She cried out in pain, but took hold of his hair and pulled him toward her. They tumbled to the ground.

The tumble interrupted the kiss. Their breathing had become ragged, aggressive. Exhalations scented with odors of longing and love washed over their faces and bodies. Elise now lay on top of him. She nuzzled his neck, tasting the hint of salt from the day's exertions, then the sweetness of his skin once the saltiness was gone. Teasing, taunting, she kissed his throat. She felt him swallow and her heart exploded with the dearness, the preciousness of him. Her possession. She provoked him, running her tongue along the rise of his Adam's apple. But the provocation was squelched under the knowledge that for her, anything more than what they'd just now enjoyed required a marriage ceremony and a ring.

She stopped and breathed, "Oh Lendar, I love you. I want a wedding at my grandparents' ranch."

He seemed to stiffen.

Elise lifted her head and studied his face.

His eyes were unreadable, a storm of conflict and consuming desire.

Elise murmured. "A Christian wedding."

He pressed her head to his chest. Through the thumping of his heart she heard him say, "Elise...I have waited so long..."

Her face was wet, her eyesight blurred. "Why me, Lendar? Why me? I am nobody special. Not only that, I'm a failure."

Lendar struggled to look her in the eye, but they now seemed too entangled. "Let's sit up."

"Ok."

They scrambled up, stepped back to the ridge and settled side by side, their legs dangling. Elise felt that though her thigh pressed against his and his shoulder rubbed against hers, she was too far away.

His fingers brought her mind back into unity with his. He cupped her jaw, one hand on either side, turning her face to shine in his gaze. Elise basked, her whole being directed through her cheeks, her lips and eyes, upturned toward Lendar, soaking in his aura, wanting more and more and more.

Lendar traced the edge of her nose with his thumb. "I've told you that the Most High gave me a vision over twenty years ago when this trip to earth was nothing more than a scheme. In the vision, I saw you standing on that sidewalk; I saw the buildings and the gas powered vehicles. I saw the sun touching your hair, the red highlights like fire. And I saw the little boy and I knew his name was Max. I knew you were a student at University of New Mexico. It seemed to me that as we conversed we joined into one spirit. And then I awoke.

"I lay in blissful languor in the feeling of connection, the joy of loving until it began to fade, then I dashed up to the cockpit where my lord, prince Anwic, keeps the holographic globe the Somainai made during their visit to earth in the 1860's. But of course, there was no University of New Mexico at the time and Albuquerque was a dusty, adobe village.

"At first, I was disappointed, but then I realized that if you were alive during the days when that globe was created, you'd be dead before I could meet you. My devastation was replaced by hope and delight in the kindness and generosity of the Most High.

"Prince Anwic intruded into my thoughts, asking me if I'd come up to the cockpit to work or I was there to gawk at the globe. In that moment, I forgot the vision. It had been slipping away already, my connection to your spirit lost like a drowning man who loses his grasp on his savior's hand.

"The dream never came fully to mind again until that night in the restaurant when you left the image of yourself with Max sitting in his stroller outside that store on my links unit. When I saw that picture again in your presence, I recognized you. It was a recognition one might feel upon seeing his reflection in a mirror after years of blindness. It was a recognition a man might feel when he sees his newborn child. You, heart of my heart and flesh of my flesh and Max, our son, though born by another."

Lendar's piercing eyes searched her, his voice had faded to a whisper, his face edged closer and closer until his nose dented her cheek and his kiss took her mind far away into a new reality. A place where she had never been, yet a place where she had always belonged. She belonged to Lendar Marl.

His lips turned soft and pulled away. His words came from that secret place, they flew like arrows into the reality of an alien space ship. His voice, though barely audible, carried the confidence and authority of a solo instrument on its own after a great symphonic surge of sound. "You are my destiny."

He stroked her eyebrow with the back of his index finger. "You think of yourself as ordinary, but the gold of your loving heart glows bright and your unguarded, honest soul attracts me like sweet fragrance. And like a man mesmerized, or a moth to a flame, I am drawn to you. I can no more resist you than I can resist the clamoring of my empty belly or my parched mouth in thirst. I must have you." His mouth covered hers like a branding iron, burning and marking her as his own. His hand roamed over her shoulder and down her arm. His embrace crushed her, as if he would press her body through his skin and bones into the core of his being.

She was senseless, separated from reality, adrift in Lendarness. Then she heard him say, "No one like you could exist in my world. Only the Most High, working here on earth, through His Anointed and by His written Word could shape a woman like you from the trials and failures you've endured.

"No female like you could exist in my world where culture is stilted and static, where women must be treated like precious glass and they learn to manipulate and twist men. Stultified religion and erroneous ideas of God do not make for women such as you. Your dynamic Savior shines through you, freeing you to be more yourself than you could possibly be anywhere else. You're not possible anywhere but here."

His hand tangled anew in her hair, he pulled her head back and peered into her eyes as if he could make his stare into lasers penetrating even further into her soul. "And that could only happen here, on planet earth, the point of origin, the place of birth and rebirth, the center of the universe where the Most High has incubated and brought forth His greatest Gift to all beings created in His Image. And you, Elise, you are a singularity of beauty, natural grace, fortitude, intelligence, guilelessness and vessel of the Most High. You are mine, His gift to me and I intend to have you and keep you until the day I die."

Elise did not think it possible, but his next kiss transcended all previous kisses. Colors exploded in her mind's eye transmuting into music and from there into magnificent flavors. Beauty overwhelmed her until she wondered if she could breathe, or even if she were still breathing. Perhaps she had died, drowned in a sea of ecstasy.

She wondered if her eyes would be able to see the natural world again, if perhaps they had been ruined by the brilliance of this moment, burned blind, sight turned inward where Lendar's heart pulsed in unison with hers.

She wondered if her bones still existed. Until now, they'd never altered or alerted her to their existence unless bruised or broken, but she felt as if they'd been changed into "fingers" capable of touch where the brilliance within, the flavors and the music played over their newly formed nerves like teasing breezes at once wonderful to avoid and too much to bear.

Each moment, the kiss brought new eruptions of joyful music throughout her being. And Elise knew her life had only just now begun.

Marilyn W Lathrop lives in southeastern New Mexico where the stars can still rule the skies.

Marilyn would like to thank her husband and family for their indulgence and listening ears. Thanks to Bev Coots and all the readers who have made suggestions and to you, dear reader, of this book. But most of all, thanks be to God.

Find Marilyn W Lathrop on Facebook; marilynwlathrop.com; overtheedgescifi.blogspot.com

To order signed copies e-mail or write:

Felix River Publishing
P.O. Box 351
Dexter, NM 88230
felixriverpublishing@gmail.com

www.ingramcontent.com/pod-product-compliance
Lightning Source LLC
Chambersburg PA
CBHW061923170626
46813CB00006B/2281